SONS OF THE CITY

Scott Flander

SONS OF

THE CITY

A NOVEL

WILLIAM MORROW AND COMPANY, INC.

New York

It is the policy of William Morrow and Company, Inc.,
and its imprints and affiliates, recognizing the importance
of preserving what has been written, to print the
books we publish on acid-free paper, and we exert our best
efforts to that end.

Library of Congress Cataloging-in-Publication Data

Flander, Scott.
Sons of the city : a novel / Scott Flander. —1st ed.
p.   cm.
ISBN 0-688-16429-3 (alk. paper)
I. Title.
PS3556.L346S66   1999
813'.54—dc21   98-50416
                                                          CIP

Printed in the United States of America

First Edition

1 2 3 4 5 6 7 8 9 10

BOOK DESIGN BY JENNIFER ANN DADDIO

www.williammorrow.com

For my parents,
Judy and Murray Flander

ACKNOWLEDGMENTS

This book owes a lot to two good friends: Marc Kristal, the finest writer I know, and retired Philadelphia Police Sgt. Joe Escher, a cop's cop if there ever was one.

I'm grateful to my agent, Barbara Lowenstein, and to my editor, Claire Wachtel. Thanks also to the others who helped along the way, including Mike Lynsky, Ginny Bazis, Karen Stallone, Marisol Bello, Jim Nolan, Kitty Caparella, Vince Kasper, Yvonne Latty, Dan Hawes, and Dr. Gilbert Palley.

SONS OF THE CITY

ONE

I was hoping to have a quiet evening, no shootings, no foot pursuits, no 302s taking off their clothes in the middle of Baltimore Avenue and claiming to be the original Adam from the Garden of Eden. But this was the night that Mickey Bravelli was holding his big fund-raiser at Lucky's Little Italy, and my brilliant lieutenant wanted me there.

Somehow his tiny brain remembered that I had come to the 20th from the Organized Crime Unit. Eddie, you know their names and faces, he said.

Yeah, unfortunately, I said.

So instead of leaving me in peace, he told me to spend the night outside Lucky's, keeping an eye on things. Never mind that plainclothes guys from my old unit would be there, which meant we really didn't need a uniformed presence. Never mind that I was a sergeant, and had a whole squad to watch out for. The lieutenant didn't care.

Just sit in your patrol car across the street from the restaurant, he said.

Just bend over so I can stick my foot up your ass, I didn't say.

Lucky's was in the heart of Westmount, an Italian neighborhood of narrow brick row houses and corner stores in West Philadelphia. Whenever anyone in Westmount wanted to throw a big party—a wedding reception, a fiftieth anniversary—they booked the Roma Room at Lucky's.

Tonight, it was reserved for Bravelli and his friends. One of his guys was being tried for the fourth time for bribing a judge—the first three cases had ended in mistrials—and he had run out of money for lawyers. Bravelli was holding a $250-a-plate dinner to help him out, and who was going to say no?

I decided to take Nick along for the ride. Nick was my younger cousin, and he was also in my squad. You're not supposed to supervise your relatives, but the bosses conveniently forgot that when they decided to dump me in the 20th.

Throughout the evening, Nick and I watched a steady stream of Bravelli's pals arrive at the restaurant. Most of the younger guys wore black—black suits, or black sports jackets with turtlenecks. Their girlfriends were all wearing short, supertight dresses with beads and rhinestones, with slits all over the place and necklines so low their breasts were practically hanging out.

The older guys, with their thinning hair and bulging jowls, looked like they had just thrown on whatever was handy in their closet—rumpled blue or gray sports jacket, white shirt, no tie. They generally walked in together in groups of three or four, like ducks heading for the water, their bellies sort of leading the way.

I was hoping the mob fashion show would cheer Nick up, but he was only half paying attention. He seemed lost in his own world, the way he had been for the past six weeks, ever since his father—my uncle Jimmy—had tripped over a bucket of tar on a row house roof in Westmount and cartwheeled over the edge. Nick had been on the roof, he had seen it happen. And he blamed himself for not being able to save his father, in the way people are always blaming themselves for things they can't control.

"Hey, Nicky," I said, "you know any of these guys?"

He shrugged. "Yeah, some of 'em. At least the young ones. We all sat next to each other in homeroom at West Philly."

"These lowlifes actually went to high school?"

"That's where the girls were. That's why we all went."

"And you became a cop, because we all know how much the girls like a man in uniform."

Nick gave me a small smile, then glanced over at the people going into Lucky's.

"What the hell we doin' out here, Eddie?"

"Watching the evening's entertainment."

"I don't mean just tonight," he said. "I mean every night."

A big Cadillac was pulling up to the red canopy that led from the sidewalk to Lucky's front door. Some young guy I'd never seen hopped out, ran around to the passenger door, and opened it. This girl got out, this beautiful girl, maybe twenty-four, with long brown hair. She was wearing a short, light blue dress, it just made you fall in love with her. As she got out, and her boyfriend was closing the car door, she turned away from him, toward the street, where she thought no one was looking, and spit out her gum.

Nick was staring at his feet. "You ever sorry you became a cop, Eddie?"

"C'mon," I said, "you can't be tired of the job already, Nicky, you've only been a cop for four years. Most guys don't get bitter and cynical for at least five years."

Nick gave a laugh. His mother and my mother were sisters, but when people saw the two of us together, they couldn't believe we were related. Nick's father was Italian, and that half had gotten the upper hand when Nick was born. He had a dark face, jet black hair, and big round brown eyes, the kind girls loved.

My father, on the other hand, had given me his thick brown hair, green eyes, and square jaw. I was also a hell of a lot taller than Nick, and more inclined than he was to get a little exercise once in a while.

Nick turned to me. "It's all your fuckin' fault, you know."

"What is?"

"You're the one who said I should become a cop."

"I never said that. You came to me, you said, What's it like being a cop?"

"And what'd you say, Eddie?"

"I don't remember."

"The fuck you don't. You said it was like being part of a big family. Where everyone takes care of each other."

"Well, maybe I did say that."

Nick shook his head. "It's all just bullshit, Eddie. Guys don't watch out for each other here."

"Some of them do."

"What about Henry Bowman? You think he cares?"

Bowman was our pea-brained lieutenant.

"People like him don't count," I said.

"What about Joe Gorko? I'm gettin' my ass kicked in front of a house on Pine the other day, I call for an assist, Gorko shows up, sees he'll actually have to get in a fight, and then he drives right by, pretendin' like he doesn't even see me. Fuckin' coward."

"People like him don't count."

"Yeah, well, who fuckin' does count, Eddie?"

"How about your partner? Steve would do anything for you."

"Yeah," Nick said, looking down. "He would." Neither of us said anything for a couple of minutes, and it was Nick who finally spoke.

"Don't you ever clean out your fuckin' car?" He was looking at the trash around his feet. There were Dunkin' Donuts bags, and McDonald's wrappers, and a grease-soaked paper bag that probably once held a cheesesteak.

"Aw, Thompson left his shit here again?" I said. "That fat fuck."

"He eats this much every day?" Nick was stirring the pile of trash around with his left shoe.

"That's nothin'," I said. "That was probably just breakfast."

"Damn."

"You know, Nicky, when you first become a cop, you think you can clean up the city. Then after you're here for a while, you realize you can't do that, so you say, I'll just clean up my district. But you can't do that either, so you say, OK, one corner, I know I can keep one corner clean. Finally you get to the point where you say, Screw it, all I'm gonna do is keep my car clean. And you can't even fuckin' do that."

Nick put on a thin smile. "But it's like a family, right?"

Everyone going into Lucky's had to walk past the overly excited TV reporters who had set up camp next to the red canopy. It looked like a Hollywood premiere—the TV reporters had absolutely no idea who was connected and who wasn't, so they filmed everybody coming in. It could have been a waiter late for work, the TV cameras suddenly turned on him like he was Al Capone.

All the guests were greeted at the door by a short guy in a lime green suit. This was Spock. Technically he was an associate of Bravelli's crew, but he was somewhere between a gofer and a mascot. When I was in OC—that's what we called the Organized Crime Unit—we picked Spock up a few times for questioning. The conversation usually went like this:

"What's your name?"

"Spock."

"What's your real name?"

"I just tole ya, it's Spock."

"What are you, a fucking Klingon?"

"No, I'm Italian."

"Really? What part of Italy do the Spocks come from?"

"I ain't never been to Italy."

"How about outer space?"

"I ain't never been there, neither."

Tonight it looked like he was the emcee at Lucky's, smiling, saying hello to all the guests, ushering them to the door. I half expected to see him carrying around a microphone.

It was a warm June evening, and curious neighbors were gathered in clumps on the sidewalk across from Lucky's. The restaurant faced a block of two-story row houses that had plain concrete steps instead of porches. Some of the houses had been converted into modest neighborhood businesses—a small Italian bakery, a florist, a beauty supply shop—and the owners lived on the second floor.

Many of the onlookers tonight were worn-out housewives in their forties or fifties, giggling with each other like high school girls. In their midst I saw Doc Bizbee and two other plainclothes guys from OC I didn't recognize. I guess they were getting new people all the time. All three were wearing golf shirts and faded jeans and white sneaks, my old uniform. They were gathered around a freshly painted bright orange fire hydrant like it was a campfire, their arms crossed, trading stories while they casually watched the goings-on across the street. I was thinking that if I hadn't been busted out of the unit six months ago, I would have been with them now.

As if on cue, a brown Plymouth pulled up and stopped next to ours. It was not a pleasant sight: Captain Lenny Lanier, the Organized Crime Unit's boss, was behind the wheel. I had forgotten he would be here, I had probably just blocked it out. Lanier pushed the button that lowered the passenger window, and waited until it was all the way down.

"How's it going, guys?" he asked.

I just looked at him, not saying anything. He was an ugly bastard—dark circles under his eyes, and a perpetual five o'clock shadow, no matter how often he shaved. I had always wondered why someone with a face like his would ever be made captain.

"How you doin', Eddie?" he asked.

"What do you care?"

"Now, c'mon, Eddie, don't be that way."

"Exactly how do you want me to be, Captain?"

Lanier tried to smile, which with that face was always a mistake. "I'm sorry it had to happen the way it did."

"Yeah? Well, bite my ass, Captain."

The smile disappeared. I guess it finally dawned on him that I wasn't going to suggest we go get a beer. He powered up the window and pulled off.

Nick and I looked at each other, and said at the same time, "Fuck him."

I smiled at Nick. He was a good kid.

My eye caught some movement in the rearview mirror. Three men in dark suits, coming up the sidewalk from behind us. Without thinking, I put my hand on my gun. They were radiating danger, you could almost see it shooting through the air like tracers.

"Here they come," I said to Nick, as they walked by our car. It was Mickey Bravelli, with two guys from his crew. One of them was Frankie Canaletto, his lieutenant. Last I heard, the DA's office was close to charging him with murder for an old unsolved mob hit. The third guy was Goop, Bravelli's musclebound driver and bodyguard.

Bravelli was in his early forties, and he had an athletic look, like a tennis player, though I doubt he ever even saw a tennis game in his life. There weren't exactly a lot of tennis courts in West Philly.

He had gold chains around his neck and his hair slicked back. So did Canaletto, who always walked around with his chest stuck out. Even Goop had the gold chains and the slicked-back hair. That was the look.

Bravelli led the way as the three of them crossed the street at an angle in front of us, heading toward the red canopy. They all turned to see who was in the police car, and it took Bravelli about two seconds to recognize me. He had seen me plenty of times when I was in OC, but I was always in plainclothes.

Without stopping, Bravelli gave me a puzzled look, like he was asking, What are you doin' in uniform? Like he was actually concerned about me. But I could tell by his mocking eyes that he thought it was funny to see me sitting there in my little police car.

They kept going. And as the three of them neared the canopy, the TV crews spotted them and swung their cameras around like a flock of birds suddenly shifting direction. Bravelli, striding toward the entrance, smoothed back his hair with both hands and straightened his tie and his suit jacket. I realized then why he had come on foot—if he had pulled up in a car, he would have been on camera for only a few seconds. But walking down the street with his men, like he was leading a gang of gunslingers into town, he could be the star of his own movie. Sure enough, the TV crews couldn't get enough of him—their cameras picked him up as he strutted across the street, and stayed glued to him until he was through the front door.

There was an emergency tone on the radio—priority call.

"All units, we have Ninth District cars in pursuit of a black Mercedes heading west on Walnut from Thirtieth. Wanted for a founded carjacking."

Nick looked at me. "Maybe he'll turn off of Walnut."

"Yeah," I said. "And maybe he won't."

We were on Walnut at 72nd. The pursuit was more than forty blocks away, but it was heading straight toward us.

"We could pull the car into the middle of the street," Nick suggested.

"And what?" I said. "Be a one-car roadblock? What are we gonna do, hold up our hands and say, Could you please stop?"

I knew that as the Mercedes flew down Walnut, it would pick up every police car in the district. Which meant that if the pursuit got this far—and it would only take three or four minutes—they'd all be screaming by Lucky's at ninety miles an hour.

And there, halfway out into the street, were four TV camera crews, side by side, all getting the same pointless shot of the front of the restaurant, all about to be mowed down. I jumped out of my car and ran down the middle of the street toward them. Nick was instantly at my side, and we both turned up the handheld police radios on our gunbelts.

"He's past Thirty-fifth!" someone yelled over whooping sirens.

"Thirty-sixth! Now Thirty-sixth!" shouted another voice.

Jesus, he was moving fast.

I reached the camera crews. "Get out of the street, now," I ordered.

We tried to herd them toward the sidewalk. A perky-looking blond TV reporter in a red dress and bright red lipsticked lips put her hand on her hip.

"Officer, we have every right to be here—"

"We got a high-speed pursuit coming right down Walnut," I said, trying to stay calm so they would be calm. "Get out of the street."

I could hear on the radio that they were past 45th. The perky blonde looked over my shoulder at her cameraman. "Eric, let's get a good shot of it."

"Now!" I yelled.

"OK, OK," she said, almost pouting.

Tim Timberlane, a jerkoff TV reporter from Channel 7, had his hand to his earplug and was yelling into his microphone, "I wanna go live, I wanna go live."

I had seen Timberlane a lot on TV. A real smarmy guy about twenty-seven with a talent for showing cops in the worst possible light. No matter what the story was, we were always the bad guys. A true asshole.

The other camera crews were drifting toward the sidewalk, but Timberlane wouldn't move. We began to hear the sirens.

"Get out of the fucking street!" I yelled at him.

He still didn't move. I couldn't believe anyone could be this stupid. I just grabbed his arm and started pulling.

Timberlane didn't take his eyes off the camera. "We're being harassed by the police, right here on live TV, you're seeing this live. Officer, will you give us your name, can we have your name, please?"

The pursuit was less than two blocks away, its chorus of sirens growing louder each moment, beginning to drown out everything.

I was trying to drag Timberlane and his cameraman to the sidewalk, but they kept resisting, they didn't want to move. And then I turned and there was the Mercedes, heading right at us, right in our lane. Shit, I thought, he's going to get us all.

The driver must have suddenly seen us as well, because he jerked the wheel and the Mercedes swerved across two lanes of Walnut. It was going out of control, and started clipping all the guests' parked Lincolns and Cadillacs, BANG, BANG, BANG, and then it jerked back across Walnut toward us and Lucky's canopy.

Timberlane and his cameraman finally started running, leaving me for an instant facing the Mercedes, meeting the eyes of a terrified black teenager behind the wheel. I jumped back, falling onto the street, and the Mercedes whooshed by, brakes screeching. People dove out of the way as the car jumped the curb, knocked down the brass poles supporting the canopy, then slid along the restaurant's red stucco front wall, shooting out sparks and leaving a trail of the car's black paint. The Mercedes probably would have kept going forever, but it hit a brass standpipe coming out of the wall and bounced back across the sidewalk, spun halfway around, and lurched to a violent stop.

All over the street, police cars were squealing to a halt. The doors of the Mercedes popped open and two black kids jumped out. Both had guns, big ones. They looked around and saw that in a moment they would be trapped on all sides. And they started running toward me.

I grabbed my gun and tried to get on my knees, so I could at least get off a shot. I looked around for Nick, he was pulling his gun out. But it wasn't me the two young carjackers were heading for, it was the restaurant. They darted under the half-fallen canopy and disappeared through Lucky's front door.

Nick reached me and grabbed my arm, boosting me onto my feet. By now, cops were jumping out of their cars, unholstering their guns.

Nick and I ducked under the canopy and pulled open the door. My view was blocked by the big fountain at the entrance, and we heard the chaos before we saw it—shouts of men and women, tables being overturned, plates crashing.

As I swung around the fountain, I saw the two carjackers careening toward the rear of the massive dining room, knocking into tables, pushing back waiters. They seemed to be headed toward the kitchen, straight back, but they suddenly darted to the left, toward a set of closed rough-hewn wooden doors. They probably didn't notice the hand-lettered sign over the doors, but I did. In a smooth, cursive script, it said "Roma Room."

The kid in the lead pulled open one of the wooden doors, and they both dove inside and disappeared as the door closed behind. Bravelli and his guests were about to get a very big surprise.

We barreled past a blur of families who were already half on their feet, clutching white tablecloths that were turning red with spilled wine. There was no direct path to the Roma Room, only around this table, back around that one. At last I reached the door. Holding my gun in my right hand, I grabbed one of the big wooden handles with my left and pulled. Nothing. Maybe you were supposed to push. I tried that, nothing again, then tried the other handle, pushing and pulling, knowing the doors were locked, not accepting it.

"Police!" I yelled. "Open it up."

Something was happening inside, I could hear it through the doors. Shouting, yelling, something heavy falling. I was waiting for gunfire.

Nick was right there with me. "How could it be locked?" he asked.

"You think I know?"

Cops were piling around me. Three or four of us grabbed the handle together and pulled as hard as we could.

"Now push," I said.

From inside, we heard the crash of glasses and plates, and some kind of slapping sound, like a beaver's tail hitting the water.

We all pushed, and still the door didn't move.

"I don't fucking believe this," I yelled in frustration. "Let's try through the kitchen."

A few moments later I was leading a dozen cops past big pots of steaming spaghetti sauce. We headed in the direction of the Roma Room—basically, to the left—but the kitchen was like a maze. Bread warmers, walk-in freezers, boxes of potatoes stacked to the ceiling. Twice we hit dead-ends.

A chef was staring at us.

"Where's the Roma Room?" I yelled at him. He blinked and his mouth dropped open. We all waited, waited, waited. He blinked again.

A few feet away, a wide-eyed Hispanic guy was watching us, frozen in the act of pulling silverware from a dishwasher.

"Roma Room," I said. "Where's the door?"

He shrugged. *"No Inglés."*

"Roma!" I shouted at him. "Roma! Is Roma fuckin' English?" He shrugged again.

We tried another route, past a wall of employee lockers, and this time we saw a set of swinging stainless-steel doors with small windows at eye level.

"Gotta be it," I said, and we charged ahead, pushing through the doors into the Roma Room. We were on the far end, but in the center we could see ten, fifteen guys crowded together, kicking and yelling at something. When they spotted us, they hurriedly backed off, like jackals temporarily abandoning their kill. It didn't take long to see what they had been doing. Lying on the floor were the two carjackers, their faces bloody and contorted in pain.

One was balled up in a fetal position, holding his side, tears and blood dripping onto the polished hardwood floor. The other was on his stomach, his left hand up, his head turned the other way. His eyes were squeezed closed, like he was waiting for the next kick. Their guns were gone.

"Call Rescue," I told Nick.

I scanned the room. It was quiet now; all the men were back at the big round tables with their wives and girlfriends. They looked at us innocently, like they had showed up just a second ahead of us, and were as surprised as we were to see these two black kids bloody on the floor.

"Anybody want to tell me what happened here?" I asked, knowing it was a stupid question.

"I didn't see nothin'," said a young guy sitting nearby, all serious. He looked around. "Anybody see what happened?" He waited a moment, then turned back to me apologetically. "I don't think nobody here saw nothin', sergeant. Sorry we couldn't be more help. Have a nice day."

A few titters came from around the room. They knew they were going to get away with it, they didn't doubt it for a moment. Now I had no choice but to nail as many of them as I could.

Goop was sitting at another nearby table. I definitely remembered seeing him in the group kicking the kids. I could start with him.

"OK, Goop, let's go," I said. "Stand up."

"Huh?" He couldn't believe it.

"Stand up."

"You don't got to do it, Goop," someone yelled.

I turned toward Nick. His regular partner, Steve Ryder, was with him now. He must have been part of the pursuit.

"Nick, Steve," I said. "Lock this guy up."

Goop seemed offended. "Wha'd I do?"

"What do you think?"

Nick and Steve reached to grab him, but he jumped up and took a few steps backward, knocking into the next table. "I ain't goin' nowhere," he snarled.

Guys began standing at all the tables, and some of the ones at the far corners of the room were already starting to head in our direction. Most of the cops who had come into the room had already left, and there were only about seven of us now, standing together. There were maybe a hundred of these guys. Not the best of odds, and they were probably better armed than we were.

The kids were still lying on the floor, but now they were watching us. You could see them asking, in silent questioning, What is this wasp's nest we've stumbled into?

Bravelli's men were closing in on us, tightening the circle. Nick had his hand on his holstered gun, and he glanced at me. "Now I know how Custer felt."

The doors from the kitchen popped open, and Tim Timberlane

came through, followed by his cameraman. The camera light flipped on, bathing the room in a garish glare.

"Get them out of here," I yelled. But who was I saying that to? All the cops were with me, the only people by the door were mob guys. We watched as four or five of them politely pushed Timberlane and his cameraman out of the Roma Room and back into the kitchen. I had to admit, they were a lot nicer about it than some of my guys would have been.

Maybe the camera would have helped us, maybe Bravelli's people would have backed off rather than taken a chance of starring on the six o'clock news. I didn't care—whatever was going to happen was between us and them. It was private.

I turned away from the kitchen doors, back to the menace at hand. And standing there was Bravelli himself, looking a little impatient, like his linguine was getting cold.

"I think it would be better if you just leave now, North," he said. "And take these two Comanches with you."

I ignored him, and turned to Nick. "Other than Goop, who else was kicking the kids?"

"What's your fuckin' problem?" Bravelli asked. "We did you a favor. Hey, nobody got hurt, right?"

I looked at the two kids on the floor. "Almost nobody."

"They didn't deserve it?"

"You don't even know what they did, why they ran in here."

"Like it makes a fuckin' difference? They come in with guns, there's women in here. You can't do your job, North, we will."

"So this is just more of your vigilante shit, is that what's going on?"

Bravelli shrugged, like he didn't know what I was talking about. But he knew. More and more during the last two months, people in the Italian neighborhood had been taking the law into their own hands. Whenever blacks were caught breaking into houses or trying to steal cars, people wouldn't call the police—at least not right away. They'd dispense their own justice, and by the time we'd arrive, the blacks would be half dead.

We all knew Bravelli was behind it. He was the one egging the neighbors on, saying it was up to them to keep the scum out of Westmount. Sometimes his guys even provided the muscle. I had no idea what Bravelli got out of it. Maybe he was just trying to be a local hero.

Standing there looking at Bravelli, there was no way I was going to back down. Even if all we got was Goop, that'd be enough.

Nick had his handcuffs out, ready, and I nodded to him to go ahead. Nick tried to grab Goop's arm, but Goop—more annoyed than anything else—put his palm on Nick's chest and pushed hard. Nick ended up three feet back, and he almost tripped over one of the carjackers.

My cops were getting a little nervous. Bravelli's guys were moving closer, they were absolutely unafraid of us. I didn't want to take my gun out—my cops would have followed my lead, and then there would have been guns all over the place.

For some reason, Bravelli's eyes settled on the silver nameplate over the badge on Steve's blue police shirt.

"Ryder," he said, taking a step forward to get a closer look. "Hmmm. Police Commissioner's son, right? I heard a lot about you."

Steve stood his ground, and just stared at Bravelli. I always thought it was amazing how much Steve resembled his father, how with their easy good looks, their blue eyes and thick, dark eyebrows, they seemed like father-and-son actors out of Hollywood.

Bravelli didn't take his eyes off of Steve, it was weird. I stepped between them and got in Bravelli's face.

"Leave him alone," I said.

"It's OK, Sarge," said Steve.

Bravelli looked at me and shook his head. "Yeah, Sarge, it's OK," he mocked. "Except that you should have left when you had the chance. Now you're way outnumbered."

"Really?" I asked, and then clicked the microphone on my shirt lapel. I bent my head to the microphone, still looking at Bravelli, and tried to sound slightly bored. "Radio, this is 20-C Charlie, I need an assist in the Roma Room at Lucky's."

I straightened my head back up. "OK, let's do a count, Bravelli. We got seven thousand guys. How many you got?"

I knew I wouldn't have long to wait—plenty of cops would still be hanging around outside the restaurant. Two burst in from the kitchen, and then two more, and there was a ⟨ wooden doors.

"They're still locked," said Nick, but burst open, and blue shirts were flowing into at me, like, How come we couldn't do that?

Bravelli's men just stood there, afraid to try a unwilling to retreat. Bravelli looked very pissed, which good for the first time all night.

Lanier appeared next to me. "Everybody OK here?" he as⟨ ⟩, looking around.

"We're all fine and dandy."

Two paramedics with orange first-aid boxes picked their way through the crowd and reached the two kids.

"OK," said Lanier, "now I want everybody out."

"Sure, Captain. Right after I lock up about a dozen assholes for assaulting my prisoners."

"No," he said. "Once Rescue gets these two out of here, we're leaving."

"Captain . . ."

"No," he said again. "There's already a media cluster-fuck outside. I'm not going to let it get ten times worse."

I knew Bravelli was looking at me, waiting for me to glance over, for our eyes to meet. I wasn't going to do it.

Other paramedics were arriving, and everyone—cops, mob guys—watched as the kids were loaded onto stretchers and carried out of the room. When they were gone, Lanier turned to the largest group of cops and announced, "I'm canceling the assist. We're all leaving."

Then he turned and walked out. Bravelli laughed, and I couldn't help it, I looked at him.

"You really are a fuckin' failure at everything, aren't you?" he asked me. Then he snapped his fingers, as if he had just thought of something. "Hey, North, why don't you go to work for the Parking Authority, I bet you can handle writing tickets. If my dumb brother-in-law can do it, anybody can."

One of his pals standing near me started laughing, and I practically had to call on God to keep from smashing my first into Bravelli's face.

almost dark when we got outside. As I walked alone toward patrol car, Lanier intercepted me.

"I just wanted to let you know, Eddie, this wasn't personal."

"Sure, Captain. Like getting me transferred wasn't personal, either."

"Eddie, we've been over this—I had to report those calls to the bosses."

"No one has to report anonymous calls, Captain, and you know it. And now I'm not even in your unit anymore, and you humiliate me in there tonight, in front of all those lowlifes. You know what, Captain? You are the biggest asshole in a department of assholes."

I didn't wait around for his reaction, I just turned and headed for my car.

TWO

When they kicked me out of OC and busted me back to patrol, they could have sent me to any district in the city. They picked the 20th, probably because it was just about the furthest place from my house up in Northeast Philadelphia, which meant a pain-in-the-ass commute. That's how the Department usually expressed its sense of humor in dealing with people it didn't like. If I had lived in the 20th, they would have sent me to Canada or someplace.

I wasn't about to admit it to anyone, but I actually liked working in the 20th. A lot happened there, which was not a bad thing, at least if you were a cop.

It was a real cross section of the city, and had just about every kind of neighborhood. It started in Westmount, which was the largest Italian section outside of South Philly. Hardly any crime ever happened there, other than the occasional mob hit.

As you headed east, toward the skyscrapers of Center City, you went through black West Philadelphia, a succession of poor and working-class neighborhoods. Crime did happen there, plenty of it, but there were a lot of good people, too. It was a shame to see them when they came home from work and found that some crackhead had broken down their door, torn their house apart looking for money, and then taken the VCR on the way out.

Finally came University City, the area around the University of Pennsylvania and Drexel. Penn liked to call itself a "campus in an urban setting," which meant that it was a place where rich kids from the suburbs took money out of ATMs in the middle of the night, and then walked away counting the twenties. They were so dumb even I wanted to rob them.

University City was a collection of student apartment buildings, grungy beer-and-pizza joints, Indian restaurants, and computer stores. A little further from campus were several neighborhoods with large, leafy houses where the professors lived, along with people like newspaper editors and architects. Plenty of big trees your dog could pee on.

At the eastern end of the district was the Schuylkill River, the boundary with Center City. About the only time we ever actually went to the river was when some homeless guy decided he just couldn't take life anymore, and jumped in from the Walnut or Chestnut Street bridge. Neither bridge was really very high, but in West Philadelphia everyone just did the best they could.

I didn't calm down from what happened at Lucky's for hours, and it wasn't until the next night, as I cruised through the streets of West Philadelphia in my patrol car, that I finally began to relax. Maybe it was because everything was so familiar—the row houses and the stores, even the young black guys on the corners, laughing and drinking their beer from bottles in paper bags. Out here, you knew the rules. You knew whose side everyone was on.

About nine-thirty that night, I decided to stop by district headquarters to see if Nick was around. I was hoping maybe I could take another shot at cheering him up. As usual, Sammy was in the operations room doing paperwork at his battered gray-metal desk. And, as usual, he had tuned the TV to a cop show.

Sammy was a regular inside guy, one of the cops who sorted through incident reports and dealt with any members of the public who might wander in. He was a towering blond with a thick mustache, and always reminded me of a Minnesota lumberjack who should be eating pancakes. Except that he wore a blue uniform instead of a red flannel shirt, and I never caught him trying to cut down any of the scrawny trees in West Philly.

"Sammy," I said. "You seen Nick?"

"Unbelievable," he said, pointing to the TV. "This cop stops a

stolen car and says to the guy, 'Could you get out of the car, please?'
He actually said please. And this show's supposed to be realistic."

"Sammy," I said again. "Nick around?"

He shrugged. "Must be out on the street. Look, now he's calling
the guy sir." Sammy looked up at me. "My father's the only one I
call sir."

I headed over to the Shop-Now supermarket on the edge of University
City, I figured some of the guys would be there. The store closed at
9 P.M., so at night the empty parking lot basically became a cop hangout. If you needed to talk to someone in the squad, that's where you
told Radio to have them meet you. A lot of times we'd sit there in
our cars when things were quiet, eating our cheesesteaks and catching
up on the latest gossip.

As I pulled into the darkened lot, I saw two police cars and a brown
unmarked car parked together. Something strange was going on, though
at first I couldn't tell what it was. Nick, Steve, and Buster, another
one of my cops, seemed to be doing something to the unmarked car.

When I reached them I had to laugh—they had covered every one
of the car's windows with big orange stickers that said "TOW." The
stickers were the kind we slapped on a windshield to let the Parking
Authority know we wanted a car towed. You only needed one sticker—
they were pretty big—and these guys had used about two hundred. It
wasn't hard to figure out what was going on.

I pulled up next to the other cars and got out. "Who's inside?"
I asked.

Steve put his finger to his mouth to shush me. He had a mischievous
smile on his face, and his blue eyes were glittering with excitement,
like a kid on Christmas morning.

"It's Little Napoleon," he said, keeping his voice low. "Sleeping like
a baby."

"You got a captain in there?" I was impressed. Little Napoleon was
what everyone called Casimir Razowski, a short little dickhead who
actually did look like Napoleon, or at least the pictures of him in the
liquor ads. He was in night command, one of the people who was

supposed to keep an eye on things when the regular captains went home. Except that the only thing Little Napoleon ever kept an eye on was his watch.

I walked up to his car, a standard city-issue Plymouth. Buster and Nick were covering up the last little gaps on the back window. If Little Napoleon woke up now, he'd be in complete darkness, he wouldn't know where the hell he was.

"He's been coming here every night this week," said Steve. "He just sleeps for the whole shift. I have the feeling this is going to be his last night."

"What he means, Sarge," explained Buster, "is that he wants Little Napoleon gone so *he* can come here to sleep."

"Wait, I thought both you guys came here to sleep," I said.

Buster got an indignant look. "You kidding? I always go behind the old Pepsi plant."

Buster was a big, likable guy, always chomping on his gum and grinning his lopsided grin. He seemed less like a cop than a big-league ballplayer just off the bus from Kansas or someplace.

He also had the loudest mouth in the squad, which he actually put to good use when he was driving 20-17 car. Nothing in that trash heap worked—not the siren, not the horn, not even the red-and-blue emergency lights on top. Other guys driving it couldn't figure out how to make a car-stop. They'd see someone run a red light, and just let them go. But Buster would stick his head out the window and yell, "YO, PULL OVER!" And they would.

I noticed the silver nameplate on Buster's chest. Instead of "BROWN," it said "KIRK." I looked at Steve's nameplate, then Nick's. They were both "KIRK."

"Where'd you get those?" I laughed. Kirk was the name of our captain, Oliver Kirk. I knew the idea was that if Little Napoleon woke up and read one of the nametags, he'd call up headquarters and yell he wanted the ass of some cop named Kirk.

Steve's eyes glittered again. "Place up on Castor Avenue, they're the same ones who supply 'em to the city. I got a friend who works there."

He reached in his front pants pocket and pulled out a whole handful of nameplates. They all said "KIRK."

"Want one?" he asked.

I laughed and shook my head no. I liked Steve, it didn't really bother me that he was the class clown of the 20th. Here he was the Commissioner's son, and he was forever coming up with stuff like this. What made it strange was that he had the potential to be a great cop. Steve had wonderful instincts—he could look at three guys standing on a corner, and say, the one in the middle is carrying a gun. And he was always right.

But he never seemed to take the job seriously, he was always screwing around. Maybe that's what happens when your father's the Commissioner. It couldn't have been easy—any success would be attributed to the father, any failure would show that the son just couldn't measure up. Maybe Steve, in a weird way, was just trying to be his own man.

He looked at me warily. "This OK with you, what we're doin'?"

"Sure," I said. "You guys are restoring my faith in the Police Department."

They laughed and went back to work on the stickers. It was funny—with the four of us standing there talking, you could almost forget that Little Napoleon was in the car. I gazed at the line of row houses across the street, and thought that if anyone looked out their window, they'd just see four cops bullshitting in the middle of an empty supermarket parking lot.

Steve had used up all his stickers, and now was turning his attention to me. "You may be interested to know," he said, "that Michelle's on her way over here."

"Your sister?" I asked, as casually as I could. Nick and Buster were trying not to smile.

"Yeah," said Steve. "You know she's in the Twentieth tonight, right?"

"No," I said. "I didn't know."

"Ortiz went home sick. We were short a sergeant, so they called Michelle over from the Twelfth." That was a neighboring district, and we often used each other's sergeants.

"What, when did this happen?" I asked. "I was just talking to Sammy, he didn't say anything."

"Couple of minutes ago," said Steve. "Michelle just paged me, she said Donna's showing her around the district. I told them to stop by here."

"You want her to see how we do things in the Twentieth, huh?"

Steve smiled. "So, you going to ask her out?"

I gave him a blank look, like I didn't know what he was talking about. Nick and Buster had big smiles now, they were just having a good old time.

I was a little nervous, I hadn't counted on seeing Michelle again so soon. We had met only three nights ago, at a retirement party for a detective from Central. It was held at River Fever, a huge club down in Essington that overlooked the Delaware. A real pickup place—the dance floors were jammed with hungry-eyed guys and girls from across the river in Jersey. But the retirement party had reserved the outdoor deck, which was actually pretty nice. It had a bamboo bar, and palm leaves, and a warm breeze coming off the river.

Everyone at the party was standing around, talking shop, and someone introduced me to Michelle. We just started talking, and by the end of the evening we were at a table by ourselves, in the dark, away from the others. It was one of those deals where you feel you've known the person forever, where everything just seems so natural and relaxed.

Like her brother and father, Michelle had the family's dark eyebrows and high cheekbones, and blue eyes that were so alive they just seemed to talk to you. Her face was narrow, like a model's, but it wasn't hard, it seemed to have a gentleness to it. And she had shoulder-length brown hair that was so luxurious it looked like something out of a shampoo commercial.

She told me she had just made sergeant the week before, and was starting her new assignment at the 12th. She knew she'd be filling in at the 20th from time to time—which meant she'd be supervising her brother.

"Think that'll be a problem?" I had asked her.

Michelle just smiled. "I did it all the time when we were growing up."

I asked Michelle how much older she was than Steve.

"Four years. But what you really want to know is how old I am now, right?"

I nodded with a sheepish smile.

"I'm thirty-one," she said. "And you're what, about thirty-five?"

I nodded again. "Good guess."

"You're kind of a serious person, aren't you?" she asked.

"Why do you say that?"

"I don't know, you just have a way of looking at people that's so intense. The way you kind of scrunch up your forehead."

"I didn't know I did that."

"Well, you do. But it's not a bad thing. I kind of like it."

Sitting there in the darkness by the water, we totally forgot about the party, forgot anyone else was around. About midnight, when she said she had to go, I asked her whether she wanted to get together sometime.

"Sure," she said, then smiled. "But aren't we doing this backwards?"

"What do you mean?" I asked.

"Well usually, two cops meet on the job, and then get together off-duty. So since we're meeting off-duty, where are we going to go on a date, a hostage situation?"

I laughed. "That's a good idea. We could have dinner first—Italian hoagies in the patrol car."

"We hear the hostage call," said Michelle. "We rush to the scene . . ."

"We talk the gunman into surrendering . . ."

"Right," said Michelle. "By offering him our food."

"And then," I said, "the three of us go get some water ice for dessert."

Michelle nodded approvingly. "Sounds like the perfect date to me."

I looked at her. She was great, I couldn't believe my luck. I hadn't met anybody like her in a long time. Maybe not since Patricia.

Of course, all the other cops at the retirement party saw the two of us talking and laughing together, and apparently we became a big topic of conversation. By the next day, everyone in the district had heard there was something going on between Michelle and me.

Now in the supermarket parking lot, Steve, Buster, and Nick were looking at me, waiting for me to reveal all. I felt like I was back in seventh grade.

There was loud rumbling and clanking, and we all turned to see a police tow truck pulling into the lot and heading toward us.

Steve almost giggled. "This is going to be great," he told me. "We're having our sleeping captain towed to the impoundment lot."

The tow truck backed up in front of the Plymouth, and the driver, a stocky Italian guy, climbed out.

"This is Dominic," said Steve. "Friend of mine."

We all nodded hello. Steve quietly explained the situation to Dominic, whose eyes widened when he got to the part of who was actually inside the car.

"Yo, Steve," he said, "I don't wanna get into any more trouble, why do ya think I'm in the Tow Unit to begin with?"

"Don't worry," said Steve. "In order for Little Napoleon to jam any of us up, he'd first have to explain what he was doing sleeping in his car in the middle of West Philadelphia at ten o'clock at night."

It was a good point. Dominic walked over and started hooking up the Plymouth, and we watched as another police car pulled into the lot.

"Looks like Michelle and Donna," said Steve.

It was the first time I had seen Michelle in uniform, and it was a treat. Police uniforms are designed for men, and they tend to flatten out the curves of most women. Michelle's blue uniform just brought out her curves, which she had a lot of, all over her body.

Michelle walked over and said hello to me, and I said, "Welcome to West Philadelphia." But I was thinking, damn, I ain't never seen no cop like this before.

It would have been hard to imagine a more dramatic contrast between Donna and Michelle. Donna was a short, chain-smoking, smart-ass, frizzy-blond-haired cop who grew up on the streets of Philadelphia's working-class Port Richmond section. She had a soft, friendly face—it was her personality that was rough around the edges.

Donna was Buster's usual partner and, as we all knew, his girlfriend. They tried to keep it a secret, but we could tell, just by the way they acted together.

Michelle couldn't help noticing the stickers all over Little Napoleon's car.

"What is this?" she asked.

"Shhhh," said Steve. "It's a captain, sleeping. We're having him towed."

"Why?"

"Because," Buster said solemnly, "he is an interloper."

"Get outta here," Donna said, and laughed. "You don't even know what that means."

"I used it right."

"Sure you did. Gimme a cigarette."

Buster obediently reached into his blue shirt pocket, pulled out a cigarette pack, and handed it to Donna.

Michelle was watching, amused. I wanted to talk to her, alone. About what, I didn't know, but it didn't matter.

A call came over our portable radios, report of woman screaming inside a house, 5823 Tyler. It was Nick and Steve's sector, Radio gave them the assignment. Steve clicked on his radio and acknowledged the call. "Twenty-fifteen, OK," he said, but he made no move toward his car.

Michelle looked at her brother, puzzled. "Aren't you going to go?"

"No rush, it's just a crackhouse. We get that call every night. There's nobody screaming, neighbors just want us to show up and scare the druggies away. This is much more important."

"Is this what you guys do every night?" Michelle asked.

"Oh, no," said Buster. "We can't come up with ideas this good every night."

"But Steve is always the ringleader, right?"

"Yep," said Buster. "Steve's the expert on the fun, and me and Nick are the experts on the women."

Donna snorted and turned to Michelle. "The only thing Buster knows about women is from those pipehead hookers on Sixtieth Street."

"Don't knock it," said Buster.

"Hey, Buster," Donna said, "didn't I hear you trying to bum five bucks from someone, 'bout an hour ago?" She looked at us. "The hookers charge five bucks, Buster's asking around for five bucks. Think it's a coincidence?"

Michelle smiled at me. "Are they like this all the time?"

"All the time," I said, and then thought, why not ask her out now? I'll just take her aside and ask her.

Steve reached into his pants pocket and pulled out a couple of nameplates. "Here," he said to Michelle and Donna, "put these on."

Donna laughed when she saw the name and grabbed one immediately, but Michelle hesitated. "This is the captain's name?" she asked.

"Yeah," said Steve. "Isn't it great?" He saw her expression, then added, "Or are you going to be a sergeant now?"

Two sets of blue eyes locked onto each other for a moment, and then Michelle walked over to the Plymouth. We all thought she was going to pull open the door and wake up Little Napoleon. But she just looked at all the stickers, then turned to face her brother.

"You missed a spot," she said.

Steve gave a relieved smile and took a look at where she was pointing. "Damn," he said. "Buster, get me a sticker."

"Next time, Steve," said Michelle, "call me first. That is, if you want it done right."

"Hey, I did OK before you came out here."

"Really? How do you run down the street with your shoelaces untied?"

We all looked at Steve's shoes—the laces of both were actually untied. Steve quickly bent down to tie them, and looked up at Michelle.

"I was always surprised you became a cop," he said, still bent down. "Police cars don't come equipped with lighted makeup mirrors."

"At least I answer my calls when they come over the radio," said Michelle.

I half wondered whether Little Napoleon was already awake, and was just sitting there listening to this shit.

Nick asked Steve something, and Buster had turned to Donna, so for the first time Michelle and I were able to talk.

"I had a good time the other night," I said.

Michelle smiled. "So did I."

We took a few steps away from the others, it was like Michelle was thinking the same thing I was. We both just wanted to be together.

When we turned, though, Steve, Nick, Donna, and Buster were suddenly standing right next to us, with innocent looks on their faces.

"Ignore them," I said, and we turned our backs and walked some more. When we stopped again, they were still with us, as if we hadn't even moved.

"Where we goin', Sarge?" asked Buster. "Pittsburgh?"

Another call came over the radio, someone was complaining about a neighbor's loud music. Donna was assigned to handle it, which meant that Michelle would be going, too.

"You want to grab a beer after work?" I asked her.

"Sure," she said.

"That sounds great," said Steve. "We'll all go."

Michelle looked at her brother and shook her head. As she got into the car with Donna, he was just smiling at her, you could tell he was asking her to smile back. And as the car pulled away, she did, very slightly.

When they were gone, I turned to Steve and Nick. "You guys better take care of that crackhouse call. Radio's going to want to know where you are."

"Yeah, sure," said Steve. "Dom, you ready?"

Dominic had hooked up the car and was sitting in his truck, just waiting to get out of there. "Yeah," he said out the window. "Just put in a good word about me with your father."

Steve laughed. "You think he listens to me?"

Dominic shifted the truck into gear and started pulling the Plymouth away. Steve was beside himself with joy. "Man, I can hardly wait until Little Napoleon wakes up."

He didn't have to wait long. As Dominic drove out of the lot, he cut the driveway too close and the right wheels of the truck bumped down over the curb, followed by the right wheels of the Plymouth. A few seconds later, the car's window came down about six inches, and stopped, jammed on the stickers. There wasn't enough room for Little Napoleon to stick his head out the window, all you could see was his mouth, yelling at the tow truck. If Dominic heard anything, he was pretending not to. The last we saw of them, the tow truck, the Plymouth, and Little Napoleon's big mouth were all sailing merrily down Spruce Street.

Ten minutes later I was back in my patrol car, cruising aimlessly past the night-darkened row houses and storefronts of West Philadelphia, thinking about Michelle. I could hardly wait to see her again, even if we'd be surrounded by a bunch of leering, beer-guzzling cops. I checked my watch—just after ten, less than two hours to go.

"ASSIST! ASSIST!" came a shout over the radio. There was crackling, then dead silence. Shit, that didn't sound good, it didn't sound good at all. I wasn't sure about the voice, it might be Nick. Were he and Steve OK? I reached an intersection, and slowed to a stop, waiting to see which way I should go.

"Unit?" the dispatcher asked. She sounded as worried as I was.

There was more crackling, an unintelligible yell, then silence again. I pictured cops throughout the district, one or two in a car, listening. Probably some had stopped, like me, waiting. It seemed like forever. Finally, there was a burst of static, then: "Officer down! Officer down!" It was definitely Nick's voice. "5-8-4-3 Tyler. Call Rescue! Officer down!"

I was fifteen blocks away. I took them as fast as I could, sixty, sixty-five, seventy mph. At that speed, trees and houses rush past in a blur, you don't notice your siren or the flashing blue and red lights on the buildings as you pass by. All you can do is concentrate on the next intersection: if it's a green light, you try to go even faster; if the light is red, you slow a little, just enough to see whether you'll be hit, then you step on the gas and pray.

I had the green light at a wide intersection a few blocks from Tyler, and I knew I'd be there in a moment. Out of the corner of my eye, I saw another patrol car screaming toward me from the left. I jerked the wheel as hard as I could to the right, spinning the car in a tight circle. Whoever was in the other car did the same thing. Two cop cars, spinning like pinwheels in the middle of an intersection, inches from each other. We both came to a stop at the same time. I didn't recognize the guy—he was from another district—but we sat there for a moment, looking at each other in relief.

I could hear on my radio that the first cars wer
scene, they were yelling that a cop was down. I shot ou
tion, and the streets flashed by, and then I was in fror
house, and out of my car, running up the sidewalk tow
of cops gathered on the wooden front porch.

Steve was sprawled face up, next to the open front do .. Michelle
was already there, kneeling beside him, pressing her hand to the side
of his head, blood seeping out between her fingers.

"Please," she said, taking deep breaths, "God, please!"

THREE

Donna was on the porch, too, and she bent down and gently pulled Michelle back. Michelle's hands, covered with blood, kept reaching toward her brother. In the light of a streetlamp I could see dark red blood oozing from a bullet hole in the right side of Steve's head, matting his hair, creating rivulets on the wooden porch planks. His police radio, still turned on, echoed the chaos around him.

Nick was reeling around the porch, dazed, like a confused dog over its fallen master. "Where's Rescue?" he shouted into the air. "Where are they?"

Michelle fell back on her brother again, and again Donna had to pull her away. It was awful. Through the front door I could see cops searching the dimly lit living room, and I heard the thumping of feet going up and down stairs. Buster came through the doorway onto the porch.

"Place is empty," he said, holstering his gun. "We checked upstairs, the basement, round back in the alley."

Nick was still pacing the porch, and I grabbed his shoulder to stop him.

"Nick, what happened?"

His eyes were full of anguish, and he stepped back, breaking my grip. "Where's Rescue, Eddie? Where's Rescue?"

I was beginning to wonder that myself. There was no sign of one of the Fire Department's boxy red ambulances. I looked back at Steve. The porch floor was covered with blood. We didn't have time to wait. I glanced at the street and spotted V.K. and Larry's white police van.

"Let's get him in the wagon," I yelled to the cops around me.

Four of us picked up Steve and carried him down the steps and then to the van. We opened up the rear doors and put Steve in, laying him on the cold metal floor. Michelle, her blue shirt red with blood, climbed in and cradled her brother's head in her lap. She was talking to him, saying something softly over and over, I couldn't hear what it was. Donna got in the back with her and we closed the door. V.K. and Larry got in front, and the wagon took off.

All I could think of was that this was somehow my fault. I'm the fucking sergeant, I should be able to keep my cops from getting shot. Maybe there was something I should have said to Steve, something I should have taught him, that could have prevented this from happening. Wasn't that what I was supposed to be doing out here, keeping my cops safe?

I felt like throwing up. I wanted to go somewhere, to just get away and think about what a fuckup I was. What made me believe I could be a sergeant, be responsible for other people's lives?

But I knew I couldn't leave, I had to stay and do my job. Focus, I told myself. Focus on what you have to do now.

Nick was standing a few feet away, still dazed.

"Now, what the fuck happened here, Nick?"

"I don't know," he said. "I was around back, I heard a shot . . ." He paused to steady himself.

"Take your time," I said.

"So I came through the back door, through the house, when I got to the front, the door was open, there was Steve . . ." He broke off again.

"You see anybody?"

"A black guy, running down the street . . . but I didn't go after him, Eddie. Steve was shot, I got on the radio, I didn't know what to do."

"You did the right thing, Nick, you called for help."

That seemed to calm him a little.

"This guy you saw," I said. "Any flash at all?"

Nick shook his head. "Just a black guy, I really couldn't see anything more. I should have gone after him, Eddie, I'm sorry."

"No, Nick, you stayed with Steve, like you should have."

I got the attention of a handful of cops standing in the front yard. "Start knocking on doors, see if anybody saw anything."

They fanned out on both sides of the street. The block was lined with trees and wide three-story row houses, all with porches that were divided off from one another by metal or wood railings. This had once been a prosperous black neighborhood, but it was falling on hard times, and people were moving out. A crackhouse in the middle of your block can do a lot of damage.

Bowman, the lieutenant, was coming up the sidewalk. "Captain's on his way in from home," he said.

Bowman had been transferred from the 26th in North Philly about three months before. It only took us a couple of days to peg him as one of those cops who become supervisors so they can rest. He usually hung around the operations room reading his hunting magazines, and he wouldn't go out unless something big happened. Then when he got to a scene he'd be pissed at us, like his attitude was, Why can't you keep things quiet? Tonight he had a real worried look on his face, and I think he knew he wasn't going to be getting back to his magazines anytime soon.

I told Nick to tell us what happened, from the beginning.

They got the call about the woman screaming, he said, and when they got here, Steve knocked on the front door, and Nick waited by the back door.

"That's the way we usually do it at this place," he said.

"Usually?" I asked.

"Yeah, we're always hoping that one of these days, when Steve knocks on the front, some guy with the stuff is going to run out the back, we'll get a drug pinch."

I was furious. "Without any fucking backup?"

Nick looked at the ground.

"That is so fucking stupid, Nicky," I yelled. "What the fuck were you thinking of?"

"Usually nobody answers the door, so we just leave. We never go in." Nick's eyes pleaded with me to understand.

"So this time," Bowman said, "some crackhead opens the door and blows your partner away."

Nick looked at the ground again.

Buster was coming up to us. "Hey, Sarge, we got a neighbor, real good witness. She heard a shot, looked out her window, saw a guy running down the sidewalk."

"Any flash?"

"Yeah, lotta detail."

"All right, put it out."

Buster tilted his head to talk into the mike clipped to his shoulder. A moment later, the dispatcher's rapid but controlled voice came back across a sea of radios.

"All units, flash information on a founded shooting of a police officer, 5-8-4-3 Tyler, approximately ten minutes ago. Looking for a black male, twenty-five years of age, five eleven, 160 pounds, wearing a black baseball cap, red T-shirt, dark pants, and white sneakers. Last seen running west on Tyler from that location."

Cops were streaming back to their cars and squealing off into the night. Everywhere there was movement, lights, sirens, people yelling into the radio. When an officer gets shot, his squad moves through the grieving process quickly, and right now we were in the stage of being very fucking pissed off.

Cops were still inside the crackhouse—that was stupid, they were stomping all over the crime scene. I climbed back on the porch and stepped through the front door.

"I want everybody out of the house," I yelled.

The place was pretty disgusting. The living room floor was covered with all kinds of trash, newspapers, McDonald's wrappers, balls of tin foil, beer bottles, a box of kitty litter filled with cat shit. There were a couple of old couches, half the cushions gone, and a battered wooden coffee table covered with junk.

I knew from Nick and Steve that a man and a woman actually lived here. But it wasn't really their house anymore. They had started letting other people use the place in exchange for drugs, and pretty soon the whole house got taken over by crackheads.

Marisol Cruz, one of my cops, was standing by the door.

"Look what we found, Sarge."

She pointed to a gun lying on the floor. A snub-nose, probably a .38.

"Don't let anybody touch it until the detectives get here," I told her. She nodded OK.

I went back outside, found Bowman, and told him about the gun. Detectives from Southwest were on their way, he said. Bowman was staring out onto the street, and I followed his line of vision. A TV news van was pulling up, the first, I was sure, of many. I told a couple of cops to stretch some tape—the yellow kind that says "POLICE LINE— DO NOT CROSS"—from tree to tree in a big circle around the front of the house.

I wanted to call the hospital, see how Steve was doing, and I remembered there was a pay phone in front of the bar on the corner. As I headed down the sidewalk toward the bar, I saw the white shirts arriving: captains, inspectors, chief inspectors. Commissioner's son gets shot, they start calling everybody in.

The phone was all beat up, and I was amazed I even got a dial tone. I called HUP, the Hospital of the University of Pennsylvania, and got through to the emergency room. I identified myself, and asked if there were any 20th District cops around. I was surprised when Michelle came on the line.

"He's just going into surgery," she said. "I keep asking how he is, and they won't tell me, they just say they're doing all they can. I don't know what that means. Do you know what that means?"

I said I didn't.

"My father's on his way here, maybe he can find out."

I told her everyone was praying for Steve, and hung up.

When I got back to the crackhouse, a small crowd was gathering, and three or four television crews were standing in the street filming the porch with their harsh bright lights. Just in time for the fucking eleven o'clock news. I was glad the TV cameras were too far away to see the blood.

Buster's voice suddenly came over Police Radio: "We got 'em!"

Typical of Buster. Forgets to say who or where he is.

"Unit coming in?" the dispatcher asked.

"This is twenty-oh-seven," said Buster, out of breath. "We got 'em, Six-two and Locust. Matches the flash perfectly."

That was about nine blocks away. Was it possible we had actually got the shooter? I got on the radio and told Buster to bring the suspect to Tyler Street, we'd have the witness ID him here.

A couple of minutes later, Buster pulled up. There, in the back of his car, was a young guy in a red T-shirt and black Yankees cap, angry as hell. There was something wrong, though. He didn't look like a crackhead, he didn't look like he belonged in that house. His eyes were too clear, his clothes were too nice. But I didn't care, I was excited, we all were. We all wanted the asshole that shot Steve.

Two of my cops were escorting a middle-aged black woman down the steps of her front porch. With the description she had given us, obviously her eyes were good, but there was something else I was worried about. She might get intimidated by the suspect and change her mind, and I didn't want to lose our only witness. We had to keep the suspect from seeing her face. I told the cops to bring her directly behind the patrol car, and then about four of us stood in front of her, so she could sort of peek between us. As Buster got the guy out of the backseat, we shined our flashlights right in his eyes. He came out blinking, blinded by the lights.

I could hear the woman gasp. "That's him," she said. "That is definitely him."

We had the motherfucker cold.

"That's my son," a woman somewhere yelled. "That's my son you got there."

Now what?

A thin, haggard black woman was coming toward us. "That's my boy you got there," she yelled. "He didn't do nothin', why you got him?"

"Ma'am," I said, "we have a witness."

"What witness?" She spotted the older woman. "Now Miss Jones, don't you recognize my boy, this is my boy Charles."

So much for keeping the witness anonymous.

"Ma'am," I said, "this woman saw your son running from the crime scene."

"What crime scene?" she yelled. "He was just walking out the house, he didn't no sooner get out the door when we heard this loud bang. We thought it was a firecracker."

"How long from the time he left the house until you heard the bang?" I asked.

"Wasn't no time. Happened in the same second, the same second."

"Was there anybody else in the house with you?"

"Everybody was there. Cousins, aunts, uncles . . . listen, Mr. Policeman, you got to let my boy go."

I turned back to the older woman and asked, "Ma'am, where did you first see the suspect?"

"Right there," she said, pointing to the sidewalk in front of a house three doors down from the crackhouse.

"And that's right where we live," said the suspect's mother.

Miss Jones came out from behind us and walked right up to the suspect. "Oh, it *is* Charles," she said. "I'm sorry, child, I didn't know it was you." She turned to me and added, "I watched this boy grow up. He's a good boy."

Buster and I looked at each other with the same thought: we were screwed. Our only lead was wrong, which meant we now had no idea who we were hunting for.

Now, we'd be stopping every black guy who looked even a little suspicious. And it's not like it's done politely. You see a guy walking down the sidewalk a few blocks from the crime scene, maybe acting a little nervous, you can't just roll down your window and say, Excuse me, sir, are you by any chance the gentleman who discharged a firearm in the direction of one of our police officers?

If he's the shooter, he'll run. And if he's got a gun, he may figure he's got nothing to lose, and all of a sudden you've got another cop shot. So you have to get the drop on him. You jump out of the car fast, with your gun in your hand, and before he knows what's happening you push him up against the hood and pat him down. Then you can ask him where he's coming from and where he's going.

All this meant that a lot of black guys were going to be very unhappy with us. And that meant, I knew, the black community was going to be all over our asses.

I told the cops to take Miss Jones back home, and then I turned to our former suspect. Donna switched off her flashlight, but Buster was so frustrated he kept shining his light in the guy's eyes.

"Damn, why you blinding me?" he said. "I didn't do nothin'."

"Buster," I said, and made a motion with my thumb like I was switching off a flashlight. He finally turned it off.

"Why were you running?" I asked.

"Hey, when shooting starts in this neighborhood, you don't stand around, you get as far away as possible. Them bullets don't have no names on 'em."

"You see anything?"

"I didn't see nothing. My feet were doing the seeing for me."

I turned to Buster. "Get the cuffs off, but take him to Southwest anyway."

"You arresting me?" the guy asked, as Buster fished out his hand-cuff key.

"No," I said, "but you're a witness. The detectives are gonna want to talk to you."

"You're just doin' this because I'm black."

"You can shut up now," I said.

"I ain't shuttin' up. You motherfuckin' cops violated my civil rights."

His hands were free, and he was rubbing his wrists like he had been manacled for the last ten years.

"All you cops are fuckin' racist."

The TV crews heard the commotion and started over.

"All right!" someone in the crowd yelled. "Go, Homicide!"

I stared at the guy. "Your nickname is Homicide?"

He took a step forward so he could see my nameplate. "Your name is North? What are you, a fucking compass?"

All of a sudden we were blinded by television lights. I quickly turned and walked away, and I could hear him saying, "That's right, they violated my civil rights. A black man can't walk down the street without getting harassed."

Captain Oliver Kirk, the only guy who could legitimately wear one of Steve's nameplates, pulled up and got out of his black Plymouth. He was in uniform—white shirt with the badge on the breast pocket and double gold bars on the shoulders—but he had a rumpled look, like he had got dressed in a hurry. His curly red hair was sticking out in all directions.

Bowman walked up, and the two of us filled the captain in. We told him that all we had so far was the gun. Detectives had already bagged it up and brought it out.

I wanted to go over to HUP to see if there was anything I could do for Michelle. Bowman hesitated a little—if I left, there'd be more work for him—but Kirk said go ahead.

I looked back at the house. It was weird—there were so many people here, cops, neighbors, reporters. But Steve was gone, and the asshole who shot him was gone. This was just the empty shell of something that had happened. All we could do was look at it, examine it. In a way, it wasn't even real anymore.

I found Michelle in a third-floor waiting area, down the hall from the operating room. She was standing silently with her father, and I hesitated a little before walking up to them—maybe they didn't want to be disturbed. But Michelle looked up and spotted me, and waved me over.

"Any word?" I asked.

She shook her head no.

"Sir," I said to her father. "I'm Eddie North, Steve's sergeant. I just wanted to see if there's anything I could do."

"Thank you," he said, and we shook hands.

Ben Ryder was a big, broad-chested man in his mid-fifties, still with powerful muscles, still with the striking good looks he had passed along to his children. Whenever I had seen him before, usually on TV, he was wearing a suit. Now he had on a navy golf shirt and khakis. I was always a little caught off-guard by his command presence. You knew that when he walked into a room, he could gain the respect of everyone there by his appearance alone. I could see why most cops considered him intimidating.

A few minutes later, Michelle's mother arrived, a middle-aged blonde with a big purse, holding back tears. She hugged Michelle, then the Commissioner. I remembered Michelle telling me that her mother and father were divorced, but you couldn't tell, the way they held each other. At least for the moment, they were a family again.

I told Michelle I was going to wait outside, and she nodded and took my hands in hers.

"Thanks for coming, Eddie," she said, trying to smile.

I took the elevator downstairs and left the hospital through the emergency room entrance. The sliding glass doors whooshed open, sending me out into the warm night.

Off to one side, TV crews were setting up a bank of cameras, probably getting ready for some sort of press conference. There were reporters all over the place, trying to get comments from everyone who went in and out, including me when I passed by. I just ignored them.

Some of the cops from the 20th were standing next to their patrol cars under a lamppost in the hospital lot, smoking and talking quietly. Donna was there, and V.K. and Larry, and Marisol, and Paulie Rapone. Dave Larkin grew up with Steve, he was there, too. When I walked up they looked at me, silently asking whether I knew anything.

I just shrugged and said, "Nothing yet."

Suddenly, we were blinded by a TV light. It was that jerkoff reporter Tim Timberlane. He didn't give a shit about Steve—he just wanted someone to help him look good on the eleven o'clock news. It wasn't going to be me.

"Sergeant, what can you tell me?" he asked.

"For starters," I said, trying to look past blue spots, "I can tell you to go fuck yourself."

The cameraman had the sense to turn off the light, but Timberlane didn't give up. "We just want to know how you feel," he said.

I forced myself to keep my mouth shut. I didn't like that camera there.

Buster took a couple of steps forward and put his face in Timberlane's face. "No one wants to talk to you," he said. "Bye."

"But . . ."

"Bye."

Timberlane noticed that camera crews were surrounding someone outside the emergency room entrance, and he and his cameraman took off in that direction.

"Something's going on," I said.

An inspector was walking toward us, I couldn't remember his name. "You the people from the Twentieth?" he asked.

"Yeah," I said.

"Commissioner sent me out here to let you know."

Donna saw the look on his face, and cried out, "Oh, my God."

The inspector hesitated a moment, and then said, "Steve Ryder has just died."

In my mind, I saw Michelle's hand on Steve's head, trying to hold in the blood, trying to hold in the life. She couldn't do it. No one could.

Donna and Marisol started crying first, then some of the guys. No one said anything. Ever since Steve got shot, we were moving too fast to feel anything. But now we all just stood there, wiping the tears away.

When I got home that night, I sat on the couch in my darkened living room and had a beer, then another, then another. But I knew that no matter how much I drank, it wouldn't be enough.

I still lived in the small row house Patricia and I had bought years ago. She moved out after the divorce, and I was glad to be able to stay there. It was in Oxford Circle, a peaceful neighborhood in Northeast Philadelphia that had at least a couple of cops living on every block.

Of course, we all knew each other. We had backyard barbecues in the summer, and on Sunday afternoons in the fall we'd all get together to watch the Eagles on TV until it was time for the guys on four-to-midnight to head into work.

If you ever needed help—shoveling your car out of the snow or putting up a new rain gutter—there was always someone around. It didn't matter that they worked in different districts, or that this one was a patrolman and that one a lieutenant. You were among people who understood you, understood the life of a cop.

Sitting there in my living room, I wondered whether I really wanted that life anymore. How could it be worth it, when you had to watch your friends die?

FOUR

The day after a cop is killed is always the worst. You stand there at roll call and see that someone's missing, and you realize he'll never be there again. You don't feel like going back out onto the street, but you know you have to, that's your job.

At least there was one good thing about coming into work—we could talk to each other about Steve, trade stories about him. Buster said, Remember that night Steve found a big toy stuffed lion in a Dumpster, and stuck it in the back of a wagon? Whenever we'd open the back doors to put prisoners in, they'd scream in terror. That was classic Steve.

Like most district headquarters, ours was pretty cramped, and we had to hold our roll calls in a dimly lit, green-tiled room that doubled as a municipal courtroom. In the front of the room, two steps up, was an old judge's bench and an American flag on a wooden pole. Sometimes at roll call the captain or one of the lieutenants would stand up there and address the troops, but I usually just stood in front of the guys at ground level. It seemed a lot less trouble.

Shortly after 4 P.M., the twenty-eight men and women in my squad assembled for roll call. No one bothered to line up in rows, the way you're supposed to. People were pretty much standing around in groups of two or three, with their friends.

I didn't feel like talking, so I just told everyone to stay sharp going in on disturbances, which is what we called domestic disputes, and on man-with-a-gun calls, and any other time we rolled in on something that might suddenly turn deadly. I said we shouldn't get so caught up in what had happened to Steve that we'd be putting our own lives in danger.

They were all very quiet. Donna was still crying a little, and Buster's smile was gone, he looked heartbroken. Nick kept his eyes on the ground, I don't think he once looked up. I had called him at home that morning, and told him he didn't have to come into work. He showed up anyway.

I dismissed the squad, and they filed into the operations room to get their portable radios from the bank of chargers on the wall. They talked among themselves a little and then finally walked out into the Yard, climbed into their patrol cars, and headed out onto the street.

As I was about to join them, Dee-Dee, the captain's secretary, came into the operations room.

"Oh, you're still here, good," she said. "Captain wants to see you."

I followed her down the hallway. She turned left to go back to her desk, and I took a right and walked through the open door to Oliver Kirk's office. I've been inside a lot of captains' offices, but never one like Kirk's. Most of the time, you'll see plaques on the wall from the mayor or from some community group. Then there's usually a map of whatever police district it is, with red or green pushpins showing drug pinches or maybe reported burglaries.

Kirk's office, on the other hand, was the bridge of the starship *Enterprise.* When he first got promoted—and became Captain Kirk— guys started leaving *Star Trek* stuff in his office as a joke. He'd come in, and there'd be a little James T. Kirk action figure sitting on his empty chair. He loved it, and even started collecting the stuff himself. Now everything in his office had to do with *Star Trek.*

On the walls were color stills from the original *Star Trek* series, along with a row of oil portraits of the *Enterprise* crew, which he had painted himself. They weren't bad—you could actually tell who was who. By the door was a clock in the shape of the Star Trek insignia. Next to it was a glass display case with weapons and other devices. And in a back corner of the office, next to the window, was a lifesize cardboard cutout of James T. Kirk himself.

People who didn't know Kirk came into his office and immediately assumed he was a nut. We used to joke that Spock—Bravelli's Spock, not the real one—would be right at home here.

The first time I was in his office, Kirk proudly showed me what everything was. And he admitted that when he was a kid, he used to watch the TV show all the time. I could picture it—Kirk as a twelve-year-old boy, with the same curly red hair he had today, sitting in front of the TV set, eyes wide open, as his hero led the *Enterprise* to glory. Naturally, his nickname in the 20th was "James T." Sometimes we'd forget and call him that to his face, and he never seemed to mind.

As I walked in, Kirk motioned for me to sit. It was just a regular chair, not a *Star Trek* chair or anything.

"How you doin', Eddie?" he asked, and I could tell he wasn't doing too good himself. It's hard for a sergeant to lose one of his men, but it's hard for a captain, too. Maybe harder.

"He was a good kid," Kirk said simply.

"Yeah."

We looked at each other. What else was there to say?

"Homicide making any progress?" I finally asked.

Kirk shook his head. "No, and there's some trouble. The black community's getting hot about all these ped-stops. People are calling their church leaders, the church leaders are calling the politicians. It's not good."

"Yeah, I thought that might happen," I said.

I knew that all day today detectives and street cops had been questioning young black guys hanging on corners. We no longer had much hope of coming across the shooter himself—he was probably hiding in another crackhouse somewhere. Our only hope was that his name—or even his nickname—would spread on the street.

When someone commits a crime that makes the papers and television, they have a hard time keeping it to themselves. They want to point to the TV and say, See that, I did that. It makes them feel powerful, like they're really somebody. Eventually they tell someone, and that person tells someone else, and pretty soon it's not a secret anymore.

Most of the guys we were questioning were known drug dealers and crackheads and assorted lowlifes, but some of them were also regular young guys. It wasn't fair, and you really couldn't blame them for complaining. I certainly wouldn't have wanted to get stopped by the cops just for walking down the street. But if there was another way of finding Steve's killer, I didn't know about it.

"Eddie, the reason I wanted to talk to you. We had another vigilante attack in Westmount."

"Today?"

"Yeah, this morning. Black guy robbed an Italian grocery on Cedar, ran out and jumped in his car, car wouldn't start."

"Don't tell me," I said. "Instead of running, he kept trying to get the car started."

Kirk looked at me in surprise. "You already heard about this?"

"Just a lucky guess."

Kirk smiled. "Anyway, the owner came out and started yelling, and pretty soon there was a crowd around the car. They dragged the guy out and almost killed him. He's at St. Michael's now."

"Any of Bravelli's people involved this time?"

"You kidding? Nobody saw nothin'. Street full of shoppers, they all happened to be looking the other way."

"You want me to drop by?"

"If you would. The detectives are all tied up on this thing with Steve."

"I understand."

"Talk to the store owner, he's not a bad guy. He didn't want to say anything this afternoon, but things have quieted down, maybe he'll open up a little."

I never did talk to the store owner. I didn't even make it to the store. The closest I got was a few blocks away, at the corner of 80th and Locust, where a cluster of Italian bakeries filled the air with warm, sweet smells.

I was stopped at the light, gazing to my left at the pastries in the window at Carlino's on the other side of the street. I noticed that the image of my patrol car—with me in it—was reflected in the bakery's glass door. You don't get to see yourself like that too often, and I was actually looking at the door when it opened and Canaletto and then Bravelli stepped out onto the sidewalk. A black Cadillac Seville had been sitting at the curb just around the corner on 80th, and the moment Bravelli emerged from the bakery, Goop hopped out of the driver's seat and quickly pulled open the back door.

As Canaletto got in the other side, Bravelli spotted me, and paused. We just looked at each other for a few seconds, stone-faced, neither of us giving away anything. Then he abruptly turned and walked over to the Cadillac and got in. Goop—resplendent in a highway-worker-orange jogging suit—closed the door and got back behind the wheel. A few moments later, the car eased away from the curb.

Maybe I should have just let it go. I didn't really want to be in Westmount—I wanted to be back in West Philly, trying to find the guy who shot Steve. But when I saw Bravelli, somehow all my anger got transferred right onto him. He was the reason this job was fucked up, he was the reason that everything went wrong, and that good people like Steve got killed. I knew it didn't fit together like that, but I didn't try to make sense of it. Whoever shot Steve was nowhere around; Bravelli was right here. And right now, he would do.

I took a sharp left onto 80th, pulling behind the Cadillac, and flipped on my overhead red and blue lights. Somewhere inside of my head a voice was saying, wait, you have to have a plan, you can't do this without a plan. But I just pushed that aside. And as the Cadillac's brake lights came on and both our cars slowed to a stop, I could feel the adrenaline starting to kick in.

It was a typical Westmount street, narrow row houses one after the other on both sides. I got out of my car and walked toward the Seville. When I reached the driver's window, I almost yelled into Goop's face. "Everybody out of the car."

"What's your friggin' problem?" Goop asked.

"Everybody out."

"Yeah? You're supposed to say sir."

"No, I'm supposed to say asshole. Now, get out of the fuckin' car, *asshole.*"

"And if I don't?"

"It's OK, Goop," a voice from the back said, and the rear doors opened. I had to be careful—I was going to have three guys out, with no backup. My goal was to get Bravelli alone, but first I had to make sure no one was armed.

"What happened, North?" Bravelli said as he climbed out of the Seville. "Get lost on a doughnut run?"

"Behind the car," I said. "All three of you." They walked to the rear of the car, half laughing, playing along for a while. Both Bravelli and Canaletto were wearing white shorts and pastel knit golf shirts.

"Hands on the trunk," I ordered. Goop and Canaletto obeyed, but Bravelli hesitated. He was glancing around at the nearby houses, where people were gathering on their porches and at their windows to see what was going on. I knew he was worried about losing face. Good.

I quickly patted down Goop's orange jogging suit.

"What, you want to feel me up?" he sneered. "You a fuckin' homo?"

"Hey, Goop," I said, finishing up with him, "Was that a baby carrot in your pocket, or are you just glad to see me?"

Canaletto snickered. Goop gave him a dirty look, then sputtered a "fuck you" in my direction. I moved on to Canaletto. No gun.

"You're next," I said to Bravelli. He took a step back, like I somehow wasn't permitted to touch him. "You want to fuckin' pull us over," he said, "do it somewhere else, not in our own fucking neighborhood."

"Really? Well, guess what? I'm pretty sure I can pull you over any fucking place I want."

I turned to Goop and Canaletto. "You two, back in the car. I'm going to search your boss, and then all three of you assholes can go." They quickly complied, figuring that the sooner they got in the car, the sooner this would be over.

Once Goop and Canaletto were back in the Seville, I spun Bravelli around and pushed him against the trunk, and made a big show of frisking him. He was spewing obscenities, but I took my time. More people were gathering.

"Yo, leave him alone," someone yelled. I turned. On the sidewalk, standing in front of the growing crowd, were four Italian guys in their early twenties, dressed in sleeveless white T-shirts and baggy shorts. Just corner boys, I thought, all they know how to do is spend their lives sitting on steps, playing cards and bullshitting and drinking beer.

Bravelli wasn't armed, either. Now I could get started.

"Heard your boys beat up another black guy today," I said.

He looked puzzled for a moment, then understood.

"That's what this is about? You got to be friggin' kiddin' me, you should be thanking the people who are doin' your job for you."

"Don't worry about how we're doing our job."

Bravelli half laughed. "You still haven't found the moolie that whacked your cop, have you?"

"I would strongly suggest you shut the fuck up about that."

"I heard you're gettin' a little help."

"Help from who?"

He gave a little asshole smirk. "Like I said, you can't do your job, somebody's gonna do it for you."

That was enough. I shoved Bravelli hard against the trunk, and when he bounced back up, I slammed my fist into his face. It felt great. He kept his balance, but looked at me with astonished eyes and tried to speak.

"What the fuuu—"

"I told you to shut the fuck up about that, didn't I?"

The doors of the Seville popped open, and Goop and Canaletto jumped out, their faces contorted in anger. They quickly got between me and Bravelli, protecting him.

"Police brutality!" someone in the crowd called out.

The corner boys were moving closer. "That fuckin' cop is beatin' Mr. Bravelli," one of them yelled.

I pushed Canaletto to one side and sent my fist toward Bravelli's face again, but Goop batted up my arm and then pushed me back into the corner boys. They were right behind me, I didn't realize they were so close.

"Fuckin' cop needs a lesson," I heard a voice say, and then someone shoved at my back, almost sending me sprawling onto the street. I turned to face my four attackers. They all had mean, fearless looks, it didn't matter to them a bit that I had a badge. They were probably some of the ones who had been beating up the blacks.

I glanced back at Goop and Canaletto, they were ready to join in. Not including Bravelli, that made it six against one. I reached on my belt for my nightstick, but only came up with empty air. I had left the stick in the car.

"Now you're gonna take a beatin'," said one of the corner boys, a big ugly son of a bitch.

I wasn't too proud to call for help. I keyed my mike. "This is 20-C-Charlie, I need an assist, 8-0 and Locust."

No response.

"Radio, this is 20-C-Charlie. Gimme an assist, 8-0 and Locust."

Still no response. Fucking piece-of-shit radios.

"No one to help you this time," said Goop. "That's too bad."

I keyed my radio again, but the big guy yelled, "Get him, quick."

He was repulsive, he looked like a fucking hippopotamus. He lurched toward me and swung at my chin. I leaned back and a giant fist went harmlessly by, but at the same moment I felt a punch in my lower back, near my left kidney. The big one again threw his fist at my face, but he was slow and I grabbed his arm in mid-punch, stepped forward, and slammed his massive jaw. An instant later I was hit in the lower back, harder than before, and someone slammed the side of my head, and I was down on the ground, and the giant motherfucker got on top of me and started flailing my face with his fists, getting his revenge. Between the flashes of white light that came with each punch, I could see a wicked smile of dirty, broken teeth. All I could think of was, this asshole needs a good dentist.

Then there was a "thwack!"—like someone hitting a tree with a baseball bat—and the guy's jaw went slack. I saw Buster standing over him, raising his nightstick, but the asshole wasn't giving up, he was pulling back his fist to give me a final shot with all his might. I watched as Buster's stick cut down through the air, it seemed in slow motion, a foot from the guy's head, then a half a foot, then an inch, then it hit, and the stick shot back into the air like it had bounced off a rubber ball. The guy just closed his eyes and it was like a mountain falling off of me.

I couldn't get up at first. My head hurt, face hurt, my back hurt, I didn't feel so good. Buster was standing there protecting me, and

Donna was trying to help me to my feet. I could see the other corner boys racing away in all directions, and the crowd was moving back.

"Where'd you come from?" I said to Donna.

"Civilian called in an assist," she said. "We were right around the corner. You want Rescue?"

There was blood streaming from my mouth, but my head was starting to clear a little. "I think I'm OK," I said. I glanced around for Bravelli's car—where was it?

"Buster, you see a black Seville?" I asked.

Buster was chomping feverishly on his gum, looking up and down the street, making sure no one was coming back. "Not here when we pulled up," he said.

Bravelli had slipped away.

FIVE

When I got back to district headquarters, and looked at my face in the locker-room mirror, I felt like going into hiding. I knew the first thing everyone was going to ask was "What the hell happened to you?" But I cleaned myself up the best I could, and headed upstairs to the operations room.

Sammy took one look at me and said, "What the hell happened to you?" I didn't bother answering.

We had a tiny lunchroom with a sink, a scuzzy green refrigerator, and a picnic table covered with a plastic Italian tablecloth. Someone had just made coffee, and I took my mug down from its peg on the wall, filled it, and took a painful sip. The coffee was awful, like all cop coffee, but it was awful in a way that was familiar, almost comforting.

"Hi, Eddie," came a woman's voice.

I looked up. Michelle was standing in the doorway, in uniform, holding her police hat in her hand at her side.

"Michelle," I said, pulling the cup away from my face in surprise. That was a mistake—she flinched a little when she saw the raw cuts and bruises.

"They'll go away," I said, and put the cup down on the counter.

Michelle's own face had that washed-out look that comes from grief, and a paleness that her makeup couldn't hide. I wanted to hold her, comfort her, tell her how sorry I was about Steve. I hesitated, not knowing whether it would be OK. It didn't matter—Michelle simply stepped forward and hugged me. We held each other for a long time, and I could tell she didn't want to let go. Well, there was no reason to. It didn't matter if anyone saw.

"I'm going to miss him," I said softly.

"Yeah," she said through new tears. "Me, too." She finally squeezed me tight and stepped back, and she had the saddest smile.

She looked at my face again. "Eddie, are you all right?"

"Just a fight," I said. "Michelle, what are you . . ." I didn't know how to ask it.

"What am I doing here?"

I nodded. "Well, yeah. I don't think anybody expected you back so soon. You going to be in the Twelfth tonight?"

"I don't know yet. I'd rather be in the Twentieth, where I can at least help out."

"Have you talked to your captain?"

"Yeah, he said it's fine with him if it's OK with Kirk."

"I'm sure he's not going to have a problem with it. Unless . . . are you really all right to be out here?"

"I'm a cop, Eddie. This is what I do. I can't just sit at home, that's a hundred times worse."

I would have felt the same way. "If you think you're all right . . ."

"I'm fine. Well, maybe I'm not fine. Maybe it just hasn't hit me yet. But until it does, I have to be doing something."

"That's understandable. Why don't you ride with me, I'll get the OK from Kirk."

Her face relaxed and she gave me a grateful smile. As we walked back through the operations room, Sammy waved us over.

"How come you're not over at Seventy-fifth and Pine?" he asked.

"What's at Seventy-fifth and Pine?"

"You didn't hear on Radio?"

"Not on this one," I said, pulling it off my belt. "I can't even get static."

"Supposed to be a body in a car trunk," said Sammy. "Could be mob-related."

"Hmmm," I said, scratching my jaw. "Heart of Westmount, body in a trunk. Yeah, maybe just a slight possibility."

When Michelle and I got there, they still hadn't opened the trunk. Captain Lanier and Doc Bizbee and all the other guys from OC were hanging around the car, along with some cops from my squad. The object of everyone's attention was a deep blue Lexus, brand-new or close to it.

A crowd had gathered around, and as we made our way through, I caught Doc's eye. He came over, and I could tell he was pretending not to notice my face. I introduced him to Michelle, I told her that Doc and I had become good friends when I was in the unit.

"I'm real sorry about your brother," Doc said in his slow Texas drawl.

Michelle nodded her thanks, and I asked Doc what he had.

"Might be a fella inside there sleeping," he said. "A real deep sleep, if you know what I mean."

Doc had two features you noticed first: he was completely bald, and he had a big stomach under his Dallas Cowboys T-shirt, so that he was round on the top, and very round in the front. He had a soft face and an affable smile, like he had never really had a bad day in his life. Basically, he looked like a hick. You'd never know he was a sergeant. Hell, you'd never even know he was a cop. We always told Doc he seemed like he'd be more at home slopping hogs on a dusty farm out in West Texas, gettin' his giant blue overalls all muddied up. Whenever we'd ask him what the hell he was doing on the streets of Philadelphia, he'd drawl, "I belong here."

And we'd look at him and laugh and say, imitating his accent, "Why, Doc? Some of your hogs get loose?"

Today he had on his Cowboys T-shirt, as usual, and also a Cowboys baseball cap, so it looked like he happened to be on his way to a game at Veterans Stadium when he got sidetracked. The Cowboys weren't particularly popular in Philly, and more than a few people in the crowd were glaring at his cap and shirt.

Doc told me that about an hour before, someone had called Southwest Detectives and suggested that cops check the trunk of a Lexus at 75th and Pine. When asked why, the caller had replied, "All right, don't check, I don't fuckin' care, when the neighbors start complaining about the smell, don't come fuckin' crying to me." Then he slammed down the phone.

"Wonderful," I told Doc. "An anonymous caller with an attitude."

Michelle was looking at the trunk of the Lexus. "Any idea who's inside?" she asked.

Doc shook his head. "We checked the VIN. Car's stolen."

As Doc took off to talk to Lanier, Michelle and I gazed at the Lexus. "Hell of a coffin," I said aloud.

Considering that we were in Westmount, it was a good bet this was Bravelli's work. But who was inside? One thing for sure, a lot of people had come to find out. The spectators, at least three hundred strong, had pressed so close that Lanier had ordered barricades put up, yellow-and-blue police sawhorses. People had gathered behind them four-deep, craning for a view.

It was wild—men, women, even children were everywhere, hanging from windows, peering down from roofs, standing on newspaper boxes, perched on traffic lights. One young neighborhood guy had even set up a lawn chair on the top of his car, and was sitting there drinking a bottle of beer and listening to rock music on his car radio.

Lanier came over to where we were standing, and looked at my battered face with mock alarm.

"Forget to wear your seat belt again?" he asked.

One thing about trying to bust somebody's balls, you have to at least be friendly with the guy or it doesn't work. I just looked at Lanier and shook my head.

By now, though, he had turned his attention to Michelle. He noticed her nameplate, and asked, "Are you any relation?"

"This is the Commissioner's daughter," I said. I was hoping they wouldn't shake hands, but they did.

"Captain Lanier," I explained cheerfully to Michelle, "was the fine commander who had me transferred out of the Organized Crime Unit."

"C'mon, let's not get into this now," said Lanier.

"I had my own squad," I told Michelle. "And we were doing great, we were closing in on Mickey Bravelli. We had witnesses, evidence, wiretaps, everything."

"C'mon, Eddie . . ."

"But then anonymous calls started coming in saying that I was taking money from the mob. Isn't that right, Captain?"

I turned to Michelle. "Instead of treating the calls like bullshit, which they were, Captain Lanier dutifully reported them to his bosses. The next thing I know, I'm pushing a patrol car around West Philadelphia."

"It was a little more complicated than that," Lanier said to Michelle.

"It wasn't any more complicated than that," I said.

Lanier hesitated. He was obviously reluctant to leave things where they stood, but he knew arguing with me wasn't going to get anywhere.

He smiled at Michelle. "Nice meeting you, but it's time for me to get to work."

He turned and walked back over to the Lexus, where he was joined by Doc and the other detectives. The new activity was sending a surge of electricity through the crowd. Knots of young guys, who had been standing around bullshitting, turned in unison toward the barricade.

Lanier called for a nearby police wagon to be brought behind the Lexus. He wanted to at least partially block the crowd's view, and the crowd didn't like it. As the wagon pulled into place, people started booing, like they were at a ball game and the center fielder had just dropped the ball.

"Hey, c'mon, let us see!" people were yelling, as they pushed and shoved to get a view again. Doc had a crowbar in his hand, and Lanier said, "OK, Sergeant, pop it."

Doc bent down with the crowbar, and a woman in the crowd shouted, "It's show time!"

The street was suddenly quiet, like someone had pushed down all the city sounds, so that even the traffic passing at a nearby intersection seemed to glide by in silence. The crowd, hushed, strained forward toward the Lexus. Even the guy with the lawn chair had shut off his car radio and was now standing on his car.

Doc worked the crowbar for a moment, and then with a loud creak and a thump the trunk popped open, and the crowd gasped at what it saw and heard.

What it saw was a thin, nattily dressed black guy, half propped up between two large stereo speakers, his dead waxy face looking out over the astonished crowd. On his chest was a white placard, with the words, in black Magic Marker, "COP KILLER."

What the crowd heard was music, somehow set to start playing when the truck was opened, blasting from the two speakers.

It was the rock anthem by the group Queen, heard at every sporting event: "WE WILL . . . WE WILL . . . ROCK YOU!! (Stomp-stomp clap. Stomp-stomp clap.) WE WILL . . . WE WILL . . . ROCK YOU!!"

The music was so loud that Doc and the other cops staggered back a few steps, and then a huge cheer went up from the crowd, and they were all clapping and whistling and yelling approval.

"WE WILL . . . WE WILL . . . ROCK YOU!! (Stomp-stomp-clap. Stomp-stomp-clap.) WE WILL . . . WE WILL . . . ROCK YOU!!"

Doc reached into the trunk and ripped the wires from the speakers and the music went dead. The crowd booed, but then cheered again, louder than before. They were whistling and clapping in appreciation— it was a great show, and they had gotten their money's worth.

I glanced at Michelle. Her face was ashen. She just stood there, staring at the body, staring at the placard. The moment I saw it, I thought about what Bravelli had said on the street—about how we were going to get help finding who shot Steve. This was it. This was what he had been talking about.

Doc came over to us, embarrassed. "I'm sorry you had to see this," he said to Michelle. "We had no idea."

"It's all right," she said.

Doc turned to me. "Eddie, you know who that is in the trunk, don't you?"

"Never seen him before."

"Well, I have. That's Ru-Wan Sanders."

"No shit. You sure?"

"I don't know too many of those guys," said Doc, "but I do know him."

"One of what guys?" Michelle asked. "Who is he?"

"Black Mafia," I said. "Ru-Wan over there was—what, Doc, second-in-command?"

"Something like that. They're always switching around."

Michelle looked at us. "I don't understand, what does this mean?"

"It means," I said, "that there's something going on here we don't know about."

"But why would the black Mafia . . ." began Michelle.

We were all silent for a moment, taking it in. It was just too hard to believe.

"Maybe we should ask Mickey Bravelli," I said, and told them what he had said that afternoon.

Doc tilted his head and squinted, like he just had heard that a neighboring farmer was growing giant tomatoes.

"Bravelli sure found out awful fast," he said in his Texas drawl. "We didn't have a hint, not even a hint of a hint."

"Tell you what bothers me," I said. "The black Mafia doesn't have anything to do with the crackhouse where Steve got killed. It's just a place for pipers—the street dealers don't even go inside."

Doc saw where I was going. "So there'd be no reason in the world for Ru-Wan Sanders to ever be in there."

"Well, one reason," I said. Doc thought for a moment, then nodded.

"What?" said Michelle. "You guys aren't going to tell me?"

Doc and I looked at each other. He was about to say it, then hesitated, so I took over.

"Maybe Ru-Wan was there because he knew Steve was going to be knocking on that door. Maybe he was the one who made the call to 911."

Michelle put her hand to her mouth. "They were waiting for Steve?"

"It's very possible," I said. "And I think it's also very possible Bravelli knows why."

A few minutes later, we were pulling into the Yard at district head-quarters. Michelle had asked me to take her back, she wanted to talk to her father about Ru-Wan Sanders.

As I stopped the car in front of the police entrance, Michelle said, "We have to find out what Bravelli knows."

"It'd be nice."

"But there's no way, is there? Bringing him in isn't going to do any good."

"Not likely."

"How about somebody going undercover?"

I shook my head. "It could take months to get inside Bravelli's crew—if we could get in at all."

She thought about that for a while, then opened the car door. "We have to find out."

Once I had dropped Michelle off, I got back on the street and asked Radio to try to raise Nick. He didn't respond. I figured maybe he had one of our famous nonworking radios. Other cops in the squad could hear me trying to reach him, maybe one of them would get on the air and say where he was. No one did, but no big deal.

I tried the 7-Eleven at 40th and Walnut, across the street from the Penn campus. It was a favorite cop hangout, primarily because you could sit in your patrol car all day and watch a steady stream of Penn girls pass by. In the summer, when the girls all wore tank tops and shorts, the parking area in front of the 7-Eleven was like a police mini-station.

I didn't see Nick's car, but I wanted some coffee anyway. I walked in and my heart jumped a little—there was Patricia, getting a small plastic bottle of orange juice from the glass case. She turned, and then stopped in surprise when she saw me.

"Eddie. You back in uniform now?"

She looked more relaxed, prettier than when I had last seen her, when our divorce came through a year ago. Her black hair was shorter now, shiny and curled in above the shoulders. She was dressed up—tight navy blue dress, black pumps, black leather purse on a long strap over her shoulder.

"You have a job around here?" I asked.

I had almost asked her whether she was going to Penn—I knew it was her dream to go there, to get a master's in archaeology. But Penn's tuition was something like $25,000 a year, hard to afford on the salary of a fifth-grade public school teacher.

"We haven't talked for a while," she said. "I'm not teaching anymore, I'm a secretary at Penn. In the president's office."

My stomach dropped. She deserved better. She was worlds above the girls at Penn with their daddies' credit cards.

Patricia smiled. "But, I'm also in the archaeology program here." She explained to me how employees of Penn could enroll as part-time students without paying a penny.

She said she had just gotten engaged. A Center City architect. He was designing the house they eventually wanted to build.

"So in other words," I said, "we split up and the gods start smiling on you."

She laughed. "C'mon, we had some good years, didn't we?"

"Yeah, we did."

At least until we started having our troubles. I was in OC, working permanent four-to-midnight. I had to leave for work before Patricia got home from the elementary school, and she'd always be asleep when I came in.

I was in love with the job, in love with being a cop—I couldn't get enough of it. But it was like being in a self-contained world. The stuff you saw, you couldn't talk about with your wife, so you talked about it with other cops. After work, everyone in the squad would go out drinking to three or four in the morning. We were all too keyed up to go home.

I'd get up late and hang around the house until I had to go into work. Sometimes Patricia and I would go days without seeing each other—we didn't even have enough time together to fight about it. There were no kids as an excuse to stay together, and one day, she just decided to leave. It happens to cops all the time.

We talked for a while longer in the 7-Eleven. She told me her father had died five months ago, and that shook me up because I really liked the guy, we had shared a lot of beers together. Patricia said she had heard about Commissioner Ryder's son, and she asked how the investigation was going.

"Not so good," I said. "You know, he was in my squad."

"Oh, I'm sorry. One of your family."

At first I thought she was being sarcastic, but then I saw she meant it. It was something I always felt she had never understood.

"Family's important," she said. "Whatever your family is."

She straightened my collar, the way she did when I first became a cop, and then we walked to the counter. She bought her orange juice and insisted on paying for my coffee as well. When we were outside, I offered to give her a lift to wherever she was going, but she said her car was just down the block. She was on her way home.

"Bye, Eddie," she said, and stood on her tiptoes to kiss my cheek. Then she turned and walked away.

I decided to cruise by the crackhouse on Tyler Street, I wasn't exactly sure why. The block looked a lot different during the day. Kids were playing on the sidewalks; old folks were on their porches, relaxing on their metal lawn chairs. At night, the trees had created vague, ominous shadows as we searched for Steve's killer. Now they just provided a friendly shade.

I was only half surprised to see Nick's empty patrol car in front of the house. I parked my car behind his, and walked up the sidewalk. The yellow police tape was still stretched across the porch, but the front door was open. What was Nick doing in there? He shouldn't be in there.

For a few hours the night before, the house had been the center of our universe. Now, in the quiet afternoon light, it looked like just what it was: an old abandoned row house, nothing more. I stood on the porch and tried to peer through the gloom inside.

"Nick," I called. "Nick, you in there?" I stepped through the doorway and froze. Standing in the darkness was Nick, arms at his side, totally still, like he was a ghost, chained to the place where his partner had died. It was pretty spooky. As my eyes adjusted to the dark, I could tell that Nick was looking at me but not really seeing me.

"Nick," I said. He didn't move. "NICK!" He seemed startled, like I had woke him up.

"Eddie," he said in a low voice.

"Nick, what the hell you doin' here?"

He seemed puzzled. "I don't know."

"You OK?"

"Yeah. I guess so."

"C'mon, let's get out of here."

I reached out and put my hand on his elbow, to help guide him out the door. He coughed, and I caught the scent of warm beer. I didn't say anything at first. I just led him out onto the porch, under the yellow police tape, and down the steps. He blinked in the bright sunlight, and tried to shade his eyes.

"Nick, you hitting the bars at four in the afternoon, in uniform?"

He shrugged.

"What'd you do," I asked, "just walk in, sit down and order a beer?"

He looked back at me, unwilling to argue. I thought I would be angry, but I wasn't. If I were in his situation, I might have spent the afternoon in a bar myself.

"Why don't you go home," I said. "Get your car at headquarters and just go, don't talk to anybody."

He nodded obediently, and I walked with him to the curb. When we reached his patrol car, I said, "Nick, something weird happened today." I told him about Ru-Wan Sanders showing up in the Lexus trunk. That got Nick's attention, I could see his clarity starting to return as he listened.

"Did Steve ever mention the black Mafia?" I asked.

"You kiddin'? He probably didn't even know who they were."

"That's what I would have figured. But you know how Steve sometimes took the car out on the street by himself, and left you at headquarters for a while?"

"Yeah, I guess."

"Where did he go?"

Nick shrugged. "I don't know, he never told me, he didn't want to tell me. He'd just get this smile—you know, the Steve smile, the one he gets when he's up to something—and he'd say, "It's my little mystery, Nick."

"You'd think he'd at least tell his partner," I said.

"Yeah, you would, wouldn't you?" said Nick. "I don't know, Eddie, I don't know why he didn't confide in me. But now I can't ask him, can I?"

SIX

Like a sleeping lion that has been unwisely awakened, Commissioner Ben Ryder rose up with sudden fury at the black Mafia. Late that afternoon, he assembled the media outside police headquarters in Center City and vowed that the criminal organization would be shut down, obliterated. No longer would it be allowed to kill cops.

Those sentiments, naturally, were greeted warmly by the press, the public, and the Fraternal Order of Police, though word spread through the Department grapevine that some top commanders were questioning the Commissioner's wisdom. There was no real evidence yet that the black Mafia had killed Steve—wasn't this just a knee-jerk reaction?

It wasn't hard, though, to figure out why the Italian mob would rat out the black Mafia. The two organizations were deadly rivals, and if Bravelli saw an opportunity to bring down heat on the black Mafia, he wouldn't hesitate to use it.

But there was one major problem with the police going after members of the black Mafia. We didn't know who the hell they were.

There were only a few we could even identify, like Ru-Wan Sanders, and we could only guess at their roles. Doc had once been assigned to make an organizational chart of the black Mafia, with little boxes showing who reported to whom. I thought he did a pretty good job, considering that none of the boxes had any names.

Part of it wasn't our fault. Every so often, leaders of the black Mafia would go off to jail on drug charges, and the organization would seem to dissolve. It would always reemerge, though—just as strong, with a new set of leaders. Sooner or later, of course, the old members would get out of jail and want their jobs back, and a certain amount of gunfire would ensue. Doc wouldn't even bother to get his chart back out.

But we weren't entirely free of blame. Cracking down on the Italian mob was much more glamorous, and got bigger headlines. For up-and-coming prosecutors and police commanders, that's where the glory was—not in making drug and gun pinches in poor black neighborhoods. Now, we were paying for our neglect.

The Philadelphia Police Department, however, was not about to let facts get in the way of an investigation. And so for the next two days and nights, we locked up everyone even rumored to be part of the black Mafia. And who knows? Maybe we accidentally snagged somebody who was.

One thing was certain: a lot of young black guys in the neighborhood were getting a firsthand look at the inside of a police station. It was a good bet that not everyone was being treated gently, and if the black community was hot before, now it was steaming.

Then Nick made things a lot worse.

It happened on Wednesday, the day of Steve's wake. We were growing angry and frustrated that no progress was being made. All the arrests, all the countless hours of questioning, had come to nothing. Even the gun from the crackhouse had yielded nothing—no fingerprints, no way to trace it.

That day, I had the bright idea of asking for Jeff Bouvier's help. Jeff was a young black guy in my squad who was maybe the smartest cop I ever met. He had a way of rapidly sizing up situations and then dealing with them, fearlessly and efficiently. In the movies, cops are always getting people to hand over their guns rather than shoot. That never happens in real life—we're usually crouched around the corner of a building, calling for backup. But I had seen Jeff do it, twice. People just trusted him.

We gave him the nickname "Commissioner," because that's what we all figured he'd be someday. He didn't like it, but that was too bad. You don't get to choose your own nickname.

Jeff had grown up in West Philadelphia, and knew a lot of the guys on the street. He'd arrest somebody, stick him in the back of the police car, and on the way in to the district they'd talk about what was happening with friends from high school.

That Wednesday after roll call, I took Jeff aside and asked him whether he knew any of the guys in the black Mafia.

"Sure, Sam Epps. Though I think he calls himself Hakeem somebody now. He just got out of prison, maybe six months ago."

"And he's in the black Mafia?"

Jeff thought about that. "Well, he was, before he went away. I don't know about now."

A slight detail, maybe, but one I wasn't particularly worried about at the moment. We could bring him in, sweat him a little, see what we could find out. Anything would be better than what we had.

So, Jeff, Nick, and I went off to find Hakeem somebody. Jeff said he had recently seen the guy hanging out at 52nd and Market, so that's where we went first.

There were nicer shopping areas in Philadelphia than the 52nd Street strip—places like Chestnut Hill, where doughy-faced white couples in shorts slurped ice cream cones and strolled past designer clothing stores.

In West Philadelphia, things were a little different. This was where poor and working-class black people went to get bargains on makeup and shoes and paper towels, and loud music blasted from every third or fourth store. And always, there was tension on the block—the tension of survival.

Hakeem was right where Jeff said he'd be, standing on the crowded corner of 52nd and Market, next to the newspaper stand, calling after every young woman who passed by.

Nick was in his police car, Jeff was with me. When we pulled up a couple of stores away and got out, Jeff pointed to Hakeem.

"There he is. Guy in the glasses and goatee."

"Let's go get him," said Nick.

As I was deciding whether to call in another unit, just in case Hakeem tried to run, Nick started to walk toward him.

"Nick, hold up," I said. But he just kept going. And before I could call out again, Nick walked right up to Hakeem, and with a fierce, quick motion, punched him in the mouth. Hakeem went down like a rock.

This was not a good thing. The street was crowded with people—old guys, teenagers, women holding shopping bags with one hand, kids with the other. They had all just seen a white cop go up to a black man and hit him in the face without a word.

Fortunately, Hakeem wasn't hurt too badly, and Jeff and I were able to get him on his feet. When I glared at Nick, he seemed surprised.

"Just wanted to make sure he wasn't going to give us any trouble."

I looked around, and everybody had just stopped what they were doing, they were all staring at us.

We handcuffed Hakeem and took him to Southwest Detectives. And that's where we discovered that he had already been brought in, the day before. And that since he had been released from prison, he had gotten a good job, and had stayed out of trouble, and had nothing to do with the black Mafia anymore.

All of which, as I loudly explained to Nick later, we could have found out without knocking Hakeem down in front of an audience. I told him he should be very glad that Hakeem probably wouldn't file a complaint. Hakeem was no doubt aware that known criminals who file complaints against cops—even for legitimate reasons—usually find themselves getting harassed at least ten times a day by the cops' pals.

Nick didn't consider himself lucky, he just didn't care. He was absolutely unrepentant.

O n Thursday, four days after he was killed, Steve got a hero's funeral. That morning, more than three thousand cops lined the street outside St. Gregory's Church on Bustleton Avenue, a mile or so from the Ryders' home. The summer air was warm and hazy, and seemed to have a natural silence that everyone could feel.

Michelle had asked Nick and me to be pallbearers, and of course we said yes. I was extremely relieved that my deep blue dress uniform still fit. I hadn't worn it in six years, since Tommy Moran's funeral. I was a pallbearer at that one, too. Simple car-stop, bang, Tommy was dead. He was a good guy, a good friend.

Now it was Steve's turn. The evening before, Nick and I had helped carry his casket, covered with an American flag, into the church for his wake. For half the night, the line of cops filing in stretched halfway around the block.

This morning, another stream of mourners was making its way up the steps and through the open doors. And as I stood on the steps with Donna and Buster and the rest of the honor guard from the squad, I was a little surprised to see so many politicians. I had wondered whether they would come—whether anyone would come. Ever since Ru-Wan Sanders had made his surprise appearance in the trunk, a dark question had swirled through the Police Department, spinning through every division, every station house, every group of cops standing together.

It was a simple question, simple and horrible: was Steve Ryder a dirty cop?

Homicide detectives had come to the same conclusion Doc and I had—that it seemed unlikely Steve's death was random. It also seemed unlikely that the black Mafia would have targeted a cop unless it felt it had a very good reason.

Why would the black Mafia have taken such a chance? Steve was just a patrolman, he couldn't have done much to hurt them. But there was another possibility: perhaps Steve was somehow involved with the black Mafia himself. Perhaps he had been working for them, and had crossed them in some way. That was the kind of crime these people would not be able to forgive.

Some of the politicians told the papers—off the record, of course—that they were reluctant to attend the funeral, but felt it would look worse if they stayed away. After all, there wasn't any proof about Steve, at least not yet.

And so we watched them file into the church, all solemn and sympathetic and totally full of shit. It was pretty awful.

Once the services began, I walked in by myself and stood in the back, in an alcove under the balcony. It was nice and cool, the way churches always are, and there seemed to be a light breeze coming from somewhere. In front of the altar was Steve's casket, still draped with the flag, surrounded by flowers.

"It is a loss for all of us, for all of Philadelphia," the priest was saying. "Steven Ryder was more than a friend, a brother, and a son. He was a son of the city."

We shouldn't ask why Steve was taken, the priest continued, because God had a good reason, even if we didn't know what it was.

That's what they always said. Maybe it was supposed to make the family feel better, but it didn't do much for me. I wanted to know. I walked back outside and waited with the others for the service to end.

Finally it was over, and the church doors opened, and I went back inside. When I reached the casket, the Commissioner nodded to me. Michelle, who like her mother was wearing a simple black dress, gave me a brave smile.

Nick and I and the other pallbearers lifted the casket and carried it down the aisle and out the doors of the church. Captain Kirk was leading the honor guard, and as we started down the stone steps toward the silver-gray hearse, he shouted, "Atten-shun!"

The honor guard snapped a salute, and held it. The order echoed down the street, and each unit, one at a time, came to attention and saluted. Three thousand cops, from Philadelphia, from up and down the East Coast. It was pretty impressive. But how many of them were here only because it was expected?

In the procession from the church to the cemetery, Nick rode with me in the front seat, and Donna and Buster sat in the back. I'd been to cop funerals where there would only be a hundred or so police cars, but today there were more than a thousand, snaking through the streets, red and blue lights flashing. Every intersection along the route was blocked off, and at many of them, drivers were out of their cars, watching. All along the way, neighbors gathered on porches and front lawns.

"I wonder what they're thinking," said Donna.

"They're wondering about Steve," I said. "They're all wondering about Steve."

Steve's grave site was shaded by a green canopy, which somehow seemed at odds with the surrounding gray sea of granite markers. In the shade were three rows of folding chairs, filled with family members. At least a third of the men wore police uniforms—the family was full of cops. Behind the canopy, at the head of the grave, were a dozen large floral displays. One was an American flag, another was a big police badge made of carnations—Steve's badge number, 34907, was in blue on a field of yellow.

There were two other groups near the canopy, and I wasn't happy to see either of them. One, of course, was the media, the reporters with their notebooks, the photographers in their khaki vests, already hungrily snapping photos. And, as always, the television cameras, this time a forest of them on tripods, poised in wait for the grieving family.

Strategically placed next to the media was the other group: the politicians, seated on folding chairs. In the front row was the mayor, and next to him the governor. There were others I had seen in the papers or on TV: Philadelphia's newly elected DA, city council members, state senators. It was hard to look at them and know that some didn't want to be there. Maybe none of them did.

Nick and I headed for the hearse, where the other pallbearers were standing quietly. A red-cheeked young cop, walking in front of us, seemed surprised to see Steve's casket still inside, and he stopped short. He lingered for a few seconds, then crossed himself and moved on.

Buster and Donna joined the front lines of the army of blue that was forming into a massive phalanx, fifty across, scores deep. It took another half hour before everyone was in place, and suddenly the cemetery became very still. Michelle and her parents emerged from a black limousine and joined the other family members at the grave site. From somewhere, a bagpiper began playing a mournful "Amazing Grace."

Nick and I and the others carried Steve's casket to the canopy, then gently rested it on the canvas straps suspended above the freshly carved grave.

I glanced at Michelle. She had her arm around her mother, comforting her. The Commissioner, wearing a dark suit rather than his uniform, was stone-faced. He must have known about the questions and the doubts. Now, I thought, he had to endure them as he put his son in the ground.

I was jerked into the moment by rifle shots, and it took me an instant to realize it was the twenty-one-gun salute. On a grassy incline, seven cops with rifles fired into the air, once, twice, three times. Then two buglers we couldn't see played "Taps," one echoing the other. Each note seemed to float in the air—almost as if you could see it before it faded. And then the funeral was over, and the great mass of cops behind me began breaking up.

I walked over to Michelle. Her eyes were red, but she was no longer crying. Without a word, she reached out and hugged me for a long moment.

"If you need me for anything . . ." I said.

"Actually, can we talk later?"

"Sure, anytime."

"At your house? Maybe around seven?"

I tried not to sound surprised. "Of course. Absolutely."

She said she didn't know where I lived, so I pulled a pen and small notebook from my breast pocket and wrote out my address. Someone was standing next to me, waiting to talk to Michelle. The new DA. Short guy with wire-rim glasses and a soft, pink face. I handed the address to Michelle, nodded to the DA, and took off to find Nick, Donna, and Buster.

T he four of us all had the day off, so we had a long lunch at a diner near the cemetery, then headed back to district headquarters to pick up our cars. When we pulled up, there was a clump of television camera crews at the front entrance. Probably looking for quotes about Steve. If anyone asked, I'd tell them he was a good cop, that we'd all miss him.

But when we got out of the car, and headed toward the building, we could see that the reporters weren't talking to cops. They were interviewing City Councilman Barney Stiller, the most powerful black politician in Philadelphia. And there weren't just a few reporters surrounding him, there were a lot. They didn't all happen to show up here at the same time, I realized. This was a press conference.

"What the hell is he doing here?" asked Nick. "I sure didn't see him at the funeral."

Stiller was a tall, imposing man, a former pro football player, and he towered above the cameras. We moved just close enough to hear what he was saying.

"We're very sorry about the young police officer's death," Stiller said, like he was giving a speech. "And, out of respect for his family, we wanted to wait until after the funeral to make any statements."

"Get ready for the 'but,' " said Donna.

"But," said Stiller, "the time has come to speak out. We can no longer tolerate the police harassment of black men in West Philadelphia. Nothing, not even an officer's tragic death, gives police the right to mistreat our community's young sons."

Buster was incredulous. "He wants us to be nice to the black Mafia?"

Stiller was too far away to hear Buster, but when he spoke next he gave an answer.

"The police claim they're just going after people they already know are criminals. But in reality, totally innocent black men are being rounded up like animals and questioned for hours without regard to their lawful rights. Some are even being struck down on the street."

I glanced at Nick. He was listening to Stiller nonchalantly, like he just happened to be a passerby and that last remark had nothing at all to do with him.

"Today," Stiller was saying, "we are announcing a people's protest. We are calling on everyone—men, women and children—to join a march on the Twentieth Police District this Saturday afternoon. It will be peaceful—but it will be powerful."

"Remind me to call in sick Saturday," Nick said.

"Yeah," said Buster, "I think my grandmother's going to die Friday night."

"Your grandmother died last month," said Donna.

"That was my other grandmother."

"You said that one died last year."

"Yeah," said Buster, taking out a cigarette, "but this is my other-other grandmother."

"Cigarette," said Donna, and he handed her his pack without thinking. They were both single, just boyfriend and girlfriend, but they were like a couple that had been married twenty years.

We stood in the Yard, and watched the rest of the press conference from out of earshot.

"He should have been at the funeral," said Nick. "He's an asshole."

"He may be an asshole," I said, "but he's right about what he's saying. We're screwing this thing up."

SEVEN

Michelle didn't show up at my house at seven. About a half hour later, though, someone did knock at the door, a woman I'd never seen before. She was a classic Westmount Italian girl: lots of curly hair, half covering her face, heavy eye makeup, bright red lipstick. She had on skintight, soft, powder-blue jeans, and a black-lace halter that sort of draped over her breasts and fell short of her waist, showing her smooth stomach. I stared at her for ten seconds before I realized it was Michelle.

"Hey, can't I come in?" she asked.

"Yeah, sorry," I said, motioning for her to enter. Once she was in the living room I just stared at her some more. I kept expecting her to tell me what was going on, which she didn't do.

"Can't I sit down?"

"Sure, let's go back to the kitchen, I'm just making myself a sandwich. Sorry the place isn't cleaned up more."

"Looks fine to me."

Michelle followed me to the kitchen, and I pulled out a chair for her at the small, square, wood-topped table parked in the corner.

"Want a sandwich? I'm making ham and cheese."

"No thanks."

"How about a beer?"

"You have any wine?"

"Just beer."

"Beer's OK."

I pulled a bottle from the refrigerator, twisted off the cap, and handed it to her. I caught a slight whiff of fresh soap, like she had just come out of the shower.

"You look like a girl I used to date," I said. In fact, she looked like *every* girl I used to date, until I met Patricia.

She smiled and held up the beer bottle. "Could I have a glass?"

I opened a cabinet, found a glass that looked like it might work for beer, and handed it to her.

"So, are you going to tell me?" I asked.

"Tell you what?"

"Why you look like this."

"I will, in a minute."

I laughed. "OK, don't want to rush you. By the way, there's something I've been trying to check out. Every once in a while, Steve would disappear for an hour during his shift. He'd just take off in the police car by himself."

"That was probably Wendy."

I thought for a moment. "Wendy Bass, the little blonde in the Twelfth?"

"You didn't know about that?"

"No—they had something going?"

"That's the first thing I heard about when I got put in the Twelfth, hey, you know your brother's doing a Barbie-and-Ken with Wendy Bass." That's what we called it when two cops got together romantically, a Barbie-and-Ken.

"I guess that makes sense," I said. "That's probably where he was going."

I finished making my sandwich, and sat at the table.

"I couldn't help but notice," I said, "your hair is extremely curly."

"Yeah, it's a perm. Isn't it great?"

"It wasn't like that at the funeral."

"Yes it was. I just kept it under my hat. So to speak."

"I got to be honest, with that makeup and hair, you look like you just moved to Westmount."

"I did. The day before yesterday."

When I laughed, she said, "No, I did. I got an apartment above Angela's, you know, that beauty shop at Seventy-eighth and Locust."

"You're serious."

"And, I got a job at Angela's, doing manicures. There was an apartment available upstairs, so it worked out great."

"Wait, when did you get this job?"

"Same day I got the apartment, day before yesterday."

Today was Thursday, which meant Michelle would have gotten the job on Tuesday—two days after Steve was killed. It didn't make any sense.

"What's the deal with being a manicurist all of a sudden?"

"I'm good at it. I learned when I was in high school, at my aunt's hair salon up in the Northeast. And every year I was in college, that was my summer job—doing manicures there."

"Don't you need to go to beauty school and get a license for something like that?"

"If you really know what you're doing, the salon owners don't care if you have a license."

"You're not quitting the Department, are you?"

"No, but I'm taking a leave of absence. Stress-related, because of Steve."

"So you can be a manicurist."

Michelle looked at me for a moment with a half smile. "You used to be in the Organized Crime Unit, right?"

I nodded.

"Did you run any investigations? You know, undercover?"

"A few."

"You want to run another?" She raised her eyebrows.

"What do you mean?" I asked, but my mind was racing ahead, already beginning to understand.

"You said Bravelli knows why my brother was killed."

"He may know, I'm not positive."

"I want to find out."

"By going undercover," I said.

She nodded.

"And this is your undercover outfit."

"Yeah." She smiled, sitting up straight so that she was sort of modeling her halter. Which of course just emphasized her breasts and bare stomach.

"Do you like it?" she asked.

"You have no idea."

Michelle smiled again. "Anyway, would you help me? In a very unofficial investigation?"

"Why unofficial?"

"I know my father, there's no way he'd let me do this."

"You don't think he'd find out?"

She shook her head. "I told him I'm taking a leave, that's all he's going to know."

"And you want to go undercover by yourself?"

"Not by myself. I'd like you to back me up, to be my second set of eyes."

"But what would you do undercover? It's not like you could join the mob."

"Obviously. But if I got to know Mickey Bravelli, I might be able to get him to confide in me. Maybe not right away, but eventually."

I waved my hand to dismiss the idea. "Michelle, these guys don't even trust people they've known all their lives."

"I know that."

"And the only way you could even get close to him, you'd have to be his girlfriend."

"I know that."

I could feel my eyes widen. "You want to be his girlfriend?"

"No, but I'd be willing to go out with him a few times."

I felt sick, picturing Michelle arm in arm with Mickey Bravelli.

"He'll expect you to sleep with him."

"Doesn't matter, I won't do it."

"Then he won't have anything to do with you."

"Maybe. Maybe not."

"Michelle, this is a fantasy."

She looked at me for a few moments. "A lot of people seem to believe my brother was corrupt. Do you?"

I shook my head. "I don't know."

"I don't know either, Eddie. But I have to find out any way I can. You know, it's like I lost Steve twice . . ." She broke off, shaking her head.

"What do you mean?"

"Well, once when he died, and once . . . never mind, it probably doesn't make any sense."

"Go ahead."

"Well, if Steve was into something he shouldn't have been, then he wasn't the person I thought he was. It's like I lost the brother I thought I knew."

"It does make sense, Michelle. But you're not going about it the right way. I mean, how are you even going to meet Bravelli?"

"I've already done that."

"You've already met him?"

"There's this fruit store next to the beauty shop," she began.

Now I understood. "And on the other side of the fruit store," I said, "is the clubhouse."

"Clubhouse?" she asked. "You mean, like Mickey Mouse?"

"No, like Mickey Bravelli. That's a mob hangout."

"That's probably why I saw him in the fruit store. I went there on my lunch break the first day, to get something to eat, and there was Bravelli, buying a banana."

"Lucky you."

"He looked me up and down, like, Who is this? I pretended not to notice. Mrs. Correri told me later he comes in all the time."

"Who's Mrs. Correri?"

"She and her husband own the fruit store. Anyway, I hung out in there during my whole lunch break yesterday, hoping he'd come in."

"And you got lucky again."

"Yep, and I think he came to see me. As soon he walked in the door, he looked around, like he was looking for somebody. I was talking to Mrs. Correri, and he noticed me and started staring. Finally, he came over and said hello to Mrs. Correri—he calls her 'Mama Correri'—and then he asked her, 'Who's your new customer, Mama?' She told him I was the new manicurist next door, and she introduced us."

"And?"

Michelle shrugged. "Well, that was it. He got a banana and left."

"Another banana? What is he, a monkey?"

"Anyway, I had to call in sick at Angela's this morning, you know, so I could go to the funeral, and when I called, they told me Bravelli's coming in tomorrow morning at eleven for a manicure. He specifically asked for me."

"Michelle, if he finds out who you are, he'll kill you. Your face was on the TV news tonight, I'm sure it's going to be in the papers tomorrow . . ."

"Not this face," she said, pointing. "People who don't know me won't make the connection. And anyway, Bravelli's going to see what he wants to see."

"And what's that?"

"Some new girl in the neighborhood who turns him on."

All I could think of was, That fucking asshole Bravelli is invading my life again. Here I meet this great woman, and now she and Bravelli are going to start going out together? And she's going to get killed doing it?

"No way," I said.

"What?"

"This is a bad idea, Michelle, and I'm not going to help you."

"Fine. I'll do it myself," she said, getting up from the table.

"You can't go undercover without backup."

"I'm already doing it."

"Really? Do you even know the first thing about working under-cover?" She started moving through the living room, and I followed. "Have you called any friends from your new apartment? Your phone could be tapped, you know." She kept walking. "Have you put family photos out—somebody else's family?"

She stopped at the front door and turned.

"See? This is the kind of stuff I need you for."

"You can't do it alone."

"Well, are you going to help me?"

"Do you mean am I going to help you get killed? No."

She nodded, and opened the door, and then she was gone.

I ended up going to Westmount the next morning to watch Bravelli get his manicure. It wasn't so much deciding to go as not being able to stay away.

I remembered that there was a hardware store across the street from the beauty parlor, and I figured that'd be a good place to watch from.

I drove to Westmount in my black Chevy Blazer, and parked around the corner from the store. I had on jeans and a dark green golf shirt, which is what I would have worn before going into work that day anyway. I didn't stand out, but of course I didn't blend in, either—you couldn't do that in Westmount unless you lived there your whole life.

As I walked into the hardware store, the door jangled some little bells. The store was dimly lit and cram-packed with cans of paint, black-plastic wastepaper baskets, boxes of nails, toilet seats, rolled-up American flags in boxes, even garden hoses—as if anyone in Westmount had a lawn. And everything was covered with a thick dust, like no one had stepped inside the store in twenty years.

I walked to the front windows and looked out across the street. I could see the clubhouse, the fruit store, and, directly across from me, the beauty shop. On the big front window was written in nail polish–like paint "Angela's."

"Whadda ya need?"

I turned to see a little guy about ninety years old, squinting up at me through thick, smudged glasses. His pants were way too big—they probably fit him sometime before World War II—and had to be held up with suspenders. It was like he had suddenly shrunk inside his clothes and hadn't had time to change into smaller ones. He stared at me, his lower lip sticking out, shiny and wet, in a permanent pout.

"Just looking around," I said.

He shrugged and walked back behind the counter. He was halfway through some kind of sandwich, maybe chicken salad. I watched as he picked it up with both hands and took a tiny bite, like a little squirrel. He had forgotten all about me.

I looked back out the window at the clubhouse. When I was in OC we had done surveillance on it, usually from a van parked across the street. Like most mob clubhouses, it was where the guys could get together and relax—they'd play cards, eat sandwiches, shoot the shit. The public wasn't invited. This one was in a vacant storefront, and the tiles on the sidewalk in front still had the old store's name, written in script, "Westmount Shoes for Ladies."

From the sidewalk, you couldn't see inside. There were dusty gray curtains in the windows, and the glass front door was painted black.

Hanging in one window was a big Italian flag, sagging a little in the middle. In the other was a sun-faded poster for an Italian-American parade from two or three years before.

We knew from informants who had been inside that there were a couple of tables for cards near the front, a few stuffed and folding chairs here and there, and a fairly new, regulation-sized pool table. They had some sort of video game, but supposedly the deafening sound effects drove Bravelli crazy, and no one dared use it while he was there.

You could tell it had been a shoe store—the walls on either side were still lined with slanted wooden shoe racks, still painted pink for the ladies of Westmount. Farther back, a new kitchen had been installed. That's where they made the sandwiches and kept the beer.

There was also a TV that always seemed to be on, maybe to make it harder for a bug to pick up conversations. An informant told us that one time when he came into the clubhouse, six mob guys were watching a soap opera in the middle of the day, hanging on every word.

Actually, they shouldn't have worried about us bugging the place. A couple of times we tried to get in, posing as servicemen for Philadelphia Electric, but something always went wrong.

One time Doc and I got dressed up in electric company uniforms and banged on the clubhouse door. We had toolboxes and everything— we were all set to wire the place up. But just as the door was opening, an off-duty cop from the neighborhood happened to walk by.

"Hey, Doc," he said. "When'd you quit the force?"

The door slammed shut, and that was the end of that.

I smiled at the memory, then glanced at my watch. Just about 11, time for the manicure. A moment later, Bravelli emerged from the clubhouse. I moved back from the window, though I doubted he'd be able to see in. It was dark where I was standing, and the windows were pretty dusty.

Bravelli was dressed to kill. Perfectly tailored gray nailhead suit that had to cost at least two thousand dollars. Dark shirt, long black tie. The guy was a walking cliché. When you saw Bravelli, you got the feeling he went to mob movies, saw what everyone was wearing, then went out and bought the same thing for himself. Which probably wasn't surprising, considering that he supposedly loved to watch gangster movies.

I thought he was heading straight for the beauty shop, but instead he ducked into the fruit store. It took up two storefronts, and had probably been grand in its day. But now the place looked rundown, almost abandoned. Its brown paint was peeling badly, and discarded wooden fruit crates were stacked up in the windows.

Bravelli came out of the store carrying a red apple, then disappeared into the beauty shop. A few moments later, he and Michelle sat down at a table in the window, across from each other, like they were in a restaurant. He handed her the apple. What a fucking teacher's pet.

I was surprised—Bravelli was violating a mob rule. You never sit in the window, it's too dangerous. You sit with your back against the wall, so you can see who's coming in the door. But here they were, right next to the glass, and with the sun coming in I could see them both clearly, even the expressions on their faces. It was like Bravelli was so confident on his own turf, he was almost daring somebody to come by and take a shot.

He extended his right hand across the table, and Michelle took it and looked at his nails. He said something and she laughed a little, and then she started doing something to his hand, I couldn't tell what, some kind of stroking or massaging. It made me a little sick just to watch it. I could see him talking and smiling, turning on the charm. That may work with your usual bimbos, I thought, but it ain't gonna get very far with Michelle.

I had to admit, she was right—Bravelli was seeing what he wanted to see. Now and then she smiled shyly, playing along. But a manicure was one thing, what about outside the beauty shop? She'd be on her own, in unfamiliar territory. One slipup, one small mistake, he'd know she was a cop. And he wouldn't hesitate for a moment to have her killed. I stood there in the window thinking, this is going to end in her death. Michelle is going to her death.

"Whadda ya need?"

I almost jumped a foot. The old guy was right next to me, squinting up through his thick glasses. It was like he had never seen me before.

"Nothin'," I said.

He shrugged and headed back to the counter. I started to watch Michelle and Bravelli again. What am I going to do, I thought, just leave Michelle out here in Westmount on her own? Just hope I don't hear a call over Police Radio one night of a woman found dead?

Bravelli looked out the window, and his gaze swept the street. I took an involuntary step back, into the shadows. What if Michelle saw me here, and got rattled and gave herself away?

The bells of the door jingled, and in walked Frankie Canaletto. He didn't see me. I quickly turned away, pretending to be examining some feather dusters sticking out of a big tin watering can.

"Hey, Charlie," Canaletto said to the old man, "I need me a new float for my toilet."

I glanced around and realized I was standing right in the toilet-float section. There were three of them, piled together in a wire basket at my elbow.

"What kinda toilet you got?" the old man asked in a gravelly, damp voice.

"What difference does it make? A toilet is a toilet."

"No, no," the old man said, "now they got these modern toilets, you gotta have special floats. I remember when I used to carry one kind of float, one kind was all you needed for any toilet anybody had. Then they made things complicated, they're always makin' things complicated. Look at this faucet piece here, see how they made it complicated, I remember—"

"Charlie," Canaletto said, "I don't want no faucet. I want a float. You got all kinds, right?"

"I don't got the modern ones. What kinda toilet you got?"

"I don't know, Charlie, a toilet toilet. Let me take a look at your floats."

"You probably got a modern toilet. I probably don't got what you need."

"Where's your floats, Charlie?"

"Over by the window. But I probably don't got what you need."

I could hear Canaletto's steps on the dark wood floor. I waited until he was right behind me, then I whirled around and snarled, "What the fuck are you doin' here?"

He almost fell backwards in surprise, but then he straightened and glared at me. "What are you doin', you spying on us?" He turned his head to look out the window, and immediately spotted Bravelli and Michelle in the beauty shop.

He turned back to me with a triumphant smile. "You *are* spyin' on us. Hey, Charlie," he said, keeping his eyes on me, "this guy's a cop, you know you got a cop in here?"

"Whadda ya sayin'? I don't know nothin' about him. He didn't want to buy nothin'."

"That's 'cause he's a cop, Charlie. He's spying on people."

I had to get out of there. I grabbed all three toilet floats from the basket and shoved them at Canaletto. "Here," I said, brushing past him. "Go home and clean up your shit."

When I reached the door the old man called out to me. "Hey, mister."

I turned. "Yeah?"

"You don't see what you need, just ask."

Canaletto rolled his eyes. I slipped out the door and hurried down the sidewalk and around the corner.

A half hour later, I called the beauty shop from a pay phone, I figured the manicure would be over by then. I didn't know what name Michelle was using, so I just asked for the manicurist.

"Which manicurist?" the woman on the phone asked. "We got two, ya know."

"Uh . . ."

"You want Lisa or Annie?"

"Which has the curly brown hair?"

"They both got curly brown hair."

"Which is the new one?"

"They're both new. What do you want, hon, you want a manicure? They're both good, believe me, either one, take your pick."

"Well, I talked to a manicurist in the fruit store the other day, I don't know which one it was, she said definitely to ask for her. But I'm not too good at remembering names."

"The fruit store? Probably Lisa, she's been goin' over there. Hey, Lisa!" the woman screamed. "Guy onna phone wants a manicure!"

I waited for a few seconds, then I heard footsteps and someone picking up the phone.

"Hello?"

I couldn't tell whether it was Michelle.

"This is Eddie." I figured if I got the wrong girl, the name wouldn't mean anything.

There was just silence, then: "Why are you calling me here?" Definitely Michelle.

"Do you still want me to help you?"

"Of course. But you shouldn't be calling me here."

"I know, but I didn't have any other way of getting in touch. Can you page me when you get off? I'm going into work at four."

She said OK, and I gave her the number and hung up. I was on the street when she paged me that evening, and I found a pay phone and called her back. We tried to figure out where to get together. One thing we agreed on: it had to be a place where no one from Westmount would ever go.

EIGHT

At noon the next day, I was sitting in my Blazer at Carver Plaza, a public housing project in North Philadelphia that was almost all black. Its three high-rise buildings had seen a lot of misery over the years. All the balconies were covered with wire fencing, so children wouldn't fall out, and half of them had clothes drying on lines. Probably none of the basement washers or dryers worked.

I was parked in the main lot, out of sight of the street down the hill, and I watched as a dented red-and-white United Cab approached. It pulled up next to my Blazer, and the back door opened and Michelle emerged. She had stopped using her car—it was registered under her real name, and anybody with a friend in the Police Department could run a license check.

Michelle looked sensational. She was wearing stonewashed jeans, white boots, a black blouse, and a thin black jean jacket, tightly buttoned at the waist.

I reached over and unlocked the passenger door, and pushed it open for her. She climbed in, and the first thing she did was lean over and kiss me on the lips. I almost had a heart attack.

"Hey, Eddie," she said, her blue eyes sparkling.

"Hi," was all I could say back.

"You ever try getting a cab to a housing project?" she asked. "Forget it. The first cab wouldn't take me here because of the danger I'd be in. The second one wouldn't take me because of the danger *he'd* be in. The only reason I made it was because the third guy was from Iran or India or someplace, and he had no idea in the world who or what Carver was."

"Is he coming back?" I asked.

"I told him an hour, but I don't know, one look at this place and he might already be on his way back to his home country."

Michelle still had a sadness about her, but for now it seemed to be pushed away.

"I'm glad you changed your mind," she said. "I was hoping you would."

I told her about how I had watched the manicure from the hardware store, and my encounter with Frankie Canaletto. I thought she might be angry, but she wasn't, it didn't seem to bother her.

"Actually, I'm sort of glad you were there, you know, just in case anything had happened."

"I got to be honest with you, Michelle. I know you want to find out about Steve, but I still think you're going to be in too much danger. It's not worth it."

"But you are going to help me?"

"Well, yeah, I'm going to try to keep you alive."

She smiled at me. "And I'm sure you'll do a great job."

One thing about a white guy and a white girl sitting in a truck in the middle of a black housing project, they don't exactly blend in. As Michelle and I talked some more, we watched three young black guys walk slowly in front of the Blazer. Predators who had picked up the scent.

"Look at their expressions," said Michelle. "Their brains are working overtime trying to figure us out. We must be cops, right? But if we're cops, then what are we doing here?"

"Certainly not undercover work," I said, and Michelle laughed.

"Right," she said, "so they figure maybe we're not cops, maybe we're social workers, or newspaper reporters, or people from the Housing Authority. But now their problem is, how come we're not getting out of the vehicle? How come we're just sitting here talking?"

"We might be ordinary white people who just happened to get lost in North Philadelphia," I said.

"Though we'd have to be pretty stupid white people."

"And even those guys don't think white people are that stupid, I said."

"So there's no answer. Nothing fits."

"They still think we might be cops, though," said Michelle.

"Yeah," I said, "and you know they're going to spend the next twenty minutes arguing about it."

We kept an eye on them until they were out of sight.

"So how'd the manicure go?" I asked.

"Great. He asked me to go out to dinner with him at the Bordeaux."

That was a hoity-toity French restaurant in Center City where they charged just for breathing their air.

"Oh, I've been there many times myself," I said.

"You have?"

"Actually, I've walked past there many times. I've never technically been inside. When you going?"

"I'm not. I turned him down."

"Why?"

She laughed. "You don't understand women, do you?"

"Not particularly."

"I knew he'd ask me again, and he did—he called me at the shop this morning. I said OK."

"You took a chance."

"Not really. He's used to women falling all over him. To guys like him, 'No' is . . ."

"Intriguing," I suggested.

"Exactly."

"See, I know a little about women."

"No, you know about guys. Actually, he can be quite charming."

"Charming? Michelle, he's a stone-cold killer."

"What can I say? Anyway, we're going to Lucky's tomorrow night."

"I thought you said the Bordeaux."

"When he called me this morning he said maybe I'd prefer something less formal, something in the neighborhood."

"Sounds like he's getting cheap on you."

"No, I just think he's trying to be more down-to-earth."

"Yeah, right. Did he tell you what he does for a living?"

"Well, at one point he said, 'Do you know who I am?' I just looked at him for a second, and then I said, 'Maybe, but . . . I don't know, I don't watch soap operas much anymore.' He thought that was very funny."

I just couldn't picture that asshole as a normal guy who could sit down and have a normal conversation with a woman. Particularly not Michelle. I tried not to think about it.

"Tell me about your apartment," I said.

"It's on the third floor, above where Angela lives."

"Is it furnished?"

She nodded. "And it's pretty dismal."

The living room furniture was old and scuffed up, and the whole apartment was very dark. Even on the third floor, you could smell the pungent chemicals used downstairs in the perms.

"You know," said Michelle, "it's enough to make me want to spend the night in my own apartment once in a while."

"Up in the Northeast?"

"Yeah, on Rhawn a few blocks from the Boulevard. Theresa, that's my roommate, she doesn't really know much about what I'm doing. But I told her I wouldn't be staying there for a while."

"I wouldn't go back there unless I had to," I said. "If you're going to get into the part, you've really got to do it all the way."

"Yeah, I know," she said, gazing out the truck window. I found myself looking at her face, her smooth skin, just drinking it in. She turned to me and smiled.

"Want to hear my name?"

"Sure."

"Lisa Puccini, like the composer. What do you think?"

"Mama mia!"

She laughed. "I'm actually one-quarter Italian."

"And it's certainly a very nice quarter. What about a cover story? Given any thought to that?"

"Oh, yeah, I've got it all worked out. I'm from Wilkes-Barre, born and raised. Two sisters, one three years older, one three years younger."

"What happens if you run into someone who really is from Wilkes-Barre?" I asked.

"Well, I sort of did grow up there—that's where my grandparents lived. Steve and I and our mom spent our summers up there."

"What about Lisa Puccini's parents?"

"My father worked at the post office. He's retired now, my mother has a sewing business out of the home."

"You got names for everyone?"

"Let's see. Older sister is Regina, she's married and lives in Pittsburgh, younger sister is Sandy, she's got tattoos and a pierced nose and she's the lead singer for a rock band."

"What's the band's name?"

"Um—I can't remember?"

"Not good enough. You have to know everything."

We tried to think of a good name for her sister's band, and I suggested "Turn That Damn Thing Down."

"That way," I said, "when a kid's father yells that upstairs, the kid's going to think, Boy, my dad's hip."

Michelle laughed, but said she'd have to think about it. I asked her a lot of questions about Lisa Puccini, including what she was doing in Philadelphia. Her story was that she left Wilkes-Barre to get away from a violently abusive boyfriend, and was trying to start a new life. She wanted to keep a low profile so he wouldn't be able to find her.

"Lisa Puccini" had worked as a manicurist at a beauty shop on South Main Street in Wilkes-Barre. It was an actual beauty shop, owned by Michelle's real cousin Darlene. If anyone called asking about Lisa Puccini, Darlene would say she had recently quit and hadn't been heard from.

"That's good," I said. "You've really thought this through."

I glanced at my watch. The cab would be back soon.

"Eddie," Michelle said quickly. "Look out your window."

I turned. There were the three guys, standing right there, malevolence rising from their bodies like steam. Apparently they had decided we weren't cops.

"Hey, white boy," said one of them, a short, muscular guy in a black T-shirt. "You got a cigarette?"

There was about a 99 percent chance he had a gun and was four seconds away from pulling it out. I reached under my T-shirt on my right side, pulled my Glock from its holster, and then stuck it out the window in the guy's face.

"Get the fuck out of here," I said. "We're the police."

He took a step back and then turned angrily to his friends.

"What'd I fuckin' tell you?"

"No, man," one of them said. "I was the one told you."

"You both lying motherfuckers," said the third. "I was the one said it first."

"The fuck you did."

"I'm tellin' you, I said it, I said five-oh."

They had totally forgotten we were there.

"Yo!" I yelled. They turned. My gun was still out the window. "Take a fuckin' hike."

Without a word they shrugged and ambled off, looking for something else to relieve their boredom. I put my Glock back in its holster.

"You going to carry a gun?" I asked.

"I don't think so. It'd be nice to have, but what happens if Bravelli or somebody finds it? Most women in Westmount don't have guns."

"Your decision. By the way," I said, "don't ask Bravelli a lot of questions. In fact, don't ask him any questions. If he starts talking about business, seem totally uninterested, change the subject. Particularly if it's about Steve."

"Why? If he's telling me . . ."

"It's like you turning him down for the Bordeaux. You have to convince him it's not that big a deal. If you can do that, maybe you can get him to tell you a lot more. He'll never trust you, but maybe he'll get stupid."

Michelle's cab was approaching. I made sure I had her pager number, and that she had mine.

"If you run into any problem at all," I said, "call me right away."

"I will. You know, I guess the only thing I'm really worried about is that my mother or father will find out."

"Aren't they going to wonder what you're doing on your leave of absence? What are you telling them?"

"Are you kidding? I'm not going to tell them anything—particularly not my father. He asks way too many questions. If my parents call my other apartment, Theresa will take a message for me. I'm going to keep this as simple as possible."

The cab pulled up next to my Blazer. I didn't want to let Michelle go, I didn't want to let her go back into that world. I tried not to look worried, but Michelle knew.

"I'll be all right," she said. "And thanks for not trying to talk me out of this again. It wouldn't have done any good."

"Yeah, I know."

"I just hope this works," she said. It was the first hint of doubt I had seen.

"It will," I said. "You'll do great."

She smiled and this time I kissed her. And for a moment it was just me and her, sitting in that truck, as if no one else in the world existed. Not even Mickey Bravelli.

Right after roll call that afternoon, I headed over to Barney Stiller's protest march in my patrol car. If we were expecting to get off easy, we were kidding ourselves. Four thousand marchers showed up.

It seemed that the harder we went after the black Mafia, the worse things got. We just couldn't seem to make any progress—it was still like throwing darts blindfolded. We had no idea what we were hitting, though we kept hearing the cries of the black community.

Until that summer, one of the things that had always distinguished West Philadelphia from many other black neighborhoods was that people were willing to cooperate with the police. If there was a street-corner murder in parts of North Philly, for example, just try asking neighbors for help finding the bad guy. You'd be met by a blank face and a quickly closing door. It wasn't that people there were afraid to cooperate, though some were. It was just that they didn't like cops. White cops, black cops, they weren't particular. They didn't like any of us.

In West Philly, it was different. You'd be at a murder scene, see a young guy lying dead on the street. A crowd would gather behind the yellow police tape. As you walked back to your car to get something, you'd hear a soft voice: "Officer." An elderly black man, maybe, or a young mother holding a small child. They'd motion for you to walk with them around the corner. "I saw who did it. It was that boy Darnell, he lives across the street with his mother, Mary Owens. She's a good woman, she don't cause nobody no trouble. But that Darnell, he shot this young boy down in cold blood, then ran right back into his house. Still there, probably."

You'd knock on the door and make the pinch, and the detectives would show up and just look at you in amazement.

Over the years, a trust was built up between the community and the police. They needed us, we needed them. We understood each other. But now that trust seemed to have vanished. The black community was hurt, humiliated, full of rage. Why should they help us?

I drove to Dogshit Park, where the march was to begin its twelve-block route to 20th District headquarters. Actually, the official name was Ariwanna Park, after a tribe of Indians that presumably hundreds of years ago lived on 56th Street and bought Chinese take-out from around the corner. People in the neighborhood wanted to rename it Conrad Park, after Nathan Conrad, a black Vietnam War hero who had grown up across the street. They argued that the Ariwannas had long since moved out, and hadn't left a forwarding address. City council was more than willing to make the change, but it turned out there were still a few Ariwannas left here and there, though not in West Philly, and they demanded that the park's name stay the same.

Faced with a tough decision, city council as usual ducked the issue completely. Which meant that everyone in the neighborhood called it Conrad Park, but as far as the city was concerned, it was still Ariwanna Park.

We didn't know what to call it, so we just gave it our own name. At night, purse-snatchers and other criminals were always running in there to hide, and we were always running in after them, and when we came out we usually had to scrape off the bottoms of our shoes on a nearby patch of grass. No one knew exactly who came up with our new name for the park, but I would have put him in for a commendation.

When I arrived at the park, protesters were still gathering under the trees. I pulled my police car to the curb and got out and just started chatting with people, hoping to ease the tension a little. I knew some of the people there—residents, store owners, community leaders. They were friendly to me, and I even ran into a woman who called me by name and thanked me profusely for finding the thief who stole her VCR. I didn't remember her at all. Still, most of the people there watched me with suspicion, a low anger in their eyes.

Finally, the march began, as protesters spilled out of the park and onto the street. Leading the way were two police jeeps from Traffic, side by side, their red and blue lights flashing.

There were men from the neighborhood, but also a lot of women with young kids. Some people were carrying signs with such heartwarming sentiments as THIS IS NOT A POLICE STATE and PHILLY COPS ARE RACIST. Nearly all the marchers were black, but here and there were a few young whites. They looked like Penn students, full of self-importance. I figured maybe they got in the wrong line and thought they were in a march for better cafeteria food.

One young guy near the front of the march was walking backwards with a bullhorn, leading a singsong chant with the words "GESTAPO POLICE, YOU'RE WHITE AND MALE, YOU'RE THE ONES THAT BELONG IN JAIL."

It took me a second to recognize him—it was Homicide, the guy we picked up the night Steve was shot. As I was watching him fade noisily into the distance, Marisol got on the radio and asked me to come to 64th and Pine, about halfway along the route. She was calm, but from the sound of her voice, I had a feeling there was trouble. When I got there, two boys, both about thirteen, were standing on top of Nick's car, kicking at the red and blue lights. It didn't look like the protest was exactly instilling respect for the police among the young.

One of the kids had on a red Phillies cap, the other had a red Sixers cap. Nick was furious, his face was as red as the hats. He was yelling at the kids to get off, and he was trying to grab their legs, but they kept jumping out of the way, playing a game with him. Meanwhile, the street was full of people marching by, chanting about putting police in jail, and they were all watching Nick. It was not a good situation.

Marisol and her partner, Yvonne Shelley, were standing nearby. "We figured you better handle this," said Marisol.

I walked up to Nick. "Calm down, just ignore them for right now."

Nick looked at me like I was crazy. "Just try it," I said, and turned my back on the boys. I motioned for Nick to do the same. Reluctantly, he turned around. It worked—they just stood silently on the car roof, and eventually joined us in watching the march. I told Marisol and Yvonne to take off, we had it under control. After a few minutes, the march had passed, and everything was quiet. I turned back to the boys.

"All right, time to get off."

"You can't tell us what to do," said the kid in the Phillies hat, pointing his finger at me. With that, both of them kicked at the red and blue lights again. They just had sneakers on, but they were kicking hard, and we heard a crunch and pieces of blue plastic flew across the top of the car. More kicks, more crunches, now red plastic was flying. The kids were laughing, having a great time.

"Get off my fuckin' car, NOW!" Nick yelled. They just laughed and kept kicking. Nick's face got red again, and he climbed on top of the hood of the car and took out his nightstick.

Before I could even tell him to put it away, he whacked the boy with the Phillies hat in the leg, and the kid yelped in pain and fell to one knee. He looked at Nick in astonishment, like how could he ever do such a thing. Meanwhile, his pal slid down the back window onto the trunk, then onto the street, and took off running.

"That's enough, Nick," I said.

It should have been over then. The boy in the Phillies cap had given up, he was ready to come down, just looking for a way to do it. Nick was still standing on the hood of the car, he could have just grabbed the kid's arm. Instead, he put one foot on the windshield to brace himself, and then swung his stick again, catching the back of the boy's knee. Without a sound, without resistance, the kid collapsed forward, toward Nick.

"Nick!" I yelled. I knew what he was going to do. I could see it coming. I tried to grab Nick's leg, but he had reared back, he was swinging as hard as he could, and his stick caught the kid's head with a crack. The boy fell onto the hood of the car, unconscious, blood streaming over the bright white paint.

"What the hell you doing?" I yelled.

Nick was almost surprised by my question.

"You saw him, he was fuckin' up my car, you think I'm gonna let him get away with that?"

"So you're going to get us both fired, is that it? Is that what you're trying to do?"

I looked around—there was no one anywhere. It was like a ghost town. All the onlookers on the sidewalks and the front porches were gone, they seemed to have been simply swept away by the protest march. Was it possible that no one had seen what happened?

What I should have done was call for Rescue, and then filed a full report. But had I done that, Nick would have been charged with assault and fired before the end of his shift, and I probably would have gotten jammed up for letting it happen. You just don't beat a black kid senseless at a protest march against police.

I had no doubt the Department would hang Nick without a second thought. It wouldn't matter that maybe he was acting a little crazy because his father had just died, and because his partner had just died. They wouldn't take that into consideration. They wouldn't care.

Which meant I had to choose between my cousin and the Department. It took about one second to make a decision.

"We can take him to the hospital ourselves," I said, taking another look around. "Help me get him into the car." There was still no sign that anyone had seen.

Together we picked the boy off the hood, carrying him under his arms, and put him in the backseat. He was still unconscious, still bleeding badly. I checked the trunk for the first-aid kit that was supposed to be there, and somehow wasn't surprised it was missing. I did find a reasonably clean white towel, though, and I got in the back with the kid and held it to his head.

"St. Mike's," I told Nick. "Let's go, now."

It was a small hospital, only a few blocks away. At one point I took the towel away and looked at the kid's wound.

"Damn, Nick, you really split the kid's head open."

"He had it comin', Eddie."

As we pulled up to the emergency room area, the boy was beginning to wake up. I quickly unpinned my badge and my nameplate, and dropped them into my shirt pocket. When the car stopped, I pushed opened the door and helped slide the kid out.

"Think you can make it to those doors?" I asked him, and pointed at the two large sliding glass doors to the ER. He was still groggy, and I don't think he really knew where he was. Without a word, he staggered off in the right general direction. I ran around the back of the car and jumped in the front passenger seat, and Nick oh-so-casually put the car in gear and glided back out into the street. As we made the turn we looked back and saw the ER doors close behind the kid.

There was still blood on the hood, which is not the kind of thing people wouldn't notice. The only place I knew that had a hose was the Yard at headquarters, but since that was where the march was headed, it probably wasn't exactly the best place to go. Nick said he had seen a hose behind the supermarket at 54th and Baltimore, it was probably used to clean out the Dumpsters.

We pulled behind the supermarket, and hosed off the car and cleaned out the backseat. Nick gave me a smile as he started to get back behind the wheel.

"Thanks for saving my ass, Eddie."

I grabbed his arm and pulled him back out. "You think this is a good time?" I said. "This was a fun thing that you did?"

"No, but like I said, he had it comin'."

"The fuck he did, Nick. First you deck that guy on Fifty-second, now you try to kill this kid. What the fuck is wrong with you?"

"C'mon, Eddie . . ."

"I should beat the shit out of you right here, Nick. If you weren't going through such a tough time, I swear to God I would, right here, I would just lay you the fuck out on the street."

Nick's eyes were full of surprise and hurt.

"You may not have to deal with Internal Affairs," I said, "but you're going to have to deal with me. And I'm going to be a lot fucking worse."

"What do you want me to do, Eddie?"

I just looked at him. I didn't know what I wanted him to do. And now what was I supposed to do? What could be worse than him getting fired and locked up?

Nick saw what I was thinking. "You look out for me, don't you, Eddie?"

I shrugged, like it was no big deal. But it was true, ever since he was a kid, he had counted on me. I was ten years older, he looked up to me. I was the one he could talk to. He never felt he could go to his father, or his brothers, Chris and Matt.

Nick and his brothers were the only cousins I had, and our families were pretty close. Although we lived up in the Northeast, and they lived in Westmount, we were always at each other's houses. It was like I was the Bari kids' extra brother. Chris, Matt, and Nick were all ushers at my wedding, though Nick, to his eternal sorrow, was too young to go to the bachelor party.

And though Nick always used to come to me for advice, I was never sure how much help I really was to him. There was the time, when he was in the fourth or fifth grade, that he had stolen a brass baseball paperweight off his teacher's desk. The teacher suspected another student, but couldn't prove anything.

It was just before Thanksgiving, which was at our house that year. As soon as Nick walked in with his family, he grabbed my arm and led me back outside onto the front porch.

He told me about the paperweight, and said, "What should I do, Eddie?"

I was nineteen, and here I was being asked to give moral guidance to a nine-year-old. I remember standing out there with him, watching the street get dark. It was one of those clear November evenings where you can see the stars even in the city. I couldn't wait to get dinner over with and get back out onto the street with my friends.

I thought about telling him to just admit he stole the paperweight, and take his punishment like a man. You can't let a friend take the rap. But I figured he had to come to that conclusion himself or it wouldn't be worth anything.

I ended up sounding like one of those idiot older brothers on TV. "You have to do what you think is best. Whatever feels right to you."

Nick nodded like he understood, and we went inside.

When our families got together at Christmas, I asked him how it had all turned out. He told me he had thought about what I had said, and decided to keep his mouth shut. It worked—nothing ever happened to him or his friend, and he got to keep the paperweight. Though one night he was using it to knock out streetlights, and it went through a neighbor's upstairs window. So much for imparting my wisdom.

As Nick and I drove back to district headquarters, I remembered the paperweight. In all the times I had tried to help Nick over the years, had I ever really known what I was doing?

Nothing much else happened that afternoon, if you don't count the woman who came down to file a complaint against police. Her thirteen-year-old son said he had been badly beaten by two white officers during the protest march. She happened to stop by as Barney Stiller was giving a speech to the crowd outside, and he got wind of it, and got the woman to tell her story through the bullhorn. The crowd was furious, and some young guys started yelling that they should storm our building. I thought we were going to have fright night at the 20th, but things eventually calmed down.

Kirk called me into his office, he was pissed as shit—he wanted to know who the hell those two cops were. I promised him I'd do my best to find out.

A few minutes after eleven that night, my pager went off. It was at the end of the shift, and I was coming up the steps from the basement locker room after changing out of my uniform. I checked the phone number—it was Doc, calling from his house in Fishtown. He knew I'd be getting off work now.

I walked into the operations room and used one of the black rotary phones. We were probably the last police department in the world to get push-button phones, except maybe for some little town in India that used cows instead of police cars.

"Hey, buddy, I want you to see somethin'," Doc said when I called. "Need your advice."

"What's up?"

"Still wearin' your uniform?"

"No, I just changed."

"Good. Do me a favor and take a ride by Sagiliano's. Stick your head in the door—don't go in—just look around, see what you see."

"What am I looking for, Doc?"

"You'll see. Just don't go in, OK?"

"Sure."

"I could sure use your advice on this one, buddy."

We hung up, and I headed outside to my Blazer. Sagiliano's was a corner taproom in Westmount, and everyone knew it was a mob hangout. Neighborhood people mostly came there to drink, but it was also a restaurant, and there were a few booths and tables in the back. It was the kind of place that if you sat down at one of the tables, at the next one you'd see Mama making the ravioli by hand.

I'd been there a couple of times on jobs. It had a low, wood-paneled ceiling, and the dimly lit bar was in a long, narrow U shape, so people could sit all the way around and talk to the person sitting across.

Like most workingman's bars in Westmount, Sagiliano's had no pretensions whatsoever—the counter of the bar wasn't polished oak, it was just cheap Formica, worn shiny in places by the bottoms of countless beer bottles. Against the darkened walls was the usual shuffle-board-bowling game, the video blackjack machine, the worn-out jukebox.

No one came from miles around. There were bars like Sagiliano's every few blocks in Westmount, and the customers all lived or worked close by. It was the kind of place where someone might suddenly walk out, leaving his beer half finished, his newspaper open on the counter. But he was just going home to take care of something, he'd be back in a minute. His bottle and his newspaper would be there waiting for him. The only distinction Sagiliano's had was that connected guys from the neighborhood liked to drink there, and you never got into a fight because of who might be sitting on the next stool.

I found a parking space a block away and walked up to the entrance. There was a solid wood door, so I couldn't see inside, but it seemed pretty quiet. I pushed the door open, took a step in, and—following Doc's instructions—looked around. The bar was mostly full. Older men with craggy alcohol-faces, younger guys with sleeveless white T-shirts, still dusty from the construction sites. The TV, bolted to the wall at one end of the bar, had a weatherman giving the five-day forecast. A couple of guys sitting near the entrance turned to look at me, and didn't turn away—I was a stranger.

And there, in a booth at the back, was Lenny Lanier, in street clothes, sitting by himself, a glass of beer in front of him. I saw why Doc didn't want me to walk through the bar—Lanier might have spotted me. I quickly slipped back out the door.

I didn't even wait until I got home to call Doc, I stopped at the pay phone at the 7-Eleven near Penn.

"Was he there?" Doc asked, his Texas accent making the last word two or three syllables.

"Yep," I drawled back.

"Well? What do you think?"

"I think that Lanier shouldn't be anywhere near that bar."

"It's not like he's undercover," said Doc. "If he were, I'd know about it."

"And how would he even go undercover?" I asked. "Everybody in Bravelli's crew knows who he is."

"So what's he doing there?" asked Doc.

"You tell me."

"That's what I've been trying to find out for the past two weeks."

"He's been going in there for two weeks?"

"At least. The first time I saw him was by accident, I was just checking out the bar, just seeing who was inside. There was the captain, sittin' in the back. I didn't say anything to him, I just left."

"Was he on duty?"

"No, he gets off earlier than me, 'bout seven. But it seemed pretty strange him being there. So the next night I sat in my car, I guess about a half block away, see if he'd come by after work. Sure enough, he did."

"Have you told anyone?"

"I guess I could go to the inspector, but what am I gonna say? Hell, maybe he's just drinking. Tell you what, I'm not in any particular hurry to get someone jammed up for nothing—just look what happened to you."

"Yeah. But I don't trust that bastard, Doc. I didn't before, and I do even less now."

"Think I should say somethin' to Lanier?"

"No, he knows what he's doing, he knows he shouldn't be in that bar socializing."

"So what do you think?"

"I think you should keep a very close eye on him," I said. "Anything else makes you suspicious—anything at all—then you go to the inspector. That way, you'll have two reasons instead of just one."

"Yeah, that sounds good. I know you don't like him, Eddie, but personally, I don't think he's that bad a guy."

"I wouldn't be so sure," I said. "Just watch your back."

I hung up. It was hard to believe that Lanier really might be involved with the mob. Was that why I got kicked out of OC, just as I was closing in on Bravelli?

I remembered that night in Lucky's, the night Steve died, how Lanier had stepped in to prevent me from arresting anyone in Bravelli's crew.

Was it possible?

NINE

I saw Lanier again the next night. In another place I didn't want him to be.

This time, it was outside Lucky's, just before Michelle and Bravelli were set to have their little dinner. I was cruising around the neighborhood in my patrol car—actually, trying to pass by Lucky's as often as I could without making it obvious. I told myself the reason was that if Michelle spotted me, and knew I was around, she might feel safer. But I knew that what I really wanted was a glimpse of her, just to make sure she was OK.

It was during my third or fourth swing by Lucky's that I noticed the brown Plymouth sitting by the curb on the nearby cross street, 70th. I couldn't see who was inside, but it was an unmarked police car, no doubt about it. I circled the block, got onto 70th, and drove past the Plymouth. As I did, I saw Lanier's ugly face looking back at me.

He must have gotten word Bravelli would be here tonight. I circled around again, and this time parked on 70th about a half block behind his car, out of sight of Lucky's. As I walked up toward the car from behind, I could see Lanier watching me in his rearview mirror. I was heading over to the driver's side to talk with him, but he called out "Get in," and pointed to the passenger's seat. I didn't really feel like sitting in the same car as Lanier, but it was better than standing out in the street.

Lanier turned to me when I got in. "You trying to ruin my surveillance, Eddie?"

Of course, the answer was yes. Instead, I said, "I just wanted to see what you're doing here, Captain."

"Why?" He seemed genuinely surprised.

"Just curious."

"You know how it is, Eddie, I can't talk about jobs."

We both saw it at the same time, the black Cadillac Seville, coming down Walnut, passing by us, pulling over to the curb in front of Lucky's.

Goop got out from behind the wheel and opened the back door on his side, facing the street. Michelle emerged, wearing a red, sleeveless dress.

"You know, she looks a little familiar," said Lanier. "You ever seen her before, Eddie?"

I pretended to study her as she waited for Bravelli to come around from the other side.

"No," I said. "She's definitely a new one."

"I know I've seen her," said Lanier. "I don't know where, but I have, and I don't think it was a very long time ago."

It wasn't. Lanier had spent at least three minutes talking to Michelle when Ru-Wan's body was found in the trunk. Now he was a half block away, and an inch from recognizing her, disguise and all.

For some reason, Michelle and Bravelli were still talking by the car. I tried to will them into the restaurant. Goop was already waiting for them by the front door, ready to open it. Get over there, I thought.

"This is driving me crazy," said Lanier. "I know I've seen her."

"Just another Westmount girl," I said. "I'm sure Bravelli goes through 'em like water."

Finally, Michelle and Bravelli did move around behind the car, and toward the canopy. Keep going, I thought, don't stop, just keep going. Goop held the door for them, and they disappeared inside.

"I'm going to find out who she is," said Lanier. "It's going to drive me crazy until I do." He turned to me. "That ever happen to you, Eddie?"

———

hadn't expected this. If Lanier did learn the truth, I had to know right away, I had to be able to warn Michelle. Doc was my best shot—Lanier might mention it to him.

But that meant I'd have to tell Doc about Michelle. I hadn't wanted to tell anyone, I'd always assumed I'd be the only one who knew who she was. But it couldn't be helped now, I knew that.

And so I told Doc the whole story. He understood. He was already trying to stay as close to Lanier as possible, to find out what was going on with him. He promised to let me know whenever Lanier talked about Michelle.

From that point on, my stomach didn't stop churning. Michelle started going out with Bravelli almost every night. Much of the time, Lanier—shadowed by Doc—was somewhere around. Doc had quickly realized that Lanier was obsessed with learning who the woman with Bravelli was. He pushed Doc to find out everything he could about her.

I told Michelle about all this, but it didn't seem to bother her.

"If Lanier figures out who I am, I'll make a decision then," she said. "Right now, I'm not going to worry about it."

She didn't seem to be worried about anything. Two weeks after her date at Lucky's, we met again at the Carver housing project. She was jazzed.

"I'm making fantastic progress," Michelle said when she got in my truck. "I am really good at this. I think I must be a natural."

"So Bravelli's going for it?" I asked.

"Are you kidding? He's crazy about me. Every time we go out he gives me a gift. See? You like this necklace?"

It was a silver and gold job that had to cost at least a thousand.

"Great," I said, trying to sound like I meant it.

"He calls me all the time, every day he sends flowers to me at Angela's—every single day. Actually, it's getting a little embarrassing, because everybody who comes in wants to know who they're from, and they start asking questions. Though I guess that's good, because the word's getting out"—and here she started with a Southern accent—"Mickey Bravelli's trying to win my heart."

She held her hands to her chest and fluttered her eyelids.

"Give me a fucking break," I said.

"Actually, it's been a lot of fun. Like when we go into Jumpin' Jiminy's, everybody knows him, and he's got me on his arm, and he's kind of showing me off. But I can tell, he's really trying to impress me. He's more worried about what I think than what the other people think."

Jumpin' Jiminy's was a dance club in Center City, on the Delaware River. Bravelli had taken Michelle there a half dozen times in the last two weeks.

"Why do you think he's so attracted to you?" I asked.

She gave me a look. "Thanks a lot."

"I mean, you're not from the neighborhood, you're really not from his world . . ."

"Actually, I think that's why he's interested in me. I don't fall all over him, I don't act impressed around him. It's like when he told me what he does for a living."

"He told you?"

"Yeah, a couple of nights ago. We went to a Phillies game, and then we got some water ice at this place on Oregon Avenue. You know that little park across the street? We went over there and sat down on a bench, and Mickey said, 'It's time I told you what I do. I want to know if you got a problem with it.' "

"Mickey? You're going to call him Mickey around me?"

"What do you want me to call him?"

"How about shithead?"

"C'mon, Eddie. Anyway, he said, 'Did you ever see the movie *The Godfather?*' I just played dumb, I said I'd heard of it, but never saw it. So then he asks, 'Not even Part II?' I say no. 'Not even Part III?' I shake my head no again.

"Then he says, 'You had to see *Goodfellas.*" And I said, 'That was that old movie with Jerry Lewis and the wicked stepmother, right?' Mickey's mouth dropped open, it was really funny. So then I said, 'No, I guess I'm thinking of *Cinderfella.*' "

I laughed. "Did he get it?"

"No, but he was very patient. He went through a long list of movies, I guess every mob movie ever made. I kept saying, Nope, Nope, Nope. Finally, he said, 'Do you ever see comedies?' I said Sure. So he says, 'How about *Married to the Mob?*' And I said, Yeah, I've seen that.' And he said, 'Well, that's what you'd be if you married me.' "

"How imaginative."

"So I asked him, had he ever thought about going to college and getting a real job?"

"You said that?"

"Yeah, he laughed. I think he actually liked me asking that. I just think Mickey feels—"

"Michelle, do me a favor."

"All right. Bravelli feels."

"Thank you."

"I just think he feels he can relax around me. You know, he can be more himself."

"Has he tried anything with you?"

That stopped her.

"Eddie, I'm undercover, I'm playing a part."

"Oh, so now you're going to sleep with him?"

"No, I'm not going to sleep with him, I told you I wasn't going to do that." She was pissed.

"Sorry."

"In fact, I think that's another one of the reasons he's attracted to me. Because I *won't* sleep with him. You know, that first date, after we went out to Lucky's, he asked me whether I wanted to come over to his house. I said no. Second date, I said no. Third date, I said no. I think he was starting to get upset, like he was about ready to say, Forget this girl. But then, when I kept saying no, I think he respected that. He still asks every time we go out, but now I think he expects me to say no. It's almost as if I were to say yes, he'd like it, but he really wouldn't like it."

"Because then you'd be like every other woman he goes out with."

"Exactly."

"Well, it is true about these guys," I said. "They look for a different kind of woman to have their kids than to be their girlfriend."

"Maybe that's what he sees in me. A possible future wife."

"Can I throw up now?"

"Hey, I think it means I'm doing a good job."

"Yeah, maybe. Is he talking at all? Are you picking up anything?"

"Well, not about Steve, if that's what you mean. But I can tell you that Bravelli really hates the black Mafia."

"I don't think that's top-secret information, Michelle—you know, they're competitors."

"Yeah, I know. But this crackdown my father's doing on the black Mafia? Bravelli thinks it's great."

"I'm not surprised. Are you getting anything else?"

"Well, he's really worried that Frankie Canaletto might get charged with murder."

"Good."

"I heard he killed some mob guy?"

"Yeah, over the winter," I said. "Supposedly some kind of interoffice squabble."

"Over the winter? Why would he be charged now?"

"I think it's the new DA. He just seems to be more aggressive than the old guy. You know, more interested in actually fighting crime. From what I hear, Canaletto's going to get nailed."

"Well, Bravelli's definitely upset about it. I mean, you can tell they're really close, Bravelli treats him like a brother. He said they've known each other since kindergarten."

"Where I'm sure they were model pupils. Are you kissing him?"

Michelle moved her head back a little. "Where'd that come from?"

"Just curious."

"Well, I'm not going to answer it."

"Then you are kissing him."

Michelle narrowed her eyes at me. "What if I am? What if I am? Let me tell you something, Eddie, you think this is easy? I'm putting myself in danger, I'm trying to find out about Steve—and whatever you think, that's what's in the back of my mind the whole time—"

"I know."

"—and I'm just trying to do this the best way I can, and all I'm getting from you is grief."

"Just picturing you and that asshole . . ."

"Eddie," she said, looking hard into my eyes, stopping me. "I could use your support."

I took a deep breath. I was about to continue, but she wouldn't let me speak.

"I could use your support," she repeated.

"OK," I said. I took another deep breath, and let it out. "OK."

But I sat there thinking, what if I just killed Bravelli? I could have this all over with. And I wouldn't have to worry about it, ever again.

That night about nine, Doc paged me. He said he was planning to do a little surveillance in Westmount, and he wanted me along.

"I'm working right now," I said. "I'm out on the street, in my patrol car. I'm in uniform."

"Don't worry about that," Doc said. "No one will see you. Just come on over."

Doc told me he had become preoccupied with finding out what was going on with Lanier. Every night when the captain left OC headquarters in Center City after work, Doc followed him. Half the time, Lanier went home, to his house up in the Northeast. The other half of the time, he went to Westmount.

Doc said he had been looking for a way to run an audio surveillance on Lanier. He had figured out how and where to do it, and was ready to pull the trigger tonight.

Come on over, he said again, and he gave me the address.

It was at the far end of Westmount's Locust Street shopping district. The stores began at 77th—the block with Angela's and the mob clubhouse—and extended to 85th. Those eight blocks were sort of like a small-town downtown—clothing stores, jewelry stores, furniture stores, and of course the inevitable beauty salons. Everything was closed for the night.

Doc was waiting for me at a door to some offices near the corner of 85th. He had a key to get us in, and we took the stairs to the second floor. It was an insurance office, and Doc had another key for that door.

There wasn't much to the reception area—a couple of tidy desks, both with framed family photos, and little flowers in little vases, and computers shut down and covered with clear plastic dustcovers. Doc kept the lights off, but there was plenty of illumination from the street.

I followed him down a hallway, using his bald round head—which nicely reflected the light—as a beacon.

"This place is run by a friend of mine," he explained. "Ex-Navy, ex-cop."

In the back, overlooking the alley, was what had to be his friend's office. Wood-paneled walls covered with diplomas and certificates and photos of Navy fighter planes. There was a modest desk that was just as neat as the ones out front, though it had about six different kinds of paperweights, and a model of a Navy jet on a plastic stand.

"This is it," Doc said, and waved me over to a small window that looked out to the right. The building we were in jutted out a few feet, and the side window gave us a clear view down the alley to 85th Street.

"The other side of the alley, down at the end," said Doc. "See that back entrance?"

The next street over was Manning. I tried to remember what was at the corner with 85th. "That's Sagiliano's," I said.

"Right."

"Which might explain why there's a brand-new white Lexus blocking the alley," I said.

"Never seen it before," said Doc. "But somebody's got his own personal parking space."

"What are we looking for?" I asked.

Doc told me that three days before, he had followed Lanier to the bar, and parked on the side street as Lanier went inside. About a half hour later, he spotted Lanier in the alley.

"He was talkin' to someone," said Doc. "From where my car was, I really couldn't see them too well. I could tell it was Lanier and some other guy, but I was just too far away to see a face."

"Think it was Bravelli?" I asked.

"I don't know, but I'll tell you what. The captain had to come out that back door there. And I'll bet whoever he was talking to went back in through that door."

"So this might be Bravelli's private little meeting place," I said.

"Might could be. The captain's in there now, so if he comes out tonight, we got a front-row seat."

"You got it wired?" I asked.

"Yep-sir-ee."

Doc took out his walkie-talkie, and held it near the window so he could get some light from a street lamp in the alley. It wasn't a typical police radio—this one had a numerical keypad and display panel on the front.

Doc keyed in a frequency and turned up the volume. There were low-level street noises, nothing more. Doc pointed out the window toward the back doorway of Sagiliano's.

"I don't think you can see it from here," he said, "but there's a metal box by the door, has telephone wires runnin' up to the roof. I hid my microphone in the box where the wires come out, right where the hole is."

"Where's the transmitter?"

"It's with the microphone, it's all one unit."

We took turns looking out the side window for the next hour. Whoever wasn't at the window got to sit in the insurance agent's big padded chair and play with his toy jet.

Just before ten-thirty, I saw Sagiliano's back door open.

"Doc," I said, and he jumped up and came over. Bravelli came out, and then held the door open for someone. It was Michelle. Doc glanced at me, but I kept my eyes on the alley.

Bravelli was saying something to Michelle, but we couldn't make out what it was. Doc grabbed the radio and turned up the volume.

"You just got this today?" we heard Michelle ask, pointing at the white Lexus.

"Yeah," said Bravelli. "Take a look."

The driver's side of the car faced the opposite side of the alley, and Michelle and Bravelli had to walk around. They kept talking, but they were totally out of range of Doc's microphone.

"Shit on a stick," Doc said.

I didn't like this. If Lanier was inside tonight, he would have seen Michelle.

Bravelli opened the driver's door, and motioned for Michelle to get in behind the wheel. She did, and looked around, and turned the steering wheel back and forth, and then got out. When she did, she said something and laughed, and all of a sudden she and Bravelli were kissing. My stomach dropped, I felt sick, like I was going to throw up. It only lasted a moment. When Michelle backed away, I was weak with relief.

Together, they walked around the front of the car, and Bravelli opened the passenger door. Michelle was about to get in, but then she turned and took a step toward Bravelli and said something, and then took another step, and kissed him. She put her arms around him and this time they didn't stop kissing. I closed my eyes and opened them again, and tried to convince myself that it was Bravelli who had started the kiss, not Michelle. I tried to close my eyes again, to look away, but I couldn't.

One good thing about being a cop, you get to carry a gun. I could run downstairs and out the door, and around the corner into the alley. I could be there in thirty seconds. Now's the time, I thought. Now's the time.

But I couldn't move, I just stood there, unready for murder. Finally they stopped kissing, and stepped apart. Michelle got into the car and closed the door, and we heard the "shoomp" of it shutting over the radio, and then Bravelli got in on his side, and we heard his door close, and then we heard the car starting. There was a roar over Doc's radio as Bravelli pulled the car out onto 85th Street and off to the right, and then the alley was quiet again.

TEN

I barely said anything to Doc, I just walked out of the insurance office, and down the stairs to the street. There had to be some way to fuck up Bravelli's world. Maybe I could have my cops raid the Pleasure Palace, his "massage parlor" on Cleo Street near the Penn campus. Or we could bust up his numbers operation on Chestnut. There was plenty of other stuff Bravelli's crew was into—protection, loan-sharking, meth dealing. Plenty of targets. All we had to do was choose.

But as I drove out of Westmount, I knew it wouldn't make much difference. Guys from OC, from Citywide Vice, from Narcotics, were always going after Bravelli. Parts of his operation might be shut down for a week or two, but then they'd be back in business, as if nothing ever happened.

I realized I couldn't even harass Bravelli anymore. If I stopped his car, Michelle might be inside—and I didn't want to put her in that situation.

So what could I do? Nothing?

It was a quiet night, there was plenty of time to think as I drove through the streets. Out of habit, I swung by the crackhouse. It was something I had started doing every night—I was hoping that sooner or later, the pipers who used to hang out there would wander back. Maybe they could tell us something, anything.

Kirk wanted to have the house sealed up, but I argued against it. They've got to come back sooner or later, I said. I had made sure all the crime scene tape was gone, the door was unlocked, everything was back to normal.

That night, as I cruised past the house, I realized it had been three weeks since Steve was killed. It seemed much longer, months maybe. In the evening summer breeze, the block seemed so peaceful. Had it really even happened?

There was some kind of light coming through the front window. It was so dim, at first I didn't even realize I saw it—I just had a sense that something about the house was different. I stopped the car, and looked closely at the house for a few moments. Someone was inside.

I got out of my car, took out my gun, and walked carefully up the sidewalk and onto the porch. The window was covered by a grimy window shade.

I examined the brown-painted wooden door. It had been smashed open so many times, it barely hung onto its hinges. I gave it a little kick, and it swung open.

And there, on the sagging old couch, was a black guy sitting quietly, hands resting on his thighs, like he had absolutely nothing else in the world to do.

He was maybe forty but he looked sixty, in the way that drugs can just take twenty years right out of your life. He had on brown pants that had one day been dress slacks, and a collar shirt, short-sleeved, with blue and white stripes. They looked clean, like he had been staying with somebody who washed his clothes. How about that, I thought, a half-presentable crackhead.

He was definitely not the shooter, that was obvious—he was not even remotely alarmed at the presence of a uniformed police officer holding a gun on him.

"How many other people in the house?" I asked, stepping inside.

"Nobody. Just me."

I lowered my gun. I didn't think he was lying.

"What's your name?"

"Ronald."

"Ronald what?"

"Just Ronald."

"Nobody's just Ronald. Ronald what?"

"Ronald Caruthers."

I looked around. He wasn't smoking crack, and in fact there didn't seem to be any sign of drugs in the living room at all.

"What are you doing here?" I asked.

"What am I doing here? This is where I live."

And the way he sat on the sofa, relaxed, even comfortable, he did look like he lived there. He had come home.

"You gonna make us leave again?" he asked, like he was just wondering, already resigned to the inevitable answer.

I holstered my gun. "What do you mean, 'again'?"

He looked at me, puzzled. "Do what, now?"

"You said make you leave again. Who made you leave before?"

"Cops," he said, annoyed at being asked such a ridiculous question. "When was this?"

"Right before that cop was shot here. They told me and Gail to leave."

"Who's Gail?"

"Gail's my wife."

"How soon before, like a week?"

That question took him aback. "Not a week. It was the same night."

That didn't make any sense. But I'd never seen a crackhead who was very reliable on dates.

"How do you know it was the same night?" I asked. "Maybe it was a couple of nights before."

"It wasn't no couple nights before, it was the same night. We saw it on TV at my aunt's, I said, damn, that's our house."

This couldn't be right. "What did these cops say?" I asked.

"What do you mean, what did they say?"

"What did they say?"

"They said to get out."

He looked at me like I was retarded. He had never seen a cop ask so many stupid questions.

"Uniformed cops?"

He shook his head. "No." And then, adding helpfully, like I wouldn't be able to figure it out myself, "They were undercover."

"You mean plainclothes? Detectives?"

"If that's what you call them."

Now I understood. Two guys from the black Mafia. Ronald and Gail just assumed they were the police.

"Did they say they were cops?" I asked.

"Cops never say they're cops, they just come right in."

"Then how'd you know that's who they were?"

Ronald's mouth dropped open. This was by far the dumbest question he had ever heard in his entire life.

"Two white guys walk into a place like this," he said, "I don't need to see no proof of purchase."

"*White* guys?"

"Why do you got to repeat everything I say? Officer, if you want to be a real investigator—"

"You're telling me two white detectives came in here and told you to clear out the same night the police officer was shot?"

"Now you got it. See, I knew you would, I knew you would eventually. You may not ask the best questions . . . Why you looking at me like that?"

I must have been staring right through him.

On the first floor of Police Headquarters downtown, in the Photo Identity Unit, were the mug shots of every officer in the Philadelphia Police Department. Normally, no one ever pulled one out unless something bad happened to a cop, like he got arrested, or killed, and then the photo would be copied and given to the media so the public could see what we looked like. When they sat us down and took our pictures, they should have given us little signs to hold that said, "If you're looking at this, my ass is grass."

Things would have been a lot simpler if I could have just started showing mug shots of detectives to Ronald. But sergeants, particularly inconsequential patrol sergeants, didn't have access to the photos. You either had to have a very good friend in Photo Ident, which I didn't, or approval from a commander. I didn't have that, either.

It also would have been helpful if Ronald could have at least given me decent descriptions of the two detectives. But describing "white guys" wasn't exactly his forte.

"You all look alike," he said, when I pressed him for details such as height, weight, and hair color. "You're all just plain vanilla scoops, sittin' in a bowl, if you know what I mean."

It had occurred to me that maybe Ronald's two mystery men were actually Nick and Steve—maybe they had swung by the crackhouse before they went on duty, just to see if they could get a quick pinch. But Ronald said he knew who Nick and Steve were. They were the ones always pounding on his door, saying Open up.

One thing I knew, I couldn't tell anyone else in the Department about Ronald. Something this big could never be kept a secret, and I didn't want Ronald's two detectives tracking down him and Gail for "questioning."

So for now, until I checked out Ronald's story, I was on my own. With no mug shots, no descriptions other than vanilla ice cream, my only option was to start showing Ronald detectives in person.

Part of me couldn't accept the possibility that cops had something to do with Steve's death. If it was a crackhead, or the black Mafia, that was at least understandable, you were dealing with the enemy. But cops didn't kill cops, it just didn't happen. I knew one thing—if I found out who they were, I'd be judge, jury, and executioner. They could have their fucking trial at the funeral home.

There was no question, at least as far as I was concerned, where we should start looking. And so the day after I found Ronald in the crackhouse, he and I sat in my Blazer watching the entrance of OC headquarters on Arch Street.

The unit worked out of an old, three-story brick building about four blocks from Police Headquarters, with nothing on it to indicate it had anything to do with the police. It was almost like the building itself was undercover, but what gave it away was what always gave us away—the Plymouth Gran Furys. There were five of them, all black or brown, sitting in the small parking lot to one side and along the curb out front.

Most of the guys in the unit left work about five, and we were there fifteen minutes early. I had told Lieutenant Bowman I'd be coming in late, and that someone else would have to handle roll call. He was pissed, but I got off the phone before he could tell me exactly how pissed he was.

I couldn't decide which was stranger, doing a stakeout of my old unit, or doing it with a crackhead. And Ronald wasn't even your ordinary crackhead.

"Don't you got pictures of all the cops?" he asked, as we watched the building's entrance. "Why don't I just go through them?"

"Well, we don't have photos of everybody."

"Just show me the pictures you do got."

"It's a little complicated."

"You can't get 'em, can you?" said Ronald.

"What do you mean?"

"You don't have that authority, do you?"

For some reason, I couldn't lie to Ronald.

At exactly five, the first detective came out. Stan "The Man Who Won't Retire" Allen. Stan had thick gray hair and a matching thick gray mustache, and from a distance could look imposing. But up close, you could see that his eyes were weak, and rheumy, and beaten. He already had thirty-five years on the job, far more than the number needed for retirement. But had he left, his ex-wife would have been awarded part of his pension. And Stan vowed that he would die on the job before that ever happened.

So Stan kept coming in to work, though he had long ago stopped actually doing any work. I knew there was no way he was at that crackhouse—the last time Stan had been on the street, disco was still big. I wasn't even going to bother asking Ronald about him, but Ronald volunteered anyway.

"Not that guy," he said.

During the next few minutes, Ronald said the same thing about Mike LaShane, Pete Caruso, and a young cop I didn't know.

He even said it about Norman Carter.

"But he's black," I pointed out.

"That's why I said he's not the guy."

I tried not to admit to myself that I was really just waiting for one person, that out of every cop in the city, there was really only one I wanted Ronald to see. I was so busy telling myself to be fair, not to jump to conclusions, that Lenny Lanier was out the door before I realized it.

"Not that guy," Ronald said right away.

"Take a good look," I said. "Are you absolutely sure?"

Ronald squinted at Lanier. "Damn, that's one ugly white man," he said. "I would have remembered *him*."

I was disappointed, I wanted to leave. Still, we waited a while longer, and when Doc came out I held my breath. But Ronald hadn't seen him before. He also didn't recognize any of the next four detectives we saw, which didn't surprise me, considering that the first three were black, and the fourth was a white woman, Laura Fielding.

After another half hour, I was ready to go, I didn't want to do this anymore. We were looking in the wrong place, I knew that. I also knew that taking Ronald around, trying to do this by myself, wasn't going to work. Those two detectives might not have even been detectives at all. They could have been off-duty cops, or patrol officers on a plainclothes detail. There were too many units, too many people, too many possibilities.

I did know one person, though, who could pull those mug shots, who definitely had the authority. And I didn't think he would turn me down.

At nine the next morning, I called Police Headquarters and asked for the Commissioner's office. They transferred me upstairs, to a female corporal.

"This is Sergeant North from the Twentieth. I'd like to talk to the Commissioner."

"Hold on."

A minute later, her sergeant came on the phone, and I repeated my request.

"Something I can help you with?" he asked.

"No, thanks, I need to talk to him directly."

"Hold on."

This time I had to wait three minutes before the next person picked up.

"Yeah, Sergeant, this is Lieutenant Franklin, what can I do for you?"

"Well, Lieutenant, you can get the Commissioner on the line for me."

"What's this in reference to?"

"It's in reference to a conversation I want to have with him."

"Hold on."

"No, don't put me on hold." Too late. I sat there for another three minutes.

Finally, I heard another voice. "Captain Lazzaro."

I'd never been to the Commissioner's office, but I wondered how many people worked there. It couldn't be that big.

"Captain, this is Sergeant North from the Twentieth."

"Yeah, Sergeant, how you doin'?"

"Not too good, Captain. I've just spoken to a corporal, a sergeant, a lieutenant and now you, no offense. I'd like to talk to the Commissioner about something. Is he in?"

"Not right now. Does he know who you are?"

"I'm sure he'll remember me, I was his son's supervisor. Could you give him a message that I'd like to talk to him?"

"He's going to want to know what it's about."

"It's about his son. I can't say any more, it's confidential."

"All right, I'll pass along the message. I can't promise anything."

I gave him my pager number and told him thanks.

"Hey," he said cheerfully, "that's what we're here for."

ELEVEN

That day was Westmount Sidewalk Sale Day, an extravaganza of fun and festivities for the whole family. Actually, it was just a big sales promotion for the eight-block stretch of the Locust Street business district. There were balloons tied to parking meters, banners stretched high across the street, the whole works. Most stores had tables out front with merchandise and hand-lettered sale signs.

A few of the side streets were closed down to make room for live music and food vendors. You could take a break from your shopping and get a meatball sandwich on a hoagie roll, and stand there dodging the dripping tomato sauce while you listened to a Mummers string band.

I swung by Locust in my patrol car a little after two, and decided to get out and take a walk past the sidewalk sales. I still hadn't heard from the Commissioner, and I was a little nervous being the one to break the news that cops might have been involved in his son's death.

When I crossed over 78th Street, I hesitated. This was the block with Angela's—and I had decided it would be better to stay out of Michelle's way.

As I was about to turn around and head back, my eye caught a beige Toyota Corolla parked at the curb about thirty feet ahead of me. Something about it wasn't right.

I looked more closely. Two black guys in the front seat. That wasn't unusual, there were plenty of black shoppers on the street. But just the way these two guys moved their heads, the way they looked around, my radar was going crazy.

I was still on the corner, and I got on my radio and called in the license tag. It took less than a minute for the dispatcher to get back on the air. The Toyota had been reported stolen from Center City that morning.

When I told the dispatcher the car was occupied, she didn't even have to ask someone to back me up. Cars started calling in, saying they were on their way. It was a dangerous situation, and everyone knew it.

Using pedestrians as cover, I got a little closer. The two guys in the car were looking at Angela's, across the street and a few doors down. And I saw why: Mickey Bravelli was sitting at the table by the window, getting a manicure.

I had to move fast. I really didn't care about Bravelli—if these guys whacked him, I'd give them a standing ovation. But sitting across from him, giving him the manicure, was Michelle. I stepped into the entryway of a clothing store and got back on my radio.

"This is 20-C-Charlie, expedite backup. The two suspects in the Toyota may be armed."

When I looked back, Bravelli wasn't in the window anymore. The table was empty. How could that be? I had only looked away for a few seconds. I could hear the Toyota's engine starting.

I clicked my radio mike. "This is 20-C-Charlie, put out an assist, 7-8 and Locust."

I pulled out my gun and started running toward the Toyota. Bravelli was already coming out of Angela's front door, and as he did, the Toyota pulled out into the street.

It was too late, I couldn't stop it. As the Toyota passed in front of Angela's, the driver pointed a machine pistol out the window and started firing at Bravelli. Bullets shattered the glass door behind him and peppered the wall, and I was praying none would find Michelle's window.

Goop burst out of the fruit store and onto the sidewalk, he had a gun in his hand, and now he was firing at the Toyota as it picked up speed.

Usually when there's a drive-by shooting, it's the passenger who does the shooting. In this case, though, Angela's was on the driver's side, so he had to do double duty, driving and shooting at the same time. Which was pretty stupid, considering that Locust was two-way—and the car could have just as easily approached Angela's from the opposite direction.

And the Toyota's driver proved conclusively that he couldn't steer and shoot at the same time. He was trying to fire back at Goop, but he was veering too far to the left, and he just drove the car across the oncoming lane and then up onto the sidewalk. The car glanced off a light pole and gently spun around and backed into a store window, as if that had been the driver's intention. The sidewalk was crowded, but the car missed everyone—people dodged out of its way gracefully, almost unconcerned, like they were practicing some new kind of dance.

I ran into the street, toward the Toyota, my gun in the air. I caught a glimpse of Bravelli, dazed but unhurt, and Michelle's window, intact. I didn't see her anywhere.

Goop had begun jogging toward the car as well, but when he saw me he slowed, and I gave him a look that said, Stay right the fuck where you are. He stopped short and lowered his gun, waiting to see what was going to happen.

There was a loud whoop-whoop of a siren right behind me. I glanced over my shoulder, it was Randy Trover and Dave Larkin. The Toyota was facing out toward the street, and the driver was trying to get it unstuck from the store window.

But they saw me coming at them, saw Randy and Dave's car, and they bailed out. In a moment, they were sprinting down the street away from me. I was running after them, hoping Randy and Dave might be able to catch them in their car. But traffic was stopped in both directions, they were locked in tight, and Randy and Dave had to jump out and join the pursuit on foot.

As I passed the smashed Toyota I saw, on the ground, the driver's gun—it was a TEC-9, a 9mm machine pistol.

I couldn't believe how fast the two guys were. When they reached the cross street, 77th, the one who had been the driver disappeared around the corner to the left. The passenger cut across the street to the right, heading down 77th in the opposite direction. I yelled for Randy and Dave to go after him, I'd get the driver.

When I reached the corner, and swung to the left, I realized I wasn't the only one in this foot pursuit. There were five or six young white guys running behind me. "Get 'em!" they were yelling. "He shot Mickey Bravelli!"

For a moment I wondered whether they meant me. But they were focused on the black man in the baggy green shorts, running ahead of us down the middle of 77th.

"Stay back!" I yelled at two young guys to my left. One of them had long, flowing blond hair, like a rock star, but his face was hard and when he looked back at me his eyes were full of menace.

He ran past me, and pulled in front, like he was getting ahead of me in traffic. He was wearing shorts, and on the back of his calves were tattoos of giant eyes, one on each leg, as dangerous looking as his real ones. And they were looking up, right at me, as I ran.

One by one, the others passed me as well. I had on my gun belt, my nightstick, my bulletproof vest, my hard shoes, they just powered by me in their shorts and sneakers and strange tattoos.

There was no question that they would catch him first. And now there weren't just five or six anymore, other neighborhood guys were joining the chase, not even knowing what the black guy had done.

The driver took a right at one corner, a left at the next. He was almost a block away from me now, I was losing him. But his other pursuers were getting closer, like a pack of wild dogs about to take down their prey.

I was getting out of breath, I didn't know how much further I could keep running. And they were all getting too far away. A block later, I didn't see where any of them had gone.

Some people were out on their porches, looking toward an alley, and I ran down the street until I reached it. And there they were, halfway down the alley, a dozen of them, in a tight circle. It was exactly like Bravelli's men around the black kids at Lucky's. It was happening again.

There was a loud gunshot, and suddenly the pack was scattering, running out the other end of the alley. When I reached the driver, he was lying on the ground, trying to catch his breath, holding his right shoulder with his left hand. His orange tank top was turning red under his fingers. Still, he didn't seem to be badly hurt.

"They shot me," he said in astonishment. "What'd I do to them?"

I couldn't say anything, I was just trying to get my own breath back. I kept my gun aimed at him, and knelt and patted down his green shorts. No weapons. I got him to use his free hand to empty his pockets. All he had was a pack of cigarettes and a lighter, which I sat on the pavement next to him. I got on my radio and called for Rescue.

The guy looked about twenty-five. He had a shaved head, muscular arms, boyish round face. From what I could see, he had probably been shot by a small-caliber bullet that had gone into the fleshy part of his shoulder. There was a lot of blood, but it didn't look serious. He seemed to be more annoyed than in any great pain.

"Can I have my cigarettes?" he asked casually. I handed them to him, then gave him his lighter. Guy gets shot, at least he deserves a smoke.

He gave me a friendly smile of thanks. This was nothing to him. Steal a car, try to whack someone, crash the car, run from police, get chased and shot by white vigilantes. All in a day's work.

"Why'd you shoot at Bravelli?" I asked.

"Motherfucker killed Ru-Wan," he said matter-of-factly, lighting a cigarette.

"You missed, you know."

He seemed surprised for a moment, but then he shrugged. Hit, miss, didn't make any difference to him. Nothing made any difference. A sudden anger rose inside of me.

"Why'd you use a garbage gun?" I asked, almost spitting out the words at him.

"Huh?"

"Why'd you use a TEC-9? It's a fucking piece of shit. What'd you expect to hit?"

He looked at me and narrowed his eyes. What was going on here?

"Why didn't your passenger do the shooting?" I asked. "You were coming at Bravelli from the wrong direction. What are you, a fucking idiot?"

"I'm not an idiot," he said defensively. A police car and a wagon were pulling up.

"What do you fucking call it, then? You can't even do a drive-by shooting. What was this, a drive-crash shooting?"

The guy's mouth was half open. V.K. and Larry were coming over from the wagon, and he glanced toward them hopefully.

"You fucked up, you know that?" I was yelling now. "You had a golden opportunity and you fucking blew it."

He just stared at me.

"You OK, Sarge?" Larry asked.

"Yeah, it's under control," I said, trying to calm myself down. "Once we get this asshole out of here, I guess we'll have to try to find the other assholes who shot him."

"I'm not an asshole," the guy said.

"Take my word for it," I said. "You're an asshole."

"What about Larchwood Street?" V.K. asked.

"What's on Larchwood?"

"This guy's partner ran into a house, got himself a hostage. Fifteen-year-old black girl."

The scene at Larchwood was a zoo. Unlike my guy, the passenger hadn't been chased by anyone but Randy and Dave, so he was able to get much farther—across 67th Street, out of the Italian section and into black West Philadelphia.

He ducked into a house on Larchwood Street near 65th, apparently hoping to run out the back. We found out later that the back door had a deadbolt that locked from the inside with a key. But the key was hidden, and the guy was trapped.

The only person in the house was a fifteen-year-old girl, sitting in the living room watching TV, and the guy dragged her upstairs, to the second-floor front bedroom. Randy and Dave were out front, on the street, and for a moment they weren't sure which house he had run into. Then the guy opened the upstairs window, and showed them the girl, and said he'd kill her if they came in. For good measure, he fired a wild shot that went through the roof of a parked car.

Captain Kirk was already at Larchwood Street when I arrived. He told me that a squad from SWAT was on its way, and he was trying to track down someone in Hostage Negotiations.

If the guy had been alone, we could have just waited him out. Sort of like the old joke, a man holds a gun to his head, threatens to shoot, and tells the cops, Don't laugh, you're next. But this guy was pointing his gun at a hostage, which meant we didn't have forever.

We had another problem: crowds were already gathering behind the yellow tape at each end of the block, and they were hot. During the foot-pursuit, the guy had occasionally turned to fire at Randy and Dave as he ran. They fired back, which wasn't such a good idea. There were a lot of people on the street, particularly kids.

Fortunately, Randy and Dave didn't hit anybody. But you had the sight of two white cops, blazing away with their guns as they ran after a black guy in a crowded black neighborhood. Not the kind of thing to help police-community relations.

As we stood down the street from the house, separated from the crowd by the yellow police tape, first one bottle, then another came at us. One young woman, holding a small child in her arms, called out to me, "You could have killed my baby, you know that?"

I glanced over at her. She couldn't have been more than seventeen. Her black sundress barely hung on to her scrawny frame, but her face was full of fury. I didn't know what to say to her, and she shrugged, like she didn't expect me to say anything.

"You police just don't care at all, do you?" she asked.

I figured the television reporters would be pulling up in about five minutes. Maybe a little longer—after all, they had to spray their hair before they came out.

An hour later nothing had changed, except that we were all on live TV. One section of the yellow tape had been designated for the media, and we could see the TV reporters giving their breathless updates every few minutes. They must have thought they had hit the lottery: a botched hit on a mob boss had led to a tense hostage situation with racial overtones. This was why ratings were invented.

SWAT was on the scene and in control now, and a hostage negotiator had arrived. He had a portable cell phone, and was calling the phone at the house every few minutes. Each time, the guy would pick up the phone and say "Hello," like he lived there, like he had no idea who might be calling.

When the negotiator would identify himself, the guy would immediately say "Fuck you," and hang up. But every time the phone rang, he'd pick it up again. Maybe he was expecting a call from Publisher's Clearing House saying he had just won $10 million.

I'd never seen this hostage negotiator before. He was in his early fifties, black, a little overweight, neatly trimmed mustache, clear eyes. You looked at him and could tell there was no way he could ever be bullshitted. He was wearing plaid shorts, sandals, black socks that stopped just below the knee, and a light blue Caesars Atlantic City T-shirt with a fresh mustard drip right in the front. I had no doubt he had been cooking hot dogs on the backyard grill behind his row house when he got the call. One moment he's grabbing the pickle relish from the refrigerator, the next he's trying to keep a fifteen-year-old girl from getting killed.

We still hadn't found any of the guys who had shot the Toyota's driver. Not that I expected we would—they were probably all inside their houses, watching us on TV.

"Hey, Eddie."

I looked up, it was Nick.

"I heard about the drama you got goin'," he said brightly. "Which is the house?"

"It's about halfway down the block," I said, pointing. "Dark brown brick, black metal railing on the steps, gunman in the window. The usual."

"Yeah, I see it," said Nick. He seemed very cheerful, almost chirpy. This wasn't Nick, even on a good day.

"You on something?" I asked.

"You mean like drugs?" He laughed. "Look at my eyes, do these look like drug eyes to you?"

No, they didn't, they looked normal. There was no alcohol on his breath, either. Maybe Nick wasn't drunk or high, but then it was something else.

"How long has everybody been out here?" he asked, glancing around.

"Over an hour."

"Oh, man, you should have called me sooner. I'll get 'em."

And with that, he started walking down the middle of the street toward the house.

"Nick!" I yelled. "What the hell are you doing?"

"Don't worry, Eddie," he said over his shoulder. "Be back in a minute."

Kirk appeared at my side.

"What's going on?" he demanded.

I couldn't give him an answer. I yelled to Nick twice more, but each time, he turned and waved and gave me a big smile.

Finally, I ducked under the tape and ran after him. We were a few doors down from the house when I reached him and grabbed his arm.

"Nick," I said. "Where you going?"

"It's no big deal," he said, almost surprised that anyone would think it was. "Somebody's got to go get this guy, right? I don't mind doing it."

We were still in the middle of the street, maybe forty feet to one side of the house. Close enough to see the upstairs window, close enough for the gunman to see us. His face appeared for a moment, then vanished.

Nick turned and walked the rest of the way to the house, leaving me there. The gunman was back again, this time holding the girl half in front of him as he pointed his gun out the window, first at me, then at Nick.

"Get back or I'll shoot," he yelled.

It was Nick he was more worried about. Nick was now in front of the house, casually walking toward the porch like he was just going to visit a friend. He didn't even have his gun out.

The guy fired a shot at him, and missed, then fired again. Nick kept walking, like nothing was happening, like he was Superman or something, and the bullets were bouncing right off him. Then he was on the porch, out of sight of the shooter, and he simply opened the door and walked in. I glanced up at the window. The gunman had a panicked look, then he was gone.

This was insane. What did Nick think he was going to do? And what was I going to do, stand there with my thumb up my ass while my cousin got blown away?

I ran toward the house, listening for gunfire, and then I was on the porch, and through the open door and into the living room. A music video was blasting from the TV.

There was a loud thrashing and thumping upstairs, and I ran toward the staircase and smashed my shin against a heavy coffee table. I took the stairs two at a time, and as I came up the staircase I could see, in the front bedroom, the guy lying facedown on the carpet and Nick straddling him, cuffing his hands behind his back.

Nick looked up and smiled at me when I came into the room, it was like he had been expecting me. The girl was cowering in a corner, hugging herself, shaking, crying with open eyes. She was wearing a blouse and skirt, she looked like she had just come home from school.

Nick stood, then grabbed the handcuff chain and pulled the guy to his feet. I'd never seen a prisoner so shamefaced. He wouldn't look at Nick, he wouldn't look at me. Thirty seconds ago he had a hostage, he was in control—suddenly he's captured by a cop who doesn't even bother to take his gun out of its holster.

"Told you I didn't mind doing it," said Nick, with that bright, eerie smile. He picked up the guy's pistol from the floor and started taking him out of the bedroom.

I walked over to the girl. "He hurt you?" I asked.

She shook her head no, and I helped her over to the bed. "Can you just sit here for a second?" I said. "I'll get someone up here to take care of you."

I stuck my head out the window and gave Kirk the thumbs-up. Cops started streaming under the yellow tape and running toward the house.

Nick, meanwhile, was taking the guy out the front door. He was so casual about it, he looked like he was just going out for a stroll. Think I'll get a beer, oh, by the way, here's that barricaded man you wanted. And here's his gun.

A crowd of SWAT cops converged on the guy, and hustled him into the back of a police wagon that had pulled up in front of the house. I spotted Donna, and told her to go upstairs and try to comfort the girl.

Some of the SWAT guys were giving Nick dirty looks. Saving that girl was their job, not his. Who the hell did he think he was? I heard one of them mutter something about disciplinary action.

But Buster, Randy, and Dave had come up to the house, too, and they gave Nick high-fives. Nick was smiling, enjoying it.

Like nothing, nothing at all, was wrong.

Later, just about everyone who had played a part in the day's events made an appearance at the 20th District. It was like the cast of a play coming out for a curtain call.

I had to go upstairs and get interviewed by the detectives, and so did Nick, and Randy and Dave. Bravelli and Goop were brought in to give their statements, and the two guys from the Toyota were being interrogated as well—I was right, the driver's gunshot wound had been minor. The doctors took the bullet out and released him into police custody, like what he had come in for wasn't anything more serious than something stuck between his teeth.

Even one of the punks who had chased down the driver was there. It was the blond guy with the eyes on the backs of his legs. His mother had seen the story on TV, simply assumed her son was involved, wormed it out of him, and drove him to the district. He admitted he was part of the chase for a while, but claimed he wasn't there in the alley when the shot was fired and didn't know who was. Even his mother couldn't make him rat out his friends.

Detectives asked me, do you recognize the guy, and I said, Gee, I think so.

I didn't get out of there until about ten. As I was leaving, I saw something so strange, for a second I didn't know what I was looking at. Just inside the front entrance, Ronald the crackhead was arguing with Goop.

I knew that Goop had just been released. Detectives had wanted to charge him with reckless endangerment, but the DA's office said to let him go. He had a license to carry the gun, the prosecutors pointed out, and had fired it only after Bravelli was fired upon. It would be hard to get a conviction, they said. Which of course was bullshit. They were just cowards, they didn't want to take the chance of losing a case.

Goop was a member of today's ensemble, but what about Ronald, what was he doing here? He wouldn't let Goop out the door. Every time Goop tried to slide past him, Ronald moved to block his way. Goop was twice the guy's size, he could have snapped him in two. But perhaps bearing in mind that he was in a police station, and that he had just narrowly avoided being charged, he was actually behaving politely.

When I walked over, Ronald glared at me.

"You cops are all the same," he said. "You all just have to lie, don't you?"

"What are you talking about?"

"Like you don't know."

Goop was avoiding my eyes, trying to get out the door.

"Hold up, Goop," I said. "Ronald, you want to tell me what's going on?"

"City came by today, said they were boardin' up my house, said I had to get out."

"I'll take care of it, Ronald, but . . . why are you talking to this guy? Don't go anywhere, Goop." He was still trying to get past Ronald.

"I'm just tryin' to get someone to let me stay in my own house," said Ronald. "This detective here won't even speak to me."

"What detective?"

"Him, right here." He pointed to Goop.

I laughed. "He's not a detective."

"Yes, he is."

"What makes you think he's a detective?"

Ronald was puzzled. "What do you mean? He was one of the ones that made me and Gail leave the house that night."

I looked at Goop, he looked back at me. I could see him consider for a moment whether to make a break for the door, but I held his eyes, it was like holding a gun on him. He wasn't going to move.

TWELVE

Bravelli again. Everywhere I turned, there he was. Goop in the crack-house meant that Bravelli didn't just know about Steve's murder, he was part of it.

In a way, I was relieved. For me, the idea that cops had cleared out the house for Steve's killer had knocked the solar system out of kilter. Planets had been spinning around all over the place, out of control. Now things were back in order: cops get killed by the bad guys, not the good guys. Maybe not a pleasant thought, after all, but that's the way it was.

Except that in this case one of the bad guys was Mickey Bravelli. And all I wanted to do was go up to him, put a gun to his head, and just pull the trigger.

I turned Goop over to Homicide, and got Ronald to tell the detectives what he told me. It now seemed clear the black Mafia and the Italian mob had teamed up to murder Steve. They probably had a falling out after the killing, and Ru-Wan ended up in the trunk. Detectives still couldn't say why Steve was killed in the first place, but the assumption was that he had wandered into some very deep shit.

Goop, naturally, was no help at all. He was more than willing to talk all night about the shoot-out on Locust, and even took undue credit for the Toyota's abrupt crash. But when asked whey he was at the crackhouse, he played dumb. That wasn't me, he said. That must have been someone else.

Of course, we couldn't charge him with anything. All he had done, as far as the law was concerned, was tell people to leave a house. Unless we could connect him with the crime, there was no way we could prove conspiracy. It was very frustrating to watch him walk out the door, to watch that fuck-you smile he threw at me over his shoulder.

But Goop's life was going to change. In the same way that we had harassed—or at least had tried to harass—the black Mafia, I knew we were going to go after the Italian mob.

I wanted to tell Michelle, tell her that the charming guy she was going out with maybe wasn't so charming after all. But I couldn't reach her that night—I paged her four times, she didn't call me back.

I figured that she was probably out with Bravelli, and didn't have a chance. But why didn't she call me when she got back to her apartment? You get four pages, you have to know it's important. Maybe she never went back to her apartment, or maybe Bravelli came to hers. I didn't want to think about that. I preferred to assume that Michelle simply had her pager turned off.

She finally called me, about noon the next day, at my house. She said she was at a pay phone under the tracks of the Market Street El, and had only a few minutes left on her lunch break.

"Didn't you get my pages?" I asked.

"I'm really sorry about that, Eddie, I should have called you back."

I didn't say anything, I was waiting to see whether she would fill the silence with an explanation. She didn't, she just asked why I had paged her. I told her I wanted to talk face-to-face, could we meet somewhere tonight?

She said no, she was having drinks after work with some friends, and then going out to dinner with Bravelli.

"I think this is a little more important than drinks and dinner," I said. "Cancel out."

"I'm not going to do that," she said flatly. "Just tell me over the phone."

So I did, I told her all about Ronald and Goop. When I had finished, Michelle was silent for a while, all I could hear was the background noise around her, a car horn, people talking.

"I'm going to have to think about this for a while," she said at last.

"Maybe you should get out."

"Why should I get out? Isn't this all the more reason to keep going?"

"But if he had something to do with Steve . . ."

"Then I should stay in and find out what it was."

"Unless you get so upset that you can't think clearly."

"I can think clearly, don't worry about that. I told you, I just have to let this sink in. I have to get back to work, OK?"

"Michelle, wait. I talked to your father last night."

Silence. Then: "What . . . why?"

I told her how I had been trying to reach him, and that when he finally called me back last night, at the district, I was able to tell him about Goop.

"He was very grateful," I said. "He remembered me from the funeral. You know, he asked me whether I had heard from you."

"What did he say?"

"Just that. Had I heard from you. I said no. What's going on, aren't you talking to him?"

"Oh, both my parents have been calling my apartment up in the Northeast, leaving messages. I just haven't had a chance to get back to them."

"Is that a good idea? Aren't they going to worry about you?"

"They'll live. You didn't say anything to my father about me, did you?"

"No."

"Good. You may not agree with how I'm handling this, Eddie, but I know you're not going to betray me."

And what was I going to say to that?

That night, as I was cruising in my patrol car past the Penn campus, a familiar voice came over Police Radio: "Well, do you want to?"

That sounded like Buster, but who was he talking to? Another voice responded, "Do you?"

That sounded like Donna.

"If you do. Gimme a cigarette."

Well, it was definitely Donna and Buster. But they were riding together—what were they doing talking to each other over Police Radio?

"So, you do want to?" Buster asked.

"I guess . . . yeah, if you do," said Donna.

"OK, let's do it."

"What if we get caught?"

"We're not going to get caught, OK?"

The dispatcher's voice broke in: "All units, check for a hung carrier."

Those two knuckleheads were just riding along in their car, talking, they had no idea they were going over the radio. It wasn't hard to figure out what had happened. A patrol car's radio has a handheld microphone about the size of a hockey puck, with a button you push when you want to transmit. A lot of guys are in the habit of keeping their mike next to them between the seats, but if it gets wedged in, the button can accidentally get pushed down. And you'll be transmitting without even knowing it.

"You ever done it before in a police car?" Buster was asking.

I hoped he wasn't talking about what it sounded like he was talking about.

"No," said Donna. "Have you?"

"This'll be my first time."

"Yeah, right, like I believe that."

"Gimme a break, you think I go around having sex in the back of police cars all the time?"

I almost ran my car off the road. I could just imagine who was listening to this—not only every cop in the district, but supervisors, maybe even commanders. And then all the civilians with scanners—like newspaper reporters listening for shootings, tow-truck drivers waiting for wrecks, retired guys sitting in their living rooms, killing time . . .

The dispatcher came on again. "All units, we have a hung carrier."

"No shit," I said, half aloud. The dispatcher could break in all she wanted, I doubted it would make any difference. When you're transmitting you can't receive, so unless Donna and Buster happened to have their portable radios turned on, they wouldn't be able to hear the warnings of a hung carrier.

"I just don't want anyone seeing us," Donna was saying.

"No one's going to see us—as long as we find the right place."

If the bosses find out who you are, I said to myself, the only place you two are going is the Front. That was our disciplinary board. So far, though, they were in the clear—they hadn't called each other by name. Three police districts operated on this radio band, the 18th and 20th in West Philly, and the 12th in Southwest. Despite what a lot of cops thought, there was no way a transmission could be traced back to a particular car.

"How about by Penn's ice rink?" Buster suggested.

This was great—now they were actually talking about where they were going to go to have sex. I had to hand it to Buster, though, the ice rink wasn't a bad idea. It was on the eastern edge of the campus, not far from the river, and you could park behind it, on a lower level, and not be seen from the street. Some nights, when it was quiet, we'd go down there and have snowball fights with the snowdrifts of crushed ice dumped from the Zamboni.

"Forget that," said Donna. "You never know when some hockey team is gonna come by for a practice."

Good point, I thought. I had forgotten that there were people coming and going at strange hours.

"OK, then you pick a place," said Buster.

"How about Cobbs Creek Park? That road down there is pretty hidden by the trees."

Not a good idea, Donna, I said to myself.

"You never heard about that park guard?" Buster was asking.

"What park guard?"

"You never heard about that?"

"What, are you deaf? I just said I never heard about it."

"I thought everybody knew about that."

"Well, I ain't everybody," said Donna. "You gonna tell me or what?"

"This park guard was down there one night, just sitting in his car, someone just came right up and blew him away."

"Maybe we should skip that one," said Donna.

"You think?"

I had been worrying about Michelle all day, but now I was beginning to relax a little. And as diversions went, this one was pretty good. I even wanted to have some fun with it. I got on the radio, and asked to have Nick meet me at the 7-Eleven by Penn. I also called for Jeff and his partner, Mutt.

Mutt's real name was Alan Hope, but since Jeff was Jeff, he had to be Mutt. He was a big, stocky guy from Mayfair, a working-class white neighborhood, and he only cared about four things in life: the Phillies, the Eagles, the Flyers, and the Sixers. All he wanted to talk about was sports. No matter what the conversation was, he'd always bring it around to what this team or that team was doing.

He'd listen to sports-talk radio in his patrol car, and then pull over to a pay phone and call and start arguing on the air. He had a crewcut and enormous forearms, like Popeye, but he was a lot smarter than most people thought.

I got to the 7-Eleven first and parked along the curb in front of the store. A minute later, Nick pulled up behind me. He could hardly get out of his car he was laughing so hard. "This is fan-fuckin'-tastic," he yelled. "I hope somebody's making a recording of this."

Jeff and Mutt were right behind Nick, and they were cracking up, too. We all gathered in front of my car, half sitting on the hood, listening to the *Donna and Buster Show* on our handsets.

Mutt couldn't believe our good fortune. "This is somethin' to tell your grandchildren about," he said. "This is gonna go down in history."

It was a warm night, and though it was summer, there were still some students around the campus. Two pretty young women in super-short gym shorts and tight T-shirts passed in front of us, heading toward the 7-Eleven. We all paused to admire the scenery.

"I knew I should've been a U. of P. cop," Nick said, as we watched the girls disappear into the store.

We all smiled. This was the old Nick, this was the way he had been before his father died, before Steve died.

I waited until the girls were safely out of sight, then got everyone's attention again. "Here's what we're gonna do," I said. "When Donna and Buster pick a spot, we get there first. They come around the corner, we turn on our lights and sirens and scare the shit out of 'em."

Everyone agreed that this was an excellent plan—though first we had to figure out where the hell Donna and Buster were going. We sat there and listened as they considered and rejected three more places to get laid—the golf course (too out in the open), under the 30th Street train station (too many homeless), and in the parking lot behind the zoo's giraffe habitat (too weird).

"You know where I'd go," said Nick. "The parking garage under the Civic Center. No one's ever down there."

It was amazing—five seconds later, Buster said, "I got it—under the Civic Center."

Nick smiled at us knowingly. "Great minds . . ."

"You're an idiot, right?" Donna was asking. "You ever been down there?"

"Yeah . . . ?"

"You happen to notice all the little TV cameras?"

"Oh, yeah," said Buster. "I guess that is pretty dumb."

"You think?"

I looked at Nick, he gave a shrug and a half smile. "Well," he said, "maybe not-so-great minds."

The dispatcher cut in again. "Twenty-C-Charlie."

I keyed the mike on my shoulder. "Twenty-C-Charlie."

"Requesting assistance in identifying and locating the hung carrier."

We all looked at each other and laughed. I recognized the dispatcher as Debbie, one of the regulars on the Southwest Division band. She didn't have to ask who was on the air—she had been around for years, she knew the voices of all the cops. Which meant there was probably an angry captain or two standing over her shoulder.

"What are you going to tell her?" Jeff asked.

"The truth, of course," I said, and keyed my mike. "Radio, I don't think the hung carrier is in the Twentieth, you might want to check the other districts."

"OK, C-Charlie," Debbie said.

Nick and Mutt were smiling at me. Jeff wasn't sure quite what to think. Didn't matter—my job was to protect my cops, not dime them out.

We hadn't heard anything from Buster or Donna for a couple of minutes, and Nick started to get a little worried.

"They better not be off the air," he said. "This is too good to waste."

"I got it!" Buster almost yelled. "The perfect place we can go."

But he didn't say where, he just drove on in silence. So we just sat there, listening to dead air, our dreams of the big surprise fading fast.

Then Donna came on again. "I forgot to tell you, I ran into Michelle today."

My heart took a nosedive into my stomach.

"Michelle?" Buster asked.

"At least I think it was her. She really looked different, she had a perm, her curly hair was all over her face. Jeez, where you goin'?"

"I told you, it's the perfect place. Where'd you see Michelle?"

"I was driving through Westmount on my way to work, I stopped by that fruit store, you know, on Locust? She was coming out as I was going in, I think she was pretending not to know me."

I was having trouble breathing. I didn't know who might be listening to this.

"That's strange," said Nick. "I thought I saw Michelle in Westmount, too, the other day. But I wasn't sure it was her."

I looked at Nick, Jeff, and Mutt. "We got to find these jokers before the bosses do. Let's split up, start looking."

Nobody moved.

"Let's go," I said impatiently.

"Go where?" Nick asked.

"I don't know, just get in your fucking cars and go."

They glanced at each other, and moved away from my car. They knew something was going on, but they didn't know what it was.

I was just about to get in my car—though I had no idea which way to go—when my pager went off. It was Doc's number, with 911 after it—an emergency. I was only a few steps from a pay phone, and I called the number.

"You listenin' to this?" Doc asked in a low voice, like he didn't want to be overheard. There was real worry in his voice.

"Yeah," I said. "I'm going to try to find them."

"Well, you better do it quick. Lanier's in his office, listenin'. He's got this funny look on his face."

"Do something to distract him. Shoot him or something."

As I hung up, Donna was saying, "You sure about this? I don't want anyone seein' us."

"Look around," said Buster. "Ain't no one gonna see us."

It was quieter in the background, Buster had probably stopped the car, maybe even turned the engine off.

"See?" said Buster. "I told you I was a fuckin' genius."

Nick, Jeff, and Mutt were looking at me, waiting to see what was next.

"I told you guys to get on the fucking street. Now go!"

They didn't argue, they got in their cars, and we all took off at the same time.

"So I went up to Michelle," said Donna.

"Let's talk about her later," said Buster.

I stepped on the gas, pushing past the campus bookstores and coffeehouses. But where was I going? Where the hell was I supposed to turn?

They were quiet again, they were probably kissing. Good, I thought, let 'em kiss, let 'em fuck, just keep Donna's mouth shut.

"Michelle was so nervous," Donna broke in, a little out of breath. No, I thought, Donna's the one who's nervous, so all she wants to do is talk.

"Aw, c'mon, relax," said Buster. You could hear the frustration in his voice. He wasn't any more happy than I was.

"You know what was weird about Michelle?" Donna was asking. "It was like she was trying to be someone else."

I felt sick. This was not happening. There was a sound in the background over the radio, getting louder. It was a deep, rapid thumping.

"What do you mean, someone else?" asked Buster, curious now. "Like she was working undercover?"

"Thought you weren't interested."

The thumping noise seemed familiar, what was it? Then I realized—that was the sound of a helicopter passing over. But it wasn't passing over, the noise level stayed exactly the same. Which meant that if it was a helicopter it would have to be hovering right over Donna and Buster's car. That didn't make sense, what would a helicopter be doing hanging around in West Philadelphia?"

"Chopper Alley!" Nick shouted over the air.

That was it—the medevac copters coming into HUP usually had to wait for clearance, sometimes you could see them hovering over the railroad tracks that ran between the river and Penn. We all called it Chopper Alley. I wasn't happy Nick had just told the world where Donna and Buster were, but at least now I knew.

It wasn't far from where I was—just down Civic Center Boulevard to the parking lot where we had our after-work summer keg parties. A dirt road led up an embankment to the railroad tracks, and once you were up there, the trees were tall enough so you couldn't be seen from below. Buster was right, it was perfect.

I flipped on my siren, praying its whoop-whoop-whoop would cut far enough through the night air for Donna and Buster to hear.

"Somethin's going on," Donna said.

It was working.

"Whatever it is," said Buster, "they're comin' this way."

I sped past the parking lot and bounced up the embankment through the darkness. When I reached the tracks, my foot was still all the way down on the gas pedal, but I was going too fast, Donna and Buster's car was right there in front of me. I slammed on the brakes and jerked the wheel, and then I was heading back down the embankment, not on any road now, just through trees and thick brush, and big rocks were banging and scraping on the bottom of my car.

"Holy shit," I heard Buster say.

It lasted only a few moments—I came out onto another dirt road at the bottom of the embankment, and I was finally able to stop. I jumped out of my car and saw Donna and Buster running down the hill toward me.

"Sarge!" Buster yelled. "You all right?"

I took a deep breath and waited until they reached me. "Your mike's been on for the last twenty minutes," I said. "Everything you've said has gone out over the air."

Even in the darkness, I could see them both turn pale.

"Everything?" Donna asked.

"Yep. And now everyone knows where you are. So get back up to your car, shut off your mike, and get the fuck out of here before the fucking Commissioner or someone shows up."

Buster was already jogging back up the hill, and Donna turned and followed. "Meet me at the Shop-Now," I yelled after them. "We gotta talk."

On the way, I stopped at a pay phone near the Civic Center and called Doc.

"I couldn't get him away from the radio. Eddie, I'm real sorry, I tried everything."

"You think he knows?"

"It's hard to tell. I could see the gears in his head turnin'. He's been real quiet in there."

A few minutes later we were all at the supermarket parking lot—me, Donna and Buster, Nick, Jeff and Mutt. I told them that Donna was right, that it was Michelle she had run into. And she had also guessed right about Michelle working undercover.

"I didn't want to tell you guys about it, for obvious reasons. But you've seen her once, you may see her again, maybe hanging around Mickey Bravelli."

"That's what she's doin'?" Donna asked in astonishment.

"Yeah," I said. "She's trying to find what Bravelli knows about Steve."

"That lady has brass balls," said Buster.

"If any of you see her," I said, "you don't know her. OK?"

They all nodded. Donna lit a cigarette, and I noticed her hand was shaking.

"Did I say too much about Michelle, you think?" she asked me.

"Maybe not. But there's no way to know."

Donna grimaced. That wasn't the answer she wanted.

When I reached Michelle by phone later that night, and told her about Lanier, she shrugged it off.

"I'll just have to take my chances," she said.

"Michelle, he's been watching you for two weeks. He's going to figure out who you are, sooner or later. If he hasn't already."

"But maybe he won't."

"That's a very big maybe."

"Eddie, I'm making too much progress to stop now. I have to keep going."

"He may already know who you are."

"Fine. Then so be it. I'm just going to have to take that risk."

THIRTEEN

As worried as I was about Michelle, I couldn't ignore what was happening to Nick. He seemed to be getting worse. One moment he's OK, the next he's walking up to a house with bullets coming out the window at him, like he's on some kind of suicide mission.

I had been avoiding talking to his mother, hoping things would change. But I finally concluded it wouldn't be a bad idea. Aunt Janet was a smart woman, she'd know what to do.

I went over to her house around noon the next day. She lived by herself on 80th Street in Westmount, in the row house where Nick and his brothers had grown up. I felt bad that I hadn't stopped by more than a couple of times in the two months since Uncle Jimmy's funeral. But when Aunt Janet opened the door she screamed my name with delight, and gave me a big hug and a kiss on the cheek. She immediately sat me down at the kitchen table and made me a ham sandwich on white bread. She even gave me some milk in one of the tall, blue-metal glasses that I remembered from when I was a kid. I'd spent a lot of time in that kitchen, downed a lot of milk and ham sandwiches.

Aunt Janet was a tall woman, and had a very dignified bearing. People who didn't know her well thought she was a little aloof, but she was just the opposite—warm, open, understanding. Her short hair was getting gray, but Aunt Janet was still full of life, always trying new things. A couple of months before Uncle Jimmy died she took an art class in which they sketched nude models. When Uncle Jimmy found out that some of the models were male, he ordered her not to go, but she just laughed and went anyway.

She seemed so different from my own mother, who had become just another neighbor lady in fluffy house slippers whose kids have long since grown. No expectations, no surprises, just a comfortable life of bus trips to the casinos and plenty of air conditioning in the front room where the TV was, and getting Uncle Jimmy to put in a powder room on the first floor last year so she wouldn't have to always walk up the stairs.

I ate my sandwich while Aunt Janet washed some dishes. Something was different about her, and it took me a minute or two to realize what it was. She wasn't singing. Usually when she did the dishes she sang some tune very softly. It was one of the things that had always made me feel so comfortable here.

"How you doin' these days?" I asked. "You doin' OK?"

She turned and smiled. "That's sweet of you to worry about me. You ever see Patricia anymore?" They had always gotten along, and Aunt Janet often told me she was very sorry we split up.

"Yeah, in fact I ran into her a couple of weeks ago. She's getting married again."

"Well, good for her. What about you—when you gonna get married again?"

"Maybe never."

"I bet you're seeing somebody, aren't you?"

"I wish I was."

"Really, what's her name?"

"There's no name."

"You can tell me."

"You're barking up the wrong tree. Hey, listen, I really came over to talk to you about Nicky."

The playful smile left her face and she looked down at the green tile floor. "I'm worried about him, too," she said. "He just is not getting over his dad's death."

"Or Steve's," I said.

She wiped her hands on a dish towel, then pulled out the chair across the table from me and sat down.

"It's affecting his work, isn't it?"

"Yes, it is," I said. "In fact, I'm thinking of taking him off the street."

"Can he do some paperwork or something, behind a desk?"

"Well, that's the problem. Guys are going to think he's getting a break because he's my cousin. Then they'll stop talking to him, stop being friendly. It could make things a lot worse."

"Can't you do anything, Eddie?"

"I don't know. Has he talked to you at all about it?"

Aunt Janet shook her head. "He won't open up. Maybe he will with you."

"I've tried."

"Keep trying. You know he worships you." She put her hand on my hand. "Ever since you were kids, you know that."

"What am I going to do, take him to a ballgame?"

She thought for a moment, then smiled. "That's a good idea, Eddie, that's an excellent idea. Nicky loves baseball, just like his father did."

That's how Nick and I ended up sitting in the rain that night at Veterans Stadium, getting soaked to the bone and watching the Phillies get their butts kicked.

Our seats were out in the outfield, in left, but at least we didn't have to see the expressions on the Phillies' faces as they struck out, one by one. It started raining, not heavily enough to stop the game, but steadily, and it was like there was a mist between us and home plate. It was warm, so we didn't mind getting wet, but as the game wore on and the Phillies fell further and further behind, most people left for good. Nick and I just sat there, eating our four-dollar hot dogs and drinking our five-dollar beers, watching the green artificial turf get darker and darker.

For a while we just talked about minor stuff, office gossip, nothing serious. By the sixth inning, we were the only people left in our section, there was just no one else around. We moved up to the front row, as close to the field as we could get, and put our feet up on the rail.

"Nick," I said, once we were settled into our new seats. "You never did tell me about how Uncle Jimmy died."

"Sure I did."

"Well, two sentences maybe. But not how it happened."

"Why do you want to know all that for?"

"I don't know, maybe it'll make it easier for me to deal with it. It's hard to accept that he's gone."

Nick watched the game in silence for a while, then finally turned to me.

"It never would of happened, Eddie, if he didn't keep makin' me go up on the roofs. He should've just let me be a cop."

I knew that was something Uncle Jimmy was never willing to do.

When he decided to retire, he tried to get one of his sons to take over the family roofing business. All three Bari boys had worked on the roofs in high school, and even after they got out. Sometimes I joined them to pick up a little extra money. Nick hated it more than any of us. He hated the tar steam, hated having to get the tar off his clothes and his face and hands. He said that whenever he'd go out with a girl, he was sure she could smell the tar on him.

Uncle Jimmy had first tried to get Chris to become his partner. But he didn't get far—Chris was already a successful electrician, and didn't want to get back on the roofs. So then my uncle turned to Matt, the middle son. But Matt had his heart set on becoming a chef. He was going to restaurant school, and working part-time in the kitchen at Lucky's.

That left Nick, and Uncle Jimmy started putting tremendous pressure on him to take over the business. Nick told his father a million times he wasn't interested, but it was like Uncle Jimmy had cotton stuck in his ears.

Aunt Janet always said Nick became a cop because of me, but I knew a big part of it was wanting to be finally free of his father. Uncle Jimmy never forgave him for it, he even stayed away from Nick's graduation at the police academy.

We sat there watching the game a little longer, then Nick said, not looking at me, "You really want to know what happened?"

"Yeah, I do."

It took him another three minutes to begin.

"It was a Thursday, my RDO." That was Regular Day Off. "My father calls me at five-thirty in the morning and says he wants me to go with him on a job. I told him I had worked till midnight the night before and me and some of the other guys from the district had gone out drinking till about three in the morning.

"You know my father, he was the type of guy, you could tell him that stuff, and it was like he wasn't even listening. 'I need you on a job,' he says. 'Three guys called in sick. I got to get on the roof myself. I need one more man.'

"I could hear my mother in the background telling him to leave me alone. But my father only ever heard one voice: his own, you know that. I felt like asking him, Did you call Chris? Did you call Matt? But he would've just said, Oh, they work today. Like he ever called them, even on Saturdays. He always called me, just me.

"What could I do, Eddie? Whenever he asked me, I couldn't say no. He was my father. I had to go, I always had to go. It got to the point where I was afraid to pick up the phone. It was driving me crazy. It was like he had something in his head that prevented him from letting me live my own life. I used to picture myself as a cop, forty-five years old, my father still calling me to go work a roof. He just wasn't going to let go.

"One time I talked to my mom about it, she said she'd talk to him. I don't know what she said, but for the next six months he never called me about a job. Whenever I'd stop by the house for dinner or whatever, he never brought up the subject. But I knew my father. I could tell he was thinking about it. I knew that sooner or later he would start calling me again.

"And of course he did. The first time, I just flat-out refused. I told him I was a cop, not a roofer. Of course he hit the ceiling. 'You're too good to be a roofer, is that it? You're too good to help your father when he needs your help?' So I went over and did the job. Whenever I'd stop by the house, me and my father would always argue and end up yelling. Mom tried to stop it, but as soon as she left the room we'd start yelling again.

"He'd always say, I was his last hope. If I didn't take over the business, he'd have to sell it, and everything he worked for his whole life would be gone. Like that was my fault. I tried to tell him that he should just take the money and enjoy it, but he always yelled back at me, 'It ain't the money. It ain't the money.' But, you know, Eddie, he never said what it was, never. Eddie, look!"

One of the Phillies had hit a deep drive right at us, and we jumped to our feet. It looked like we'd be able to just reach out over the rail and grab the ball, but as it sailed through the air, the rain seemed to get in its way, pushing it down toward the earth. The Astros left fielder was waiting when the ball gave up the fight ten feet in front of the warning track. Nick and I looked at each other, shrugged, and sat back down.

We watched the game for a while without saying anything. Nick was building a neat little stack of empty beer cups at his feet.

Finally, he looked at me, and asked, "Want to hear the rest of the story?"

"Sure."

"Like I said, the morning that he died my father called me up about five-thirty. I think I was still half drunk, I only had about two hours of sleep, I told him to get someone else. He said he couldn't get no one else, and if he didn't he would lose the job. So I said, so what, what's the big deal about one fuckin' job. Can't you lose one fuckin' job?

"I had never cursed in front of my father like that. He got real quiet, and then he said, 'The job is at 7923 Pine, does that mean anything to you?' I said no, and he said, 'Have you ever heard of Mickey Bravelli? Well, this is the house of Mickey Bravelli's mother. You want me to tell Mickey Bravelli I couldn't put a roof on his mother's house because my son was too lazy to get out of bed in the morning?'

"My first reaction was to say, yeah, what do you care about Bravelli, let him get someone else to give his mother a new roof. But I couldn't say that, I didn't want to put my father in that situation.

"So the next thing I know it's seven in the fuckin' morning and I'm up on Bravelli's mother's roof. Fortunately it was the flat kind, those are easier to do. There were two other guys there who worked for my father, Johnny Presario and Ralph Knox, I don't know if you know them. Good guys. So it was just the four of us, but that's all you really need.

"I didn't say nothing to my father all morning, I just did the work. But I was mad the whole time. I was thinking, why do I have to be up here? Why can't he get enough people so that when they call in sick, he doesn't have to call me? Why does he always call me, why not Chris, why not Matt? Why doesn't he let me live my own life? I just kept getting madder and madder. It got to so I wouldn't even look at my father. He didn't notice, which got me even more upset. We stopped for lunch at eleven, and I'll tell you, I was about ready to explode.

"Ralph had went down to the corner to get me and Johnny and him some hoagies, and we ate on the steps of a house across the street. Usually we would of hung out in front of the house we were working, but considering whose house it was, we decided not to.

"My father didn't eat with us. He said he had some work at the office and drove off in the truck. It was a nice break not having him there, and I started to cool down a little. I figured just four more hours and I could go home.

"Just as we're getting back on the roof, my father comes back. He starts climbing the ladder, but then Mickey Bravelli drives up, so my father gets back down and starts talking to him. After a couple of minutes, my father calls out, 'Yo, Nick,' and I come over to the edge of the roof and he waves me down. 'I want you to meet someone,' he says. So I climb down the ladder and take off my gloves and my father says, 'Mr. Bravelli, this is my son Nick, my youngest.'

"That was the first time I had ever met him, and you know, Eddie, I remember thinking, this guy's nothin' special, just another criminal, just another asshole like the kind I lock up every day. My father said why don't you get back on the roof, so I climbed back up the ladder.

"OK, after a while my father comes up on the roof, and says that Mr. Bravelli has gone inside his mother's house. He says that this Bravelli is going to invest some money in the business. I just look at my father like he's crazy.

"'Listen, Nick,' he says. 'I want to buy a couple more trucks,

SONS OF THE CITY   151

expand the business. Right now, I only got three crews. With this money, I can build it up to six. Double the money I'm takin' in.'

" 'You gonna go partners with him?' I ask. ' 'Cause if you are, you ain't going to double your money. He's going to take all the extra.' My father shook his head. 'No, we got a deal. I pay him back such and such a month. I got it figured out.'

"The whole thing didn't make no sense. My father was almost sixty years old. Instead of thinking of retiring, here he was talking about expanding the business. There would be no way he could keep track of everything unless he hired someone to help him. My father was still looking at me. His eyes were kind of soft, if you know what I mean, like they used to get when I was a kid and he would say, 'Let's go buy you a baseball glove' or something like that.

"I got a knot in my stomach. I knew what was going on. My father wanted me to be the one to run the business. That was the whole reason he got me to come today. That thing about three people being sick was probably bullshit. He wanted me to meet Bravelli and then make the pitch to me. And you know what? I was right. The very next thing my father said to me was, 'You come work with me, Nicky, I'll give you half of the business, yours to keep. And when I retire you get the whole thing.'

"I told him for the eighty millionth time that I was a cop, not a roofer. So he says, 'Forget about that cop bullshit, you can make a lot more money with me. That's why I got Bravelli—with him we can build up the business, we could be the biggest roofers in Westmount.'

"I couldn't believe it. Nothing I was ever going to say was ever going to convince him. He wanted what he wanted, and he didn't care about no one else. 'You never listen to me, do you,' I said. And he said, 'I know what's best for you. Come work with your father.'

"I told him this was my last time on a roof. I said, 'I'll finish this job, but that's it.' So now he's yelling. 'Whaddaya mean, that's it? I got it all planned out.' I started yelling back at him.

"I said, 'Chris didn't want to be a roofer, you said OK. Matt didn't want to be a roofer, you said OK. Why does it have to be me?'

"So my father said, ' 'Cause you're all I got left. I need you. Your father says he needs you and you just turn your back on him.'

"Eddie, I was tired of him puttin' this guilt trip thing on me. I just walked over to the ladder to get off the roof. So I'm walking over there, and my father catches up with me and grabs my arm. He's yellin', 'Where do you think you're goin'? I worked out a deal with Bravelli. What am I gonna tell him?'

"So I yell back, 'You want to put me in business with a gangster? What kind of father are you?'

"So he yells, 'Don't you ever talk to me like that. Don't you ever talk to your father like that.'

"I've never seen him so upset, even when my brothers and me were kids and got into trouble. I knew he couldn't see straight, and I had a sort of feeling, like that he was so upset he might fall. Right then, I should've tried to calm him down, tell him I would think about it, apologize for the way I was acting. If we were going to argue, we shouldn't do it on the roof. That was the first rule—don't do nothin' on the roof that could get someone hurt.

"All it would have taken was for me to say, 'OK, I'll think about it. I appreciate what you're doing.' But I was upset, too. Like father, like son, you know. So I didn't say nothing. I didn't really think he would fall.

"OK, what happens next is that he turns away from me real quick, and walks toward the ladder. I knew he wasn't watching where he was going. Right before he reaches the ladder he turns back toward me and yells, 'Don't you ever talk to me like that again.' And when he turns back around he trips over an empty tar pail.

"It was like I knew it was going to happen, Eddie. It was so weird. I thought he might catch himself, but he was too close to the edge. He went over, looking up like he was looking at the clouds. I wanted to grab him back but it was too late, he was too far away, and then I couldn't see him no more. I looked over the edge and he's lying on his back next to the step. The roof is three stories high. I get down the ladder as fast as I could and as soon as I got to my father I can tell he's dead."

Nick looked at me for a moment, then turned away. I knew then that he would blame himself the rest of his life, it didn't matter what I said, what anyone else said. He would carry it with him until he himself was in the ground.

FOURTEEN

My pager woke me the next morning, its beeeep, beeeep, beeeep boring a hole through my head until I opened my eyes and slammed my palm down on my alarm clock.

Beeeep, beeeep, beeeep.

I found my pants, found my pager still hooked to the belt, checked the page, didn't recognize the number, and went back to bed.

Ten minutes later, it woke me again. Same number. I should have just turned the pager off and got some more sleep, but I was curious. Someone really wanted to reach me.

"This Eddie?" a voice asked, when I called the number.

"That's right."

"Hey, pal, long face no see."

Sounded like Max Tuba—he had his own special way with the English language. I wasn't sure it was him, though. Max was an old mob snitch, but I had long ago lost contact with him.

"Is this who I think it is?" I asked.

"Is that a trick question?"

"Is what a trick question?"

"Sometimes," he said.

"What?"

"Exactly."

"What?" I asked again.

"Exactly," he said. "Sometimes 'What?' is a trick question."

It was definitely Max. Our conversations always sounded a little like Abbott and Costello.

"I got to talk to you, pal," he said. "How about lunch?"

"Listen, I'm not in the Organized Crime Unit anymore."

"I know that. You're in the Twentieth. I don't care, I still got to talk to you."

I hesitated. I couldn't imagine what Max could tell me that would be very important.

I heard a woman's voice in the background, and then Max said, "Gotta go. How about our McDonald's on Ridge, at high noon?"

I told him OK. At least he had picked a classy restaurant.

When I pulled into the McDonald's a few hours later, I spotted Max's big yellow Lincoln Continental in the parking lot. The bright sunshine glinted off the Lincoln's shiny chrome bumpers and side-view mirrors, and slid off the roof and hood in all directions, so that it looked like the car was generating its own light.

I parked my Blazer a few spaces away, and headed for the entrance. The smell of French fries washed over me in a wave, opening my nostrils and making my mouth water. Nothing like McDonald's fries. It was one of those clear July mornings that can trick you into thinking the summer's never going to get stifling hot. I had on khaki shorts and a light blue golf shirt, and as I walked through the lot I enjoyed the feel of the cool breeze on my arms and legs. I almost forgot why I was there.

Almost. The sight of Max waiting in line snapped me out of it. Max was in his late twenties, and was big, hulky, not really all fat or muscle, but something in between, like he was just born that way and couldn't help it. His face, which was big to match his big body, had a warmth and expansiveness, like it could draw you in, envelop you before you knew what was happening. Today, Max had on a gigantic red sweatshirt with the sleeves ripped off, gray sweatpants with the legs pushed up to just below the knee, and spanking-new white high-top basketball shoes. Could have been just another happy-go-lucky overage Philly corner boy.

Max spotted me and gave a big toothy smile.

"Yo, Eddie," he said in his deep South Philly voice. "You can stand with me."

I glanced at the man in line behind him, a quiet-looking bald guy, cradling a book on computers under his arm. He looked way up at Max and then down at the floor and started blinking a bunch of times.

Max paid no attention. He was next at the counter and carefully gave his order to a pimply kid in a maroon McDonald's outfit.

"Two Big Macs, two large fries, two milk shakes—one vanilla, one chocolate—two apple pies."

He turned to me.

"You want anything? My treat—on the house."

"Fries and black coffee."

Max ordered for me and then asked the kid whether the shakes were low-fat.

"Well, sir, they're lower fat."

"I don't want no lower fat ones. I want the low-fat ones."

"Sir, I'm sorry . . ."

"Check in the back, maybe you got some."

The kid nervously scratched his neck. A thin young woman with a pinched face and a greasy maroon sun visor appeared and asked Max if there was a problem. I glanced around for a place to sit down. This kind of thing happened every time we came here.

The first time was about three years before, when Max had just become an informant and we needed a place to meet. How about the McDonald's on up Ridge Avenue, he suggested. I tried to talk him out of it. Even though that was on the northern edge of the city, far from Westmount, I was worried about someone chancing by. Anybody could get the sudden urge for a Big Mac. But Max insisted no one he knew had ever been up this far—usually his friends never left the neighborhood except to go to prison or maybe the Jersey shore.

I had asked him where on Ridge Avenue the McDonald's was.

"Never been up there," he said.

"Then how do you know about it?"

"I *don't* know about it," Max said.

"Max, is there a McDonald's up on Ridge Avenue?"

"There has to be," he said. "There's McDonald's everywhere."

This was classic Max: he was proposing that we meet at a place he was only guessing existed, but which turned out actually did, because he was right: there *is* a McDonald's everywhere.

I glanced over at the counter, where the drama was continuing. There was a lot of talk about low-fat and lower-fat and what about no-fat and can you mix the chocolate and vanilla and do you have carrot sticks they're supposed to be healthy no we don't have them anymore sir, and finally Max was lumbering away with a tray piled high with his trophies from the war.

We found a booth around the corner near the rest rooms, and settled into the hard plastic yellow seats. There was no one around.

Max pulled the lid off one of his milk shakes, tilted the cup over his mouth, and just poured the whole thing down his throat.

"Max, you don't even know what those things taste like, do you?"

"What do you mean? They taste like milk shakes."

Max was a mob associate, which meant he wasn't actually a member, he wasn't a "made" guy, but he was part of the larger organization. He reported to Canaletto, and his job was to be a salesman. Whenever the mob would have something that "fell off the back of a truck," Max's job was to find a buyer. Once he did, he'd haggle out the price, take the cash, and arrange for delivery.

It was easy work, unless the buyer happened to be an undercover cop. Which was how I met Max. He was already on ten years' probation for receiving stolen goods, and he took my suggestion to become a snitch rather than an inmate. For a few months after that, he'd meet me at the McDonald's and pass along information—after he ate all the food in the place.

One day he didn't show up for a meeting, and I lost all trace of him. He just dropped off the radar. I always wondered whether he got whacked, maybe for snitching. Part of me felt bad about that, because I liked him.

"Where have you been?" I asked him. "It's weird, Max, but I've actually missed you."

He smiled for a moment, but then turned serious. "I messed up on a couple of jobs, and they didn't want nothin' to do with me no more. I'm sort of workin' my way back."

"Good for you." I meant it.

"But you gotta know right off, Eddie, I ain't a snitch no more. I got some information, but it ain't snitchin'."

I nodded, as if that made perfect sense.

"I'm doin' odd jobs now, you know what I mean? Whatever they want."

"Sure."

"Like, one of these jobs was takin' the big guy's computer into the shop."

I knew he meant Mickey Bravelli. People in Bravelli's crew never mentioned his name in public, in case law enforcement was listening in. Of course, Max was now sitting across the table from law enforcement, but he didn't seem to factor that in.

"What computer?" I asked.

"The one at his house. I went and picked it up yesterday and took it to Hotshot. It was broke or somethin'."

Hotshot was a computer store near Penn. It was really a front for Bravelli's central bookmaking operation.

"What's on this computer?"

"How would I know? They want me to take it in, I take it in, I don't ask questions. But maybe something good's on it. If I was you, I'd go right over to Hotshot and grab it."

"Maybe I will, Max, thanks."

"Don't say I never did nothin' for you."

"OK, I won't. But if this isn't snitching, Max, why are you telling me?"

He drained his second milk shake. "Because of one of the other jobs they had me do."

I waited.

"I need your help, Eddie, I figured maybe if I did somethin' for you, you'd help me out."

"I might."

Max smiled, like I had already said yes, which I hadn't.

"What was the other job?" I asked.

I could see he didn't want to tell me, he really didn't.

"Go ahead," I said. "Just say it."

"All right. OK. All right, I'll say it. I was with Goop that night."

"What night?"

"The night that cop got killed. Me and Goop went to that house, got these two people out."

"That was *you?*"

Ronald was probably the only person in the world who would have thought that both Goop and Max were cops. To him, all white people really did look alike.

"I didn't know what was going to happen, Eddie, I swear to God, I swear on a stash of Bibles. I just did what Goop said."

"But you knew there was going to be a hit."

Max tried to gauge how much he needed to say to me.

"It's better if you tell me everything," I said.

"Yeah OK. I figured they were going to whack somebody, but I thought it would just be some moolie. I mean, look at the neighborhood we were in."

"But why'd they kill Steve Ryder? Why'd they pick him?"

Max fished around in all his McDonald's wrappers for something else to eat, and when that failed, he examined both his empty milk shake cups. Finally, he looked up at me.

"I didn't want to tell you this, but I will. We were all in the clubhouse watchin' the news, and the funeral comes on, you know, the funeral of that cop. And the big guy says, "I hope Ryder learned his fuckin' lesson."

"Did he say what lesson that was?"

"No, and I wasn't gonna ask him. I didn't want to become a lesson myself."

A pregnant woman was coming our way, leading a little blond girl by the hand. They brushed past and disappeared into the women's rest room.

"Who was the shooter?" I asked Max. "Ru-Wan Sanders?"

"Where'd you get him?"

"Remember, Max? He was the one who showed up dead in a trunk with a sign on him that said "Cop Killer." You didn't forget already, did you?"

"No, no way. But I think that was just a game the big guy was playing."

"What do you mean, a game? The shooter was somebody else in the black Mafia?"

"I'll tell you, Eddie, dimes to doughnuts, from what I heard I don't think the black Mafia had anything to do with that."

"Yeah, but the shooter was black."

"You don't think the big guy can find one of them to do a piece of work for him?"

"So you're saying Bravelli just wanted to make it look like it was the black Mafia?"

"Pretty smart, huh?"

"Actually, yeah. It throws suspicion off of him, and gets the Commissioner to go after his enemies."

I remembered Michelle talking about how happy Bravelli was with the crackdown on the black Mafia.

But why was Max telling me all this?

"You know, you didn't have to come to me, Max," I said. "We had no idea you were part of this—maybe we never would have found out."

"Sure, I know. But what if you would've? I mean, without me telling you. What would've you done?"

I thought about it. "We probably would have charged you with every back crime we're holding over your head."

"And then I'd be in jail, right?"

"Hell, I would hope so."

"And the big guy would figure you'd be trying to get me to rat him out."

"Which we would."

"I don't think he'd like that. In fact, he already told me I can't be trusted as far as I can throw him."

"He said that?"

"Right in front of everybody. We were all coming out of the clubhouse one day, I forget what we were talking about. He says, Max, if everyone here got locked up, I'd bet you'd be the first person to snitch."

Bravelli was smarter than I thought.

"Can you believe he said that, Eddie?"

"Max, you *are* a snitch."

"I was a snitch. Not no more."

"So Bravelli should trust you now."

"Yeah, he should."

"Max, you're ratting him out right now."

"But that's only because he thinks I'm a rat."

"Whatever you say, Max."

"The bottom of the line is that if you throw me in jail, the big guy's gonna think I'm snitching on this thing with Goop. And that's gonna be the end of Max Tuba, Man About Town."

"So in other words, you're ratting Bravelli out so he won't think you're ratting him out."

"Now you got the whole picture postcard. I'll tell you everything I know, everything I don't know. But you got to promise—you got to promise—you won't let word get out that I was in that house."

"It might be out of my hands, Max."

He looked at me, pleading. "Why do you think I came to you, Eddie? I can trust you. I mean, nobody ever found out I was a snitch, right?"

"You and me are the only two people who know."

"So you got to protect me now. I'm a confidential informant, right?"

I thought about it. "All right, Max. I'll make sure we keep you out of this."

He looked very relieved.

"By the way," I asked him, "what does Bravelli's computer look like?"

"You can't miss it," he said, excited now to be helping me out. "It's white."

"Max, all computers are white."

"Really?"

"Yeah, really."

He thought about that. "Oh, yeah," he said, "it's got a lot of little yellow things on it."

"What yellow things?"

"You know, those little yellow things."

"Max, I don't know what you're talking about."

"Those tiny pieces of paper, you know, you stick 'em places."

"Post-It notes?"

"No, Eddie, it's not a cereal. It's somethin' you write on."

"I get it, Max."

"You sure?"

"Pretty sure."

With Max, you could never be sure.

Hotshot was run by Bobby Mono, Bravelli's uncle. He was an old-time made guy, very highly respected, and Bravelli put him in charge of his gambling operations.

Throughout Philadelphia there were a number of independent bookmakers handling basketball games, baseball, everything. Bravelli took 10 percent of their profits in exchange for letting them stay open, but he also provided a valuable service. Sometimes the bookies got so much action on a single bet, like on a playoff game, that an upset would wipe them out, put them in deep debt. So Bravelli—as part of his fee—let them edge off some of those bets to the mob. If there was an upset, the mob would pay everyone off and the bookmaker would be OK. If the mob lost big, well, it had deep pockets. It could never go broke.

Mono was the guy who supervised this loose-knit confederation. He and his people handled the edged-off bets from the bookies, and made sure they were paying their 10 percent.

The Organized Crime Unit had never hit Hotshot, though at the time I was transferred we were close to going in. We had been wiretapping the place, trying to collect enough evidence for a search warrant. We already had a pile of transcripts from the phone tap. My favorite was a conversation between Mono and Spock, who was calling to place a couple of bets on horses at Philadelphia Park. Normally Mono didn't deal with gamblers directly, but he would take bets from his fellow mobsters, who needed a bookie they could trust.

When people called Hotshot to place bets, they were supposed to use computer terminology. The problem was, not too many of the people in Bravelli's crew were computer-literate. Including Spock, who couldn't even stay with his code name, Dirty Harry. Here's how the conversation went:

SPOCK: Hey, Bobby, this is Harry.

BOBBY MONO: Harry? Harry the fuck who?

SPOCK: You know, Harry . . . Harry . . . Fuck, man, Harry.

MONO: I know 10 fuckin' Harrys. Which fuckin' one are you?

SPOCK: Uh, Dirty Harry, Dirty Harry. How many Dirty fuckin' Harrys do you know?

MONO: Oh, it's you, you dumb fuck. Listen, pal, I got Harrys crawling up my ass.

SPOCK: (Unintelligible).

MONO: I know what you mean. (Unintelligible).

SPOCK: (Laughs).

MONO: What do you need?

SPOCK: I want to buy three computers, they all gotta come from Philadelphia.

MONO: Today?

SPOCK: Yeah, I'm fuckin' buying today.

MONO: What's your first one?

SPOCK: Starting with the 1-RAM.

MONO: OK.

SPOCK: I'm picking the 6 MEGS.

MONO: OK.

SPOCK: You got that? I'm putting my money on the 6 MEGS in the 1-RAM.

MONO: Yeah, I got it. 1-RAM. 6 MEGS.

SPOCK: No, the other way around.

MONO: Doesn't matter, Harry. How much hard drive do you want?

SPOCK: I want 200 hard drives on the 6.

MONO: OK, 200 hard drive.

SPOCK: Next is the 5-RAM. I like the 12 MEG in the 5-RAM.

MONO: The 12 MEG.

SPOCK: Yeah, yeah, I been watchin' this one for a while. I'm goin' big, I want 500 on it.

MONO: OK, Harry, 500, you got it. Anything else?

SPOCK: Let me see now, let me see now, yeah, yeah, in the 7th RAM, I want to put 300 hard drives on the 2 MEG. On the fuckin' nose.

MONO: Computers don't have noses, Harry.

SPOCK: Mine fuckin' better.

The moment Max had mentioned Bravelli's computer, I thought of Doc. He was OC's computer geek, and I knew that once he heard about this, he'd be salivating.

After I left Max at the McDonald's, I called Doc and told him we needed to talk without Lanier around. He said to come on by the office, Lanier was gone.

When I got there, I laid the whole thing out, though I didn't say who my confidential informant was. I was right, Doc was beside himself.

"Shoot, man, let's go get that thing."

"Doc, we'd need a warrant to even get in the place. And Lanier would have to sign off on it."

"No, he wouldn't. I can get one without a commander's approval."

"You must have a friend in the DA's office."

"Eddie, I got friends everywhere."

I wasn't going to argue with him. With that warrant, we could go into Hotshot and confiscate a few computers—including the one we wanted most.

That night, West Philadelphia found another reason not to like cops. This time we didn't bash anybody over the head, or shoot at anybody, or even lock anybody up. We just got some bad luck. But if we had set out to enrage the black community—if that had been our only goal for the night—we couldn't have done a better job.

It began, as bad luck for cops often does, with an assist-officer call. Two women were pummeling each other on a sidewalk in West Philadelphia, and Yvonne and Marisol were dispatched to escort the two combatants to their respective corners.

Naturally, once the police arrived, the two women joined forces to defend their God-given right to kill each other, and attacked Yvonne and Marisol with their full fury.

Yvonne took a punch to the side of the head and went down immediately, and when she tried to stand up, she got a kick that cracked a rib. Then both women came after Marisol, who was barely able to put out a call for help on the radio before she went down as well.

Paulie Rapone wasn't far away, and he flipped on his lights and siren and hit the gas. He would have done the same thing for anyone in the district, but he might have been going just a little bit faster because it was Yvonne and Marisol.

Until a year or so before, Paulie was just another older white cop who complained all the time about the Department's changing complexion. He believed affirmative action was ruining the Department, filling the ranks with minority cops—particularly females—who lacked the training, the dedication, and the instincts of old-school guys like him. He would barely speak to Yvonne, who was black, and to Marisol, who was Latino, and so they in turn wanted nothing to do with him.

One night, though, Yvonne and Marisol saved his life. He had been chasing a drug dealer, and the dealer turned on him and somehow got Paulie's gun away. He was about to shoot Paulie in the head when Yvonne and Marisol ran up and together knocked the guy to the ground. They said it was no big deal, but he never forgot.

And so when he heard Marisol's call for help over the radio, he pushed his car in that direction as fast as it would go. He was four blocks away, flying through the intersection of 48th and Spruce, when he hit the old man.

Paulie had the light, even the most angry witnesses later admitted to that. But it was dark, and Paulie's car seemed to come out of nowhere. And it wasn't even Paulie hitting the man that people felt was so outrageous, so inexcusable. It was what happened after that.

Paulie saw the man at the last second, an old black guy with a cane, stepping out quickly into the street. Paulie swerved to the left, hard, but he was too close, and the right front corner of his car caught the man and simply flicked him into the air. He was so light, Paulie barely even felt the impact.

There wasn't much Paulie remembered after that. Later, he recalled losing control of the car, and struggling desperately to keep from slamming broadside into a streetlight. But he had no memory of the crash, or of calling for help, dazed and bloody, before he passed out.

We now had two assist-officer calls at the same time. There were a lot of cars coming in, everyone in the district, and they should have split up, fifty-fifty, on the two assists. But there was chaos on the radio, and for the first few minutes, Donna and Buster were the only ones who arrived to help Paulie.

What they saw when they pulled up at 48th and Spruce was a police car wrapped around a streetlight, its windshield cracked from the inside, its red and blue lights still flashing.

They didn't see the old man—he had been hurtled over a row of parked cars, onto the sidewalk, out of sight. They didn't even know he was there. And so while life slipped out of the old man, Donna and Buster stayed with Paulie. It wasn't until a woman finally ran up to them, screaming and pointing, that they realized what had happened.

Of course, the neighbors didn't know that. All they saw was two white cops helping one of their own, ignoring the black man that cops had just run down. And still it got worse. When the Rescue unit pulled up, the paramedics saw the same thing Donna and Buster had—the police car. And they ran to help Paulie first.

Word spread quickly through the neighborhood that night and the next day. There was no way the black community was going to forgive us—particularly after the papers reported that the old man had died on his way to the hospital. It never would have happened, people said, if the old man had been white.

It turned out that Paulie wasn't seriously hurt, and that Yvonne and Marisol were OK as well. But the people of West Philadelphia didn't care about that. We were the enemy.

That's when the first beer bottles started getting thrown at passing police cars, exploding onto windshields with the sound of gunshots.

FIFTEEN

That night, Michelle wanted to see me. Could I meet her at her old apartment up in the Northeast? I got off at eleven. I told her it would have to be after that.

"That's great," she said over the phone. "I'm really looking forward to seeing you again."

I got there around eleven-thirty. It was a garden-apartment complex off Roosevelt Boulevard, one of those generic, three-story, brown-brick jobs that could be anywhere in the country—Atlanta, Minneapolis, San Diego. This one happened to be across the street from a video store that also sold handmade water ice from a window.

The apartment was on the third floor. I rapped on the door a couple of times with the little door knocker, and Michelle answered.

"Hi, Eddie," she said, giving me a hug. "Wait'll you hear, I've got a great story to tell you."

I wanted to say I had missed her, I wanted to kiss her, but she was already leading me into the living room.

"C'mon in, I want you to meet Theresa."

Michelle was still dressed, but Theresa was in a pink terry cloth bathrobe. She had one of those faces you call cute—sort of big, round, playful eyes, pug nose, cheerful high-school smile.

Michelle introduced us and we shook hands, and I could tell Theresa was thinking, So this is the guy she was telling me about. I wondered what Michelle had said. Theresa got me a bottle of beer and then disappeared into a bedroom, and I sat down on the soft pink couch.

Michelle was wearing jeans and a white T-shirt with a pocket, and though her hair was still curly, she looked less Westmount and more Northeast, more at home. I caught a faint scent of her perfume. It reminded me of the night we met, she must have been wearing it then.

"Eddie, you're never going to believe what happened," she said, plopping down across from me in a padded white swivel chair. "But how have you been?"

"Good," I said. "I've been fine."

"How's Nick doing, any better?" I had been keeping her posted on the trouble I was having with him.

"I don't know," I said. "I guess I'm still pretty worried about him."

She nodded, concerned.

"So," I said, "what's this thing that happened?"

She popped up out of her chair and walked over to her purse on the kitchen table.

"You're going to love this, Eddie." She opened the purse, took out a plain white envelope, and walked back over and handed it to me. I looked inside as she sat back down on the chair—the envelope was full of hundreds.

"There's three thousand dollars in there," she said proudly.

"You steal this?" I smiled. I expected her to smile back, but she was thinking about my question.

"I don't know," she finally said. "But you can tell me what you think."

A couple of mornings before, she said, Bravelli was going through the *Philadelphia Post,* looking for the latest story on the racial tension in West Philadelphia.

"Mickey said—"

"Bravelli," I corrected.

Michelle shook her head. "All right, Bravelli said what he'd really like to see are riots."

"Riots?"

"Yeah, he's hoping all this anti-police stuff is going to get out of hand."

"Because he doesn't like cops."

"Well, yeah, but he says that if you put national attention on West Philadelphia, the black Mafia will just fade away."

"Interesting theory."

Eventually, Bravelli started reading the paper's gossip column, by Jay Bender. One of the items was that some Japanese investors were considering buying Bikini Planet, one of the waterfront clubs on the Delaware. Bender said the "rumored" price for the club was $3 million, and mentioned that the Japanese were staying at the Fitler Hotel while they were making up their minds.

"He was looking at that paper all morning. You could see his mind working, he was coming up with something."

"All morning," I repeated. "Where was this, at the clubhouse?"

"No, no," she said, "at his house. Anyway—"

"Was this like really early in the morning?" I asked.

Michelle looked at me. "Are you asking whether I spent the night there?"

"I guess I am."

"Is that what you really think of me?"

"No, but . . ."

"Look, I didn't spend the night at his house, and I'm not sleeping with him. I told you, that's one of the reasons he respects me."

"And he's stopped pressuring you?"

"No, he still is. I think he can't quite believe he's got a girlfriend he doesn't sleep with. It's like, this couldn't possibly happen. I'm sure he'd never admit it to anyone."

"I see. So he considers you his official girlfriend." I tried to keep the anger out of my voice, but I knew Michelle couldn't miss it.

"You're jealous, aren't you?"

"Of course, Michelle. What do you think?"

She relaxed a little and smiled. "You're funny, you know that, Eddie?"

"Yeah, I'm a regular laugh riot."

Michelle smiled at me for a while longer. Then, as if the last conversation had never taken place, went on with her story.

After Bravelli had finished reading Bender's column, he went into the next room and talked on the phone for about half an hour. When he came back he asked her if she wanted to make an easy few thousand dollars.

"Doing what?" Michelle had asked.

"You got to say yes first," said Bravelli. "You got to agree before I can tell you what it is."

"That's pretty stupid," said Michelle. "Who would go for that?"

Bravelli just gave her a blank look and said, "Well, we all do."

"Could you at least give me a hint?" Michelle asked.

Bravelli started laughing. "A hint? You want a hint? What do you think this is, a fuckin' game show?"

That made Michelle furious.

"I told him he couldn't talk to me like that. I said, 'You treat me with respect, or I'm gone.' He got very apologetic, and said he'd never do it again."

Bravelli told Michelle he had worked out a "genius plan." Was she interested?

Michelle asked whether it was illegal.

"What the hell kind of question is that?" Bravelli yelled. "Of course it's illegal. How you expect us to make any money?"

"That's it," Michelle told him. "I'm out of here." She got up and started walking out the door.

"But he called you back."

"Of course."

"Suppose he had just let you go?"

"He wouldn't have done that, Eddie. He's never been in this situation before. He's never had a woman who's forced him to act like a regular person, instead of some image that he has to live up to."

"Mickey Bravelli could never be a regular person."

"Part of him is, though. And I think he wants someone to help him bring that out. He knows he's not going to ever do it himself."

"Oh, my heart aches for the guy."

Michelle rolled her eyes, then continued. After she agreed to go along with the plan, whatever it was, Bravelli got on the phone and told Frank Canaletto to come over.

When he arrived, Bravelli finally laid out his idea. He wanted to persuade the Japanese investors to forget about Bikini Planet, and to instead buy Jumpin' Jiminy's, the club on the waterfront that he and Michelle went to all the time.

They'd pose as the owners, get the Japanese to agree to a sale, then take their deposit check and disappear. It'd be up to the real owners to deal with the mess that followed.

"These Japanese, they should go for Jumpin' Jiminy's," Bravelli told Michelle. "It's newer. They like new stuff."

"How are you going to get them to believe you own the club?" Michelle asked.

Bravelli smiled at her. "You and Frankie."

Canaletto, he said, would play the role of the owner of Jumpin' Jiminy's. He'd call up the Japanese at the Fitler and invite them to take a look at the club.

Michelle's job was to pose as the club's manager and give the Japanese a tour of the place, sort of a sales pitch.

"Having a woman in this is what's gonna make it work," Bravelli told her. "These Japanese don't know how to deal with American women, it just confuses 'em."

"Where'd you hear that?" Michelle asked.

"I read it somewhere."

Michelle told Bravelli she probably wasn't the right person for the job.

"I've never done anything like this before," she said.

"Don't worry," said Bravelli. "All you got to say is, 'Here's the friggin' restaurant. Here's the friggin' bar. Here's the friggin' outdoor deck. That water there's the friggin' Delaware River.' "

"What about the real manager?"

Bravelli told her not to worry about that, either. He knew the assistant manager, that's who he was talking to on the phone that morning. The club's manager had the night off, and the assistant manager would let Michelle and Canaletto take over.

Canaletto picked up the phone and called someone he knew at the hotel to get the names of the Japanese, and then rang their room. They agreed to take a look at Jiminy's, and Bravelli sent a black stretch limo to pick them up. It turned out there were three of them, an older guy and his two sons.

Michelle, wearing a blue silk dress, met them at Jumpin' Jiminy's front door.

"Bravelli buy you the dress?" I asked Michelle.

"Yeah. So?"

"Go on."

"Well, the father didn't speak any English at all, but the sons were very fluent." Michelle said she showed them around, and as she did, she called all the bartenders and waiters and waitresses by name.

"How'd you know who they were?" I asked.

"It was easy—they all had nameplates, like cops."

The Japanese seemed very impressed, and asked to take a look at the books. Michelle led them to the back, to the manager's office, where Canaletto was sitting behind the desk. Canaletto opened up the books for them, and handed them the report of an accounting firm that showed Jumpin' Jiminy's to be in great financial shape. The assistant manager had laid all the stuff out in advance.

Then, Canaletto and the Japanese started haggling. Bravelli had no idea how much the club cost, but he figured that if Bikini Planet was going for $3 million, Jumpin' Jiminy's was worth at least that much. So he told Canaletto to offer a better deal than Bikini Planet—$2.7 million.

The Japanese took the bait. They first offered $2.4 million, and the two sides finally settled on $2.6 million. The Japanese evidently thought they were getting an unbelievable deal. During the day Bravelli had got one of his lawyers to draw up papers for the sale, and the Japanese were ready to sign them on the spot.

"Canaletto was such a pro," Michelle told me. "I knew he was making it up as he went along, but after a while, even I started believing him."

The Japanese agreed to make a 10 percent deposit—$270,000—to be put into an escrow account. Canaletto told them to make the check to a title insurance company that was actually a bogus firm set up by Bravelli. One of the sons wrote out the check, on a New York bank.

Then, both Canaletto and Michelle escorted the father and his two sons to Jumpin' Jiminy's front entrance, where the stretch limo was waiting to take them back to the hotel.

The moment it was out of sight, Goop pulled up in the Seville, and they all got the hell out of there.

Goop took them right to Lucky's, where Bravelli was waiting to start the celebration. They all sat at their regular table, and Bravelli ordered two bottles of Dom Pérignon. When Canaletto handed over the check, Bravelli actually kissed it.

"I'll deposit it tomorrow morning," said Bravelli. "It should clear in a couple of days."

Everybody was drinking champagne and laughing, and then Canaletto's cell phone rang. It was the Japanese, calling from the hotel. Canaletto didn't say anything, he just listened, growing more and more angry.

Finally, he yelled into the phone, "We still got your check." The Japanese guy said something else, and the veins started popping out in Canaletto's forehead. "We'll be in touch," he said, and pushed the button that ended the call.

"We all waited," said Michelle. "Finally he calmed down and said, 'Those little Japanese fuckers are trying to fuck us over.'"

The phone call, said Canaletto, was from one of the sons. If Jumpin' Jiminy's didn't give the Japanese $10,000 in cash, they'd go to Jay Bender at the *Post* and say they backed out of the deal because of rats.

"Rats?" said Bravelli.

"Yeah," Canaletto said, and then went into a Japanese accent: "We going to say big rats. Dirty rats. Run all over restaurant. Come right out of water, eat food in kitchen. No one ever come to restaurant again."

"They didn't see any rats," Michelle said. "I was with them the whole time."

"Of course they didn't see no fuckin' rats," Canaletto said. "They just want the ten thousand dollars."

"We have their check," said Goop.

"Check no good," Canaletto said in his Japanese accent. "Check never any good."

"Those motherfuckers are fuckin' scammin' us," said Bravelli.

"Can you fuckin' believe it?" said Canaletto.

"Who the fuck do they think they are?" said Bravelli.

Michelle said they sat around the table, pissed as hell, trying to figure out what to do. Canaletto wanted to go over to the hotel and kill them. Bravelli thought for a while, then asked Michelle if the Japanese had mentioned whether they had already looked at Bikini Planet.

"They said they went over there three days ago."

"Tell you what," he said to her. "You stay here, have a nice dinner. We'll be back in a little while."

An hour later, Bravelli, Canaletto, and Goop came back into Lucky's, smiling and looking very proud of themselves.

"More Dom Pérignon," Bravelli said as the waiter held out his chair. "We're going to finish the celebration."

Bravelli described what had happened. The three of them had gone to the hotel and instructed the Japanese to give them the cash they got from Bikini Planet. Bravelli's hunch was that the Japanese had also used the same extortion scheme on Bikini Planet, and may have already got the money.

At first, the two Japanese sons claimed they didn't know what Bravelli was talking about. Eventually, though, they admitted everything.

I laughed. "I'm sure some very effective interrogation techniques were used."

The Japanese had the money in a suitcase. One of the sons laid the suitcase on the bed, opened it slightly, reached in, felt around for a while, and pulled out a couple of bound stacks of hundreds.

"You gotta be kiddin' me," Bravelli told the son. He pushed him away from the bed and pulled open the suitcase all the way.

"There was at least fifty thousand, probably more," Bravelli crowed. "We only had time to do a quick count. They probably been pullin' this scam all the way up and down the East Coast."

Before Bravelli left the hotel room, he told the Japanese to keep quiet about the whole thing, and he strongly suggested that they not try to spread any negative publicity about Jumpin' Jiminy's.

"Why would Bravelli care about the club?" I asked.

"I wondered the same thing. You know what he said, Eddie? He said, 'This is *our* fuckin' scam. If the club gets screwed, it gets screwed *our* way.' "

Later, when they were back in the car, Bravelli gave Michelle the envelope with the $3,000.

"You did good, Lisa," he told her. "We're all very proud of you."

"You *did* do good," I said.

"It just seemed so natural," she said. "I don't know how else to put it."

I laughed. "You think you're a natural criminal?"

"No, but . . ." She crossed her arms, thinking. "Do you remember me telling you how it seemed like I had lost Steve twice? That I felt I never really knew who he was?"

"Right, I remember that."

"Well, when I was helping out with Jumpin' Jiminy's . . . I don't know, I felt like I was getting closer to Steve. It was almost like I was getting him back."

"I'm not sure I know what you mean."

"I don't know if I can explain it. Steve was obviously drawn to something. I think I'm kind of drawn to it in the same way. Maybe I don't understand him totally, but I think I'm beginning to."

"Except that we're not sure what was really going on with Steve."

"I don't know," she said, looking down at the floor. "He and I are a lot alike. We were a lot alike."

"So is this about Steve, or about you? Are you trying to find out about him, or about yourself?"

"Both," she said, considering the idea. "I think both." She looked up at me. "I know it sounds weird."

"There's something I have to tell you," I said. "I'm hearing now that Mickey Bravelli may have ordered Steve's killing himself. It turns out that the black Mafia may have had absolutely nothing to do with it at all."

"Do you think it's true?"

"I think it's very possible."

Michelle looked at me, thinking. "I still have to finish the job I started."

"I think it's time to end it, Michelle."

"No, it's not time to end it at all. Let me tell you why I called you over here, Eddie. It wasn't really to talk about Jumpin' Jiminy's. I just told you that story so you'll understand my decision."

"What decision?"

"I've decided to do the rest of the investigation by myself."

"Excuse me?"

"You've really been a great help, Eddie, and I appreciate it. I just don't think I need you anymore."

"How can you not need me? How can you not need backup?"

"I just don't. I've given this a lot of thought."

"What's going on, Michelle? You have a thing for Bravelli?"

"No, I don't have a thing for Bravelli."

"I think you do. And that fucking asshole scumbag may have killed your brother."

"You have to trust me on this, Eddie. I know what I'm doing."

"Do you? I think you're getting too caught up in this whole thing."

She stood. "I have to get up early tomorrow, Eddie."

I got to my feet. "Michelle . . ."

"Good night, Eddie."

I was going to lose her, I could feel it. Do something, I told myself. You have to do something. I cold feel my heart pounding. I took a step toward her, and she took a quick one back, almost tripping over the coffee table. I have to risk everything, I thought, and I took another step forward, and this time she stood her ground, and the space between us vanished, and I put my lips to hers. There was a moment of warm contact, a light touch like a flower petal, and she moved her head away. Too bad.

But then she turned her face toward me and our lips met again, and this time she didn't pull away. There was a noise, Theresa was coming back into the living room. Michelle and I quickly parted and looked at her, embarrassed.

"Sorry," said Theresa, "I didn't know I was interrupting." She gave Michelle a girl-to-girl look, like I wouldn't notice, and turned and scurried back into her room.

But the moment was over. Michelle walked me to the door, and I didn't know what to say, I didn't know what had just happened between us, or what hadn't happened.

We said good night, and I turned and headed down the steps, thinking about the kiss. The door closed behind me, with a click, and I stopped short, suddenly filled with dread.

It had been a goodbye kiss.

When I got home, I went to my hall closet, opened the door, and flipped the switch that turned on the overhead light. On a high shelf were two boxes of Christmas tree ornaments, and I reached up and took them down, then knelt on the living room floor and opened them up. At the bottom of one, underneath the bulbs and tinsel and small colored lights, was a Nike shoe box. I pulled it out, and took the top off.

Inside was a shiny black 9mm semiautomatic pistol, almost brand-new. I had taken it from a mob punk, Junior Vincente, when I was in OC, and I had just never bothered to turn it in. I really didn't know why at the time, I just figured someday I might need a gun that couldn't be traced.

That someday was getting very close. I had to get Michelle out of danger. I had to get her away from Bravelli forever.

I dreamed of Michelle that night. We were swimming in a lake, splashing water on each other. She was smiling at me, laughing as she splashed. She had forgotten all about Mickey Bravelli. And she was never going back to Westmount, ever again.

SIXTEEN

Some people in my position might not have hesitated to kill Bravelli. No muss, no fuss, end of problem. What was the big deal? But I just wasn't ready, not as long as there might be other ways of bringing him down, like the computer. I spent a lot of time wondering whether my hesitation was really a weakness. I worried about it. But in the end I decided that all I could do was the best I could.

The next morning, Doc got the warrant signed by a judge. We were set. Now all we needed was backup troops. Doc didn't want to take anyone from OC—Lanier might hear about it.

No problem, I said. We'll just take some of my guys. After roll call I rounded up Donna, Buster, Jeff, and Mutt in the Yard. I wanted Nick along, too, but I hadn't seen him at roll call.

"What do you think's on the computer?" Donna asked.

"Maybe names, maybe financial records," I said. "Maybe just something about himself that we can use against him."

"Would Bravelli be stupid enough to put that on a computer?" Buster asked.

The rest of us, at the same time, all said, "Yeah."

A half hour later, Doc and I met my cops at Dogshit Park.

"Anybody know whether Nick ever came in?" I asked.

"Yeah, he's in today," said Donna.

"We saw his car," said Buster. He looked at Donna. "It was parked on Cedar, wasn't it?"

"Tyler," said Donna.

"No," said Buster. "I think it was Cedar."

Donna looked at me, shaking her head, and then did a Buster imitation: "Yeah, Sarge, I think we saw him up in North Philadelphia. Or maybe it was in Michigan."

I asked Donna what block of Tyler Nick's car was on.

"Fifty-eight hundred," she said.

That's what I was afraid of. Nick was back at the crackhouse.

I told everyone to head over to Hotshot and park around the corner, I'd go get Nick. Sure enough, his car was in front of the crackhouse, just like it had been before.

At least Nick had the place to himself these days—Ronald wasn't going to be coming back. A neighborhood group, thrilled to have the crackhouse finally out of operation, had persuaded the city to seal it up with cinderblocks within the week. I had heard from a neighbor that Ronald and Gail had set up housekeeping in an abandoned row house six blocks away.

I walked up the sidewalk to the house and then up the steps to the porch, and called Nick's name, just like before. When I pushed the door open, there was Nick, in his uniform, standing in the darkness at the foot of the stairs.

"What are you doing, Nick?"

"I like it here in the dark."

His breath smelled of beer.

"You drunk again?"

"Just leave me alone, I'm fine here."

I suddenly felt very tired, like the darkness of the crackhouse was an enormous weight, pressing down on me. I wasn't going to be able to help Nick, I knew it then. I wasn't going to be able to give him the kind of help he really needed. Other cops had lost partners, other cops had lost parents—maybe, like Nick, even at the same time. But most cops eventually recover, they get back to normal. I had no idea why Nick couldn't seem to be able to do that. Maybe in some way he was weaker. Maybe he just didn't have the kind of strength most people have.

I was too weary to yell at him, to even say anything at all. As I silently helped him out of the crackhouse and into the bright sunlight, I realized that his career as a cop was probably over. I'd take him off the street, get him into some kind of treatment, but I already knew that wouldn't be enough. It was sad.

For now, though, I had to decide whether to go ahead with the raid of Hotshot with six people instead of seven. I went over the plan in my head, figuring out where everyone would be. It could be done.

Nick, for his part, would be sitting by himself in my patrol car. I didn't want to leave him at the crackhouse, but I couldn't take him with us into Hotshot. Nick kicked and screamed, of course. When I met the others around the corner from Hotshot, and he found out what we were planning, he wanted to go with us. But he had to listen, frustrated, as Doc and I discussed some final details with the others. I didn't tell them why Nick wasn't going along, but they could smell the beer on his breath, they could figure it out.

A few minutes later, nightsticks in hand, the six of us quickly streamed through Hotshot's front door. If this had been any other kind of raid, we probably would have had our guns drawn. But I didn't expect anyone inside to be armed, and I didn't want any of our guys shooting. If a college student in the store got hit, that would be the end of any plans I had for the rest of my life.

I was in first, leading our raiding party toward the back of the store, where we could see a set of swinging black-rubber doors.

Buster peeled off and strode over to a guy behind the counter who looked like the manager—he was tall, maybe forty-five, with black-rimmed glasses and a big shock of graying hair that he hadn't bothered to comb.

"Hands where I can see 'em," he said, poking the guy gently with his nightstick. "You touch a button or something, I'm gonna touch your head with this."

There were a couple of college kid customers playing video games, and Donna got them out. But we had another obstacle: a lumbering, heavyset guy in a bulging white dress shirt who had moved to block the swinging doors. Maybe he was supposed to be a salesman, but he looked more like somebody's bodyguard.

'We'll take this computer," I said, pointing to one on a long table. He glanced at the computer, confused, and then back at me. As he did, Jeff and Buster passed by on either side of me and—holding their nightsticks in front of them like they were up at the plate bunting—simply bulldozed him out of the way.

I told Donna and Mutt to keep the front room under control, and then Doc and I swung open the double doors, with Jeff and Buster right behind. It was some kind of repair area—there were disassembled computers all over the place. None had any little yellow pieces of paper. A young black guy in dreadlocks and a sixties red tie-dyed shirt was bent over one of the computers with a screwdriver, and he looked up in surprise.

Farther back, there was a door to yet another room. That had to be where Bobby Mono ran his operation. It also had to be where Bravelli's computer was—I knew that something so valuable would be kept in a secure location.

But the moment I saw that second door, I knew we had screwed up. It was made of thick steel, and even if we had brought along a battering ram or crowbars, it would have taken forever to get it open.

"Just knock," said Doc.

I looked at him. He raised his hand and made a knocking motion in the air. I shrugged and knocked lightly on the door.

Nothing.

I knocked again, a little louder—but not much. I wanted Mono to think maybe it was the repair guy with a question.

The door started to open, and we heard a gravely voice.

"How many fuckin' times do I have to tell you—"

It was Mono. He stopped when he saw my uniform. But before his brain told his hands to close the door I pushed it all the way open, and he stumbled back.

Mono looked like a broken-down plumber nearing the end of his career. His face was splotched with red, and he had dirty gray hair, bifocals, and a sour expression. It was quite a shock—the last time I had seen him, just a couple of years before, he was a sharp-looking old guy.

The only other person in the room was a girl, about nineteen, sitting at a computer. She had short black hair, a face that was almost pretty, but was a little too hard, and she was wearing jeans and a skimpy orange bikini top that showed off a very nice set of attributes. When she saw us, she started typing quickly on the keyboard. I grabbed her by the arm and stood her up.

"Owwww," she whined in a half-nasal Westmount accent.

"Leave her the fuck alone," spat Mono. "You got a fuckin' warrant?" He put his arm around the girl, protecting her.

"Who's this," I asked, "your granddaughter?" From the look on Mono's face I could tell it was a good guess.

"Who the fuck are you?" he demanded, making sort of spitting noises. He looked at my nameplate. "North?" he said. "That's your name, North? Where's the fuckin' warrant, North?"

Doc pulled a folded sheet of paper out of his back pocket and handed it to Mono.

"Here you go," he said.

"We're going to take along a few of these computers as evidence," I told Mono.

"Evidence of what?" Mono demanded.

I looked around. There were a half dozen computers, seven or eight phones. They all seemed to be hooked up, they were part of Mono's operation. Where was Bravelli's computer? Max said he hadn't taken it back to Bravelli's house yet, but maybe somebody else had.

There was one computer box on a table off to the side, its cover off, its guts exposed. The cover was lying upside down, and I picked it up and turned it over—and there were the yellow Post-It notes. I read a couple: "Get car washed." "Pick up cell phone."

"Excuse me," the girl said, walking over. "Excuse me, excuse me, excuse me, excuse me."

I looked at her. "You got to go to the bathroom?"

She was trying to act tough, she had her hands on her hips, but it just sort of made her attributes stick out even more.

"Excuse me," she said. "This is private property."

I ignored her and put the cover on the computer box. There was a screwdriver and several small screws on the table, and I started putting the thing back together. I didn't know much about computers, but I did know about screws.

"Look at that," said Buster, chomping his gum. "Sarge is one of those computer nuts."

"Grandpa!" the girl yelled. "Do something."

I glanced at Mono. He seemed paralyzed, but his granddaughter wasn't going to just stand around and watch us. As I finished with the last screw, and picked up the computer, she stood in front of me, blocking my path.

"You can't take that."

"Buster," I said, "would you cuff this girl?"

But before he could, she reached out and pulled the computer box right out of my hands. Damn, I thought, and I grabbed it back, and there we were, me and this nineteen-year-old girl, wrestling over a computer, and I couldn't take my eyes off her orange bathing-suit top. It just wasn't a fair fight.

There was a small explosion, and we both turned. Nick was in the room—he had just put his nightstick through a computer screen. Without a word he swung at another screen and there was another explosion, and then he swung at another, and another, smashing them as hard as he could.

"Nick!" I yelled. "Out!" Mono was standing there with his mouth open, and the girl was getting hysterical.

"Stop it! Stop it!" She wouldn't let go of the computer.

Nick came over to help me, but as he reached for the girl's arm, she ripped the computer from my hands again and swung it around and drove it into Nick's stomach.

"You fuckin' bitch," he yelled.

He came at her and she pushed the computer into his chest again, hard.

"Bitch!" he yelled again, and he brought his stick down hard on the computer. She was losing her balance, the computer was slipping from her grasp. I quickly grabbed it out of her hands, and she fell back onto the floor, onto her butt. But it was like she was made of rubber—she bounced back up and tore into Nick, clawing at his face with her fingernails.

Nick slapped her, and she started to fall back again, and he grabbed her arm and started dragging her toward a half-open door in the back. On the other side of the door you could see a toilet and a sink. Nick was going to lock her in the bathroom.

"Let me go!" she screamed. "Let me go!"

Nick pulled her the last three feet to the bathroom and threw her through the door. She fell to the floor with a groan, and I expected Nick to slam the door shut. But instead he stepped into the bathroom with her, and then slowly closed the door behind him.

"Oh, shit," said Buster.

The girl started screaming again, not in anger now, but in fear, panic.

"Susie!" yelled Mono, trying to get past Jeff.

I ran to the door and grabbed the handle. Locked.

"Open up, Nick!" I yelled. "Open up."

The girl's screams were getting louder and they were mixed with panicky sobs. It wasn't a heavy door, I knew I could break it down. I gave the computer to Doc, backed up a couple of steps, and launched into the door with my shoulder. It popped open and there was Nick, pressing himself against the girl's bare breasts, trying to pull down her jeans. I caught a glimpse of the orange bikini top, wadded up on the floor.

"Nick!" I yelled. I tried to pull him off her and then Jeff rushed in and together we got him away from the girl, and out of the bathroom.

The girl was crying hysterically, covering her breasts with her arms. I swung Nick around, and his eyes were just empty, like there was nothing in there at all.

I turned to Buster, who was at my side. "We got to get him out of here, now."

Buster and I each grabbed one of Nick's arms and hurried him through the double doors toward the front, with Doc, carrying the computer, right behind. Mono was yelling. "You motherfuckers, you're all dead! I'll fuckin' kill every last one of you."

We pushed through the work room, carrying Nick quickly along. Mono was trying to get a glimpse of Nick's nameplate, but we were moving too fast.

"I want this one's name," Mono was yelling. "What's his name?"

We were almost at the front door, and Mono stopped short and yelled at me with tremendous fury.

"What's his fuckin' name, North? You tell me his fuckin' name."

I didn't even turn to look at him, I just got the door open and pushed Nick through, and then we were all spilling out onto the sidewalk, into the soft light and warm breeze of the late afternoon.

When we got back to our cars, I waited with Nick on the sidewalk until the others drove off. Then I turned to him.

"Fuck you, Nick," I yelled, and sent my fist flying into the side of his face. He fell back onto the sidewalk, more astonished than hurt.

"What the fuck were you doin' back there?" I yelled down at him. "Do you really not care whether all your friends go to jail?"

He got to his feet.

"If that girl files charges," I said, "we're all going to jail for attempted rape. You know that, don't you?"

"C'mon, you saw what she did to me . . ."

"Shut the fuck up. I'd love to file a report on you, Nick, I really would. But that would automatically mean an investigation. And at the very least, we'd probably all get fired."

Nick was silent now.

"The only thing going for us," I said, "is that if Bobby Mono gets Internal Affairs in there, that place'll be shut down. Fortunately for us, it's a fucking bookie joint. We'll go down, but he will, too."

"So he might keep quiet?"

"You better fucking pray he does, Nicky. And in the meantime, you're off the street. Forever."

"Eddie . . ."

"You might as well take that fucking uniform off right now,

Nick. Because as far as I'm concerned, you're never going to put it on again."

I had told Doc I'd meet him at OC headquarters so we could look at the computer, but I didn't go over there right away, I was too upset to even think. I drove around for half an hour, replaying the whole scene again and again, cursing myself for not being able to stop Nick. How did I let him get so far out of control?

Finally, my breathing returned to normal and my head cleared a little, and I drove over to Arch Street. Lanier was off that day, so we didn't have to worry about him walking in.

When I got there, Doc was in his windowless office, hooking up his own keyboard and monitor to Bravelli's computer. There was a knock on the open door, and Lanier stuck his head in.

"Hey, guys, what's cooking?"

"Thought you were off, Captain," Doc said.

"I am, I'm not supposed to be here, I just came by to pick up some papers."

Maybe Lanier was simply trying to be friendly. Maybe he still somehow believed that one day I'd be his pal. On the other hand, by now Bravelli had probably heard we had his computer. And that meant Lanier might know, too.

"Doc's just taking a look at my computer," I said, trying to sound bored.

"Really, what's wrong with it?" Lanier asked. He stepped into the room. "I might be able to help."

"Thanks anyway, Captain," said Doc. "I think we have it under control."

Lanier didn't take the hint. "Mind if I watch? Maybe I can learn something."

Doc shook his head no. "This could take a while, Captain. I'm sure you got better things to do."

I turned to Lanier. "I got to be honest with you, Captain. There's some very personal stuff on this computer. It's bad enough having Doc look at it, I'd rather not have anyone else see."

"What do you mean, personal?" Lanier asked with a smirk. "You been downloading porn? Hey, I'm a big boy."

He just wasn't going to leave. I stood there staring at him, waiting for him to turn around and walk out the door. Finally, he did.

I closed the door and turned to Doc. "Is he still trying to find out who Bravelli's new girlfriend is?"

"You tell me. Ever since that night he was listening to your two cops on the radio, he hasn't brought the subject up. Not once."

"That was a week ago, Doc. You think he knows?"

"Your guess is as good as mine, Eddie. The man's hard to figure out."

It didn't take long for Doc to discover there wasn't much on Bravelli's computer after all.

"Looks like he got rid of everything but his program files," Doc said, disappointed. "And he wiped it all clean."

"What does that mean?" I asked.

"It means Bravelli knows more about computers than I gave him credit for. There's nothing here."

He was still playing around with the computer, but I was ready to leave. The whole scene at Hotshot was for *this*?

"Wait a second," said Doc. "Bravelli's got a Web browser here."

"I assume you think that's good."

Doc looked at me with his sly Texas smile. "Let's see if Mr. Bravelli has mail."

Doc called up the browser, got on the Internet, and clicked a box to download any new E-mail. Two messages were coming across, both sent the day before—after the computer was already at Hotshot.

Doc opened the first. It read:

You? What's this world coming to? Seriously, Congrats. Sure, I'll be there. Wouldn't miss it.

Then the second:

This is wonderful news, Mickey. And no I'm not jealous (well maybe a little). I can hardly wait to meet Lisa. She sounds like a wonderful girl. I guess she'd have to be to want to marry you! (Just kidding.) How did you ever get her to say yes? (Kidding!)

Love, Jill

Doc turned to me. "Did you know about this?"
I read the second message again, and then for a third time.
"Did you?" Doc asked.
I didn't answer. I didn't want to answer.

SEVENTEEN

That evening, I got another call, this time from Max. Bobby Mono, he told me, had died of a heart attack.

"You go into Bobby's store this afternoon?" Max asked me.

"Possibly."

"With some of your guys?"

"Possibly."

"And one of them tried to rape his granddaughter or somethin'?"

"Yeah, possibly."

"Well, you must have really yanked his key chain, Eddie."

Right after we left, Max said, Mono started suffering severe chest pains. Someone called an ambulance, but he was dead before they could get there.

"The big guy's after you now," Max said. "He ain't too happy about Bobby, and he ain't too happy you ran off with his computer."

"What do you mean, he's after me?"

"He's got a contract out on you. That's why I'm calling, to give you the tip-off."

"You happen to know whether the girl's going to file charges?"

"From what I heard, the big guy told her not to, he said nobody goes to the police on this one. He's gonna handle it his way."

"OK, Max, I appreciate the call."

"It's like what they say, Look before you leap."

"OK, Max."

"So before you leap, you know, look where you're goin'. OK?"

"Yeah, Max. OK."

An hour later, the Commissioner called district headquarters and left a message for me.

"Can you come up to my house tonight?" he asked when I called back. "I'd like to talk to you."

He wouldn't tell me what it was about.

"I'd rather go over that with you in person," he said. "Could you stop by as soon as possible?"

Ben Ryder lived in the Far Northeast, a part of Philadelphia designed to fool people into thinking they were living in the suburbs rather than the city. It was a vast expanse of single-family homes and row houses stretching to the Bucks County line, and was a particularly appealing place for cops and others who would have fled Philadelphia if they could.

Most cops would never live in Philadelphia if there wasn't a residency requirement for all city employees. Cross the city line and you got less crime, better schools, cheaper car insurance. Many of the houses in the Far Northeast were nicer than in other city neighborhoods, but many of them also cost more than the average cop could afford.

When Patricia and I were looking for a house, we went up as high in Northeast Philadelphia as we could, as far away from the crime and grime as possible. Our price range for houses got us only as far as Oxford Circle. A comfortable neighborhood, but nothing like the tantalizing Far Northeast.

The Commissioner lived so far up in the Far Northeast he was practically out of the city. His backyard ended at Poquessing Creek, which marked the Bucks County line. That's how you could tell he was a city employee. As police commissioner he had the money to make it to the very last yard of the city, but even *he* couldn't get across that line.

The Ryder house was a light blue, three-bedroom rancher, an average, everyday suburban house, nothing fancy. I was surprised to see my Chevy Blazer in the driveway. Actually, it wasn't my Blazer—I was driving that one—but it was the same year, same model, same black with red trim. There was one big difference—his had a million antennas. Probably $10,000 worth of radio and cellular telephone equipment in there.

The Commissioner met me at the door. When I saw him I realized I had been expecting a maid or a butler or something. On the job, a Police Commissioner always has a couple of aides around. People to get him coffee, or to run down to the corner and get a newspaper, or to act like pompous assholes when a captain or some other commander calls. Stuff like that.

But the Commissioner opened the door himself, it was just him. He was still imposing, but he had a relaxed, friendly look, and for the first time I thought of him as just Michelle's dad. He shook my hand and invited me in, and as he was closing the door he noticed the identical Blazers in the driveway.

"Either you've got a black Blazer," he said, "or mine just fuckin' gave birth."

He led me through the living room into a den. I guess I sort of expected it to look like his office at Police Headquarters—giant shiny desk, giant leather chair, American flag by the window. Not that I'd ever been in his office, or would ever see the inside of any commissioner's office in my lifetime.

On one wall of the den, over the couch, were a couple of framed prints of ducks. But on the other wall was the evidence I had been looking for that this was not the house of an ordinary person.

Four sleek televisions sat side by side on a long, black metal stand. Next to them, on another long stand, were three telephones—two black, one red—a powerful police scanner, two portable police radios in rechargers, and three or four portable telephones, all recharging. The fucker was wired up.

He pointed to the couch and said please sit down, and then he sat in an upholstered chair across from me. For a moment, he seemed like any other cop at home.

"Where's Michelle?" he asked suddenly.

"What do you mean?"

"Sergeant, I don't want any bullshit from you. I want to know where Michelle is."

"Why do you think—"

"I said no bullshit. I know what Michelle's been doing, Sergeant. I know she's in Westmount, and that she's working undercover. Doing what, I can't imagine. But I do know you're involved."

I kept my mouth shut, and watched his eyes get angry.

"Did you put her up to it?" he asked. "Because if you did . . ."

"I didn't put Michelle up to anything," I said.

"That better be the truth."

"From what I know of Michelle," I said, "it's pretty obvious she does what she wants to, not what people tell her to."

I was hoping the truth of that would calm him a little, and it did.

"Just tell me where she is," he said.

"Can I ask you where you're getting your information?"

"Theresa Fox."

The Commissioner told me he had been trying to get in touch with Michelle for the last couple of weeks. Usually he'd leave messages at her apartment in the Northeast, and she'd call him back in a day or so. But lately she hadn't returned any of his calls, and he started getting worried. Last night he had stopped by the apartment and got the landlord to let him in. There was no sign of her. He knocked on neighbors' doors. No one had seen Michelle for several weeks. That got him really worried.

He went back into the apartment and just sat there until Theresa came home, and then he started questioning her. Theresa said she hadn't heard from Michelle, but from the tone of her voice, her hesitations, the Commissioner knew she was lying. He had interrogated hundreds of suspects during his career, and Theresa was no match for him. She eventually told him that Michelle was on some kind of undercover investigation in Westmount, though she didn't know what it was about or where Michelle was staying. Theresa did know that I was helping her.

I listened as the Commissioner laid all this out. When he was finished, he said, "Now you tell me what's going on. And no bullshit."

I had promised Michelle I wouldn't tell her father, but I didn't think I had to keep that promise any longer. She was in over her head. And I needed all the help I could get.

"She is working undercover," I said. "Though it's her own personal investigation. She wants to find out what Mickey Bravelli knows about Steve."

The Commissioner's eyes widened and his mouth half dropped open. "Michelle is undercover in the Mafia?" he asked.

I nodded.

"Has she made contact?"

"You might say that." I gave him a brief account of the past few weeks, how she had become Bravelli's girlfriend. I left out the part of her planning to get married to Bravelli, though. I couldn't bring myself to tell him that.

"Jesus," the Commissioner said when I had finished. Then, almost in a whisper. "This is my fault."

He was silent, looking at the wall. I waited.

"I'm getting her out of there," he finally said, turning back to me. "Where is she?"

"Westmount."

"I know that. Where in Westmount?"

"She has an apartment there."

"Where? I'm going to go get her."

"If she's not home," I said, "you're going to blow her cover, and maybe get her killed."

He took a deep breath.

"Commissioner," I said, "let me talk to her first, I'll tell her you know what's going on, that you want to see her."

"All right, we can do it that way," he said, relieved that I was willing to cooperate. "But I'm counting on you. We've got to get Michelle out of there."

The Commissioner was saying "we." That was a good sign.

EIGHTEEN

For the next two days I tried, without success, to reach Michelle. She wouldn't talk to me on the phone at Angela's, she wouldn't answer my pages. There was only one other way to get in touch with her.

On the third day, I went to work in civilian clothes—jeans and a dark green polo shirt—and didn't bother changing into my uniform. I explained to Lieutenant Bowman that I was going to spend the evening talking to black community leaders, and I figured there'd be less tension if I wasn't in uniform.

Bowman nodded his approval. "Smart thinking, North," he said. I told him I was going to use my Blazer rather than 20-C, my patrol car, and he said that was a good idea, too.

Jeff and Mutt overheard our conversation.

"Hey, Sarge," said Jeff. "We can't get our car to start, mind if we take yours?"

"You want 20-C? Knock yourself out."

As soon as it was dark, I drove into Westmount, and headed down Locust. I slowed as I passed Angela's—the beauty shop was dark, though the lights were on in Michelle's third-floor apartment. I had planned to get out and ring her bell, but the sidewalk was more brightly lit than I remembered. That wasn't good, I might be easily recognized.

A small light came on in the beauty shop; a woman was walking around inside. I caught a glimpse of her face—it was Michelle, alone. I quickly swung my Blazer around the block, and into the alley behind the shop. I knew each store would have a back door, I was just hoping I could figure out which one was Angela's. There was one that said "Correri's Fruits," and the next one over was a red-painted emergency exit. It had to be the one. I rapped hard on the door.

No response. I banged again, trying to sound impatient, like maybe I was Angela or somebody. Finally I could hear Michelle pushing the horizontal handle on the other side of the door, and it cracked open. There was only darkness, then Michelle peered out in surprise.

"What are you doing here?" she whispered.

I reached my hand up and pulled the door open and stepped inside. When the door clicked shut behind me it was almost pitch-dark, with the only light coming from the lamp Michelle had turned on in the front of the shop.

"You have to leave," she said, raising her voice a little. My eyes were slowly adjusting to the gloom, I couldn't see much more than her backlit profile.

"Are you really getting married to Bravelli?" I asked.

"Shhhh. Angela's upstairs, nobody's supposed to be down here now."

"I want to know. Are you getting married?"

"I can't talk about it now," she whispered back. "I have to get back upstairs."

"I'll go with you."

Her head twisted a little in surprise. "You have to leave, now."

"Your father knows you're here."

"Did you tell him?"

"You want to talk down here?"

She looked around, then shook her head. "OK, we'll go up to my apartment. But you can't stay for more than a minute."

"Fine."

I followed her upstairs. As soon as we were inside her apartment, she closed the door and turned to me.

"How does my father know I'm here?"

"He got it out of Theresa. He doesn't know exactly where you are, just that you're on an undercover investigation somewhere in Westmount. He got in touch with me, he wanted me to help find you."

"What did you tell him?"

"I told him I'd pass along the message."

"He must have asked you what I'm doing here."

"Yeah, he did."

"And?"

"I told him you were trying to find out about Steve. I didn't go into any detail, but I basically told him what you're doing."

"Why did you do that, Eddie? We talked about that, you said you wouldn't." She seemed almost too upset to be angry.

"He doesn't know where you are."

"It doesn't matter. He's going to do everything he can to get me out of Westmount."

"Are you going to call him?"

"No, I'm not going to call him. What I'm doing here isn't any of his business. You can tell him that when you talk to him again. Which I'm sure you're going to do."

The phone on the coffee table rang, Michelle grabbed the receiver. "Hello?" She listened, then said "OK," and hung up.

"That was Mickey," she said. "He's coming by to pick me up. You're going to have to leave, right now."

"You still haven't told me, Michelle. What about this marriage thing?"

"It's none of your concern. Everything's under control."

"What does that mean?"

She pulled open the door. "It means it's time for you to leave, Eddie."

"Michelle," I said. She was staring out into the hallway, where I was supposed to be headed.

"Michelle," I said again. I wanted to know there was still a connection between us, I wanted to see it in her eyes. But she wouldn't look at me.

There was a loud, brief ringing. The doorbell. Michelle's face filled with panic.

"It's Mickey!" she whispered, quickly closing the door. "He must have been over at the clubhouse."

"Go ahead down," I said. "I'll lock up behind you."

"No, no, he's coming up here."

"You have to buzz him in . . ."

"The lock's broken. He always comes up."

"Always?"

She gave me a fierce look. We could hear the downstairs door opening, and then slamming shut.

Michelle started dragging me away from the door. "You're going to have to hide."

"I'm not hiding from that scumbag."

"What, I'm supposed to get killed?"

We could hear Bravelli coming up the stairs, fast.

"All right," I whispered. "Where?"

She opened up a closet filled with dresses and other clothes, and started pushing me in. It was like I was in a sitcom or an old joke—husband comes home, boyfriend hides in the closet . . .

Except I wasn't the boyfriend and Bravelli wasn't the husband. At least not yet.

I squeezed in between the dresses and she closed the door and I was suddenly enveloped in darkness. There was only a thin line of light coming from under the door. I heard a quick knock and Bravelli coming in the apartment. I found myself listening for a kiss, but I couldn't tell, they started talking right away.

"It'll just take me a second to get ready," Michelle said, and then I heard her footsteps pass by the closet. She's getting ready, with me in here?

I could hear Bravelli padding around the living room. If this were really a sitcom, right about now I'd be trying to suppress a sneeze. But I didn't have to sneeze, or cough, I could stay where I was, silent, for as long as I needed to. I wondered how familiar he was with this place. Had he spent the night here?

Michelle's footsteps came past the closet. "I'm ready," she said.

"I wrote you a poem," Bravelli said.

"Really?"

"Yeah. Here, go ahead and read it."

There was silence, and then Michelle said, "Oh, that's sweet, Mickey, thanks."

"Hey, Leez, why don't we just stay in tonight?"

Leez? Why couldn't he just call her Lisa?

"Stay in?" Michelle asked.

"Yeah, you know. We can order a pizza, rent a video."

"I don't want to stay here, Mickey, let's go out."

"Aren't you the one who's always sayin' we don't have to go out all the time, you're always accusing me of havin' to put on a show?"

"Usually, yes."

"And you know what? I kind of like the idea of just takin' it easy sometimes. Most girls don't want to do that."

"Any other night but tonight, Mickey."

"Oh, so now you're gonna be like all the other girls?"

"Is that what you really think?"

"No, maybe not. But I don't want to go out. And I don't want to argue about it no more."

I put my hands on the closet door, ready to push it open, ready to come out of the closet and grab that motherfucker by the throat and squeeze until he had no more breath and no more life. But I didn't push, I just stood there in the closet with all those fucking dresses and let my chance go by.

"Fine," Michelle was telling Bravelli. "You can stay here and read the latest issue of *Today's Manicurist,* and I'll go see the movie by myself, and then I'll have a nice dinner and then maybe I'll go out for a drink."

"Oh, that's very funny, Leez."

"You coming?" Michelle's voice was echoing in the hall—she was already out there, waiting for him.

"Yeah, yeah," he said reluctantly, and then the door closed, and I was alone, so angry with myself I was almost shaking. I pushed open the closet door and stepped out. I couldn't leave the apartment just yet, I'd have to wait a few minutes. I walked around, trying to calm down. The living room windows were half open, and a warm summer breeze was blowing in, billowing the gauzy white curtains. From time to time I could hear a car passing by on Locust.

Michelle had rented the place furnished, and there was an upholstered blue couch and brown chair, and a couple of coffee tables and lamps, and they were all plain and depressing. I pictured some old guy silently living out his days here, year after year, until one day an ambulance comes to take him to the hospital, and a week or so later there's an ad in the paper about an apartment for rent over a beauty shop.

Off the living room, separated by French doors, was the darkened bedroom. The bed was neatly covered by a blue comforter, and there were three or four fluffy pillows and even a small white stuffed bear.

Here's where Michelle spends every night, I thought. I wonder what it would be like to sleep here. I sat on the edge of the bed, and then gently lay back. The room was dark and cool, and I closed my eyes and imagined that Michelle was lying next to me. It'd be nice to be here with her, I thought, we could just lie here in each other's arms and listen to the traffic and drift off to sleep. Just drift off, in the cool darkness . . .

My pager started vibrating, and I quickly sat upright. What the hell was I doing? I looked at the phone number—it was the district, probably Sammy. I straightened the pillows a little and then walked out into the living room, to the phone on the coffee table. I punched in the number, and Sammy answered.

"What's up?" I asked.

"Where are you?"

"Why, what's going on?"

"They've been trying to call you on the radio. We got some trouble on the street."

I had left my portable police radio in the Blazer.

"Just tell me," I said.

"You better get over to Sixty-fifth and Baltimore, they got a big crowd. Somebody hit V.K. on the head with a bottle. It was pretty bad, they had to take him to HUP."

On my way out, I saw the poem. A sheet of lined paper, lying on a small bookcase by the front door. The words were printed in blue ink from a cheap ball-point pen.

ON A DESERT ISLAND WITH YOU

If I were stuck on a desert island
You're the one I'd want with me
We'd lie out on the sun-warmed sand
And gaze out at the sky-blue sea

When rescuers would come, and say,
We have a ship to take you home
I'd say no thanks, please go away,
And then your hair I'd gladly comb

I never made it to 65th Street. Neither did Jeff and Mutt. Just about the time I was getting back into my Blazer, they were heading down Chestnut in my car, crossing 67th, the border between Westmount and West Philadelphia. Whites lived on one side of 67th, blacks on the other. On both sides of the street were stores, with people living above. During the day, blacks and whites freely shopped on both sides of 67th, talked, joked, traded stories with each other. A stranger might have thought it was an integrated neighborhood. But at night, the blacks all went to their homes on the east side of the street, the whites all went to their homes on the west side. I never understood it, but it had been that way for as long as anyone could remember.

At the moment Jeff and Mutt reached the dead center of the intersection, a high-powered rifle bullet ripped through the air and into the driver's door. Jeff, behind the wheel, stepped on the gas, but a second shot went through the open window and into his neck. Blood was spurting out everywhere, and Mutt had to grab the wheel to keep the car from smashing into a light pole.

I had just got into my truck and turned on my police radio when the call came over. Mutt was on the air yelling, "Officer down, officer down," and it was happening again, everything going into slow motion like it did when Steve died, and I drove as fast as I could but it wasn't fast enough, it was like trying to get somewhere in a dream and you never do.

When I got there, Jeff was still alive. Mutt had dragged him out of the car and laid him on the ground, and he was using a towel someone had found to try to stop his neck from bleeding. Mutt was yelling at Jeff to hold on, hold on, but Jeff's eyes were closed and I doubted he could hear.

Buster came up and said let's take him in a wagon, but a fire station was only a couple of blocks away, and the Rescue unit was just pulling up. We moved aside to let the paramedics do their job, and they worked quickly, strapping an oxygen mask over his face, sticking needles in his arm, putting thick pads over the torn flesh in his neck. There was blood all over Jeff's blue uniform and under his head, just the way it had been with Steve.

The paramedics were ready, and Mutt, Buster, and I helped them get Jeff onto the flat board, and then from that onto the stretcher. The clean white pillow started turning bright red, and as the paramedics lifted the stretcher, its legs—with wheels at the bottom—popped out and extended. They wheeled Jeff toward the back of the Rescue unit, and I ran over first to make sure the doors were open enough.

It wasn't until Rescue screamed away that we had a chance to look around and talk to witnesses. No one had seen a gunman on the street, so we figured the shots probably came from a roof. I got the Fire Department to send over a ladder truck to get us up on the tops of all the houses. We were only checking the west side—the black side—of 67th. That's because we all assumed the shooter was black. Jeff and Mutt had been coming from the white neighborhood, and as soon as they hit the black neighborhood, Bang. It was an easy assumption to make.

But as I stood there in the intersection, it occurred to me that the shots could have come just as easily from the white side of the street. I asked Mutt to show me exactly where their car was when the shots were fired. He walked to the middle of the intersection, looked around, and said, "Right here."

"Did Jeff turn his head after the first shot, do you remember?" I asked.

Mutt thought, then nodded. "He did look over his shoulder, yeah."

"Like that's where he thought the bullet might have come from?"

"Exactly like that."

If Jeff had looked over his shoulder, then he was looking at West-mount. And if that's where the bullet had come from, that meant the shooter had to be white. No black person was going to be hanging out on a roof on the white side of the street.

I got sort of a weird feeling on the back of my neck. Bravelli and his crew knew I drove 20-C car—its identification was on the front, the back, the sides. They knew I drove these streets five nights a week. Wait a few hours, and there was a good chance you'd see 20-C cruising through 67th and Locust.

It was perfect: Bravelli could have someone shoot me, and do it in a place that would make everyone think the shooter was black.

I reached into the car and got a flashlight, and walked over to the Westmount side. A lot of neighbors were on the street now, and I asked whether anyone could let me up on their roof. An old couple, in their eighties, lived a few doors down from the corner. They said they'd take me up.

They led me through their living room past the blaring TV, and then up a flight of stairs to the second floor. The woman, who was wearing a pink robe over her nightgown, opened the door of a tiny back bedroom and flipped on the dim ceiling light. There was a small bed with a red satin bedspread and ruffly pillows and a couple of stuffed animals, and you could tell it hadn't been slept on in many years.

"Your daughter's room?" I asked the woman. She smiled and nodded.

"Margaret," she said. "Oh, but she's grown now."

I had to maneuver between the bed and an old polished-wood dresser with a sort of lace mat on top, covered with tiny pink and purple glass figurines and other doodads. The old man tried to open the window, but his thin arms just couldn't do it. He looked back at me apologetically, and I took a step forward and easily slid the window up. It opened onto a roof—probably over the couple's kitchen down-stairs—and from there I went up a set of wooden steps to the top roof.

I took out my gun and switched on the flashlight, and went from one roof to another until I reached the building at the corner, overlooking the intersection. And there, right where the roof swept around the corner, I spotted a 7-Eleven coffee cup on its side and the metal glint of two rifle shells. There were also a half dozen fresh cigarette butts on the roof ledge. The guy had waited around for a while. I wondered how he had managed to get on the roof with his rifle and his coffee.

Kirk was on the radio, asking whether there was any word on Jeff's condition.

Mutt was at the hospital with Jeff, he got on the air.

"He's gonna be all right," said Mutt, excited to be announcing the news. "He's gonna make it."

I had tensed up when Kirk asked about Jeff, and now I felt weak with relief. I looked out over the intersection. Near the light pole was my car, where Mutt had brought it to a halt. On the car's roof, *20 C* was painted in giant black letters, like on an airport runway.

I saw that, and knew for certain the shooter had been aiming for me.

NINETEEN

I didn't get home from work until two in the morning. Fortunately, I had the day off. I slept for a few hours, made myself some breakfast, then headed to the hospital. Jeff was awake when I walked into his room, and his mother and father were there. I noticed a couple of flower baskets on the windowsill, and I knew that by the end of the day the place would be crammed full of them, along with balloons, cards, and the occasional skin-magazine-hidden-in-the-newspaper gift.

I shook hands with Jeff's father. He was very striking, with silver-gray hair and intelligent eyes that gazed out over half glasses. I remembered Jeff once saying that his father was a college professor, Villanova or someplace, he taught history or science, something like that. The father said he had heard a lot about me, and I assured him that anything good probably wasn't true.

Jeff's mother had sort of a college administrator air about her, though she seemed a little brusque, like she would have no problem firing somebody, I'm sorry but we've already hired your replacement, by the way your stuff's in boxes out in the hall, have a nice day. But with her son lying there in the hospital bed she seemed so vulnerable. They both did.

Jeff's neck was all bandaged up. When I asked him how he was doing, he smiled and gave a thumb's up sign. His father told me that the bullet had narrowly missed his larynx. Although the doctors didn't expect any permanent damage, because of the swelling Jeff wouldn't be able to talk for a while. I asked the mother and father whether I could speak to Jeff alone for a couple of minutes. They said certainly, and went for a walk to the hospital cafeteria.

When they were safely down the hall, I looked at Jeff and just shook my head. "Can't talk, huh? How come something like this never happens to Buster?"

Jeff gave a soundless laugh.

I sat down in a chair next to the bed and told him about how I found the shell casings on the roof.

"You're here because of what happened at Hotshot," I said. "I'm very sorry, Commissioner."

He shook his head, like, forget it.

"One thing you don't have to worry about," I said. "We'll take care of Bravelli for you."

Jeff tightened his lips a little.

"You're worried," I said.

He nodded.

"About me."

His mouth twisted into a give-me-a-break look.

"About the rest of the squad."

He nodded.

"Getting hurt like you because of how I'm handling all this."

He nodded again, solemnly.

"So you think I should just forget about Bravelli?"

Jeff considered that for a moment, then shrugged. I thought about telling him that a commissioner couldn't be indecisive, but I figured what the hell, he's in the hospital all shot up, I'm not going to bust his balls. Anyway, I was the one who had to come up with the answer, not him.

My next task was to tell Ben Ryder that his daughter had absolutely no desire to talk to him. I called his office, they said he was giving a luncheon speech to the Urban League at the Bellevue Hotel in Center City.

When I slipped in the back door of the banquet room, the Commissioner was behind a podium on the dais, spreading his deep, silky voice across the room. Several hundred black men and women, seated at large round tables, were just finishing their lunches, and waiters and waitresses in beige uniforms were coming around with silver coffeepots and large trays of pie slices.

The Urban League was a collection of the most powerful blacks in the city—politicians, business leaders, heads of various organizations. And the Commissioner was assuring them that the Police Department was doing all it could to prevent a full-scale riot in West Philadelphia.

"We're trying to get the word out that we want to work with the African-American community," the Commissioner was saying. "This is a partnership. We need to trust each other."

Around the tables, Philadelphia's black movers and shakers, the men in conservative suits, the women in red or white dresses, listened intently. But they had crossed arms and stone faces, and I had a feeling they didn't believe a word he was saying.

As I watched the Commissioner, I wondered whether he really believed he could get through to these black leaders, or whether he was just going through the motions. I couldn't tell.

Finally, he spotted me, and I pointed to the door, meaning I needed to talk to him outside. He nodded and went on with his speech. I found a spare chair near the back corner, next to a makeshift bar. A blond girl in an apron was trying to wrestle a cork from an oversized bottle of white wine. Her mouth, painted with bright red lipstick, was half open in the effort, revealing a well-chewed wad of gum wedged between her upper and lower back teeth. She was wearing heavy makeup, though she didn't need any.

Girls who grow up with money and education can keep their looks for a long time. But girls like this, from rough-and-tumble neighborhoods, only have a few years, maybe from high school to their first kid. Then they lose their looks fast, and by twenty-seven seem tired and haggard and don't even bother to cover up the dark circles under their eyes. I was sorry to see this girl waste her brief moment of beauty under a pound of makeup.

"Mind if I sit down?" I asked her. She finally popped the cork out, and nodded at the chair.

"You with him?" she asked, glancing up at the Commissioner. She was chewing her gum again.

"Sort of," I said.

On a low table between me and the bar was a large white plastic container filled with ice and a lone bottle of Rolling Rock, dripping with condensation. I glanced at the girl.

"Go ahead, take it," she said. "But I need three bucks."

"Maybe later," I said.

She shrugged and we both looked up as the audience erupted in applause. The Commissioner had finally stopped talking. He said "Thank you" a couple of times, looked directly at me, and then headed toward the side door.

"Gotta go," I said to the girl, and slipped back out the door.

The Commissioner was anxiously waiting for me in a wide hallway. "You've talked to Michelle?" he asked.

I nodded. We found a brightly lit conference room that was all set up for the next day—in front of each chair at a long table were little notepads, hotel pens, and small dishes of hard candy. I half sat on the edge of the conference table.

"You want to sit down?" I asked, pointing to a padded chair.

He shook his head no. "You see her today?" he asked.

"Last night," I said, and told him about my visit to her apartment. "She won't listen to me," I said.

The Commissioner looked at me, his jaw tight. "This never would have happened if you had come to me right away."

What could I say? That I should have dimed out his daughter from the start? He finally sat down, plopping heavily in one of the blue-cushioned swivel chairs around the table.

"We don't have much time," he said. "Right before I came over here, I got a call from the *Philadelphia Post*. Actually, from their gossip columnist, Jay Bender. He was asking about Michelle."

"In what way?"

"He told me there's a woman reporter on the paper who saw Michelle working in a beauty shop in Westmount and recognized her. Apparently they went to high school together."

"That's not good."

"He said Michelle pretended not to know who the woman reporter was. But the woman told Bender, and now he says he'll probably write about it in tomorrow's paper."

"Saying what?"

"Saying that the Police Commissioner's daughter is hiding out in Westmount under an assumed name."

"And that's supposed to be a big story?" I asked.

"You know how it is, they just want to sell newspapers."

"So what'd you say?" I asked.

"I asked Bender not to run the story. He wanted to know why, I said, 'I'm sorry I can't tell you.' He didn't like that."

"How come this reporter and Bender can't figure out that Michelle's working undercover?"

"I don't know. Because media people are stupid? From what I've seen, most of them have no common sense at all, no understanding of how the world operates. And they certainly don't understand cops."

"Maybe you should just tell them what Michelle's doing."

"Absolutely not. I don't trust these people one bit—they're gossips, that's what they do for a living. You think they wouldn't let it out somehow?"

"So are they going to run the article?"

"Bender said he's going to leave it up to the paper's editor. I've already put in a call, I think I may be able to convince him."

"Michelle needs to know about this."

"Can you get word to her?"

I shrugged. "Like I said, she won't listen to me. Maybe you can give it a shot."

"How? You said she's not going to call me."

"That's right," I said. "But I think I've figured out a way we can get you two together."

That evening, Commissioner Ben Ryder collapsed in his office and was rushed to Thomas Jefferson University Hospital, a few blocks from police headquarters. There was a press conference at Jeff, with hospital officials saying the Commissioner had suffered an apparent heart attack. There were unconfirmed reports that a priest had been brought in. Radio stations were running updates every fifteen minutes, and the mayor issued a statement saying the city's prayers were with its police commissioner.

About 8 P.M., I watched as Michelle stepped off the elevator at Jeff's Cardiac Care Unit. She looked around for a moment, spotted the nurses' station, then hurried over. I had been sitting in a small waiting area off the main hallway, watching the desk through a potted plant. Michelle was wearing blue jeans and a white blouse and no makeup at all, as far as I could tell.

One of the nurses pointed at the Commissioner's room. It had a large window facing the nurses' station but the blinds were drawn, and the door was closed. Michelle walked to the door, put her hand on the metal handle, then froze. She cocked her head and slowly turned and looked right at me. Then she wheeled back around and opened the door.

I walked over and leaned against the door frame, arms crossed, listening. My eyes met those of an older nurse, who was sitting at the station, watching me impassively. All I heard inside were muffled voices, and then the door opened. Michelle didn't look even remotely surprised to see me standing right there.

"You might as well come in, too," she said. "No reason to hide out in the hall."

I stepped into the room and closed the door. The Commissioner was sitting on a ledge near the back window, which looked out into the night at another wing of the hospital. He was wearing street clothes—tan slacks, baby blue button-down-collar shirt. The bed was neatly made, unused. Nearby was the chair where he had sat waiting for Michelle. Within reach, on a low table, was the hardcover book, a police novel, he had been reading.

"This was your idea, wasn't it?" she asked me.

"Yes, it was," I said. "I was hoping your father—"

She turned back to him. "And you think this is a funny trick? Making me think you were about to die?"

"I'm sorry, honey, it was the only way to see you. I talked to your mother today, she said you haven't been returning her calls, either. Michelle, you've been worrying us both to death."

"Did you tell Mom what I'm doing?"

"Of course."

"And you don't think that's going to worry her even more? This is why I didn't want to say anything to you."

Michelle turned to me. "And I can't believe you're conspiring with him against me, Eddie."

"We're not against you," said her father. "We had to let you know about this *Post* story."

"What *Post* story?"

"Didn't a reporter come into your shop?" he asked.

Michelle stared at her father. "That was Holly Troutman. She's going to write a story?"

"It's going to be in Jay Bender's gossip column," her father said.

Michelle shook her head in anger. "I can't believe they're going to write something."

"Is it definite?" I asked.

"I'm afraid so," the Commissioner said. "I got the editor on the phone, he was a real jerk. I told him that if the story ran, my daughter's life would be in danger. You know what he said? He said this was about the tenth time I'd tried to get a story killed, and each time I used the same 'excuse'—he called it an 'excuse'—that someone's life would be in danger."

"Is that true?" Michelle asked her father.

"No, it's absolute bullshit. I've called that editor about stories no more than four times in, what, the two years I've been Commissioner? Did I tell him cops' lives were in danger? Of course—if you don't say something like that, they don't give a shit, they just put whatever they want in the paper."

"So now he doesn't believe you this time," Michelle said.

"No. He was a real jerk about it."

"So when's it going to run?" I asked.

"Tomorrow."

We were all silent, thinking. Michelle nodded, like she was making up her mind, then said, "I'll be all right."

"What do you mean, all right?" her father said. "Once they find out who you are . . ."

"You don't have to worry, I know what I'm doing."

"Really?" I asked. "You want to tell your father about how you're getting married to Mickey Bravelli?"

"What?" the Commissioner yelled.

Michelle's eyes narrowed at me. "You can't keep your mouth shut for five minutes?"

"I've heard enough," the Commissioner said. "We're going home, now."

Michelle looked at her father for a moment, then walked up and hugged him.

"Daddy, I'm glad you're OK. I was really worried." She kissed her father on the cheek, and then reached for her purse. I figured she was going to get a Kleenex, but she took a couple of quick steps and was at the door.

"But the next time you're sick," she said to her father, pointing like a schoolmaster, "you better damn well be sick."

She took one last look at me and just shook her head, and then before either of us could move, she was out the door.

"Michelle!" the Commissioner called, and he burst out the door after her. I was right behind, and together we watched Michelle slip into the elevator and quickly press the button. We were still ten feet away when the doors gently slid closed.

That was it. That was our last shot. Michelle wasn't going to listen to me. She wasn't going to listen to her father. And if that story appeared in the *Post,* she'd never survive.

There were no more options to explore, no more possibilities to exhaust. I left the hospital and went straight to my house, and then straight to the closet, and pulled down the box of Christmas tree ornaments. And then I had Junior Vicente's gun in my hand.

I got a bottle of beer from the refrigerator, and sat down at the kitchen table to look at the gun. It had a purpose now. It had a reason for being so precisely designed, so carefully made.

I had figured that if I ever reached this point, I'd be consumed with self-doubt, maybe too paralyzed to move. But it turned out to be just the opposite. I actually felt freer than ever. Bravelli was just a bug that needed squashing.

The phone rang, it was the Commissioner.

"I'm going to have a plainclothes detail watch Michelle twenty-four hours a day," he said. "I want you to tell me where she's staying."

"If anyone sees them . . ."

"You think I'm going to let that happen?" he almost yelled. "This is my daughter we're talking about."

I knew he was right, Michelle was going to need protection.

"The apartment's at 7728 Locust," I said. "Third floor. Make sure they never let her out of their sight."

"Let me worry about that, OK, Sergeant?" He hung up.

Ten minutes later, he called back.

"She's not there," he said. "If she came by after the hospital, she's already gone. Where else would she be?"

"How about her old apartment up on Rhawn?"

"I've got a car there now. Theresa says she hasn't seen Michelle all week."

"I don't know where else to look."

"Let me know if you get any ideas. I'm going to have people watch both apartments, just in case."

"Not a bad idea."

"I don't know what I was thinking," he said. "I should have had someone keep an eye on her from the moment she left the hospital." I thought he was going to say something else, but he stayed quiet for a few moments, then hung up again.

I knew I could solve the whole problem once I found Bravelli. I paged Doc. Maybe he would know where the asshole was.

He called me back a minute later.

"What are you doin' at home?" Doc asked. "You sick?"

"No, got the night off. I'm looking for Bravelli. Any ideas?"

"Yeah. Sagiliano's. That's where I am, watching the alley."

"Bravelli's out there?"

"No, but his white Lexus is," Doc drawled.

Twenty-eight minutes later, I was standing next to Doc, looking out the alley window of the insurance office. The Lexus was still there. Lanier was inside the bar, too, Doc said. Doc's walkie-talkie, picking up the sounds of the alley from the hidden microphone, was set up on a filing cabinet next to us.

I had Junior Vicente's gun in my side waistband holster. It was the only gun I had with me, it was the only gun I would need. The last time I stood at the window, I wouldn't have been ready to use it. Things change.

Not that I was going to put a bullet in Bravelli's head with Doc watching. I had no desire to spend the rest of my life sharing prison showers with musclebound apes who hated cops. But once Bravelli left Sagiliano's, I could follow him, see where he went. I could wait for the right moment.

As I looked out the window, I tried to calculate how long it would take to run downstairs, jump in my Blazer, and get to within sight of the alley entrance. Too long, I decided. It'd be better to wait in my truck near the entrance to the alley.

"See ya, Doc," I said.

He turned to me in surprise. "Where you goin'? You just got here."

"I think I'm a little too tired for a stakeout. I had to work pretty late after what happened to Jeff."

"Suit yourself. What'd you want with Bravelli, anyway?"

"Nothing, forget it."

Great, I thought. What's Doc going to think when Bravelli turns up dead an hour from now? Murder was turning out to be a lot harder than I thought.

"I don't know, I guess I just wanted to make sure we were keeping an eye on him. And obviously you are."

I was heading down the hall toward the secretaries' desks when Doc called me back.

"Wait, Eddie," he said.

When I rejoined Doc at the window, Lanier was standing in the alley next to the Lexus. He had on blue jeans, a maroon polo shirt, and sneakers, and if he was trying not to look like a cop, he wasn't doing a very good job.

"He just came out," Doc told me. "We'll see what happens next."

We didn't have long to wait. The back door of Sagiliano's opened, and Michelle emerged, wearing a short black dress and heels. She was clearly surprised to see Lanier.

"You're Michelle Ryder, aren't you?" Lanier asked.

My heart froze.

"Who?" Michelle asked.

"What are you doing here, Michelle?"

"You're mistaking me for someone else," we heard her say. Their voices were tinny, but clear. "I don't know who you are."

"No, we've met. You remember me, don't you? Captain Lanier?"

Doc glanced at me. "Bravelli's going to be coming out any minute."

What was I going to do, shoot Bravelli *and* Lanier?

"I think you've got the wrong person," Michelle said, reaching for the door handle to go back in.

"Michelle, does your father know you're dating Mickey Bravelli?"

She pulled the door open. "You've made a mistake. My name's Lisa." And she went back inside.

Lanier looked at the closed door for a moment, then turned away.

"You think he's going to tell Bravelli?" Doc asked.

"He better not."

Lanier walked over to the Lexus and leaned against it, and we watched him light a cigarette. The back door of Sagiliano's opened again, and this time, Mickey Bravelli came out.

"Yo, watch the car," he said. Lanier stood upright and said something we couldn't make out.

Bravelli was close to the microphone, and we didn't have any problem hearing him respond. "Well, keep somebody else's car warm."

"Finally, I'm seein' them together," said Doc, jubilant. "I knew if I came here often enough, sooner or later . . ."

Bravelli seemed in a hurry. "They said you wanted to talk to me."

"That's right," said Lanier, walking up to him. "You know who I am."

"Yeah, so? You been coming around here all the time. Ain't there no bars around where you live?"

"You know that my job is to put you in jail."

"So?"

"Maybe it doesn't have to be like that."

"What are you talkin' about?"

"Maybe we can work out a deal. You know, you help me, I help you."

Bravelli looked at Lanier for a long moment.

"What do you think I am, stupid?" he finally said.

"No. All I'm saying is—"

"You probably got this whole place wired up, you probably got people listening to everything we're sayin'."

"There's nobody listening."

"Either arrest me or get the fuck out of here."

"That's the point, I don't want to arrest you. I think we can work together."

Bravelli looked around, then spoke to the large, unseen audience he imagined was in the alley. "I'm a law-abiding citizen. I don't know what you're talking about."

He turned back to go into the bar.

"Wait," said Lanier, trying to figure out what else he could say.

"I ain't gonna wait," said Bravelli. "And there ain't no reason for you to drink beer here no more. That bartender, he don't like cops. You don't want him spittin' in your beer, do you?"

Bravelli opened the door and walked back inside Sagiliano's, leaving Lanier alone in the alley. He stood looking at the door, you could tell he was deciding whether to go in after Bravelli. He decided against it, though, and walked out of the alley.

"What the hell was that all about?" Doc asked.

"Don't ask me," I said. "I'm just glad he didn't mention Michelle."

"It's amazing," Doc said. "I come here every other night for two weeks, nothing happens. Then I see two things in one night. 'Course, I don't understand either one of them . . ."

Again Sagiliano's door opened. Michelle and Bravelli were coming out.

"So, which ones are we going to?" Michelle asked him.

"Why don't we start at the Taj Mahal?" Bravelli said. "Then maybe we'll hit Caesars and Trump Plaza."

"Fine."

"And guess what? I want to buy you a really nice dinner, Leez, with candlelight and everything. You can have whatever you want."

"That sounds lovely, Mickey."

They continued talking as they moved toward the car, though they were soon out of range of the microphone. It didn't matter, I knew where they were going—Atlantic City.

Which meant I didn't have to rush out of here in front of Doc. And he wasn't going to make the connection once Bravelli was found dead.

After all, what was one more mob hit in South Jersey?

TWENTY

Traffic on the Atlantic City expressway was light, and I sped past the darkened blueberry fields and through the New Jersey Pine Barrens. There was plenty of time to work out how I'd kill Bravelli: once I found them in the casino, I'd wait for them to leave, then follow them to the parking garage. I'd come up behind Bravelli with Junior Vincente's gun, two shots, pop-pop, one to take him down, the second to make sure. Michelle would be upset, but that couldn't be helped.

She was deluding herself. Bravelli would never forgive her betrayal once Bender's story hit the street. There was probably even a chapter on that in the Official Mob Handbook. Rule 235: Someone betrays you, kill 'em. If it's your grandmother, just make sure you're in the will first.

Near the end of the expressway, I could see the brightly lit casino-hotels, all lined up along the ocean like they were intentionally trying to block everyone's view. There was no doubt which casino was which—on each was its name in giant red letters you could see miles away: Caesars, Trump Plaza, Tropicana. It was like *The New York Times* Large Type Edition of casinos.

My first stop was the Taj Mahal. It was the gaudiest, ugliest, most pretentious casino in Atlantic City—just Bravelli's speed. I parked my Blazer in the Taj's monstrous garage, and headed for the casino floor.

I cruised through the cluster of craps tables, then past the long line of blackjack dealers, then onto roulette and baccarat and the other games. The casino wasn't crowded yet, so it was pretty easy to get a look at everyone there. No sign of Michelle or Bravelli. The slot machines were in four major areas, and it didn't take long to glide through each. Not bad, I thought—I'd covered the whole floor in twenty minutes.

I made quick tours of Caesars and Trump Plaza as well. But by the time I got back to the Taj to begin my second round, it was far more crowded than before. Atlantic City was kicking into high gear for the night, and the casinos were becoming swirling streams of gamblers. By my third trip through the Taj, just after midnight, faces were blurring together. All I saw were row after row of flashing, clanging slot machines, and craps tables surrounded by shouting men, and endless blackjack games, each half hidden in a thick cloud of cigarette smoke.

I'll never find them, I thought. I don't even have a chance of finding them. But then I had an idea: maybe I could catch them as they came back from Atlantic City. They'd almost certainly be coming down Walnut—it was the only major westbound street with timed lights. Everyone took it. All I'd have to do is wait at 67th, where Westmount began, and watch for the white Lexus.

I got back into town a little over an hour later, and swung by Bravelli's house, just to make sure the car wasn't there, then over to Michelle's apartment. Her windows up on the third floor were dark, though that didn't tell me anything.

Then I spotted the Organized Crime Unit's beat-up white van parked directly across the street from the clubhouse. Not a bad idea, I should have thought of it myself. Everyone in Bravelli's crew would recognize that van—in fact, I knew that was the idea. The mob guys would assume that police were doing surveillance on the clubhouse, not watching the apartment two doors down.

At least I didn't have to worry about blowing their cover. I got out of my Blazer and walked up to the van. There was no one in the front, but I knocked on the passenger door. It was dark inside—for a moment

I thought it might be empty. But then I could see someone coming from the back, climbing into the passenger seat. It was Doc. He rolled down the window.

"What are you doin' here, Eddie?"

"Has she come back yet?"

He shook his head. "Not yet."

"Who you got in there?" I asked.

"Take a look." Doc opened the door, and I stuck my head in. On the metal-mesh benches in the back were three black-suited guys from SWAT, drinking coffee and holding automatic weapons on their laps. One was looking out the van's back window at the street in front of Michelle's apartment.

A few minutes later, I was parked in my Blazer on 67th facing Walnut, waiting for the Lexus. Maybe those SWAT guys would be able to protect Michelle, maybe not. And suppose she didn't go back to her apartment—then they wouldn't be of any help to her at all.

As I sat there, I realized that just two blocks to the north, at 67th and Chestnut, was where Jeff had been shot the night before. I knew there'd be no sign now of what had happened at that intersection. Everything had been swept away. But that's how it always is—someone's gunned down on the sidewalk, and that night or the next day, the TV cameras find the splotches of dried blood. Soon, though, a neighbor comes by and hoses off the sidewalk, or it rains, and people walk over the spot like nothing had ever happened there. The only reminder is a remnant of yellow police tape still tied around a stop sign or street light.

If you're a cop in one place for a while, you can go down any block and say, a woman was shot in that house; an old man was stabbed on the sidewalk here; the intersection coming up was where Darren Roberts of Two Squad got broadsided one night by a drunk driver. Every cop has a living street guide in his head. Everyone else just sees empty streets and sidewalks.

Eventually it started getting light. From the apartments over the stores, and the row houses down the block, men with white T-shirts and jeans and brown work boots emerged, carrying lunch pails or small red Igloo Playmate coolers. The black construction workers came out on one side, the whites on the other. As they got into their cars and pickup trucks, they stole glances at each other across the street, but didn't say anything, didn't even nod hello. They all had to know each other—hell, I bet they usually gave each other rides to work—but today there was an invisible wall that no one seemed willing to push through. And that surprised me, that the black community's anger was no longer limited to the police.

I was starting to get a little sleepy, and it was hard looking at every car coming down Walnut. After a while I tried just watching for colors, just looking for white, letting the other colors fade by. Yellow, green, light blue, deep green, black. It was very relaxing, very peaceful. The cars were swooshing by, their sounds growing softer and softer . . .

A bus honked its horn from far away, and I opened my eyes and had to blink and squint to keep out the bright sun. The sidewalks were full of people. I glanced at the clock on my dashboard: 10:52.

I started the Blazer, and screeched onto Walnut, then raced down to a nearby 7-Eleven. The newspapers were right inside the door, I grabbed a *Post* and started looking for the gossip column. As I flipped through the pages, I caught sight of Jay Bender's smirking photo next to his name, which was written in huge letters. I scanned down to the fourth item. There it was:

> *We all were saddened by the senseless death five weeks ago of Police Officer STEPHEN RYDER, son of Commissioner BEN RYDER. Now, apparently, Stephen's sister, Sgt. MICHELLE RYDER, has left the force.*
>
> *Michelle was recently spotted doing manicures at Angela's, a beauty salon on Locust Street in the city's Westmount section. As she goes from clipping criminals to clipping nails, we wish her the best of luck in her new career.*

A true pinnacle of journalism. I had no doubt that by now, Bravelli had seen the article. I pictured in my mind someone in his crew reading the *Post* over coffee at the Walnut Diner, yelling "Holy shit!" and then leaping up to run to the shiny new pay phone by the door.

The other manicurist at Angela's had quit, so Michelle was the only one the place had. It wouldn't be hard for Bravelli to figure out who Lisa Puccini really was.

I threw the paper back on the pile—I wasn't paying for that crap—and walked back to my Blazer, furious at myself. I had the chance yesterday, I thought, I should have called Bender and told him that if he printed the story, I'd kill him. He didn't know who I was. Why hadn't I thought of that?

My first instinct was to get back over to Michelle's apartment. A minute later I was there, swinging around the corner onto Locust.

The white van was gone. Had something happened to Michelle? I found a pay phone nearby and called Doc's number at OC. Doc isn't here, Stan Allen told me. He's out on the street.

I paged Doc and keyed in the number of my pager. Then I called the Commissioner's office. He wasn't there, all I could do was leave my pager number with the sergeant.

Where was Michelle? I went across the street to the door leading up to her apartment, then up the stairs. Her door showed no signs of forced entry, at least that was good. I pounded on the door, called Michelle's name. No answer.

I went back downstairs and into Angela's, breathing in the odors of sweet shampoos. Three women were cutting customers' hair; one turned and gave me a can-I-help-you look, with the relaxed confidence of an owner. She was willowy, with short dark hair and big round brown eyes, and she paused, mid-snip, as I approached.

"Are you Angela?" I asked.

"Yeah?" Her eyes narrowed. Obviously I didn't come in to get my hair cut.

"You seen Lisa today?"

"Who are you?"

I pulled out my wallet and showed her my badge. She stepped away from her customer, and sort of half pushed me toward the front desk. The other haircutters were looking.

"You see the *Post* today?" I asked.

Her lips got tight. "Yeah, I seen the *Post*."

"You know Lisa was going out with Mickey Bravelli."

"Yeah, I know."

"I have to find her before Bravelli does."

"What was she doin' workin' here, playin' a joke? You don't joke around with these people." It was like she was insulted anyone working for her could be that stupid.

"Have you seen her?" I asked.

"She was supposed to be in at nine."

"Can I check her apartment?"

Angela snorted. "I ain't lettin' you up there."

"What if she's lying there dead, and it comes out that you wouldn't give police access."

Angela bit her lip. "Karen," she called over. "Give Miss Caparella a *People* magazine to read. I gotta go upstairs for a minute."

Michelle's apartment was dark, and we went from room to room, with Angela switching on and off lights. It was like she was showing off the place to someone who might rent it.

Nothing seemed disturbed. If any of Bravelli's people had been in here, they had been very neat about it. I checked under the bed and in the closets, including the one I had hidden in.

My pager went off.

"Do you mind if I use the phone?" I asked Angela.

"It's Michelle's phone, not mine."

I called the number. It was Doc.

"What happened?" I asked. "How come you're not in front of the apartment?"

"The detail was canceled," he said. "About an hour after you came by last night."

"Who canceled it?"

"We got a call from Lanier, he said the Commissioner was pulling the detail."

"Lanier? Did he say why?"

"Nope."

"And you believed him?"

"What was I supposed to do?"

"You should have stayed there until you were sure Michelle was all right."

I hung up and turned to Angela. "If you see Michelle," I said, "make sure you tell her about the *Post* article."

"Oh, I'll tell her," said Angela. "I'm going to sit her down and find out what this is all about." Her lips got tight again. "You don't know these people, you don't know what they're capable of."

Throughout the day, I made the rounds through Westmount again and again. Every once in a while I'd call Michelle's apartment, and then I'd call Sammy at district headquarters. Anybody been reported shot, I asked?

"This is the tenth time you've called," Sammy would say. "Nothing's going on. It's quiet for once."

"How about gunshots, anybody even report any gunshots?"

"Not since you called five minutes ago."

Just before six o'clock I stopped by the district. As I walked into the operations room Sammy shook his head, like, Here comes the crazy man.

"What'd you do, sleep in your clothes?" he asked.

"I think so."

"You know, they do have these modern inventions. They're called beds."

"Sammy, have I told you today to fuck off?"

"Not yet."

In unison, we both said, "Then fuck off."

He was laughing, but then he saw the worry in my face. "You gonna tell me what this is all about?" he asked.

I shrugged. "It's a very long story."

"By the way," said Sammy, "the captain's looking for you. He's in his office."

My pager went off again. I walked over to an empty desk and called the number—this time it was the Commissioner.

"Sorry it took so long to get back to you," he said. "Michelle's all right."

"Oh, man, am I glad to hear that. You talked with her?"

"Late last night."

"So you *were* the one who pulled the detail from in front of her apartment."

"Yes, of course." He seemed surprised I was asking. "From in front of both her apartments. We don't need them anymore, she's in a safe place."

"Where? Where is she?"

"That's what I want to talk to you about."

The Commissioner said he was attending an all-day conference in Valley Forge, and he had to be there for an evening session. He had a few minutes after the dinner there, and he suggested we meet halfway, on Lincoln Drive at Wissahickon Creek. We agreed on eight o'clock.

I stopped by Kirk's office. He stood up from his desk, and walked around to meet me.

"Just the man I want to see," he said. "I need you to go out on a complaint against police."

"I'm not here today," I said. "I'm off."

"Not anymore. Don't even bother with the uniform, just get right out there, it's a store at Fifty-second and Sansom, supposedly some cop beat the hell out of the black store owner. It's the last thing we need."

"Captain, there's stuff I got to do."

"I can't force you to work, I know that. But I got nobody else out there to go right now, and I don't want a fucking riot. I'm asking you to do it, for me. Take the complaint, calm things down, then get the hell out of here, go home."

Maybe I could do it, I thought. The pressure was off to find Michelle, and I wouldn't be meeting the Commissioner for a couple of hours. I had time to catch my breath. OK, I told Kirk, I'll head over there.

We were standing next to one of the glass display cases with *Star*

Trek paraphernalia, and Kirk reached in absentmindedly and lifted out a spaceship shaped like a shoe box.

"This is a shuttlecraft," he said. "The crew used it to take short trips from the *Enterprise,* you know, like when they visited a planet."

Kirk was describing it in the past tense like it was an historical artifact, the way a professor would say, "This cup was used by the Vikings to drink their enemies' blood."

"How did it fly?" I asked. Now I was using the past tense.

Kirk thought for a second, then said, "Rocket power." He seemed a little surprised at himself that he didn't know the answer right away. I nodded, like he had just told me something that was actually connected to reality.

He turned to me and smiled. "I'd love to be in one of these right now, just getting as far away from this place as possible."

"You got room for a passenger?"

"What we really need isn't a shuttlecraft," he said, "it's an escape pod."

I laughed with him. I had no idea what the hell he was talking about.

There were no patrol cars available, so I grabbed a portable radio and headed over to 52nd Street in my Blazer. I hadn't gone a block when we got a report of a second complaint against the police—this one from another store on 52nd. During the four minutes it took me to drive there, two more complaints came in from different stores. Something weird was going on.

When I pulled up, there were two ambulances already there, and another was coming down the street. People were gathering in front of a group of stores between Chestnut and Sansom, everyone was trying to figure out what was happening.

The store that had the original complaint was actually a barbershop. I pushed through the crowd inside and walked in. On the floor next to one of the barber's chairs, a thin black man about sixty, in a blood-covered barber's smock, was being worked on by paramedics.

"You a cop?" another barber asked me. I showed him my badge.

"About time you got here," he said. "One of your boys walked in here and beat Sonny over the head for no reason."

I looked down at Sonny. He was conscious, but there was blood all over the floor, soaking into the hair clippings. There were four other men in the shop and everyone tried to tell the story at the same time.

"This cop just whacked Sonny."

"It was for no reason, no reason at all."

"I saw the whole thing—he just came in here, came right in here, hit Sonny over the head. Sonny didn't do nothin', he was just standing right there by his chair."

I tried to make sense of it. "Why were the police called here in the first place?" I asked the other barber.

"Ain't no one called the police," he said. "We didn't have no trouble here."

A black woman, her makeup smeared from crying, marched into the store and started yelling at me.

"When you gonna talk to *me*?" she demanded. She had her hair pulled back and was wearing a red apron.

"Who are you?"

"Who do I look like? Your cop beat my husband half to death."

I followed her next door—it was a small deli. There was her husband, also in a red apron, lying on the floor just like Sonny. He was holding some bandages to his bleeding head.

"I'm Sergeant North," I said. "What happened here?"

"I don't need you," he said, "I need those fellows from the ambulance to get back in here."

His wife shook her head. "They come in, give my husband some gauze, and say we got somewhere else to go."

"Do you know what happened?" I asked her.

"I'll tell you what happened." Her head seemed to be vibrating in anger. "Your cop's been beatin' people all the way up and down this block."

From what I was able to put together, some officer had gone into five stores in a row, and in each one he had simply walked up to somebody, smashed him over the head with his nightstick, and walked out without a word. Barbershop, WHACK, deli, WHACK, gift shop, WHACK, drugstore, WHACK, clothes store, WHACK. Nobody was seriously hurt, but it was a mess, there was blood all over the place. All the witnesses gave the same description of the cop—Italian, dark features. They said he wasn't wearing a badge or a nameplate, but I didn't need either of those to figure out who it was.

As I walked from store to store, getting what information I could, people almost spit at me.

"You fuckin' racist cops ain't gonna get away with this," one guy shouted in my face. "We gonna fuck you up."

I wondered how long it would take these people to calm down, and then I realized, if this had happened in my neighborhood, I wouldn't calm down for about a year.

When I climbed back into my Blazer, I got on the radio and asked the dispatcher to raise Nick. He didn't respond. Probably knew I'd be looking for him. I was going to be meeting the Commissioner, I didn't have all night to go hunting through the streets of West Philadelphia. Maybe I should tell Kirk about Nick, have him handle it. No, I had to talk to Nick first, myself. You don't jam somebody up without at least giving him a chance to respond.

Buster was on the radio, asking for my location. A couple of minutes later, he and Donna pulled their car up next to me.

"Yo, Sarge, we've seen Nick three or four times this afternoon—driving around the district in his red Camaro."

"What do you mean, driving around?"

"Didn't look like he was really going anywhere. You know, just turning here, turning there."

I told Donna and Buster about the bloody store owners.

"I think Nick did it," I said. "I need you to help me find him."

Wissahickon Creek ran through the middle of the city, surrounded by sprawling woods that were part of Fairmount Park. If you hiked on one of the trails overlooking the creek, you could imagine you were in a forest somewhere, a million miles from the streets of Philadelphia.

When I pulled over into the gravel parking lot off Lincoln Drive, the Commissioner's Blazer was already there, and I parked mine next to his. At the far edge of the lot, facing the woods, was the wooden shelter where we had agreed to meet.

I didn't see anyone around, maybe the Commissioner was taking a leak in the woods. I walked over to the shelter, listening to the sound of gravel crunching under my feet. Not something you hear in the city every day.

As I approached, I heard a rustling in some bushes somewhere. The sunlight was fading, there were a lot of deep shadows, and I couldn't see far into the woods. But I figured it was the Commissioner, doing whatever commissioners do in the woods. Maybe they did what bears did in the woods, I didn't know.

There was a bench inside the shelter, so I figured I'd sit down and wait. I took one step and there was a tremendous BOOOM! and wood splinters were flying everywhere.

I've heard guns fired many times, but for a moment I didn't know exactly what had happened. Then there was another BOOOM! and a section of the shelter a foot to my right just blew apart. There wasn't much doubt in my mind now that I was being shot at.

I dove straight to the ground from the bench, like taking a dive into a pool, and then slithered to the rear of the shelter, facing the parking lot. What the hell was going on? I crouched close to the ground and peered around the corner. I thought I could see a figure in the woods, behind a tree, then I saw the flame from his gun and another shot cracked into the wood near my head. Shit, I thought, some asshole must have been hanging around the shelter, probably robbed the Commissioner, got his gun, maybe even shot him. I had left Junior Vicente's gun on the front seat of my truck, under a newspaper. It was useless to me now.

As I lay behind the shelter, I wondered why the shooter hadn't charged at me. He didn't know I was a cop, he didn't know I had a gun—or at least was supposed to. Sooner or later, though, he would come for me. And there would be nothing I could do but flip him the finger before he pulled the trigger. I looked around. About four feet from the shelter were two trees, maybe if I could make it to them, I'd have a shot of getting into the woods. Maybe I could eventually make it back to my truck.

Go for it, why not, what've you got to lose? I drove toward the trees and heard a shot and then a whizzing near my ear, like an insect.

From the two trees I took another leap, into a patch of tall bushes, and then I just started running like hell. Two more shots came after me, I could hear the bullets blast through the dense leaves. I kept running, trying not to trip over all the huge roots and fallen branches in my way. There was an embankment to my right, and I ran up it halfway and hid behind a big leafy bush, squatting as low as I could. I was thinking, What am I supposed to do now, I don't know anything about hiding in the woods. Who am I, fuckin' Daniel Boone?

It was that time of day when it seems to go from dusk to darkness in two minutes. But it wasn't like being in a real forest, where it gets so black you can't see your hand in front of your face. In Fairmount Park, the sky glowed from tens of thousands of city lights, spreading a surface illumination over the tops of the trees and bushes and branches.

I could make out the dark shape of someone coming through the woods, carefully picking his way, like someone who thought I had a gun.

He got closer, and for a moment he was out in the open, warily looking around. In the semidarkness, it looked like the Commissioner. Damn, I thought, that *is* the Commissioner, why the fuck would he want to shoot me?

I must have brushed against the bushes, because something caught his attention and he suddenly turned toward me, crouched, and took aim.

The hell if I'm waiting for this, I thought, and I took off and he just started blasting off the bullets, BLAM, BLAM, BLAM, BLAM, I could hear him crashing through the woods after me.

He must have figured out by now that I didn't have a gun. Now he knew he had me, all he had to do was get a clear shot. I was stumbling every few feet, branches were hitting my face, I was just blindly charging through the woods, trying to get away. I glanced over my shoulder. Where was he? As I turned back there was a thick branch right in front of my face, and my forehead went into it and I went down.

It didn't knock me out, but I was on my back, and as I rolled over onto my stomach I heard the Commissioner coming, cracking the dead branches under his feet, getting closer. I froze—it was too late to get up and run.

He headed right toward me, then stopped short, listening. He must have known I was nearby. But he had to be careful, too, he had to worry that I might jump out from behind a tree, and grab his gun and turn it on him.

He moved slightly and I heard a snap, maybe fifteen feet away. If it had been daylight he would have spotted me, no question. But the darkness gave me cover. It was the only thing I had.

We stayed there for a long time, I think. I breathed through my mouth, evenly, silently. I tried to keep my body relaxed. I knew he'd hear me if I shifted even slightly.

Finally he started moving again, but he was heading back, retracing his steps. After a while, I couldn't see him anymore, I could only hear his footsteps crunching the underbrush, the sounds getting lighter and lighter until they eventually faded away. Maybe the Commissioner was gone, maybe he was hiding, waiting for me to come out into the open.

I waited there for five minutes, then five minutes more. The whole time, I was trying to figure out why Ben Ryder would want to kill me. There had to be some reason, but I had no idea what it was.

Finally, I moved out from the bushes. I couldn't go back the way I had come, I might be walking into an ambush. I was able to get to the top of the ridge, where there was a narrow trail that had been rutted by mountain bikes. Maybe I could use it to circle around and get back to the parking lot.

I moved steadily but carefully, trying to stay low, so I wouldn't be silhouetted against the sky. I couldn't see the ground very well, and it seemed like I was stepping on every stick in the forest, I was making a hell of a lot of noise. But there was nothing I could do, I had to keep moving. In a few minutes I could hear the traffic again.

Down the hillside, slowly, a step at a time. I was now twenty-five feet from the parking lot. I couldn't see either of the Blazers—there was a big clump of trees blocking my view to where we had parked.

Finally, I reached the lot. My truck was still there, but the Commissioner's was gone. There was still the possibility he had just driven it a couple hundred feet down the road, around the corner and out of sight, then doubled back. That's what I would have done.

I pulled my keys out of my jeans pocket, and ran for the Blazer. With each step I expected a gunshot. I got to the door, put the key in the lock, turned it, pulled the door open, climbed in. Still no gunshots. I was OK. The Commissioner would've had me by now.

TWENTY-ONE

When your boss has just tried to kill you, it's hard to know who to turn to for advice. It's like being in a dream where you think you know where you are, but you don't quite recognize anybody or anyplace. You're just there, somewhere.

Talk to Doc, I thought. Maybe he can help you make sense of it. I drove into Center City, hoping he hadn't left work yet. As I walked into OC headquarters, Doc was coming out of his office. He spotted me and walked over.

"Funny you should walk in here," he said.

"Why, what's up?"

"Lanier just came in about two minutes ago—he's in his office. I'm going to have a little chat with him."

"About last night?"

"Yep. And actually, I'm glad you're here. I'd like you with me—he'll know that two people saw him, not just one. That OK?"

"Absolutely. Let's do it."

How was I going to have time to tell Doc about the Commissioner? We walked over to Lanier's office, he was just coming out.

"Hey, guys," Lanier said, ever cheerful.

"If you got a minute, Captain," Doc said. "Eddie and I wanted to talk to you."

"Sure," said Lanier, still friendly, but wary now. He could tell by our faces that something was wrong.

"In your office?" Doc asked. There was no one else around, but I knew Doc didn't want anybody coming in off the street and walking in on our conversation.

We followed Lanier into his glassed-in office. He sat behind his sprawling desk and motioned for us to sit, but Doc and I ignored the two padded chairs.

"Thought you might want to know, Captain," said Doc, "I've been doin' a little informal surveillance of Sagiliano's." For some reason, Doc's drawl was even more pronounced than usual. "Out back, in the alley," he continued. "Got a microphone hooked up, so I can hear as well as see."

Lanier nodded, giving nothing away. He was probably a great poker player.

"Eddie was with me last night, and we saw you there, Captain. Talkin' to Mickey Bravelli."

"Really," said Lanier. He was listening, concerned, but not as concerned as I would have expected. It was like he had just been told about a major earthquake with hundreds dead—but on the other side of the world.

"I got to be honest with you, Captain," Doc said. "From where we stood, it didn't look good."

"I wouldn't imagine it did," said Lanier.

"But, I consider myself a fair person. I wanted to give you the chance to explain yourself before I went to the Commissioner."

Lanier smiled, absolutely undaunted. "The Commissioner, huh? You're going to go to the Commissioner?"

Doc was a little taken aback by Lanier's reaction. "Well, yes, unless . . ."

"Let me show you something," Lanier said. He pulled a set of keys from his pants pocket and unlocked his top desk drawer. Then he opened a large side drawer, took out a videotape, and wheeled his chair over to a built-in bookcase where he had a television on top of a VCR. He turned them both on and slipped the tape into the VCR.

There was a blank screen for a few seconds, then an image appeared.

A brown Plymouth was approaching through an empty, trash-strewn parking lot. It looked like it had been filmed with a home video camera from the second or third floor of some building. At the bottom of the screen, in white block numbers, was the time and date—the tape had been made four years before.

As the car got closer, the camera showed it coming past a dilapidated red-brick building.

"That's the old sugar refinery," I said.

"Good eye," said Lanier.

The Plymouth stopped on the edge of the lot. A man in a leather jacket was walking toward it, though you could see only his back. When he reached the car, the window came down, and the camera zoomed in on the driver's face.

"The Commissioner," said Doc.

"Don't forget," said Lanier, "four years ago, Ben Ryder was still a chief inspector."

The man in the leather jacket pulled what looked like an envelope from an inside pocket and handed it to Ryder. Then the car window went back up, and the Plymouth pulled away. The man in the leather jacket turned and walked back toward the camera. It was Frankie Canaletto.

"You gotta be kidding me," I said.

"Keep watching," said Lanier.

The screen went blank, but then another image appeared. Same location, same camera angle. This time a black Ford Crown Victoria was coming through the lot. The date was three years ago.

Again, the back of a man in a leather jacket walking toward the car. Again, the window came down to reveal Ben Ryder's face. Another envelope. The man turned. Again, it was Canaletto. The screen went blank.

"That's when he was a deputy commissioner," said Lanier. "We've got one more."

Now a black Blazer was coming through the lot. The date at the bottom was just three months ago. The camera angle was different, and this time you could clearly see that it was Canaletto, wearing a blue polo shirt and white slacks, walking through the lot. The Blazer stopped, the window powered down. Police Commissioner Ben Ryder took the envelope.

When the screen went blank again, Lanier pressed the "eject" button on the VCR and grabbed the tape when it came out.

"It's hard to believe this has been goin' on for four years," said Doc.

"At least four years," said Lanier. "Maybe longer."

"Who made the tape?" I asked. "Internal Affairs?"

Lanier looked at me. "This didn't come from us," he said. "This is Mickey Bravelli's tape."

Lanier told us he found it during a raid of a warehouse in Southwest Philadelphia about a month before. The place was full of stolen merchandise that Bravelli's crew had taken from trucks, from the docks. Electronic equipment, cases of liquor, brand-new washing machines.

Lanier said he had come across two VCRs hooked together, set up to copy videotapes from one to the other.

"This was the tape they used to make the copy, but it was still in the machine," said Lanier. "They took the copy, left the original. Not too bright."

The two VCRs had been left on, and Lanier guessed that the taping had been done very recently—possibly the same day.

"Bravelli's trying to blackmail the Commissioner," I said.

"It looks that way," said Lanier. "And it's not a bad plan. Pay off a police commander, but tape it so you can blackmail him later."

"But this implicates Canaletto as well," said Doc.

"Doing what?" I asked. "Giving an envelope to a cop? What are you going to charge him with?"

"He's right," said Lanier. "It doesn't hurt Canaletto a bit. But it certainly makes Ben Ryder look bad—at the very least, this tape would destroy his career."

"I wonder what Bravelli's getting for his money," said Doc.

"Think about it," said Lanier. "Haven't you noticed that whenever we send a case to the DA's office, nothing much seems to happen?"

Doc and I nodded.

"And," said Lanier, "it also might explain why whenever we get close to Bravelli, we always end up having to back off. It's not like it comes down as an order. But something always happens. We have to put our resources somewhere else, or—"

"Or someone gets transferred," I said.

"Yeah, and that's what got me the most suspicious, Eddie, when that happened to you—right when you were ready to pop Bravelli. I got a call from the Commissioner himself on that one. He wanted you out of the unit, transferred to patrol. But he never said why."

"So there weren't any anonymous calls about me?"

"Who do you think told me to tell you that? And what was I supposed to do? I knew something was wrong, but I didn't have any proof."

"Until you found the tape," I said.

"Until I found the tape."

I thought about it. "But if the Commissioner's been taking payoffs, then why would Bravelli need to blackmail him?"

"That's what I've been trying to find out," said Lanier. "I've been going to Sagiliano's, trying to make contact with Bravelli, trying to make him think I'm dirty. That's what you saw me doing last night."

"So let me get this straight," I said. "Doc, you're doing an unofficial investigation of the captain. And, Captain, you're doing an unofficial investigation of the Commissioner."

They both laughed, a little shamefaced.

"You saw how successful I was," said Lanier.

"Maybe you just have an honest face," I said. "An ugly face, but an honest face."

"C'mon now, Eddie," said Lanier, but he was smiling. It was the first friendly thing I'd said to him in months.

"Something else has me worried," he said. "You saw me talking to Michelle Ryder, right? Ever since her brother got killed, she's been hanging around with Bravelli, I think in some kind of disguise. I don't know whether she's working undercover or whether she's following in her father's footsteps."

In five minutes, Lanier had gone from being an enemy to a possible ally. But until I was positive I could trust him, I couldn't reveal anything about Michelle.

"Speaking of her father," I said, "just a few minutes ago, he tried to kill me."

I recounted what had happened in Fairmount Park, and they both went pale. When I finished my story, it occurred to me that the Commissioner may not have heard from Michelle after all. Not if he was just saying that to lure me to the park.

I stood up quickly, almost knocking over my chair.

"I got to get to Westmount."

A few minutes later, I was heading through West Philadelphia. It was pretty clear that anger over what had happened on 52nd Street was spreading quickly. Everywhere, police cars were screaming around corners, up streets, into alleys.

Once I got to Westmount, I quickly made the rounds. The beauty shop was closed, and Michelle's apartment was dark. I went up the stairs and knocked on her front door anyway, yelling out that it was me.

Next stop was Lucky's. I planned to cruise by quickly, then head for Sagiliano's. But there at the curb, not far from Lucky's red canopy, was Bravelli's Seville. No one was in the car.

Stay calm, I told myself. I pulled my Blazer up behind the Seville, left the engine running, and slowly got out. Stay calm. I glided under Lucky's canopy and pushed open the restaurant's glass door. I peeked around the fountain, and through the semi-darkness I could see Bravelli's table. There he was, sitting with Canaletto and Goop, talking into a cell phone. I ducked back out the door.

This is it, I thought. I can end it right here. Just go back into the restaurant, walk right up to Bravelli, shoot him in the head, then shoot Canaletto and Goop. Then another bullet in Bravelli's head. Do it quickly. They won't have time to react.

Am I really ready for this? Yes, I told myself. Yes. If Michelle's still alive, then this is the best way to keep her safe. If not, then it's simple revenge.

But I didn't want to get caught. And if I walked inside, I'd be recognized. People who worked at the restaurant knew me. I couldn't stand outside the front door and wait, either. Someone might spot me and tip off Bravelli.

I looked around. At the end of the building, there was a passageway that ran along the side of the restaurant. It probably went all the way back to the alley. I could drive around behind Lucky's, park in the alley, come up the passageway, and wait for Bravelli to walk out of the restaurant. Much better.

I got back in the Blazer and swung around the corner, then headed into the alley until I reached the darkened walkway. It was narrower than I expected, and was full of garbage cans. I turned off the engine and killed the headlights, and pulled Junior Vicente's gun from underneath the newspaper on the front seat. The gun had a nice feel to it, I was going to enjoy seeing how well it worked.

As I got out of the truck and put the gun in my waistband, under my shirt, I felt a tremendous sense of purpose. This was what I was meant to be doing right now. For at least the moment, I had found my place in the world.

I walked through the passageway to the street, and glanced up and down the sidewalk. Two teenage girls were heading toward me, chattering away with loud voices. I ducked back a few feet into the darkness and turned, waiting until they had passed.

I took another look around the corner. It was a break for me that the Seville wasn't right in front of the canopy, but on the other side. That meant that when Bravelli and the others left the restaurant, they'd have their backs to me as they headed for their car. I could sprint down the sidewalk, come up from behind.

A familiar red Camaro was coming down Walnut, toward Lucky's, and as it passed by me, I caught a look at the driver. It was Nick. He slowed as he passed in front of the restaurant, then sped away. I didn't even consider going after him, confronting him about 52nd Street. That was the least of my concerns right now.

I glanced at my watch. Nine-thirty. I had been waiting in the passageway for a grand total of nine minutes. Time was going by too slowly. I wouldn't be able to wait here another hour, if that's what it took.

I realized with alarm that I was beginning to get nervous. Not at the prospect of shooting Bravelli and the others, but of getting caught. Don't think about that, I told myself. If you do, you might as well turn around and walk away.

My eye caught someone walking on the other side of the street, across from me, heading in the direction of Lucky's. Nick, wearing black jeans and a black T-shirt. What the hell was he doing here?

He started to cross the street at an angle, aiming for Lucky's front door. And then I realized: he had seen the Seville, just as I had. That's what he was doing all day, driving around. He was looking for Bravelli. Just like me.

"Nick!" I called in a low voice. He stopped short, in the middle of the quiet street. I called his name again, and took a half step out of the passageway so he could see me. "Over here," I called out.

He spotted me and glanced around, like he wondered who I was hiding from. I waved him over, and he jogged up to me.

"Hey, Eddie, what are you doin' here?"

I pulled him into the murky darkness of the passageway.

"What are *you* doin' here?"

"I got some business to take care of," Nick said. His eyes, even in the dim light, looked feverish.

"What kind of business?"

Nick briefly lifted his T-shirt to reveal his Glock, tucked in the side of his jeans. "Bravelli's in the restaurant," he said. "And I'm gonna get him."

No, you're not, I started to say. But how could I say that? He was only going to do what I planned to do, no more, no less.

But was it really the same thing? Somehow, it seemed crazier for Nick to want to shoot Bravelli. I had a purpose. I was acting rationally. Nick hadn't been acting rationally for weeks. I looked at him, looked at his burning eyes, and I thought, I'm not like that.

But I knew it didn't make any difference. I was in Nick's world now. I knew how it felt, I knew what it was like. Standing there in the passageway, both prepared to murder, we were like blood brothers.

"Go home," I told Nick. "I'm going to take care of it."

"What do you mean?"

"Just what I said. I'm taking care of it."

He looked at me, starting to understand, unable to accept it.

"You're not here to get him, too, are you?" he asked. He seemed almost frightened by the idea, like I had been captured by the same beast that had him.

"That's exactly why I'm here," I said.

"No," Nick said, shaking his head. This couldn't be his cousin Eddie. "You're not really going to do it."

"I am, Nick." Though I felt a tug, unseen, trying to pull me out, like someone grabbing the back of my belt. You don't want to be in Nick's world, it said. But I pulled away, so forcefully that I actually took a step forward, almost stumbling into him.

I did want to be here. I did want to kill Bravelli. Just like Nick.

"Go home," I told him. "I got this under control."

He looked at me with real worry. "I ain't leavin' you, Eddie."

"Nick, there's no sense in both of us getting locked up."

"I ain't leavin'."

"All right," I said. "All right. Then let's both do it."

Now he wasn't so sure.

"Come on, Nick. We can do it."

A black Honda Accord roared past us and up to Lucky's canopy. Two young guys jumped out and went into the restaurant. I didn't recognize them, but with their tight black shirts, their slicked-back hair, their intensity, they had to be coming to see Bravelli. I was surprised how young they both looked—was Bravelli recruiting in high school now?

What if they all came out together? There'd be five of them, that was a lot to drop. Well, I'd start with Bravelli and see how far I could get. If Nick helped, so much the better.

A minute later, the restaurant doors flew open, and the two guys came back out toward the Honda. One of them pulled open the driver's door, the other ran around to the passenger side.

"What if she's already left?" the passenger half yelled at the driver. "I told you one of us should have fuckin' stayed on Locust to watch the place."

"Just get in the fuckin' car, all right?" the driver yelled back. "We got work to do."

They both jumped in, slamming their doors, and the Honda screeched off.

I was filled with a sudden dread. Locust Street was where Michelle lived. They were going to her apartment.

It was only seven blocks to Michelle's, but it seemed like a hundred. Nick was with me in my truck. He didn't hesitate when I started running down the passageway and yelled at him to come with me.

If there were any stoplights on the way, I didn't notice them. Each intersection we hit, Nick checked his side, then yelled, "Clear!"

Finally, we were there, swinging around the corner onto Locust. We could see the Honda parked in front of Angela's. The door to the stairs that led to Michelle's apartment was open.

Something was happening—two men burst out of the doorway and fell to the ground, punching each other. I skidded my Blazer up to the curb and leapt out, Junior Vicente's gun in my hand.

It was one of the guys from the Honda, and . . . Jesus, it was Lanier. What was he doing here?

The young guy kept trying to get up and Lanier kept dragging him back down, but then Nick and I were on the guy, knocking him to the ground. Nick flipped him facedown and jumped on top of him so he couldn't move.

"Another one's upstairs," Lanier yelled, getting to his feet. "I heard a gunshot."

I ran through the doorway and pounded up the stairs, past the second floor, up to the third floor. Michelle's door had been torn open, splintered at the lock.

I swung my gun arm through first, then stepped in, ready to pull the trigger. But it was Michelle my gun was pointing at, and she had a gun, too, she was holding it with both hands, aiming right at my head.

By some miracle neither of us fired. And then I saw, at her feet, the other guy from the Honda. He was lying on the floor, writhing in pain, holding his bloody chest.

It turned out Lanier had been sitting in his car across the street from Michelle's apartment. He had seen the Honda make its first two passes, a half hour apart, and then a third, just as Michelle was coming home, opening the door at the bottom of the stairs.

"I had a feeling they might be coming back," Lanier told Michelle and me, as we all stood out front on the sidewalk. The two young guys had already been taken away—one to the hospital, the other to district headquarters—and the street was full of police cars.

Lanier said that when he saw the story in the *Post,* he was afraid Bravelli's men might go after Michelle. He knew the Commissioner had canceled the detail in front of her apartment about 6 A.M., but he didn't know why. And he couldn't get in touch with the Commissioner to ask.

"I didn't want to put another detail here without knowing what was going on," Lanier said. "But I didn't want to leave the place uncovered."

"So how long were you here?" I asked him. "Couple of hours?"

"Other than when you saw me at OC headquarters this afternoon," he said, "I've been here all day. And I only went back there to get these."

He reached into the back pocket of his jeans and pulled out two Glock clips.

"Didn't know how many bullets I'd need," he said.

"Wow," said Michelle, giving him a nice smile. "You must have really been worried about me."

"Well, I'm sure you saw the article."

"Yeah," I said to Michelle, "you did see the article, didn't you?"

"Of course."

"Then what were you doing back here?"

"I didn't want to leave this behind." She had a locket on a gold chain around her neck, and she picked it up from her blue T-shirt to show us. Inside was a tiny photo of a small boy and girl, arms around each other.

"Me and Steve," Michelle explained. "Steve gave it to me on my last birthday. And I wasn't worried about coming back here to pick it up—I had my gun."

"Fortunately," I said.

"Not fortunately. I wouldn't have come here without it. And as you can see, I put it to good use."

"But if the captain hadn't been here—"

"Then I would have shot both of them."

Lanier and I laughed.

"I'm sure you would have," I said.

"Not that I don't appreciate you being concerned about me, Captain," Michelle said.

"I'm still concerned," said Lanier. "I have no doubt that Bravelli will try again."

"I agree," I said.

"I'd like to see if we can get him locked up," said Lanier. "Maybe one of those two assholes from tonight can help us out. In the meantime, Michelle, you've really got to get out of sight. Go somewhere where they're not going to find you."

"I can't go back to my old apartment," she said. "I can't put Theresa in that kind of danger. And I'm sure they know where my father lives, maybe even my mother, too."

"I'd suggest my house," I said. "But I wouldn't be surprised if I've already been followed home at night."

"Can you get out of the city?" Lanier asked Michelle. "Way out?"

"There's always Vic's cabin," I said.

"Who's Vic?"

"Vic Funderburke, a sergeant in the Third. He's got a cabin up in the Poconos. I can use it anytime I want."

"Sounds like a good idea," said Lanier.

Michelle thought about it, then agreed. "Though I want to go upstairs for a second," she said. "I'm going to throw some clothes in a duffel bag."

When Michelle had gone back inside, I looked around. Nick was gone. Donna and Buster were standing next to their patrol car, and I asked whether they had seen him.

"I think he's at district headquarters with his prisoner," said Donna.

Good, I thought, that means he'll be tied up half the night. By the time he goes back to Lucky's to get his car, Bravelli will probably be gone. I didn't want Nick killing anybody tonight, even that asshole.

I walked back over to Lanier.

"I have to tell you, Captain," I said, "All this time I really thought you were the enemy."

"Yeah, I know you did, Eddie. But I'm not. I'm just a plain old cop."

TWENTY-TWO

In twenty minutes Michelle and I were on the Pennsylvania Turnpike's Northeast Extension, heading up to the Poconos, watching the open fields and farms give way to mountains.

Michelle was quiet for much of the ride. I wanted to tell her about her father, about the videotape, about how he had tried to kill me in the park. But she was deep in thought, like she was sorting things out, so we drove in silence.

An hour later, just past the Allentown exit, she finally spoke.

"You were right. Mickey was the one who had Steve killed."

I glanced at her. "How do you know that?" I didn't say anything about her calling him Mickey, I figured this wasn't the time.

"He told me last night," said Michelle. "I asked him and he told me."

I waited for her to go on.

"Steve was innocent," she said.

"What do you mean?"

"I mean he was innocent. He didn't have anything to do with the black Mafia, or the Italian Mafia, or anybody else."

"And Bravelli told you this?"

Michelle was silent for a while, looking out the window. Then she turned to me.

"When Mickey asked me to marry him, I put him off at first. But then I said yes—because I figured out I could use it to finally find out about Steve."

She said Bravelli called her at the beauty shop yesterday afternoon and told her he wanted to take her to the casinos in Atlantic City.

"I knew you were going," I said. "I tried to find you down there last night."

"Really? Well, it's good that you didn't, because you might have screwed things up. With that article coming out, I had only one shot at making this work."

Michelle said they had dinner at an expensive restaurant, then spent a few hours going from casino to casino. Sometime after midnight, when they were ready to head back to Philly, Michelle suggested they go to an all-night diner to get some coffee before getting on the road. She made sure they sat in a quiet booth in the back, out of earshot of the other customers.

As they drank their coffee, Michelle told Bravelli she had been following the news stories about the investigation into the killing of the Commissioner's son. Police were saying they believed Bravelli's criminal organization was somehow involved. Bravelli told her it wasn't true, the cops were just trying to make him look bad.

"So I said to him, 'I know what you do, Mickey, and that's OK, I know you're not a saint. I love you, and I want to marry you. But I need to know why you do these kinds of things.'

"Mickey looked at me for a while, I think he was trying to decide what to say. So I said, 'I trust you, and I assume that if you did this, you had to have a pretty good reason. I just want to be able to understand what it was.' "

Still, Bravelli had remained silent.

"I won't ever ask you about this kind of thing again," she told him, "I promise that. I just have to know that you had a good reason."

"Let me tell you, Leez," he said, "if I ended up doin' something like that, I would have a good reason, don't worry."

"I'm sure you would, Mickey, I'm sure of it. And if I had to guess, I'd say it was because you were trying to protect yourself."

"That's always why you do things you might not want to do, remember that. To protect yourself and your family."

"It was so you wouldn't have to go to jail for something?"

Bravelli had shaken his head. "Not me, Leez. Frankie."

"That's when I knew it was true, Eddie. He did have Steve killed after all. I started to feel sick, I was thinking, oh, my God, I can't believe this, how could I even be with this monster?"

"I would have killed the fuckin' scumbag right there," I said.

"I had to hide how I felt so I could find out more. So I said to him, 'See, this is what I'm talking about, this is why I trust you. I know how close you are to Frankie."

"I'll tell you," Bravelli had said, "when we were runnin' the streets, Frankie saved my life more than once."

"So, help me understand," Michelle went on. "You were trying to keep Frankie from going to jail? What did that have to do with the Police Commissioner's son getting killed?"

"It was just a little warning to the Commissioner."

"The Commissioner? What do you mean, the Commissioner?"

Bravelli didn't answer, he just laughed.

"What's so funny?" Michelle asked.

"That I'm even talkin' about this with you."

"You don't feel you can tell me?"

"No, that's just it. I do feel I can tell you. I feel I can tell you anything."

Michelle looked at me. "Eddie, here I am thinking, this son of a bitch killed my brother. And now this has something to do with my father, I don't know what it is, I don't think I want to know. But I have to keep going. I said, "Why would you want to warn the Commissioner?"

"You really want to know this, don't you?" Bravelli asked.

"Yes, Mickey, I do."

"OK. I told you the DA's goin' after Frankie, right?"

"Yeah, you did tell me."

"It's simple. I wanted the Commissioner to get him to back off."

The waitress came by to refill their coffee, and when she left, Bravelli began to open up more. He told Michelle he and the Commissioner had a "partnership," but the Commissioner was refusing to uphold his end.

"Do you see what he was saying, Eddie? He was saying my father was a dirty cop. My stomach was just twisting, I really thought I was going to get sick right there."

"Did Bravelli notice?"

"I don't think so, he was going on about it, he was telling me how angry he was that my father couldn't get the DA to kill the investigation."

"And he expected your father to be able to do something like that?"

"Yeah, he said my father kept insisting that it was because there was a new DA, he couldn't get the new DA to back off mob cases like the old one did. That's what he said, 'like the old one did.'"

"No wonder Bravelli didn't believe your father," I said.

"Yeah. He said he kept telling him, 'Don't give me that bullshit, Mr. Police Commissioner. You did it in the past, you can fuckin' do it now.'

"And he had some kind of leverage over my father, too. He didn't say what it was. But he said he'd already tried to use it, and it didn't work, my father still wasn't getting the DA to back off. So he had to take stronger measures. That's what he called it. 'Stronger measures.'"

"That motherfucker," I said. "He meant killing Steve."

"Yeah, that's exactly what he meant, killing my brother. Just murdering him in cold blood. He said he knew my father would get the message."

"I don't know how you were able to listen to all this."

"I don't either. And I still had to ask him about Steve. I said, 'What about the Commissioner's son? Did you have a partnership with him, too?'

"You know what he said, Eddie? He said no, he didn't even know the son. It was just a way of threatening the Commissioner."

"So Steve didn't know anything about this."

"No. My father being dirty is what got Steve killed. And then I found out something else. I don't even know if I want to tell you about it."

"That's OK."

"No, I'm going to tell you. Mickey said he got my father to believe the black Mafia did it—that's why he put that black guy in the trunk."

"So your father would crack down on the black Mafia."

"Exactly. And then later, Mickey sent someone to give my father the message that he did it after all. And you know what the message was? 'We know you have a daughter on the police force, too. We killed one of your kids, and if you don't stop the DA, we're gonna kill the other.' That was the message."

"Jesus."

Michelle looked at me. "I swear to God, Eddie, if I would have had my gun with me I would have shot him right between the eyes. I wanted to kill him right where he sat."

Michelle took a deep breath, and let it out. "I couldn't ask him any more questions after that. I just wanted to go home."

"I don't blame you."

"But there's a lot more I wanted to find out that I never did. Like, what was this leverage he had over my father?"

"That," I said, "was a videotape."

I told her about it, how it showed her father taking payoffs from Canaletto. She just kept her eyes on the floor of the truck, she didn't say anything.

I knew I also had to tell her the worst part—what had happened in the woods. She had her hand to her mouth as I described how her father had tried to kill me.

"That was my fault," she said, her voice trembling, when I had finished. "He knew I was going to tell you everything."

Michelle said that after Bravelli drove her home, she took a cab up to her father's house in the Northeast.

No wonder the Commissioner had canceled the detail in front of Michelle's apartment—she was with him.

When Michelle got to the house, her father was still awake, and she confronted him with what Bravelli had said.

"He denied everything. He said Mickey Bravelli was lying, there wasn't any deal. How could you expect a mobster to tell the truth?"

"Did you believe him?" I asked.

Michelle shook her head. "No. And he knew I knew. I could see it in the way he looked at me. My father and I have always had a very close relationship. We even joke about how each of us always knows when the other one's not telling the truth—it's a thing between us."

"What'd you do?"

"I told him he had to turn himself in. I said for Steve's sake, and for his sake. And you know what? He kept denying it.

"I'll tell you, Eddie, I completely lost it. I just got so angry, I started shouting at him. I said, 'Because of what you did, your son got killed. Your son, the good cop. How can you live with that?'

"He started yelling back, and that got me even more angry, and then we were just shouting back and forth, and I said, 'If you won't get the truth out, I will.'

"My father asked me what I meant. I said, 'I'm going to find a way to prove this. I'll tell Eddie, he'll help me. I'm not going to let you just live your life like this never happened.' "

They argued with each other for a long time, neither one giving in.

"I spent the night in my old room," Michelle said. "And when I got up in the morning, he was gone. I never thought he'd try to kill you, Eddie. I really didn't."

"There's no way you could have known."

"If anything, I would have expected him to go after Mickey, not you."

"I don't think so. It sounds like by the time he learned that Bravelli had your brother killed, he had already found out you were working undercover in Westmount. He couldn't go after Bravelli until he got you out of there first. But he could still go after me."

"I'm so sorry, Eddie."

We didn't speak much for the rest of the trip. It was about 1 A.M. when we took the Timbercreek exit off I-81 and passed through the town of Pemberton toward Lake Asayunk. I didn't tell Michelle that I had been there only once before, to go hunting, and I wasn't exactly sure which road to take. But I think she figured it out after I kept stopping and making U-turns. By some miracle I found the gravel road with the sign for the lake. There were about a dozen cabins, scattered along the lakefront, and Vic's was on the far end, apart from the rest.

They called them cabins, but they were nicer than that. Usually in the Poconos, a cabin means bare wood floors with big cracks in them, and old mattresses on bunkbeds. It's BYOSB—bring your own sleeping bag. Vic's cabin was more of a house—it was sealed up tight, and had real floors, a modern kitchen. It was small—just one bedroom—but it had a deck that extended out over the lake.

I had no idea where the key was.

"Vic told me once," I said, as I went to look under the mat, and found that there wasn't any mat. "But I think I was drunk at the time."

It was very dark, and I didn't have a flashlight in the Blazer. I got back in the truck and maneuvered it so that the headlights were pointing at the front door, but it didn't help us to find the keys.

"I wish I could remember," I said.

"Maybe we should hypnotize you," Michelle said with a smile. She was relaxing now, the tension was leaving her face.

We looked for the keys in the woodpile, on the doorsill, under the steps, everywhere. I was just about ready to propose breaking a window, when Michelle came through the door—from the inside.

"How'd you get in?"

"Simple—the key was under the mat."

"What mat?"

"The mat at the front door. This is the back door."

I thought about that for a second, and then looked at her and said, "You know what? You're right."

We turned on the lights and took a look at the place. Small, but cozy. It was a warm night, and we opened up all the screened windows to air the place out.

Vic had left some beer in the refrigerator, and we each grabbed a bottle and stood in the kitchen, talking quietly. There was a big window over the sink, and Michelle was looking through it. She was so beautiful then. I found myself thinking about our kiss at her old apartment. But so much had happened since then, she had seemed so cold, so unreachable.

"You know," she said, turning to me, "I never would have married Bravelli. Did you think I would?"

"Well, I did wonder. I mean, you really shut me out."

"I had to. I felt I was really getting inside his head, getting him to open up. I was afraid you'd get in the way."

"Was that all it was?"

Michelle looked at me and shook her head. "No, it was more than that. You're right. You probably won't understand this, but the more he opened up to me, the more I felt there was an actual human being in there. And I guess I responded to that."

"Did you fall in love with him?"

"No. But I did start letting my defenses down. I began to wonder whether maybe what he did, you know, the mob thing, maybe wasn't so bad. You saw how I was getting drawn into it—I told you what happened with me with Jumpin' Jiminy's. I really got into that."

"So what do you think was going on? Were you trying to justify Bravelli being in the mob?"

Michelle shook her head. "It didn't have anything to do with Bravelli. It had to do with Steve. You know what I think it was? If I could understand how Mickey Bravelli could be a good person and a criminal at the same time, maybe I could understand how Steve could be the same way. And then when I found myself slipping into that life, I wondered, hey, maybe I'm that way, too."

"Do you really think you are?"

"No, I don't. I know I'm not that way. Finding out about Steve and my father last night snapped me out of it. I mean, I saw Bravelli for what he was. But I'm sure that even if I never had that conversation with him, I still would have come out of it. I'm not my father. I don't have it in me to take it that far."

"You know what? I never thought you did."

"You're just saying that, right?"

"I didn't know what was going on with you. But no, I never thought you were really that kind of person. You were always Michelle."

"It's nice of you to say that."

"It's true," I said.

Michelle looked up at me. "Thanks for watching out for me, Eddie."

"Sure."

I wanted to kiss her, to put my arms around her, but I just stood there, looking stupid. It didn't matter—she stepped forward and stood on her toes and kissed me on the lips. And then I took her in my arms, and we kissed for a long time. I was just kind of melting onto the floor. It was so good to have her back.

"You know what?" she said at last. "I'd like to go to sleep, and not wake up for about three years."

"Go ahead and make it four," I said. "We've got plenty of time."

She laughed. "If you want the bedroom, I'll take the couch."

"No," I said, "you take the bedroom. I want to stay up for a while and finish my beer."

I got some sheets out of the closet and pulled the fold-out bed from the couch. As I was putting on the sheets, I watched Michelle through the doorway in the bedroom, making up the bed. She saw me looking, and smiled.

When I woke it was just getting light. I lay there for a while, enjoying the cool breeze coming in off the lake. There was a dove cooing right outside the window, and I heard the faint sound of a motorboat, somebody up early fishing. I drifted off, and when I woke again, there was a gentle smell of coffee. I sat up and looked around, but didn't see Michelle. The bedroom door was open, the bed made.

I got dressed, and as I walked into the kitchen I saw, through the sliding glass door, Michelle sitting on a chair on the deck in the morning sunlight, sipping coffee. She had made it in the white plastic coffee maker on the counter, and I poured myself a cup and stepped outside. It was warm out there, and very bright.

"Morning," I said.

"Morning."

She had on a white cotton blouse and blue jeans, which I assumed she had brought from her apartment. I brushed some leaves off a green, hard-plastic chair, and sat down. The coffee wasn't good, but it was hot.

"There's no food at all in this house," Michelle said. "We need to get some groceries."

"Fine."

"And I want to go swimming, so we need to find a place that sells bathing suits."

A little later, we got back in the Blazer and rode until we came across a grocery store down the road. Next door was a souvenir shop that sold beach-type stuff. I found a bathing suit that cost eleven dollars, and Michelle got hers for seventeen, a blue one-piece cheapie.

There was a pay phone, I called Lanier. They had brought Bravelli in for questioning, he said, but had to let him go. The two guys from the Honda weren't talking.

"Stay up there as long as you can," he said.

Michelle and I went back to the cabin and had some breakfast. Then we put on our suits and splashed around in the sparkling water, floating on our backs, listening to the laughing screams of children from the neighboring cabins.

I think that for a few hours we both tried to forget about all the terrible things that had happened. Not that we could, of course. No matter what we talked about, those things were always just below the surface.

During the afternoon, we sat sunning ourselves on the deck, and joked about how we never wanted to go back to Philadelphia.

"If we do," I said to Michelle, who was lying on a deck chair with her eyes closed, "all I'm going to do is get shot at. I wouldn't even know who was doing it—I'd be riding along in my patrol car, and the bullets would start flying, and I'd have to get on my loudspeaker and say, Excuse me, but are you a rioter, a member of the mob, or the police commissioner?"

I quickly glanced at Michelle. "Sorry."

She opened her eyes. "That's all right. I don't blame you. But you know, we do have to get back, Eddie."

"Why? Whatever's going to happen is going to happen, whether we're there or not."

"I don't know about that. I've got to try again to get my father to turn himself in."

"He's not going to do it, Michelle."

"I'll make him."

"What about Bravelli? He's still going to try to kill you."

"I'll just have to be careful. And maybe we can put him in jail. I can testify against him. I can try to get my father to testify against him."

"In the meantime . . ."

"In the meantime, I can't hide up here forever, Eddie."

"It'd be nice if we could, though, wouldn't it?"

She looked at me. "Maybe another time, huh?"

"I'll tell you what," I said. "Let's at least wait until tomorrow morning. It'll be Sunday, things will be a little calmer."

She thought about it, then nodded OK and even smiled a little. Later, we went inside, drained from the sun and the water, and had some turkey sandwiches and more beer. When we had finished, Michelle rinsed off the dishes, and said she wanted to lie down and take a nap.

I needed one, too. It wasn't just lack of sleep, it was a deep stress that had been pushed down for weeks, kept at bay. I needed to crash. When Michelle went into the bedroom, I took off my wet trunks and put on my jeans, and lay down on the couch. There was a slight breeze coming in through the screen on the sliding glass door, it felt good on my bare chest. I closed my eyes and almost instantly slipped off to sleep.

I don't know how many hours later, I opened my eyes and saw Michelle sitting nearby in a wicker chair, watching me. It was late afternoon, almost early evening; the room was bathed in the soft orange light of the sunset reflecting off the lake.

She was wearing a white linen robe that I assumed was Vic's wife's. It was open a little, enough that I could see the curve of her breasts.

"Hi," I said, lifting my head a little, then setting it back down. "How long you been sitting there?"

"Just a few minutes."

I put my hands behind my neck. "You hungry? Want to go into town and get some dinner?"

She didn't answer, she just stood up and walked over and sat on the couch. I moved my legs to give her room, and as she sat her robe opened a little and I started getting dizzy.

"I'm glad to be back in the land of the living," she said. "Especially since it means I can be with you."

She leaned down and kissed me, and it was like drinking a wonderful wine. I wanted to say that to her, but I thought it would sound ridiculous. She sat up and smiled and slipped the robe off her shoulders, and just let it drop around her waist. Her breasts were so round, so firm, and I reached out and gently caressed them, and she leaned forward so that our chests were touching, skin to skin, and we kissed and I was getting drunk in the wine.

She stood, and her robe fell to the floor, and she grabbed my hand and led me to the bedroom. She helped me take off my jeans, and we lay down on the bed, and I felt that at that moment, I had never been luckier in my life.

We made love until it got dark, and then went into town and had a seafood dinner, and when we came back, we got into bed and we didn't even take our clothes off, we just fell asleep in each other's arms.

TWENTY-THREE

We got an early start the next morning, taking with us the peacefulness of the woods and the crisp mountain air. But two hours later, as we approached the city, we saw plumes of dark, thick smoke over West Philadelphia. I flipped on the radio. They were saying that a full-scale riot had erupted the night before. Three people were dead, and fires were still burning out of control. According to the radio, the riot started after an unknown police officer clubbed Councilman Barney Stiller at a candlelight prayer march, putting him in the hospital.

I felt a pit in my stomach.

"You think that was Nick?" Michelle asked. I had told her about what happened to the store owners on 52nd Street.

"Who else?" I said. "I should have locked him up when I had the chance."

"Could you really have done that?"

"Maybe, I don't know, Michelle. But I should have done something. At the very least, I shouldn't have left him alone."

"How were you supposed to know he was going to start a riot?"

"I don't know, I don't know what I was supposed to do. But whatever it was, I didn't do it."

The radio was saying that city officials were worried the violence would spread to other areas of the city, and the mayor was calling in all off-duty police officers and firefighters. Meanwhile, the governor was activating the National Guard, and troops were expected to be on the streets by nightfall.

I had to find Nick, that was the first thing. I had to make sure he didn't hurt anybody else. I decided to go straight to the 20th—maybe somebody there would know where he was.

Michelle wanted me to drop her at her father's house. If he wasn't there, she'd take his city car, a black Crown Victoria, and start looking for him.

"He's probably in West Philadelphia," I said. "That's where everything's happening."

"Then that's where I'll go."

"You forget Bravelli's looking for you?"

"He's not going to go anywhere near those riots. I'll just stay out of Westmount."

"Michelle . . ."

"Don't bother arguing, Eddie. I'll take responsibility for myself."

The Commissioner's Blazer was gone, but the Crown Vic was parked out front. It was peaceful on that street, as quiet as Lake Asay-unk. Michelle gave me a long kiss, and then got out of the truck.

"Be careful," she said, through the open passenger window.

"Sure," I said. "Say hi to your father for me."

It was a little after ten when I got into West Philadelphia. The Penn campus was deserted—the students must have all been evacuated. The only signs of life were the U. of P. cops standing in twos and threes in front of buildings, and cruising the perimeter in their patrol cars.

It wasn't until I reached the 52nd Street shopping district that I saw the first signs of the riots. A whole row of stores on one side was blackened and gutted by fire, and flames were still eating into an old movie theater on the corner. Two engine companies and a ladder were pouring water onto the smoke and flames, and the street was clogged with thick canvas hoses and wet, burned debris. That shopping district meant a lot to the people of West Philadelphia; it was a shame to see so much of it destroyed.

I took a right on 56th toward Market. There was a group of about eight males on the corner of Chestnut, and when they saw me, they stepped into the street to block my path. Most of them had bats and metal pipes. I recognized one of them as Homicide—he seemed to be everywhere. Today he had on a T-shirt that said "The only good cop is a dead cop."

I casually stopped the truck and climbed out. They were a little surprised I wasn't frightened, but they started closing in for the kill.

A big guy standing next to Homicide yelled, "Let's get this white motherfucker."

"I don't think so," I said, holding up Junior Vicente's gun, and then pointing it in their direction.

"He's a fucking cop," said Homicide.

"Lovely T-shirt," I said to him. "Where can I get one?"

"Get ready," he said. "We're gonna make you a good cop."

He raised the pipe, and motioned for the others to follow. It was amazing, they just assumed I wasn't going to use the gun, like I'd be afraid of getting fired. This is what happens, I thought, when the criminals see that cops are always second-guessing themselves. Except that I'd much rather be out of work than dead. I fired a shot at Homicide's feet, and the bullet kicked up pieces of asphalt that peppered his high-top black sneakers. He froze.

"I got sixteen more bullets," I announced. "That's two for each of you. OK, who's first?"

Homicide just glared at me, but the rest of them all dropped their bats and pipes, and fell over themselves trying to get away.

"C'mon, Homicide," one of his friends yelled. "Dig out."

"Just you and me, pal," I said. He slowly got back on the sidewalk, not taking his eyes off me. I climbed back in the truck, gave him a final Don't-fuck-with-me look, and got going again.

I had planned to park my Blazer in the Yard at headquarters, but it was full of commanders' unmarked cars and various huge blue-and-white command-post vehicles. A half dozen empty police buses were lined up along Market, ready to take cops to trouble spots and haul away the people who got arrested.

About twenty-five cops in riot gear were clustered in front of headquarters, and it struck me that they were actually guarding the building. I wondered if there had been some kind of attack the night before. This was not a good sign.

Across the street was another police lot, but that one was packed with more riot cops. They were drinking coffee and bullshitting, waiting to be sent to trouble spots. All the on-street parking was taken. I thought to myself, Here's a question you won't find in the Police Duty Manual: When you go to a riot, where do you park? I finally found a space three blocks from headquarters. I wondered what the chances were that my Blazer would be there when I got back, and as I walked away, I gave the truck a little goodbye pat on the hood.

Headquarters was in chaos. There were white shirts everywhere, inspectors, chief inspectors, and nobody looked like they knew what they were doing.

Except Sammy. He was at his desk in the operations room, working on papers spread out in front of him. He was keeping track of all the cops and police vehicles coming into the 20th, and he was working fast, efficiently. This was a brand-new Sammy—no TV shows today.

I went down into the basement locker room and changed into my uniform. My regular gun was on the locker's top shelf, and I put it in my holster. Junior Vicente's gun went into the locker. If I was going to have to shoot anybody today, it was going to be with an official police weapon.

As I came back upstairs, Nick walked up to me. He was wearing his uniform, smiling, betraying no sign that he was the guy responsible for the city burning down.

"Hey, Eddie," he said.

"What the fuck have you been doing, Nick?"

He stepped back. "What do you mean?"

Some cops I didn't know were standing nearby, and they looked up at us. I grabbed Nick's arm and escorted him out the door. As soon as we were in the Yard, I wheeled on him.

"What the fuck do you think I mean?"

"Eddie, did Michelle find out what happened to Steve?"

"As a matter of fact, she did. Bravelli told her everything. By the way, did you cantaloupe Barney Stiller just for the fun of it?"

"Barney Stiller? That wasn't me, Eddie, I swear to God."

"How about those store owners on Fifty-second? Not you, either, right?"

"No, I swear to God. Did Michelle really find out?"

"No. I mean, yeah, she did."

"Bravelli really told her everything?"

"Yeah, everything. Why?"

"So what are you gonna do?"

"About you smashing the heads of everybody in West Philadelphia?"

"No, about . . ." He had a very strange look—confusion, fear—and without a word turned away and quickly walked through the Yard toward the street.

"Nick," I called after him. "Where the fuck you think you're going?"

What was I going to have to do, chase him down and handcuff him right there? Sammy came out the door.

"Hey, Eddie, you need to be in the courtroom," he said. "Commissioner's gonna address the supervisors."

"The Commissioner? When did he get here?"

"Just now."

I didn't need this. I didn't need any of this.

"Nick," I called again. He had reached the sidewalk and was getting into his red Camaro. I started jogging over, and he jumped into his car.

"Nick!" I yelled.

As he pulled away from the curb, he turned and looked out the open window at me, and for an instant our eyes met. It was like he was telling me something with those eyes, but I had no idea what it was.

The courtroom was filled with sergeants, lieutenants, and captains. A couple of inspectors were talking to each other next to the judge's seat. Kirk came in and then the Commissioner—in full uniform—came in behind, putting on his police hat.

That motherfucker, I thought. He tries to kill me and then he just comes in here, like nothing ever happened. He thinks nobody can touch him, he can get away with anything, even killing another cop. I wanted to take out my gun and go up to him and say, OK, asshole, let's try this again.

As he stood in front of the gathered cops he looked at me, but it was like he had never seen me before in his life. I came close to asking him loudly—in front of everyone—why he had tried to kill me. But I knew he'd deny it, he'd act like he didn't know what I was talking about.

"Today and tonight are make-or-break for us," he said.

Great, I thought, he's giving us a fucking pep talk.

"Either we stop the riots now, or they get out of hand. Either we control the situation, or it controls us. Things are quiet now, at least relatively so, and this means we have a second chance. I don't think we'll get another."

The Commissioner announced that Kirk would be the new tactical commander, considering his knowledge of the district. I wondered whether that really was a good idea—after all, those weren't Klingons out there.

But it turned out the Commissioner knew what he was doing. When Kirk began handing out assignments, he spoke with a presence I hadn't seen before. He was taking command, which is what captains are supposed to do. Damn, I thought. First Sammy, now James T. We got to start having riots more often.

Kirk said the commanders had agreed to pull back most of the officers from 64th and Locust, the center of tension and the flashpoint of last night's riot. Instead of a hundred riot police, they wanted only about six of us at the intersection, cops who knew the community and could try to keep things calm.

Kirk assigned me to lead the detail, and he told me to pick the people I wanted. We were supposed to keep an open dialogue with the merchants and residents and anyone else around. Plenty of help would be available if we needed it, he said.

"No riot gear, just your vests worn underneath the shirt," said Kirk.

I almost asked him whether he'd beam us out if we got into trouble. But I was much more worried about the Commissioner than any rioters. He was ignoring me as hard as he could, and I wondered whether he was planning to cruise by 64th and take a potshot.

All the cops I wanted with me on the detail were on the street. I had Radio get their locations, and ordered a wagon to pick them up and take them to meet me at 64th and Locust.

I asked for Donna and Buster, of course, and Mutt. I also called in Marisol and Yvonne, I had seen them calm groups of people before, they were good at it.

I wondered where Michelle was. She had probably found out by now that her father was at 20th District headquarters, which meant that she would be on her way over.

As I headed to 64th Street in my patrol car, a voice came over Police Radio: "I'm sorry, Eddie."

It was Nick.

"Unit coming in?" the dispatcher asked.

"I'm not a unit," said Nick.

Fuck this, I thought, I'm going to lock Nick up right now. Sixty-fourth Street will have to wait.

I picked up the microphone on my car radio. "This is Eddie, where are you, Nick?" I asked.

"It's dark in here, nice and dark."

Dark? He's at the crackhouse. I took a quick left at 54th and headed for Tyler Street.

Nick hadn't said anything for a few minutes, and the dispatcher had resumed the normal run of calls.

Then Nick came on again.

"Pop, I'm sorry."

A Radio Room supervisor got on the air.

"Anyone using Police Radio in an unauthorized manner is in viola-tion of section five-point-eight of the Police Duty Manual . . ."

"Steve, I'm sorry."

". . . and is subject to immediate dismissal."

I had a foreboding, a strange sense that something else was going on here. I couldn't get a hold on it, though, it was like trying to remember a fading dream that just slips through your mind like sand.

I pulled up in front of the house, there was Nick's Camaro. I grabbed my long metal flashlight, and got out and walked toward the house. The front windows were still covered with plywood, though they were now spray-painted with graffiti gibberish. When I got to the porch, I could see that the door was slightly ajar.

"Nick," I called. "Nick, you in there?"

I flicked on the flashlight and used it to push the door open a few inches. I couldn't see much, so I pushed the door harder, and as it swung open, Nick was there, pointing his gun at my head.

"Stay away from me, Eddie," he said, his arm shaking. He looked like he was about to cry. There was something very weird about this.

"Let's go, Nick," I said.

"No, Eddie. I ain't goin' nowhere."

"You gonna shoot me, Nick?"

He glanced at the gun, but kept it pointed at me.

"I didn't mean for it to happen the way it did, Eddie. I didn't mean for anything to happen to Steve."

"What're you talkin' about, Nick?"

"I had to do it, Eddie, I had to. Did Bravelli tell Michelle that, did he tell her that?"

And then I knew: this is how Steve died. He opened the door and there was Nick. Just like this.

"Oh, my God," I whispered.

"I had to, Eddie, I told you. I'm sorry." And he put the gun to the side of his head.

"Nick . . ."

He looked at me, but I don't think he heard me, his eyes were locked onto mine but they were going dead. All I could think of was that he was my cousin, and I didn't want him to die. Don't do it, Nick, my eyes said to his eyes, don't do it. In my mind we were on the porch of my parents' house that Thanksgiving when I was the only person in the world that nine-year-old Nicky believed in. I could almost smell the turkey, about ready to be served, could almost hear the adults inside talking and laughing.

Nick's eyes were still on mine, and I could see something stir in that vast deadness. It's me, Nicky, it's me. Hey, after dinner I'll show you my *Playboy*s, you can brag about it to Chris and Matt. Remember that time you asked me why sex was such a big deal? You couldn't ask your brothers—you certainly couldn't ask your parents—so you came to me. Hey, Eddie, can I ask you something? Don't tell no one I asked. When the man . . . puts his . . . you know, and the woman . . . well, you know, why do they like it so much?

Do you remember what I told you? That one day you and a girl you liked at school would get together alone and you'd both take your clothes off and you'd get to find out, and it would be like opening the best Christmas present in the world.

And I said to you, That Christmas present is out there, Nicky, just waiting.

And you asked me if Santa was a girl, and we both laughed.

Remember?

"Eddie," Nick said, but he kept the gun at his head. The floor under his feet creaked as he shifted his weight.

Hey, Nick, remember about four years later, when you introduced me to this girl from your ninth-grade math class? You were buying her a water ice at Tina's. She was really pretty, a sweet-looking girl, I remember she had long black hair and a white blouse and she wouldn't let go of your arm. You said, Yo, Eddie, I want you to meet Santa.

Suddenly the deadness disappeared from Nick's eyes, and there were a million emotions and thoughts, his whole life, I could see it, I could see it coming out, tremendous pain, anguish, unbearable, as if he had watched from outer space as the world destroyed itself in a nuclear war, watched as every human life was extinguished.

"Bye, Eddie."

"No, Nick . . ."

I stepped through the doorway and swung my flashlight at his upraised arm, as hard as I could, hearing the metal crack against bone. Nick's arm wrenched back, behind his head, but he still held on to the gun, and he tried again to put it to his head. I dropped the flashlight and grabbed his wrist with both hands, but he punched me in the jaw with his free hand, and I staggered back. I kept one hand on his wrist, and with the other punched him, and we both spun around and fell back onto the porch.

As we fell, I tried to bang his gun arm down on the wooden floor, hoping the gun would kick out of his hand, but he still held on tight. And then he ripped his arm free and I caught a glimpse of the gun rushing toward the side of my head. There was no pain—just a flash of light, then darkness.

TWENTY-FOUR

I awoke to Nick's voice. He was telling a story of some sort. At first, I couldn't get the train of what he was saying. Something about Chris and Matt and his father, something about working on a roof.

I was sitting on the crackhouse porch, facing away from the street, my back propped up against the porch railing. Nick was sitting across from me, leaning against the front of the house, his legs drawn up. His arms were on his knees, and his hands were clasped together in front. On the floorboard next to him was his gun.

I had a sense he had been talking for some time, that I had awakened earlier, had a conversation with him, and then had passed out again. I touched three fingers to my temple. It was wet, and there was a hell of a knot. I looked at my fingers—some blood, but not much. My head was pounding, but after a few seconds it eased up and settled into a dull headache.

Nick was talking about the day his father died, but the story seemed different now. He and his father were on the roof. His father told him he was going into business with Bravelli, and they argued.

"Nicky," I said.

He stopped, surprised at the interruption.

"What about Steve?"

He hesitated, and then continued his story like I had never even asked the question.

"I'm trying to get off the roof," he said. "I start to get on the ladder, and my father spins me around and grabs my shirt with both hands. I try pushing him away from me, but he holds on, yelling in my face. I don't remember all that he said, but it was stuff like I was an ungrateful son of a bitch, stuff like that."

Nick paused. "Your dad ever call you ungrateful?"

"Nick, what about Steve?"

"It don't feel too good, I'll tell you that."

"Are you going to tell me what happened to Steve?"

"I am tellin' you."

"You're talking about your father, the roof . . ."

"Eddie, all I'm tellin' you is to listen."

"Or what, you going to shoot yourself?"

"I don't know, Eddie. I thought I wanted to, but . . ."

He looked at me. "I just want you to understand, Eddie. That's why I'm tellin' you this."

I didn't say anything. He was back in his story, letting the images fill up his mind so that they had to come out. "My father is holding on to my shirt with both hands, yelling at me, and I grab his shoulders and jerk him away, make him break his grip. Then I yell back at him, 'I don't want to be a fuckin' roofer. I don't ever want to be a fuckin' roofer!' And then I push him away from me as hard as I can . . ."

He stopped talking, I didn't know why. How long had I been here? I glanced at my watch—almost noon. It had only been twenty minutes.

"I shouldn't have pushed him that hard, Eddie, I knew better. I thought he might catch himself but he falls over the edge, and I want to grab him back, I would have given anything to grab him back, but it's too late, he's too far away. Then I don't see him no more. I look over at Johnny and Ralph. They're just staring at me."

He paused again.

"I threw my father off the roof, Eddie. He didn't trip, he got thrown off."

I just looked at Nick, I didn't know what to say.

He gave a little laugh. "That's just the start of it. I come down the ladder and Bravelli bursts out the front door and says what the hell is going on. I don't say nothing. Part of me is thinking, I just killed my father. But part of me is also thinking, I'm free. Free. Then my mind just sort of shut off.

"I was sort of in a daze, I guess. Johnny and Ralph came down the ladder and told Bravelli I had thrown my father off the roof. Bravelli gets a funny look on his face and says he don't want no murder investigation at his house, and for everybody to say it was an accident. He tells Johnny and Ralph it was an accident, right, Mr. Bari just fell, right, and they look at me and then back at Bravelli and then they just sort of nod.

"I think Johnny says what about the neighbors who heard us arguing and Bravelli says he'll take care of the neighbors. Then Bravelli looks at me and says What kind of crazy fucker are you anyway? I don't say nothin.' I guess I'm crying, thinkin' of my father. Then Bravelli says, This was an accident, we're gonna make this look like an accident. You understand? I still don't say nothin', so now he yells it, "You understand?"

"Someone calls Fire Rescue, and they take my father away. Kenny Northrup and Linda Ramsey from Two Squad show up to make the report, I tell them it was an accident. So that's what they put down on the 48.

"My mom didn't say nothing, she just cried all the time. Chris and Matt wouldn't leave me alone. They kept asking, What happened, how could it happen?"

"Yeah, I remember that," I said. The night Uncle Jimmy died, all the relatives gathered over at the Bari house. In the kitchen, Chris and Matt got in a big fight with Nick, they blamed him for letting it happen. I didn't think it was fair, and I had stood up for Nick.

"I wanted to tell them the truth," Nick said, "but they would've never forgiven me, not in a million years. Mom probably would of died of a heart attack. Maybe I wouldn't go to jail, maybe they would give me manslaughter and I would get probation. But my family would never speak to me again. You remember when I left the house to go for a walk?"

"Yeah," I said. "You wouldn't let me come with you."

"I walked and walked, just trying to think of what to do. I had to make a decision. I figured if everybody thought it was an accident, then I would be the only one who knew, and maybe I could lead a normal life, you know what I mean? I might feel bad about it for a long time, but at least I would still have a family."

Nick looked at me. "I did think about telling the truth," he said. "That way I wouldn't have to hold it in no more and sooner or later everything would be OK. But, you know, that was too big a chance to take. So I decided to never tell no one, and I came back home."

Nick was silent, and I thought his story was over. Somehow what happened with his father didn't surprise me that much. Maybe I had suspected it all along, without really thinking about it.

"Nick. What about Steve?"

"I'm gettin' to that."

About a week after his father died, a couple of roofers, men who had known his father for years, stopped over at the house to see how his mother was doing. On the way out, one of them asked to talk to Nick, and took him out on the porch. The man said Mickey Bravelli wanted to see Nick, and to stop by Sagiliano's about nine.

Nick said he didn't like the idea of having to jump when an asshole like Bravelli said jump, but Bravelli knew the truth about his father, and Nick had to find out what he wanted.

"When I walked into Sagiliano's," said Nick, "someone came up and said 'This way,' and I followed him into a side room. Right before we go in, he says, 'You're gonna have to let me hold your gun.' I said fuck that, I ain't givin' up my gun. So he says, I can't let you go in. So I say, Fuck it, and I fuckin' leave, I just walked back outside. But I had to know what Bravelli wanted. So I went back in and gave this jerkoff my gun.

"OK, so I went into the back room and there's a few tables, but only one was being sat at, by Bravelli and Frankie Canaletto. Bravelli said to sit down and he asked me whether I wanted a beer. I said no, I don't want no beer.

"Bravelli told me he was sorry about my father and was I planning to take over the business. I said no, we were going to shut it down and sell the trucks and other equipment. Bravelli said that wouldn't be possible. I asked him why not. He said my father and him were partners, and now that my father was dead, he was the sole owner of the business. I just looked at him and I was thinking, what a fuckin' parasite.

"I said, 'You didn't give him no money,' And he says, 'Not yet, but we had an agreement, and an agreement is an agreement.' I said, 'Bullshit, that won't hold up in court.'

"So he says, 'This ain't going to fuckin' court. Nothing I ever do goes to court.'

"I told him my mother needed the money, and he said he don't fuckin' care. So I said, 'You motherfucker,' and I stood up and threw a punch at him. Canaletto caught my arm and twisted it back and then he punched me in the stomach. I kept my balance and I was getting ready to charge both of them when three guys who had been at the bar piled into the room. I couldn't fight all five.

"Bravelli says 'Sit down.' He was fuckin' ordering me. He says 'There's one more thing I want to tell you. About what happened to your father.' I sat back down. The three guys went back to the bar. Then Bravelli says, 'Just so you know, if you ever take a swing at me again, I'll fuckin' kill you.'

"So I said, 'Bullshit, even you wouldn't kill a cop.' Bravelli laughs and turns to Canaletto and they both fuckin' laugh. I couldn't see what was so fuckin' funny. Then the asshole says, 'I've decided we're going to have to tell the truth about your father.' He said he talked to Johnny and Ralph and told them to go to the police to say that I had thrown my father off the roof.

"I said, 'I thought you didn't want no investigation.'

"So Bravelli says, 'Somebody died at my mother's house, the police might still think it's me, maybe I had something to do with it. I figure, why should that be on me. You're the one who killed him. It should be on you.'

"I told him I wanted to keep that quiet, and he said, 'Oh, I'm sure you do. But I don't fuckin' care.' I hated to have to plead to this dirtbag, but I didn't have no choice.

"I told him that if this comes out, my family will never talk to me again, and I might as well just leave town and never come back. So he says 'You'd do anything to keep it quiet, right?'

"That's when I knew he was fuckin' setting me up, Eddie. The whole thing was a fuckin' setup. I asked him what he wanted. He smiled, like, Now we can get down to business.

"He asked me about Steve. Did I know Steve Ryder. I said yeah I know him, he's my partner. Bravelli says, 'We got a problem with this Steve Ryder. We want you to take care of him.'

Nick's story had finally led to Steve. And then I realized, this is all one story. It's all connected.

Nick said he asked Bravelli what kind of problem it was. Bravelli told him it wasn't any of his business. "I said to Bravelli, 'What do you mean, take care of him?' He said, 'You know,' and he held his hand like it was a gun, and he pointed it at me, and he went 'Pow.' I told him he was fuckin' crazy if he thought I was going to kill another cop. So Bravelli says 'If you take care of this Ryder, I'll do you a favor. I'll personally guarantee no one will ever know that you were the one that fuckin' killed your father. You won't have to get run out of town, you can stay a cop, you can have a nice Christmas with your family.'

"I hadn't drunk no beer, but I felt like I had. Then Bravelli says he'll do me another favor. He'll give me my father's business, free and clear. I said, 'That ain't your fuckin' business to begin with,' and he said, 'We went through that already, Nick. What I want is mine. What I don't want, isn't mine. It's as simple as that.'

"That fuckin' asshole, I looked at him, and he just looked back, like he already knew what I was going to do, and was just waiting, patient, for me to tell him. I looked over at Canaletto. He was drinking a beer, he was actin' like he was bored. And then a sort of funny thing happened, it's hard to explain it. I actually thought for a moment of what it would be like to kill Steve. And as soon as I thought it I knew I could do it. You know what I mean?

"In my mind I pictured driving with Steve to Dogshit Park or somewhere and then us getting out of a car and me just shooting him. But then what? How could I make it look like someone else did it?"

Nick paused to see how I'd react. And I must have had a strange expression on my face, because he said, "Yeah, that's what I was thinkin', too. Here I am not worried about killing Steve, I'm worried about gettin' away with it. And Bravelli, he's lookin' at me like he knows exactly what I'm thinkin'. It was weird, Eddie. But then I caught myself. What the fuck am I thinkin'? I can't kill Steve.

"So I decide that maybe Bravelli's bluffing about having everyone tell the truth about my father, you know, it's all bullshit. At least I have to give it a shot. So I stand up and push my chair back and say I ain't killing nobody. Do what you got to do.

"So now Bravelli turns to Canaletto and says, 'Yo, Frankie, go ahead and get 'em now.' I looked at Bravelli. What was he going to do, get someone to kill me right there? I thought, Fuck him. So Canaletto gets up and walks out of the room, and about a minute later he comes back with Johnny and Ralph. They both look pretty nervous. Bravelli says, 'I just been telling Nick here what we're all gonna have to do. I just want everybody to know, so there won't be no hard feelings. You guys tell Nick what you're going to do tomorrow morning. Go ahead.'

"Johnny shrugs his shoulders and says, 'Me and Ralph are going down to Police Headquarters and telling them what happened. Sorry, Nick.' He didn't want to look me in the eye.

"Bravelli says, 'You made arrangements to meet with a detective, right?' and Johnny says, 'Yeah, Detective Zabrou.'

Zabrou was in Homicide.

"Bravelli tells Johnny and Ralph to leave and then just stares at me. I know he's trying to force me into a decision. I'm thinkin' as fast as I can. I say what happens when the police ask Johnny and Ralph why they didn't tell the truth to begin with?

"Bravelli says, 'They'll just say they were scared to come forward. Same as the neighbors. One old guy across the street says he was looking out his window when you threw your father off the roof. He'll be a good witness.' The guy was probably on the other side of town at the time.

"Anyway, Bravelli doesn't say nothin' for a while, and then he says, 'You might be thinking I won't go through with this. But people who know me know that I don't say I'll do something and then not do it. That gets you a reputation. I don't fuckin' bluff.'

"I told him I needed some time to think about it. He said Johnny and Ralph would be going to the cops in the morning, so I didn't have much time. And he told me I wouldn't be able to call him up in the middle of the night with an answer.

"He says, 'You got to make a decision now, Nick. That's the way it has to be. Either way, I don't give a fuck.' I asked him again why he wanted to kill Steve, and he says, 'That's none of your fucking business. What's your decision? You want your family or not?'

"So I'm standing there and Bravelli keeps asking me what's my decision, he don't got all night. I'm thinking that sometimes the world works the way the world works. There ain't nothing you can do about it.

"I asked him what happens if I get caught. When I said that, he relaxed, like he had fuckin' won. He told me I wouldn't get caught. I was the only one who could get close to Steve, that's why they wanted me to do it. I told him he still had to tell me what he had against Steve. I told him I had to know. Bravelli thinks about that for a while, and then he says, 'He crossed us, OK? He said he would do something, and then he didn't do it.'

"I said to Bravelli, 'Steve was really working for you?' And he says, 'Look at it this way, Nick—you'd just be taking out a bad guy. That's what you do every day, fight bad guys, right?' So I don't know, Eddie, maybe that did make it a little easier."

Nick paused and looked at me, asking with his eyes whether I understood. I didn't understand at all, it was beyond understanding. It was sad, though, how Nick had been so willing to believe that Steve was dirty. But so had Michelle, and so had I, without much evidence.

Nick was continuing his story. He said that once he had agreed to kill Steve, he stopped worrying about whether to do it, and started thinking about *how* to do it. He decided the best place would be the crackhouse, because it would be easy to make it look like a drug dealer did the shooting.

He got Bravelli to send a couple of his guys by the house that night and clear out the druggies who lived there. Then he had someone call 911 and say there was a woman screaming in the house. Nick knew the dispatcher would send him and Steve to check it out, and since they were two-man, there wouldn't be a need for a backup car. So, as usual, Steve goes to the front door, and Nick goes around back to wait for someone to run out.

But this time, Nick doesn't wait—he comes through the unlocked back door, through the kitchen, into the living room, and when Steve bangs on the door, Nick is on the other side, waiting.

"I just stood there, Eddie. I heard Steve yell out, 'Police! Open up!' I was right on the other side of the door but it was like I was far away. I had sort of like turned off my mind before I even went into the house. It was like this wasn't really Steve banging on the door, and I wasn't really me. It was almost like I was playin' a video game, you know what I mean? It was like I was floating in the air, watching myself in the house, but I was also right there, because I had to be sharp to make sure I didn't do nothing wrong.

"I guess part of me is thinking, Steve and me are really somewhere else. This is happening, but it's not really happening. I saw a TV show one time about a kind of identical universe, you know, where everything is sort of the same, but different? When I was in the house with Steve it was kind of like that. This was what was happening in the other universe, and I was making it happen, but in some way it wasn't real. But I have to admit, something was telling me that if I went through with this, then my whole life would be switching to the other universe. Everybody else would be in the regular one but I would be in the new one, and there was no way I could ever get back. But I wasn't really thinking about that too much, because I knew if I did I would just chicken out, and also I was telling myself that I didn't really want to stay in the regular universe anyway.

"I knew Steve wouldn't hang around on the porch forever. They had said they would leave a .38 and some rubber gloves on a coffee table for me, and there they were. All that I had to do was open the door and shoot Steve. So I shut down my mind the rest of the way and put on the rubber gloves, and then I picked up the gun."

Nick paused, looked at me, then stared down at the porch, like that's who he was telling the story to.

"I pulled the door open with my left hand. When Steve saw me his mouth dropped open a little. I said to myself this isn't really Steve, it's just an image of him, and I said to myself NOW and I raised the gun and fired at his head. Steve just fell back, and for a second it was like my father dying all over again. The shot made less sound than I thought it would. It was just sort of a loud CRACK and that was it.

Nick was silent for a while, then he continued.

"I dropped the gun by the door and ran out of the back of the house. When I got outside, I yelled 'Steve!' and then I ran back through the house and looked out the front door, like I was seeing somebody run down the sidewalk. I tried to make myself see the person. Then I looked down at Steve. He was lying on the porch on his side and I could see the bullet hole in the side of his head. His eyes were closed. I said to myself, You are in the other universe now.

"Then I grabbed my radio and clicked the button and shouted, 'ASSIST, ASSIST.' I started to yell, Officer down but I realized I still had on the rubber gloves, I had to get them off me, I didn't want them on me anymore. So I clicked off the radio, and tore off the gloves and stuffed them in my pants pocket. Then I yelled into the radio, "Officer down! Officer down! 5-8-4-3 Tyler! Call Rescue!"

"I ran out onto the sidewalk, like I was looking for the shooter, and then I ran back onto the porch to wait for the first cars. I tried to keep my mind shut down. I tried to make myself believe someone else had killed Steve, not me. When everyone pulled up I sort of let my mind open up again, if you know what I mean, and I started thinking about how Steve was shot.

"I started getting really upset, because I didn't want him to get shot. Steve was a good guy, he was a good partner. He was lying there bleeding, a cop just like me was lying there bleeding. I didn't really think about that it was me who did it. I pushed that to the back of my mind. It was some other person that had shot Steve in cold blood and then just ran, it was a fuckin' crackhead. I start getting mad at this imaginary person, I'm thinking, I'm sorry I didn't kill that motherfucker when I had the chance. It was like I really did see him run away. Everybody figured it was a black guy, so I started thinking it was a black guy. I kept putting it out of my mind that I was the one that did it, I just pushed that aside because I knew it wouldn't do no good to think about it. I know it sounds weird, but I got something into my head about blacks. I was angry, I started taking my anger out on them. Like that kid at the protest march."

"And like store owners on Fifty-second," I said. "And Barney Stiller."

Nick looked genuinely surprised at the accusation. "I told you, Eddie, that wasn't me."

"Yeah, then who was it?"

"I don't know, Eddie, I just told you I killed two people. You think I'm gonna lie about beatin' somebody up?"

I shrugged. "So is that the end of your story, Nick?"

"Yeah, I guess. Except that I never heard from Bravelli after that, not a word. Johnny and Ralph, they never went to the police about my father. And you already know that me and my brothers sold all the trucks and equipment from my father's business and gave the money to my mother."

We were both silent for a long time. Now I knew why Nick wanted to kill Bravelli as much as I did, maybe even more. Bravelli held the key to his secret. And I knew why he kept coming to the crackhouse. He was trying to find the truth, his truth, here. Maybe he thought that if he came here he could change things.

Nick examined his hands. I knew he was waiting for me to say something, waiting for my reaction, maybe waiting for me to give him absolution.

He wasn't going to get it. He had betrayed Steve, he had betrayed me, he had betrayed everyone. I had held my anger back while I was listening to the story, but now it was rising up in my chest, filling my lungs.

"Stand up, Nick," I said.

He obeyed, and as he did, I curled my right hand into a fist. I was going to leave him bloody.

"You stupid fucking asshole," I said. "How could you do that to Steve? How could you be so goddamn fucking stupid?"

He looked at me, waiting for my fist, knowing it was his due. But I was thinking, I'm the real asshole. How could I have not seen what was going on with Nick, that all this shit he was going through was really something deeper? I had been blind to it. Not just since Steve was killed, but even before. All the so-called guidance I had given him over the years was worthless. Steve was dead, Nick's own life was over.

He was looking at me
what was I really going to
stranger, someone who I h

And yet there he was, N
tion, and it wasn't somethi
wanted to kill Nick for wh
everything was going to be (

Nick saw how much I was
I still hesitated.

"It doesn't matter," he sai
don't really care no more. If
long's it gonna be before she te
might as well not ever see my ι ......ɹs again."

SCOTT FLANDER

278

in right now. Once word
Commissioner's son—
with the mob—the
commanders w
forget abou
"He
thin

"Nick," I said. "Bravelli nevει mentioned your name."

He looked up at me, confused.

"No one knew what you did," I said. "Not until now."

Nick seemed about to get upset, but then he just smiled softly. "It's OK, Eddie, I'm glad I told you. I wanted to for a long time."

"Ready to go?" I asked him.

He looked at me in surprise. "Where?"

"Where do you think?"

"You're going to take me in?"

"Nick, you just can't walk away."

"Why not? You're the only one who knows. You don't have to tell no one."

"I'm not going to do that, Nick."

"I don't want my mom to know, Eddie. I don't want my brothers to know."

"It's too late. We gotta go."

A call came over the radio.

"Twenty Command, is 20-C-Charlie on the air?" It was Kirk.

"This is 20-Charlie," I said.

"How many officers do you have with you right now?"

He thought I was already at 64th and Locust.

"They're all here," I said. I knew none of my guys would get on the air and rat me out. But it dawned on me that I couldn't take Nick

spread that it was a cop who killed the
nd that the Commissioner had been working
whole Police Department would short-circuit. The
uld forget about trying to stop another riot. They'd
the cops they had left in dangerous situations.

, Eddie," Nick said. "Maybe I could stay at your place tonight,
that'd be OK?"

Him saying that seemed almost funny, but I just felt sad. He's a
million miles from reality, he still doesn't understand that I'm going
to lock him up. But maybe that's the answer, I thought—I can take
Nick in later. He's not going anywhere.

"Yeah, Nicky, that's a good idea. Why don't you head over to my
house right now and wait for me. You know, watch TV, whatever. I
think there's some beer in the refrigerator."

"That sounds good."

"And you can sleep on the couch tonight."

"Can I?"

"Sure."

"Won't be too much trouble?"

"Not for you, Nick."

He looked at me gratefully, the same way he always had. His big
cousin Eddie. His hero.

"One thing, Nicky. You're not going to . . ."

"Shoot myself?"

"Yeah, you're not going to do it, are you?"

"No," he said, shaking his head slowly. "I think tellin' somebody
what happened was a good thing, Eddie. I'm glad it was you."

"So am I, Nick."

"I'm sorry for everything, Eddie. I'll make it up to you."

"All right, Nick."

"I mean it. I'll make it up to you."

I stepped off the porch and headed to my car. It was time to get
over to 64th Street.

TWENTY-FIVE

Sixty-fourth and Locust looked like a war zone. The burnt-out hulks of three vehicles—one of them a police car—clogged the intersection, and the streets were strewn with rocks and bricks and other debris. The dozen or so stores at the intersection had all been looted, the security gates torn apart, the glass display windows shattered, everything inside thrown about.

The cops I had asked for were all there waiting for me.

"What the hell happened last night?" I said, looking around the intersection.

Donna and Buster told me they had seen the whole thing. Barney Stiller had been leading an anti-police candlelight march through West Philadelphia, protesting the beatings on 52nd Street. When it reached this intersection, the marchers halted temporarily so Stiller could talk to some people in the crowd.

"You wouldn't believe it," said Buster. "Some cop comes out of nowhere and starts wailin' on him."

Buster demonstrated the cop's technique, waving his left arm like a conductor furiously leading an orchestra, except instead of a baton swinging through the air it was supposed to be a nightstick playing paddywhack on Barney Stiller's head.

"Who was the cop?" I asked.

"We couldn't see," said Donna. "Too far down the block."

Buster said that after the cop laid Stiller out on the pavement, he just vanished, and they never got a good look at his face. Meanwhile, the marchers started going crazy in anger. Only a few cops had been accompanying the march, and the situation quickly got out of control. Donna and Buster called for backup, but the new cops arriving on the scene couldn't restore order—all they could do was help get Donna and Buster and the others to safety.

"It was pretty hairy for a while," said Buster.

At least things were quiet now. The sky was bright blue, and the air was warm. For some reason I thought of softball—it was a perfect Sunday morning, it would have been great to play today. Then I remembered that we were actually on the schedule to play the 17th District this afternoon in Fairmount Park. Maybe we could have our game in the middle of 64th Street.

Store owners had been coming by all morning to take a look at their shops. Most just went into shock. An older black woman who owned a small dress shop was standing on the sidewalk out front, tears running down her smooth cheeks.

"Why'd they do this to me?" she asked, over and over. "Why would they do this to Miss Mae—I never hurt a soul."

Yvonne, who had grown up in the neighborhood, said she had known Miss Mae since she was a kid. She went over to comfort the woman.

The six of us didn't have much to do. We were scattered up and down Locust, talking with people in the neighborhood who wanted a firsthand look at the damage. A couple of TV crews came by and filmed the intersection, and of course they spotted Miss Mae and her tears, and they made sure they got it all on tape. The TV crews looked very proud of themselves, like they had actually done something. One crew filmed me talking with another store owner, and I remembered someone saying that if you gave them the finger on camera, they couldn't show it on TV. I almost did it, but they really didn't seem too interested in me and quickly moved on.

About one-thirty, Kirk drove by to see how things were going.

"We got a police tow truck coming to get these wrecks out of here," he said. "Commissioner wants Locust opened up again. You know, at least make things look like they're getting back to normal."

"Are they?" I asked.

"Shouldn't take too long to find out," he said, and pulled off. A few minutes later the tow truck arrived, with Dominic at the wheel.

"How come you're the only tow-truck driver I ever see?" I asked.

"It's because I'm *good*," he said, climbing out of the cab. He surveyed the burnt-out cars, and his shoulders slumped.

"Yo, Sarge," he said. "How'm I supposed to tow these? They ain't got no tires. We need a flatbed."

"Can't you just drag them out of the middle of the street?" I asked. "At least over to the curb?"

Dominic stuck his finger in his ear and wiggled it around, thinking. It was like he was trying to jump-start his brain.

"Yeah," he finally said. "I guess I could do that."

He climbed into the truck and backed it up to one of the cars. When it was still alive it had been a Chevy Cavalier, but now it was just a blackened skeleton. I left Dominic to his work, and walked down the block to talk to Donna and Buster.

A couple of minutes later, we heard some shouting, and turned to look. Dominic was arguing with two young black guys. We hustled over. One of them was Homicide. Buster saw his T-shirt and his eyes narrowed in anger.

"What the fuck do you want here?" I said to Homicide.

Under different circumstances, I would have locked him up right there for what he had tried to do to me that morning. But there were a lot of people around, and they would have assumed I was just pissed off at his T-shirt. I'd probably singlehandedly start another riot.

Homicide acted like he knew I wouldn't touch him. "You can't take these cars away," he said.

"You want to tell me why?"

"They're monuments to West Philly."

"Yeah," said the other guy, who was wearing a black Phillies T-shirt. "They represent our struggle."

I just laughed. "Get the fuck out of here."

Homicide looked at me and then at Buster, who was still staring at his T-shirt. I could see Buster was making him nervous.

"C'mon, let's go," he said to his friend. "Fuckin' cops."

When they were out of earshot, I said to Buster, "Thank you for restraining yourself."

"I was about to rip that T-shirt off and then beat the shit out of him."

"Yeah, I know, that's why I'm thanking you."

Dominic was able to get the first two cars over to the curb, and we opened 64th Street to traffic. But Locust was still blocked by the burnt-out police car—Dominic was having trouble hooking it up. I watched him for a moment, and then turned and almost crashed head-on into Michelle.

"Hi, Eddie. Have you seen my father?"

"Michelle, what are you doin' here?"

"I went to Police Headquarters, they said he was at the Twentieth. I went to the Twentieth, they said he was on his way over here."

Donna and Buster spotted Michelle and came up to talk to her, and pretty soon the others did, too. My eye caught a black Seville cruising slowly through the intersection. Was it Bravelli's? I wasn't sure. No, it had to be. What was he doing here?

There was some more yelling, and I turned to see about twenty young guys marching toward us down the center of Locust. Homicide was leading the way. Who was he, a little Adolf Hitler? I got on the radio and told the other cops to rejoin me. Kirk immediately came on the air and asked whether there was trouble.

"Not yet," I said. "I'll keep you posted."

The group came up and started yelling at Dominic not to take away the police car. I told Michelle to wait over by Miss Mae's, and then I had my cops form a semicircle around the car. Dominic had finally got it hooked up, and was just getting ready to lift the front off the ground. He looked pretty nervous.

"Don't worry about them," I said. "You're doing fine."

"Maybe I should just leave it here," he said. "Why don't I just unhook it."

"You're doing fine," I said.

The shouting was attracting attention, and more and more young guys were collecting on the street. Buster came over to me, and said in a low voice, "This is how it began last night, Sarge."

I knew that if I called for help, the block would be swarming with cops. Maybe we'd be able to lock up people fast enough to keep things from getting out of hand. But it could also start another riot.

Four or five older black men, all with graying hair, came up and wanted to know what was going on. The neighborhood's old heads.

"Well," I explained, "Mr. Good-cop-is-a-dead-cop here doesn't want us to take this police car away."

"Why the hell not?" asked one of the men, who was tall and imposing, with a beard that made him look like a black Abraham Lincoln.

"It's our monument," said Homicide. "These racist cops are trying to take away our monument."

"Bullcrap," said Abraham Lincoln. He turned to me. "Officer, we don't want this thing in our street." The other men with him agreed.

Then the younger guys started yelling at the older men and we had to step between them to keep them apart. I caught a glimpse of the Seville passing by Locust again, but I couldn't pay attention to it for long. There was shouting coming from the other direction, on the back fringe of the crowd. Something was happening halfway down the block, and the crowd started sweeping back in that direction.

Buster stood on his tiptoes. "Looks like they're chasing someone."

"Dominic," I said. "Get in your truck and stay there. Don't move the car, don't move anything."

"You got it, Sarge," he said, and gratefully hopped in and slammed the door shut. I ran down the street toward the action, my cops behind me. We came upon a young black guy kneeling on the street, blood pouring from a gash on the top of his head. A woman trying to help him saw us and shouted angrily, "See what you've done."

In the middle of the block, the crowd had gathered thick around someone. They were keeping their distance from him, but slowly swirling. Everything was in motion. We tried to get through, but we couldn't get a clear look.

"It's the cop that beat Councilman Stiller last night!" a woman yelled. "I saw him with my own eyes."

"Kill the motherfucker!" someone else shouted.

Nick, I thought. Have they got Nick?

We finally pushed our way into the middle of the crowd. It wasn't

Nick at all, it was Goop—in a cop's uniform, using a nightstick to swat his attackers away like flies.

So Nick had been telling the truth. And if Goop was the "cop" who had cracked open Stiller's head, that meant he was probably also the one who had beaten the store owners on 52nd. Bravelli had said he'd like to see riots. He was certainly doing his best to make them happen.

I turned to my cops and yelled, "Lock this asshole up."

As the six of us moved forward, surrounding Goop, someone yelled, "Let's get us some cops."

The crowd was out for blood. I turned to face them, and pointed at Goop. "He's not a cop," I yelled.

The crowd was stunned into near silence.

"What?" someone finally said. "What, you think we're stupid, motherfucker?" Others took up the cry.

"He's with Mickey Bravelli," I said. They all knew who Bravelli was, and there was silence again. I took advantage of it.

"He started the riot last night. He's trying to get another one started now."

Someone behind gave me a hard shove. "You lyin' cop motherfucker!"

Goop was half raising his club at us, he didn't know what to do. He didn't have a gun, he didn't even have a gunbelt. He looked like a fucking idiot. Donna circled around behind him and pulled her gun out, but kept it discreetly at her side, pointed at the ground.

"All cops carry police ID," I yelled to the crowd. "Let's see if he has it."

The crowd wasn't ready to start believing me, and people were yelling, "You're lying to us, you're fuckin' lying."

I turned to Goop and said, loud enough for everyone to hear, "Let's see your ID."

"I don't have it with me," he snarled.

"See," I said, turning to the crowd. "He's not a real cop."

Homicide had pushed his way to the front of the circle, and now his eyes were full of hate. "All you fuckin' cops are evil," he yelled.

"We don't give a fuck. This one's real, that one's fake, we gonna fuck you all up."

"But that's wrong," came this booming voice, and there was Abraham Lincoln, suddenly towering over Homicide. I was hoping he was coming to free the slaves, which in this case was me and my cops. The old man looked down at Homicide and yelled, "You know that ain't justice."

"Fuck that, we're gonna make our own justice," yelled Homicide, and the crowd cheered. It didn't look like Lincoln was going to free anyone today.

I turned to Goop and took out my handcuffs. "You're locked up," I said, but an instant later a bottle thunked off my shoulder, it hurt like hell. Now the crowd was shoving all six of us, pushing from all directions, and I didn't see Abraham Lincoln anymore. A brick was hurtling through the air at Buster, I yelled and he saw it and jumped out of the way. Mutt and Yvonne and Marisol were together, nightsticks out, with Mutt in the middle, and they were forming a wedge to protect themselves from the crowd. I glanced over at Donna, she was still half holding her gun on Goop. I keyed my radio.

"I got a priority, this is 20-C-Charlie, my squad is under assault at Sixty-fourth and Locust. I need a very big assist, very quickly."

As the crowd moved and shifted around us, a momentary hole formed, and I could see the tow truck a half block away. The Seville was stopped next to it—I caught a glimpse of Michelle and two men . . . Canaletto and . . . it was Bravelli. They were leading Michelle into the car. Goop was just a diversion, I realized. They wanted Michelle.

And then the hole in the crowd closed back up again, like in a dream. I tried to push through the crowd, but there were too many people, too many angry faces. I keyed the mike clipped onto my shoulder.

"This is 20-C-Charlie, we need to apprehend a black Seville—"

A huge black guy reached down and yanked the radio from my belt, and started to take off. I still had the mike in my hand, and as the guy ran, the coiled cord to the radio simply popped out.

"What's the car wanted for?" I heard the dispatcher ask as the guy disappeared into the crowd with my radio. There I was, just holding the mike with a cord leading to nowhere.

Something hard hit my forehead and I went down on one knee, and there was blood streaming down my face. As I got to my feet, the crowd swarmed around me.

"Buster!" I yelled. "Buster, Donna!" But they were fighting with the crowd themselves, they couldn't help me. Faces were closing in, and now I couldn't see the others at all. Someone grabbed at my gun. I swung around with my stick and whacked at an arm, and there was a yell and the arm disappeared. Something else hit my head, and white lights were popping in front of my eyes. I fought to keep my balance, but all I saw were hands and arms, and faces filled with hate. I felt a tugging at my gun again, and again I swung my stick around. But this time hands grabbed the stick, freezing it. I twisted and turned like a hooked fish, but the crowd was all around me now, closing tightly, and I was trying to hold on to my stick with one hand, trying to keep my gun in the holster with the other, trying to keep from going down. I was hit again, and I turned and caught a glimpse of Donna, wrestling with Goop. Goop was getting her gun away from her, oh my God, I had to get there to help. But arms and fists kept coming from all over, and my gun was being pulled from the holster. I dropped my stick and grabbed the gun with both hands, pushing it back into the holster, and then there was a BOOM! from a few feet away and I was suddenly free, the crowd was pulling back.

Donna was lying face up on the ground, motionless, blood coming from somewhere in the back of her head. Goop was standing there with her gun in his hand, and he looked at Buster, who was just staring down at Donna, paralyzed.

"I ain't never killed a cop before," Goop said. He seemed proud of himself. And then he aimed the gun at Buster's head.

I had my own gun out now and I raised it and ran toward Goop, firing. BLAM, my first shot knocked him back, but he still stood there. BLAM, he jerked again and looked at me. BLAM, now he was falling backward, his eyes closing, the gun dropping from his hand.

SCOTT FLANDER

288

another, and another. Th...
way, No one in th...
...were sting...

I turned toward Donna, shaking her and calling her na... Her eyes were open in a vacant s... and I could hear people saying, "It

Police cars were screaming up to t... were jumping out. The cavalry was co... just a little too fucking late. There was s... I put my hands up, it was the blood, I had

I put my gun back in my holster and took crowd. They backed up a little. Maybe it was th... ...ace, maybe it was the fury in my eyes, they didn't know... ...nake of me, they didn't know what to expect.

"Is this what you fucking wanted?" I yelled at them. "Is this what you fucking wanted, a cop dead?"

No one answered. They just stared at the two bodies.

I kept yelling. "You take the law into your own hands, this is what fucking happens. You wanted blood, you got your fucking blood."

Homicide's tough-dude mask was gone.

"I told you that wasn't a real cop," I shouted. "And you didn't fucking believe me."

I was yelling so loud I could feel myself getting hoarse. "I hope you all are happy. I really hope you all are so fucking happy you're going to go home and laugh about how you fucking killed a cop."

"Hey, man," Homicide said. "We didn't mean for it to be no lady cop."

"Well, that's too fucking bad, isn't it?"

My foot hit an empty Diet Pepsi bottle, and I picked it up and threw it at the crowd. They parted, and watched as the bottle hit the pavement and shattered. I picked up a half brick and heaved it, and again the crowd parted, and it hit the street and bounced away harmlessly. More cops were pulling up, they didn't know what the hell was going on. Buster was still kneeling next to Donna, touching her hair softly, like she was just sleeping.

The street was littered with chunks of brick from the night before, and I picked up another one and threw it at the crowd, and then

they didn't move back, they just got out of the
the crowd protested, they didn't fight back. My eyes
from the blood, and I wiped it away with my arm.
vonne was at my side. "C'mon, Sarge," she said.

I pushed her away and found another brick, but now Yvonne and
Marisol and Mutt were stepping in front of me, surrounding me, trying
to move me away from the crowd.

And then I remembered Michelle. Pictures started coming up in
my mind, of her being beaten, her clothes being stripped off, someone
putting a pistol to the back of her head. I was frozen with guilt for
forgetting about her. How could I have forgotten her?

I told Mutt to give me his mike, and he unclipped it from his
shoulder and handed it to me. How much should I say over the air?
I gave a description of the Seville, and said it was wanted for a kidnap-
ping. I didn't say who was kidnapped.

I gave the mike back to Mutt, and started jogging toward my patrol
car. The Seville had to be in Westmount, that's where they had to be
taking her. I ran around the corner, my car was blocked in by the
police cars that had come in for the assist.

By now the street was filled with cops in riot gear. The police buses
had arrived, and cops were pouring out of them in all directions. The
crowd was melting away, disappearing. They had no stomach for this
anymore.

I needed a car. I spotted Kirk's Plymouth parked down the street,
it wasn't blocked in. I ran back to Locust, and found Kirk standing next
to Donna's body. Someone was covering it with a yellow plastic sheet.

"Captain," I said, coming up to him. "I need your keys."

"Where you goin'?"

I told him what had happened, about Goop and Donna, about the
Seville taking Michelle away. He listened and then told me I couldn't
leave the scene. He wasn't going to give me his keys.

"We got a dead cop here," he said. "And you just killed someone.
You can't leave. You're just going to have to let other people look for
the Seville."

An inspector came up, and Kirk turned to talk with him, and I
just walked away. Fuck if I was going to stay, I'd walk to Westmount

if I had to. I headed back again to the corner, maybe I could grab the car of someone coming in.

"Hey, Eddie," I heard someone call. It was Nick, still in uniform, walking toward me. Where the hell did he suddenly come from?

"I thought you were going to my house, Nick."

"I was, but I heard about Donna on my radio. And who got kidnapped?"

"Michelle. Bravelli came by here and just scooped her up."

"Oh, man. Let me help you find her."

"I don't have time for this, Nick." I started to walk away from him, then turned. "Wait, how'd you get here?"

"My Camaro."

"Are you blocked in?"

"No, not at all."

"Give me your keys."

"Why?"

"Just give me your keys."

"You gonna go find Michelle?"

"Nick, just give me your keys."

"I'm goin' with you. I'll drive."

"You're not going with me, Nick."

"I am, Eddie," he said, and something came into his eyes, not the usual weakness, but a strength that surprised me. I knew he wouldn't give me the keys. I had no choice.

"All right," I said. "Let's go."

Nick and I found the Seville ten minutes later a half block from Sagiliano's. I pulled open the car's back door and took a close look at the seat. No blood, no clumps of hair, no spilled items from a purse. Maybe Michelle was OK.

I looked around—they could have gone anywhere. After all, this was Bravelli's turf. But the bar was right here. That's where they had to be.

"You think they're in Sagiliano's?" Nick asked.

"Yeah."

"I'll go with you."

I wanted to say no, but how was I going to get rid of him? I stood there and looked at Sagiliano's, trying to decide what to do. The door of the bar opened, and Michelle came out, alone.

"Michelle!" I called. She glanced over her shoulder, at the door to Sagiliano's, then ran to meet us.

"You OK?" I asked.

"Yeah, I'm fine. He was going to kill me, Eddie, he really was." She was shaking. "Can we get away from here?"

"Sure, sure," I said, and the three of us walked quickly to the far end of the block. I kept my eye on Sagiliano's front door, though. I wasn't going to let Bravelli just walk out.

"What happened?" I asked.

"They grabbed me on Locust, they threw me in the car—Mickey kept yelling he was going to kill me, he was going to cut my throat, he was going to shoot me a hundred times, he couldn't wait to do it. Then I got dragged into the bar, into a back room. Mickey sat me down at a table, and he just pointed his gun right at my head, Eddie."

She broke off and took a deep breath.

"He said to me, 'You were the one girl, Lisa, or whatever the fuck your name is. You were the one girl. I was going to marry you, you know that? Now I have to make you dead.' I thought that was it, Eddie. I thought I was going to die right there."

She shook her head. "Damn, I wish I still smoked. You got a cigarette?"

I shook my head. When she looked at Nick, he shook his, too.

"I had to figure out what to do," she said. "So I asked Mickey, Why were you going to marry me? And he said he didn't know, it was a stupid idea. So I told him I knew why."

"What'd you say?"

Michelle looked at me. "You don't want to hear this."

"Yes I do."

"All right. I told him I was the only person who cared about the real Mickey Bravelli, the one nobody else knew. And I said whether I've been trying to find out about my brother, or whatever I've been doing, it didn't make any difference. I was still the only person. And I told him he knew it."

"What'd he do?"

"He didn't do anything. But I just stood up, and I said, 'I'm leaving now, Mickey.' And I walked out. He was pointing the gun at me the whole time, I thought he was going to shoot me. I think *he* thought he was going to shoot me. But he didn't. He just . . ."

She stopped short—the Commissioner was pulling up to the curb on the opposite side of the street in his black Blazer. He got out, and called to Michelle, "Are you OK, honey? Are you hurt?"

"I'm fine," she called back. "I'll be right there."

Michelle glanced back at Sagiliano's. "You going inside?"

"What do you think?"

She nodded. "Just be careful." She stepped off the curb and headed across the empty street toward her father. They hugged and he said something to her, and as she walked around to the passenger side to get in, she gave me a quick wave goodbye. The Commissioner got behind the wheel and closed the door, and the Blazer pulled away. He hadn't even acknowledged my existence.

I turned to Nick. He was looking at me expectantly—he was ready to go with me into Sagiliano's. What was I going to do, handcuff him to a pole? It was strange, before Steve's death, before things got so crazy, Nick was the one person I would have most wanted in a situation like this. He was the one person I knew who would never cut out on me.

I should have called for an assist, I knew that. I should have waited for an army of cops before going into Sagiliano's. But I wasn't going to wait. It really wasn't a matter of wanting to or not wanting to, it wasn't a matter of choice. There was a freight train coming down the tracks, and nothing was going to stop it.

TWENTY-SIX

You ready?" I asked Nick.

"You mean it?" He thought I was playing games with him, punishing him in some way.

"Yeah, I do. I need you."

He smiled, immensely happy. He was almost glowing.

"I won't let you down, Eddie. I promise."

We drew our guns and walked up to Sagiliano's front door. I looked at Nick. He nodded.

I pushed open the door and took four big steps in, my gun leveled, its barrel searching for Bravelli and Canaletto. There were six or seven men sitting at the bar, drinking their bottles of Bud and Miller. None of them were in Bravelli's crew, they were just drunks, no threat to us. A couple of them glanced at us, but no one showed even a hint of surprise. You could tell they were getting ready to say they hadn't seen nobody, and didn't know nothin' about nothin'. The bartender just pretended we weren't there.

Nick looked at me with a half smile, like, Could they make it any more obvious?

The bartender lifted up the hinged counter to get out, but I was right there and I jerked it back down, giving him a look that said, You ain't going nowhere, pal.

The booths in the back were empty. Nick silently pointed to an archway on the right side. Up a couple of steps was a closed wooden door. That must have been where Nick was taken to see Bravelli that night. As we moved toward the door, it opened, and Canaletto—not seeing us at first—started to walk out. But then he spotted us and his eyes got wide, and he jumped back into the room and slammed the door.

I pointed the gun at the bartender's head. "How many people are in that room?" I asked.

"Two." He didn't even hesitate, he didn't even try to be a tough guy.

I kept the gun aimed at his head. "Does that room have another exit?"

"No, this is the only way out."

"Thank you," I said, and lowered the gun, and then the door burst open and Canaletto and Bravelli sprung from it and slammed into us, sending us sprawling onto the barroom floor. What was this, a new mob tactic, did they teach it to everyone in mob school or something? They had guns out and I expected them to shoot us right there, but instead they both sprinted toward the back, into the hallway that led to the alley door.

As Nick and I were getting back on our feet, a metal barstool crashed down on the floor next to us. I looked at the bar, someone had actually thrown the stool across the room at us.

Then another one was coming through the air, and another, they were being launched like missiles, smashing into tables next to us. One barely missed Nick's head, another bounced off a wall and hit my shoulder. This was worse than Locust Street. We followed the path Bravelli and Canaletto had taken—through the hallway to the back door, and then we were outside.

Not far to our left, the alley opened out onto the street. Maybe they had run that way. I motioned for Nick to stay where he was, and I ran over and looked up and down the sidewalk. Nothing. They might have already disappeared around a corner, but I didn't think so—we weren't that far behind them. Which meant they were still in the alley, hiding in one of the countless doorways or behind the clutter of Dumpsters and empty cardboard boxes.

Instead of rejoining Nick, I ran to the other side of the alley, so that I was directly across from him. It would give us a better angle.

A Blazer was passing by on the street, it was the Commissioner. Michelle wasn't in the front seat anymore. The Commissioner saw us, saw us looking, and kept going. I couldn't worry about him now.

I nodded to Nick—let's do it. I would have liked some more help, but I didn't have a radio. I looked at Nick's belt—he didn't have one, either.

"Nick, what happened to your radio?" I called in a low voice.

He thought for a moment. "I must have left it in my car. Should I go back and get it?"

"There's no time," I said. "Either we do this or we don't."

Nick gave me a confident smile. The old Nick. "We can do it," he called.

I nodded, I felt the same way. And so we started silently working our way down the alley, holding our guns ahead of us.

And I was thinking, here I am, chasing a couple of scumbags down an alley. I've done this a million times before—going after muggers, purse-snatchers, shoplifters, burglars. This is the same thing, except now the scumbags happen to be Bravelli and Canaletto. It felt good, being so sure about what I was doing. It was like I had been a fish out of water, and for a long time I had been flopping around, gasping for breath. Now I had flipped back into the water, and I was swimming around, big smile on my fish face. And then I thought, North, you asshole, you're about to get killed, and all you can think about is that you're a fucking fish.

Where the hell were Bravelli and Canaletto? They had to still be in the alley. Maybe they had knocked on a door, got let in to the back of a store. But it was Sunday, all the stores were closed. Besides, they hadn't been in the alley that long—it would have taken a while for someone to answer a knock, we would have seen something. No, the motherfuckers were here. I glanced up and realized I was directly below Doc's secret lookout. Too bad he wasn't there now to help us.

We moved quickly, staying low, and almost before we realized it, we were halfway through the alley. Could they really have run this far? I glanced back the way we had come. Had we gone past them, missed them in a doorway? There were a lot of nooks and crannies. Nick was still directly across the alley from me, fifteen feet away. We were both crouched behind Dumpsters. He looked at me, I knew he was thinking the same thing—maybe we had gone too far. If they were behind us now, we'd be easy targets.

Forward or backward, Nick asked with his gun hand. I pointed my gun hand toward the alley ahead of us. As I stood up from behind my Dumpster I heard a sharp crack, and at the same instant a sledgehammer pounded into my chest, and I was flat on my back, looking up at rain gutters and blue sky. I couldn't breathe, it was like my whole chest was paralyzed. I've been shot, I thought, Jesus, I've been shot. I tried to draw in a breath but I couldn't do it, I was running out of oxygen. I put my hand on my chest. I felt the tear in my shirt, and through it the torn nylon of my vest, and my fingers felt the slug, still hot, embedded in the vest.

I turned my head toward Nick, he was looking at me in panic. I wanted to tell him just stay where he was, but he jumped out in the open, toward me, and there was another crack, and he spun around and fell back against the wall. I tried to yell, but I couldn't.

There was another shot, and pieces of concrete sprayed my face. I tried to look down the alley, and I thought, shit, I'm laying half out in the open. I drew in a breath and felt a sharp pain. I had to get back behind the Dumpster, out of the way. I turned on my side and raised myself up on one elbow, and I saw Canaletto step from a doorway. My hands were empty—where was my gun? I felt around behind me on the sidewalk, nothing, just broken glass. Canaletto was calmly walking toward me.

I pushed myself up so that I was half sitting now and I looked around and I still couldn't see my gun, where was it, where was my fucking gun? I turned my head and there was Canaletto, three steps away, his arms outstretched, the dark hole of his gun barrel staring at me, its empty eye asking, Are you ready? And I thought of Michelle. It was too bad I wouldn't get the chance to spend more time with her, I would have liked that.

I looked at Canaletto and tried to say "Fuck you," but I could only mouth the words and then he started to smile and then the side of his head burst open, and he looked at me as if to ask, What just happened? and then he fell straight back.

Nick was half standing, both hands holding his gun, still pointing it at the spot where Canaletto had been. Then there were two quick shots, and Nick's body jerked, and again he was thrown back against the wall, and now he was sitting up against it, like some drunk in an alley, there was blood pouring from his neck, and his shirt was turning dark red. Oh, my God, I thought, this can't be happening, Nick's going to die in this alley, we're both going to die in this fucking alley.

I had to get to Nick, I had to get over there to try to stop the bleeding. I tried to raise myself up and my hand slipped under the Dumpster and I felt my gun, I grabbed it. I got up on one knee, my chest was still killing me, but I was able to breathe now. I was getting my equilibrium. I touched the bullet in my vest again. It hadn't broken through the Kevlar, I could tell that. It hadn't pierced my skin.

A shot hit the metal by my head and ricocheted somewhere into the alley. Bravelli had to be close by. I edged back along the wall and stuck my head up over the Dumpster. There were some cardboard boxes piled high, and I peeked through a gap between the two top ones. There was a doorway, ten feet away. Had to be where he was.

I held my gun with both hands and aimed at the doorway. C'mon, motherfucker, I thought, c'mon out. There was movement in the doorway, and I saw Bravelli's head appear. I squeezed the trigger. The shot kicked into the bricks just past the doorway. Jesus, I had missed by three feet.

As I was thinking of what to do next, he suddenly came out of the doorway firing two shots at me, driving me down, and I heard his quick footsteps—he was running. By the time I was able to look for him again, he had disappeared. He had probably run only a short distance, to get better cover. But there were still doorways and Dumpsters all over the place, and now I had no idea where the fuck he was.

Nick was still sitting against the wall, hands at his sides, his eyes closed. I looked at his bloody blue police shirt, trying to tell whether his chest was moving at all. It was, he was definitely breathing.

"Nick," I yelled.

He opened his eyes and smiled at me.

"Hey, Eddie."

"Take it easy, Nicky, I'll get you help."

"I got him, didn't I?"

"Yeah, you did good, Nicky."

"Got that fuckin' asshole."

"Yeah, you got him, Nicky. You saved my ass."

"Told ya, Eddie. Told ya I'd make it up to ya." He smiled again.

"Just hang on, Nicky."

"It's OK, Eddie. Everything's OK now."

I needed to get him help right away. All these shots being fired, hadn't anyone heard and called the police? Sagiliano's was probably the only place on the alley with people inside today, and they certainly weren't going to get us help. But the shots were echoing into the air. People had to be hearing them.

I stood up and raised my gun over the Dumpster. I saw a flash from another doorway, on the other side of the alley, and the bullet hit somewhere, I didn't know where. I fired five shots at the doorway, and then three more as I sidestepped across the alley toward Nick. It was hard for me to move fast, but I was able to get behind Nick's Dumpster and kneel down. I could hear footsteps again, and I stood up and saw Bravelli's back and I fired four more shots. They all missed, and again he disappeared.

I turned back to Nick. His eyes had closed again. I grabbed his wrist and felt for his pulse. Nothing, I couldn't find it. One side of his neck was covered with blood, I could see a bullet hole. I put my fingers on the other side of his neck. No pulse.

I laid him down on the sidewalk and started to give him CPR, but when I pressed his chest, blood just came out of his neck. Got to get him help, I thought, got to get him help. But I knew it wouldn't make any difference. Nick was gone. All I could think of was, How am I going to tell Aunt Janet?

I checked my gun, pulling out the clip. Almost empty. I unsnapped the leather clip holder on my gun belt, pulled out a fresh clip, and snapped it into the gun. I had seventeen bullets, including the one in the chamber, and I wanted every one I could get.

How many rounds did Bravelli have left? I counted each shot he had fired. At least five. Six, if the one that had hit me was his. If he had a semiautomatic like mine, that meant he had at least ten left.

There had to be a way to get him. Each time I fired, I had driven him back. Maybe if I fired as I advanced, I could keep him pinned down.

It was worth a try. I came out from behind the Dumpster and started walking toward the doorway, firing as I went, BLAM, BLAM, BLAM. It was working—I was getting closer, and he couldn't fire back.

But something was happening, the pain in my chest was coming back, sharper now, each time I fired. I knew what it was: after the adrenaline had kicked in, I had been almost normal for a couple of minutes, like a football player who can stay on the field even after a serious injury. But now I was beginning to feel it, and with each shot the reverberation was like a mule-kick to my chest. And it was slowing me down.

I had to keep firing to keep Bravelli pinned, but I was going too slowly, I was going to run out of bullets before I got to him. There'd be no time to reload. I had to get there faster. Each time I pulled the trigger, I counted how many rounds I had left—eleven, ten, nine, eight, seven. I was still too far away. I'd never make it. It seemed like forever, the steady BLAM, BLAM, BLAM, I knew I was moving but I didn't seem to be getting any closer.

Still no sirens. A million shots and no one calls the police—what kind of neighborhood was this?

Six left, BLAM, five, BLAM, four, BLAM, three, BLAM, two, BLAM. Only one left. There was no way. I couldn't make it. I was dead.

Bravelli's gun flew out of the doorway, onto the pavement at my feet. What the fuck? Both his arms appeared around the corner. He was showing me he had nothing in his hands. I couldn't believe it, he was giving up. He stepped from the doorway, hands high in the air.

"OK, I fuckin' give up, OK? Don't fuckin' shoot, all right? Don't fuckin' shoot."

I glanced down on the pavement at his gun. Six-shot revolver. The asshole had run out of bullets. No wonder he was trying to get away. He stepped into the middle of the alley, hands in the air.

And I was thinking, If there was ever a time in the history of the world when a cop could get away with killing someone, this was it. No witnesses, just me and Bravelli, and Bravelli would be dead.

He had just murdered a cop, so I'd be the hero, I'd get all kinds of fucking medals. This was what I had dreamed about all along. Killing Bravelli and getting away with it, killing him because he deserved to be killed. There was still one bullet in my gun. That would be plenty.

Bravelli was starting to get uneasy. "Just lock me up, all right?" He put his hands behind his back. "Just put the cuffs on, I ain't going to give you no trouble."

Fuck the cuffs. If he went to trial, he'd come up with some "witnesses" who would say that he and Canaletto were just walking down the alley, minding their own business. And he would strut out of the courtroom and laugh in my face.

"I'm not going to let that happen," I said aloud.

Bravelli didn't know what I was talking about, but I could tell he was starting to get scared.

"Nobody's coming to help you," I said. "You're all alone."

"You can't shoot me, I surrender. You can't shoot an unarmed man. That ain't justice."

I aimed the gun at Bravelli's forehead. "Yeah? I'm gonna make my own justice."

Why did I say that? That's what Homicide had said, right before Donna was lying there dead with her eyes looking into nothing. I'm not that asshole, I thought, I'm not anything like that asshole. This isn't the same thing—this is real justice.

And then I thought of Nick, going through the world making his own justice, too. I remembered how we had both waited outside Lucky's for Bravelli, so much alike. Blood brothers. Now, it was almost as if it were Nick, not me, standing here, ready to put a bullet in Bravelli's head. I was getting everything mixed up.

Shake it off, I told myself. Just kill Bravelli. Just kill him.

But I saw the crowd again, all around us on Locust Street. Only now I was part of it, thirsting for blood, for a feast of raw death. I tried to break away, but I couldn't, I couldn't get back into myself, back to the alley where I was standing. If I pulled the trigger I was going to kill Donna, I was going to kill Steve, I was going to kill everybody.

I lowered the gun, and as I did I gradually came back into the alley, into myself. Bravelli was there crying, tears coming from his eyes. There was a big wet spot on his pants, he had fucking pissed himself.

"Please don't shoot me, please don't shoot me," he kept crying, over and over again, like a little boy.

With my free hand, I got out my handcuffs. "Lie down on the ground, face first," I ordered. He did it real quick.

"Put your hands behind your back."

Still pointing my gun at his head, I snapped the cuffs on his left wrist, then his right.

"Get up," I said.

He got on his feet. And as he straightened, I switched the gun to my left hand, and with my right made a fist and drilled it into the side of his head. My chest hurt, like I had been hit myself, a real sharp pain, and I dropped to one knee. Bravelli staggered backward, then tripped. With no way to catch himself, he fell, face first. I stood up and walked over to him and grabbed the handcuff chain behind his back.

"Get the fuck up."

Again, the moment he straightened, I hit his face with all my might, and he went down again, onto his ass. It felt good, it felt real good, I didn't mind my own pain that time.

"Get the fuck up," I said.

He just sat there.

"You got two choices, pal," I said. "My fist or my gun. Which do you want?"

He slowly got back on his feet. He was still bending over, on his way up, when my fist pounded into his right eye. He staggered back and somehow stayed on his feet, so I hit him again, in the mouth. He staggered back again, and looked like he was thinking of bolting. I raised my gun at his head, and he froze. His face was covered with blood, from above his eye, from his nose, from his mouth. His pretty face didn't look so fucking pretty now.

I finally put my gun back in my holster. Bravelli seemed to relax a little, but I drew my arm back and put all my weight, everything I had, into the next punch, right into his jaw. I heard a crack, it was one of the greatest sounds I ever heard, his fucking jaw cracking. A searing pain ripped through my chest, but it was worth it, and I fell to the ground at the same time Bravelli fell. I thought I had knocked him out, and I lay there watching him, but after a few seconds, he opened his eyes.

I tried to get to my feet, but I couldn't, and we both lay there, faces on the pavement, looking at each other. I felt like I had been shot again, and for a moment I wondered whether the bullet had somehow pushed its way into me. But I knew that wasn't possible.

It took me a long time to get up. Bravelli was still on the ground, watching me. He didn't know what was going to happen next.

I heard sirens in the distance. Help was finally coming.

I looked at Bravelli. "Get the fuck up," I said. I was afraid that if I hit him again, I'd pass out. But I couldn't not hit him. I had to keep going.

He wasn't about to get up again. Well, that was too fucking bad. I reached down to grab the handcuff chain to boost him up, and then I heard a familiar voice say, "That's enough, Sergeant."

I wheeled around and there was the Commissioner in his uniform and his Commissioner's hat. His gun was leveled at my chest. Behind him, at the end of the alley by Sagiliano's back door, was his Blazer.

I looked at him in disbelief. "You were here all along? You were here, and you didn't call for help?"

The Commissioner just gazed at me impassively. He didn't fucking care.

Bravelli was getting to his feet. He tried to smile with his broken jaw, yeah, was he glad to see the Commissioner. He walked over and stood right next to him.

"Get these cuffs off me."

Now what? Was the Commissioner going to shoot me, or get Bravelli to do it? The sirens were getting louder. It doesn't matter, I thought. I'll be dead before they get here.

The Commissioner started to laugh. "How come you didn't just shoot him?" he asked me.

What could I say?

"It's real easy," he said. "Like this."

He put the gun to the side of Bravelli's head.

"Hey!" Bravelli yelled, trying to step away.

But the Commissioner took a step to match Bravelli's step, and said, "This is for killing my son, you fucking asshole."

Bravelli looked at the Commissioner and opened his mouth, and there was an explosion and the back of Bravelli's head blew off. As he fell, you could see a big hole in his forehead.

The Commissioner turned back to me. "See? That's how easy it is."

I just stood there, looking at the Commissioner. Now he was going to kill me, blow the back of my head off. I felt the pain in my chest again, pain all over. I was tired, I wanted to lie down and go to sleep. I didn't even think about what was going to happen, that I was going to die, I just wanted to lie down.

"I didn't mean for it to be this way," the Commissioner said evenly. "I would have given my life for my son."

The air was filled with sirens now, I knew they were less than a block away, but it was too late. I tried to think of something to say, some smart-ass last words like they always say in the movies, but I was too tired even for that.

And I thought: This is how it ends.

The Commissioner's eyes met mine. "When you see Michelle," he said, "tell her I love her."

And then he put the gun to the side of his head and I watched as he quickly pulled the trigger. His head jerked in the explosion and his Commissioner's hat popped off, and then like a puppet after someone has let go of the strings, he just sort of crumpled onto the ground.

Police cars, lights flashing, were pulling into the alley on both sides, cops were jumping out, guns in hand. The Commissioner and Bravelli lay at my feet, bright red blood pooling around their heads. I turned and walked back down the alley, past all my shell casings, almost to the Dumpster that Nick lay behind. Cops were rushing toward me now.

I hesitated before taking the final step that would bring Nick into view. I was hoping that when I saw him, somehow his eyes would be open and he'd be smiling, and he'd say, "We made it, Eddie, didn't we?"

I didn't want to take that final step, I wanted to stand there forever, to keep Nicky alive forever. But I did step forward, I had to, and there he was, lying where I had left him, his arms at his sides, like he was already in a coffin.

"I'm sorry, Nick," I said softly. "I'm sorry I couldn't save you."

EPILOGUE

Sometimes it doesn't matter how true something is, people still won't accept it.

No one in the Police Department believed my story about Commissioner Ben Ryder, how he had tried to kill me and then had later stood by as Bravelli and Canaletto gunned down Nick.

Even after Lenny Lanier came forward with the videotape, no one could quite accept my account of how it all fit together. I was the only person who had walked out of that alley—I had to be covering up something, but they couldn't figure out what it was. One inspector came right out and said, "We don't know exactly what you did yet, but you're going to jail."

I was counting on Michelle to back me up. But she was so shaken by her father's death, and by the realization that she had contributed to it, that she went to her mother's house and shut herself away. And since she was the Commissioner's daughter, no one was going to push her.

So I was on my own. I spent the next twenty-four hours going over my story with captains, inspectors, deputy commissioners, people from Internal Affairs—just about everybody but the Bomb Squad.

It was Michelle who had wanted me to tell the truth about her father in the first place. When she heard he was shot, she rushed to the alley. They were trying to get me into an ambulance when she got there. I didn't want to go to the hospital, I wanted to get over to Aunt

Janet's. But the paramedics were insisting—the blunt impact could have caused heart damage, lung damage, they said. You have to go.

I spotted Michelle coming out of the alley, and I left the paramedics to talk to her. She hadn't been able to get to her father. Two commanders blocked her path, they didn't want her to see.

I told her what had happened, what her father had said. At first she was very calm. But when I told her his last words, that he loved her, she lost it, she just started sobbing.

I asked Michelle whether she wanted me to keep quiet about her father and Bravelli. Maybe we can destroy the videotape, I said.

"No," she said, taking a deep breath to hold back more tears. "No, it has to come out. Everyone has to know that Steve was a good cop. Even if my father wasn't."

"You sure?"

She nodded. "Tell them everything."

So I did. But for more than a day, Michelle kept her silence, and the Department treated me like a criminal.

She finally did come through, though, the next afternoon. I was sitting in Homicide, drinking coffee and waiting for my next round of questioners, when Michelle walked in.

"I'm sorry I left you hanging, Eddie," she said.

A captain spotted her and waved her over, and they went into a room, and pretty soon two or three other commanders showed up, and they all went in, too. They had totally forgotten about me. After a while, I just got up and went home.

I had wanted to be the one to tell Aunt Janet about Nick. I didn't want some stranger from the Department going over there and knocking on the door.

But they wouldn't let me out of the hospital—they kept me there for two hours, taking X rays, running tests. I had pleaded with the commanders to hold off the notification. Let me be the one to go over there, I said. It's better coming from a family member.

No, they said. The family has to be notified as soon as possible. And the media's hounding us for information.

Fuck the media, I said.

By the time I finally got over to Aunt Janet's, she had already heard. Matt and Chris were over there for Sunday dinner, they were all at the table when an inspector came by to give them the news.

The inspector was gone when I walked in the door. Aunt Janet was sitting on the living room couch, her eyes red, looking at nothing, her hands on her lap with a wad of tissue.

I knew I had to tell her about Nick and Steve. There was no way it wasn't going to come out now—detectives would be squeezing everybody even remotely connected to the mob. Someone would eventually mention Nick's name.

I wanted it to come from me, someone they knew. So I sat Chris and Matt down on the sofa too with Aunt Janet, and then I got a chair from the kitchen table and brought it in and sat facing them.

I told them they were going to hear some terrible things about Nick. You remember about Steve Ryder getting killed, I said. Well, you're going to hear that Nick was the one who killed him.

Aunt Janet just sat there numb, but Matt and Chris went crazy, and started yelling what was I talking about. I said it was true, Nick had told me in the crackhouse, and I went over the story with them. Or at least half of it. I left out the part about what had really happened on the roof when Uncle Jimmy died. I doubted whether the two guys up there with Nick that day would ever say anything, they didn't have any reason to. There were some things the family didn't need to know.

And then I told Aunt Janet and Chris and Matt how Nicky had gone with me into the alley behind Sagiliano's. When I got to the part about him saving my life, they all sat there, crying. And I was crying, too.

The funerals for Nick, Donna, and Mickey Bravelli were all on Thursday. Bravelli's was at St. Mary's in Westmount, and of course all the mob guys came to pay their respects. Or at least that's what they said they were doing. Actually, they were there to scope out the new job vacancy. These guys were going up to Bravelli's coffin at the altar and crossing themselves, and all the time they were thinking, Nice of you to get whacked, pal, thanks.

We just had a small service for Nick at the cemetery, in the morning. I was right about how the truth couldn't remain hidden—with Bravelli dead, some of his former pals had no hesitation about ratting him out. Of course, it got into the papers, and now the whole city knew that Nick was the one who had killed Steve Ryder.

The priests we talked to didn't want him in their church. We did find one, though, who would at least come out to the cemetery, and we picked a burial site in a quiet spot near where the woods started. Just a few people were there—Aunt Janet, Matt and Chris, my mother, and me. I wore my uniform, for Nick.

I did everything I could to keep the location of the cemetery a secret, but the media found out, and a whole pack of them showed up. They tried to get up close to the grave site with their cameras and tape recorders, and I had to go over two or three times and yell at them to stay back and respect our privacy.

Later that morning, I drove up to St. Stephen's in the Port Richmond section, where they were having services for Donna. It seemed like every cop in the city was there.

Buster never left the casket, not for a moment. He sat next to it all during the Mass, and rode in the front seat of the hearse to the cemetery. Long after everyone had left the grave site and gone home, even the family, Buster was still there.

Commissioner Ben Ryder was buried the next day. Since it turned out he wasn't exactly a model cop, they didn't give him an official police funeral, the kind Steve and Donna got. But the church was almost full, there seemed to be a lot of friends and family members. There were also plenty of police commanders and street cops. Ben Ryder had been known for being loyal to his troops, and now the loyalty was being repaid.

Michelle and her mother sat together in the front row, erect, even proudly, their heads lifted.

I wouldn't have gone to the service, except to see Michelle. I didn't have a chance to talk with her at the church, so afterward I joined the procession to the cemetery. It was a short, simple ceremony. There was no American flag covering the coffin, no twenty-one-gun salute. The Commissioner was buried next to his son. It turned out Steve had deserved his hero's funeral after all.

As I watched the service, I was thinking how Nick and the Commissioner had both decided to cross some sort of line. I don't know what you'd call what was on the other side of the line. Maybe it was just Nick's other universe.

But it was a place I couldn't go. And, it turned out, neither could Michelle.

It occurred to me that both Nick and the Commissioner had tried to come back from that place—Nick by saving me, the Commissioner by committing suicide. And as the priest spread drops of holy water on the casket, and I heard him say something about commending Ben Ryder's soul to heaven, I wondered, When you betray your soul, can you ever get it back?

Then I remembered Nick lying in the alley, saying how everything was OK. Maybe he had found some sort of peace. I wanted to think so. As for the Commissioner, I had no idea. He could have killed me, and gotten away with it, and he chose not to. I didn't know the reason he didn't, and I didn't really care what it was. I was just grateful.

After the service, I walked up to Michelle, just as I had at Steve's funeral. We moved away from the crowd so we could talk, and she said she wanted us to get together, over the weekend maybe. I told her I'd like that. Then she asked me whether I thought her father had atoned for his actions, even a little, by taking his own life.

"I was just wondering that myself," I said. "I don't know, Michelle. What do you think?"

"I don't know, either. I hope he did."

Her hope for her father was the same hope I had for Nick. I can't say why I walked out of that alley and he didn't, any more than I can say why I stopped short of the line that he seemed destined to tumble across.

But I would have pulled him back, if I only could.